ENTER THE EDGAR RICE BURROUGHS™ UNIVERSE

A century before the term "crossover" became a buzzword in popular culture, Edgar Rice Burroughs created the first expansive, fully cohesive literary universe. Coexisting in this vast cosmos was a pantheon of immortal heroes and heroines—Tarzan of the Apes™, Jane Porter®, John Carter®, Dejah Thoris®, Carson Napier™, and David Innes™ being only the best known among them. In Burroughs' 80-plus novels, their epic adventures transported them to the strange and exotic worlds of Barsoom®, Amtor™, Pellucidar®, Caspak™, and Va-nah™, as well as the lost civilizations of Earth and even realms beyond the farthest star. Now the Edgar Rice Burroughs Universe expands in an all-new series of canonical novels written by today's talented authors!

VICTORY HARBEN™

FIRES OF HALOS

EDGAR RICE BURROUGHS UNIVERSE™

The Edgar Rice Burroughs Universe is the interconnected and cohesive literary cosmos created by the Master of Adventure and continued in new canonical works authorized by Edgar Rice Burroughs, Inc., the corporation based in Tarzana, California, that was founded by Burroughs in 1923. Unravel the mysteries and explore the wonders of the Edgar Rice Burroughs Universe alongside the pantheon of heroes and heroines that inhabit it in both classic tales of adventure penned by Burroughs and brand-new epics from today's talented authors.

TARZAN® SERIES
Tarzan of the Apes
The Return of Tarzan
The Beasts of Tarzan
The Son of Tarzan
Tarzan and the Jewels of Opar
Jungle Tales of Tarzan
Tarzan the Untamed
Tarzan the Terrible
Tarzan and the Golden Lion
Tarzan and the Ant Men
Tarzan, Lord of the Jungle
Tarzan and the Lost Empire
Tarzan at the Earth's Core
Tarzan the Invincible
Tarzan Triumphant
Tarzan and the City of Gold
Tarzan and the Lion Man
Tarzan and the Leopard Men
Tarzan's Quest
Tarzan the Magnificent
Tarzan and the Forbidden City
Tarzan and the Foreign Legion
Tarzan and the Madman
Tarzan and the Castaways
Tarzan and the Tarzan Twins
Tarzan: The Lost Adventure (with Joe R. Lansdale)

BARSOOM® SERIES
A Princess of Mars
The Gods of Mars
The Warlord of Mars
Thuvia, Maid of Mars
The Chessmen of Mars
The Master Mind of Mars
A Fighting Man of Mars
Swords of Mars
Synthetic Men of Mars
Llana of Gathol
John Carter of Mars

PELLUCIDAR® SERIES
At the Earth's Core
Pellucidar
Tanar of Pellucidar
Tarzan at the Earth's Core
Back to the Stone Age
Land of Terror
Savage Pellucidar

AMTOR™ SERIES
Pirates of Venus
Lost on Venus
Carson of Venus
Escape on Venus
The Wizard of Venus

When a mysterious force catapults inventors Jason Gridley and Victory Harben from their home in Pellucidar, separating them from each other and flinging them across space and time, they embark on a grand tour of strange, wondrous worlds. As their search for one another leads them to the realms of Amtor, Barsoom, and other worlds even more distant and outlandish, Jason and Victory will meet heroes and heroines of unparalleled courage and ability: Carson Napier, Tarzan, John Carter, and more. With the help of their intrepid allies, Jason and Victory will uncover a plot both insidious and unthinkable—one that threatens to tear apart the very fabric of the universe . . .

SWORDS OF ETERNITY SUPER-ARC

Carson of Venus: The Edge of All Worlds
by Matt Betts

Tarzan: Battle for Pellucidar
by Win Scott Eckert

John Carter of Mars: Gods of the Forgotten
by Geary Gravel

Victory Harben: Fires of Halos
by Christopher Paul Carey

OTHER ERB UNIVERSE BOOKS

Tarzan and the Forest of Stone
by Jeffrey J. Mariotte

Tarzan and the Valley of Gold
by Fritz Leiber

Mahars of Pellucidar
by John Eric Holmes

Tarzan and the Dark Heart of Time
by Philip José Farmer

Red-Axe of Pellucidar
by John Eric Holmes

EDGAR RICE BURROUGHS UNIVERSE™

VICTORY HARBEN™

FIRES OF HALOS

CHRISTOPHER PAUL CAREY

Includes the bonus novelette

BEYOND THE FARTHEST STAR™

RESCUE ON ZANDAR

BY

MIKE WOLFER

EDGAR RICE BURROUGHS, Inc.

Publishers

TARZANA   CALIFORNIA

For Edgar Rice Burroughs,
who throughout his career never ceased expanding
his literary universe into new territories.

Contents

"As I rose to my feet and looked about I experienced my first startling surprise from the heavens where hung three great Suns, a large Sun and two lesser. No wonder then that the air was warm. Immediately I conjectured that I had been transported to some far distant solar system; but no, such is not the case. I wonder if I can elucidate the seeming miracle which, to us, is no miracle at all. There are, in reality, neither Time, nor Space, nor Matter. There is a Center, just what that Center is we do not pretend to know. We do not even declare that it is a Center. On the contrary it may as easily be an all-inclusive Whole. The angle of incidence theory rather tends to the latter conception; but it is easier to reason from a center than from the periphery of a vague and infinite Whole. Be that as it may, the fact remains, unquestioned and unquestionable, that there emanates from this Center outward or from the Whole inward toward the Center fluilations with varying angles of divergence or incidence, as you will.

"Only fluilations of the same angle are consciously tetecu-lent. In other words the fluilations that are you, or your trees, or your mountains, your Sun, your Moon, your Earth are identical in angle, differing only in form, frequency and speed, and because they are identical in angle you are sensible of them. Shining in your same heavens are my three Suns; but you cannot see them, nor can I see yours, nor can we see the same trees, or mountains, or rivers. Where runs a river for you stretches, mayhap, a sandy desert for me; where your oceans rise and fall rise our stately cities, perhaps."

—From *The Ghostly Script*, an unpublished novel fragment by Edgar Rice Burroughs

OMOS PLANETARY SYSTEM

FROM THE DIRECTION OF JASOOM, LOCATED
APPROXIMATELY 230,000 LIGHT-YEARS
BEYOND GLOBULAR CLUSTER NGC 7006

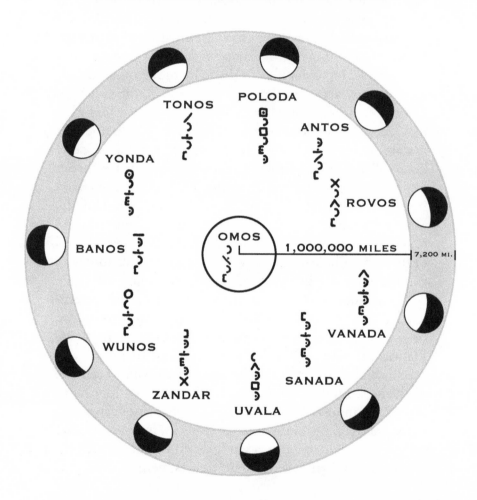

EACH OF THE ELEVEN PLANETS ORBITS THE STAR OMOS
WITHIN THE CONFINES OF THE SYSTEM'S ATMOSPHERIC
BELT. THE NAMES OF THE CELESTIAL BODIES ARE GIVEN IN
THE UNISAN LANGUAGE AND THEIR ENGLISH EQUIVALENTS.

UVALA
WESTERN HEMISPHERE

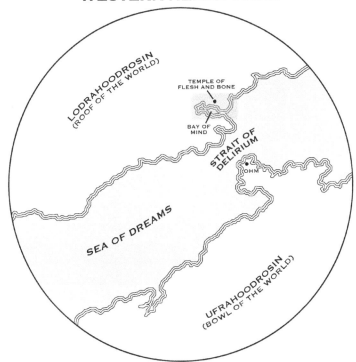

DAVROHENDUR ROVIK (LAND OF THE GUARDIANS)

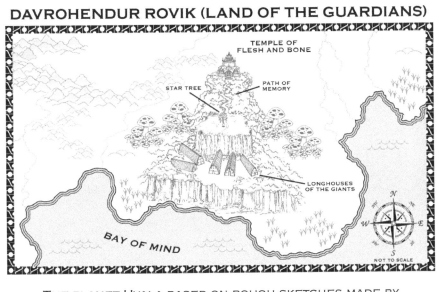

THE PLANET UVALA BASED ON ROUGH SKETCHES MADE BY
VICTORY HARBEN DURING HER VISIT TO TARZANA, CALIFORNIA.

FOREWORD

WELL, NOW *THAT'S* BETTER."
    I looked up from my office desk, startled by the unfamiliar voice. Before me stood a young woman I had never seen before—slim, athletic, of average height, wearing what at first glance I took to be a black formfitting cycling outfit, with a purple sequined stripe that ran down each side. Her complexion was a rich umber, her nose and upper cheeks accented with a hint of freckles. She had her mass of dark auburn hair tied back in a ponytail, the loose locks of which hung down before strikingly violet eyes.

"Excuse me?" I managed, not knowing what else to say, especially as my gaze fell upon the wide circle of silver metal that ringed her neck and was attached to her jump-suit much in the same manner as the grooved fitting for an old-fashioned deep-sea diver's helmet, or perhaps the helmet of an astronaut.

"I barely recognize Tarzana," the woman said, "but this office looks the same as ever. Well, a little rearranged and with a lot more *stuff* in it." When I gave her a blank look, she said, "The signal I'm beaming at your Gridley Wave apparatus must have refracted due to a phase inversion between the angles." She pointed to the locked drawer in Mr. Burroughs' old desk, in which indeed resided the very transmitter-receiver to which she had referred. "I found myself standing outside of something called a hookah lounge," she went on. "Thought I was on the wrong side of the planet for a moment. Then I saw a sign for Ventura Boulevard. I walked on until I found a familiar cross street and traced it back to Mr. Burroughs' old office. I guess it really *is* old now. I guess *I'm* old now. Sort of. Time doesn't work the way you'd think, you know."

"Wait a minute," I said, astonished, as the young woman's words seemed to shift my whole perspective of the world—no, *universe*—as if by magic. "Did you say, 'Gridley Wave'? Are you—"

"Forgive me," she said, interrupting. "I suppose I should have introduced myself. I'm Victory Harben. I believe you're the one I've been exchanging messages with through Mr. Burroughs' Gridley Wave set?"

"Victory!" I exclaimed.

"In the flesh. Well, not exactly. But the next best thing. I'm transmitting my voice and solidified image from . . . oh, let's just say somewhere *very* far away. You can thank a psychophysicist from Kjarna for giving me the idea." Suddenly my unexpected guest blinked rapidly and shook her head. "Hold on a second. I'm losing the picture signal on my end." She turned as if speaking to someone next to her who was not, in fact, there, at least from my perspective. "Tii-laa, would you please be a dear and pass me my uncertainty apparatus?"

A blue hand, clutching a gleaming, wide-barreled pistol equipped with strange copper and gold fittings, appeared out of the thin air before the bookcase in front of which Victory Harben stood. My guest took hold of the gun and the blue hand disappeared as if it had never been. She fiddled with some of the dials and fittings on the gun until a smile of satisfaction broke out on her face.

"There," she said in a pleased tone, passing the gun back to the blue hand, which had promptly appeared again, and then just as quickly disappeared after accepting the pistol, like the Lady of the Lake reclaiming Excalibur and drawing it back into the mysterious depths. "All better.

Now, where were we?" Victory walked around the large secretary's desk that had once belonged to Mr. Burroughs, sat down, and kicked up her gray metallic space boots—I can think of no better way to describe them—on top of the low, adjoining filing cabinet, making herself perfectly at home. "Oh, yes, you said in your last transmission that you wanted to hear more about my journeys through the cosmos. I'm game. But I warn you, it's a *long* story, and I'm not exactly sure how long I can keep this signal in phase."

She locked her fingers behind her neck and leaned back in the chair. "So . . . I listened to the transmission my godfather sent you about how Tu-al-sa, the Mahar queen of Mintra, swept me up in the maelstrom and hurled me from Pellucidar. Let's just say that while Jason's account is quite thorough, it's not exactly how I remember everything. He was a bit frazzled by the turn of events, after all, and rightly so, so I think it's best that I start at the beginning and give you my version of the story."

She referred to an account related to me by Jason Gridley, which I had but recently transcribed and made available to the world.* Intrigued, I grabbed a pad and a pen to take notes, and then urged Victory to go on.

"Before I begin, let's set a couple things straight," she continued. "First, my godfather and I have put into place certain special safeguards to prevent the foolhardy from confirming the authenticity of my account. Try flying an airship to the Arctic and entering the north polar opening to the hollow world of Pellucidar and you'll find nothing but lemmings, polar bears, and a lot of ice and water. Second, I am relating my account to you from what you might think of as your past. It's actually a little more complicated than that, what with the curvature of spacetime and the phasing of my signal between the angles. Comparing what time it

---

* See the bonus novelette "Pellucidar: Dark of the Sun" in the back pages of the ERB Universe novel *Carson of Venus: The Edge of All Worlds* by Matt Betts (Edgar Rice Burroughs, Inc., 2020).

is between where you are and from where I'm transmitting my image is really quite meaningless from a practical standpoint. But suffice it to say, we *are* in quite different time periods, and I started the timeline of my life close to ninety years before your present, though I'm still in my late teenage years. Confusing, I know, but you'd best get used to it before I go on any further."

She paused, gazing up musingly at the wall of dark wooden shelves beside us lined with the great author's works.

"You've read Mr. Burroughs' novels?" I asked.

"Just a few here and there when I was growing up. I was too busy reading physics and math textbooks and getting myself into trouble." She leaned over and drew a copy of Mr. Burroughs' *Tales of Three Planets* from the bookcase. "It would have done me well to have read more of them, actually. The first story in this book in particular." Her smile deepened as she paged through the volume and examined one of the maps in its front pages. Then she sighed, returned the book to its shelf, and began her story.

From here on, I shall omit cumbersome quotation marks and let Victory relate her remarkable narrative as she told it to me in her own words, prefaced only by an excerpt from a strange chronicle from another world that she felt would be of relevance to her tale.

CHRISTOPHER PAUL CAREY
Tarzana, California

PROLOGUE
EXCERPT FROM THE CHRONICLES OF YALURA

I T WAS ON THE SIXTH DAY of the fourteenth month of Hulnar when the sky darkened to a sickly green and the clouds roiled like a maelstrom, casting an ill light over the Citadel of Knives. I bade Queen Teldisforna to summon Lord Warquin at once, for I remembered well the warning given to us by the Visitor from Beyond, and who better to defend the queendom than the warrior-prince who had vanquished the indestructible Dragon Snake of Vorna?

At first, the queen laughed off my concern, dismissing the churning heavens as nothing but a summer storm that would bring much needed rain to the parched fields of her lands. But when flames of crimson and orange flicked their evil tongues from behind the clouds, she at last yielded and sent a courier to retrieve the prince.

The alarm sounded, wailing out from the temple like the shade of Pelmorshia herself from the old myths. Out rolled the colossal guns of the ancients on their great wheels of *thrixite*, and Lord Warquin ordered his knights to turn the mighty engines' barrels upon the heavens. High on the battlement I saw the prince standing tall, his cape fluttering in the howling winds, as he took command of one of the great guns. His skin glistened under his labors as his powerful muscles cranked the engine into position, a feat almost impossible to imagine, for typically the guns required the efforts of six strong men to maneuver. But such was the strength of Lord Warquin, he who had slain sixty knights of Jolemar single-handed before ascending the Great Tower of Vorna with rope and grapple and doing battle with the Dragon Snake in his foul lair.

Soon a fiendish, ear-piercing screeching from the heavens drowned out even the wail of the alarm. We all put our hands to our ears to block out the deafening noise, but it was to no avail as the infernal din seemed to come from within our very skulls. I could see but not hear Lord Warquin cry out a throaty exhortation to fire the guns. Beams of white-hot energy discharged from the wide, heavy barrels, streaking upward toward the fiery heavens.

As if enraged by the impetuous attack, the clouds transformed from sickly green to pitch black while scarlet flames lashed out like the infuriated tongues of serpents. Now a mammoth ball of fire broke through the dark clouds, a trail of black smoke and smoldering flames of orange and blue flowering from behind. The hellish bolide shot downward, arcing toward the citadel as I gripped the queen's hand, and together we shook in fear.

It could only be that bane of which the Visitor had forewarned. The Visitor had told us to plead with the one who would come, proclaiming that She, the Visitor, was gone now and that the people of Yalura had offered Her no refuge or assistance. Rather, we were to say that we had spat upon the Visitor and branded Her a Sky Witch, and would have drowned Her in the liquid iron of the giant cauldron deep beneath the keep had She not vanished from Her prison cell into thin air on the very eve of Her execution. But such would be a lie. We had not imprisoned Her, for She was a witch of neither sky nor sea nor land, but rather a friend to all Yalura—She who had used Her magic to end the famine that had stricken our land. She who had allowed our people to prosper once more. Nay, if She were a witch, She was of the good variety, and on the day She left us, taking her magical pistol of gleaming copper and bronze with Her, all of Yalura had mourned.

Perhaps it would have been better had we all died of famine, but how could we have foreseen the apocalypse that was destined to follow in the Visitor's wake.

Lord Warquin and his knights fired their great guns at the plummeting fireball, but it did not deviate from its course in the least.

The air grew hot and dry as the meteor streaked toward us, and beside me the queen sobbed as the inevitability of our deaths seized us. But both of us had misjudged the bolide's trajectory: it did not strike the citadel, but instead slammed into the great plain that lay before it, a plume of dirt and sand rising fully a *veld* high into the heavens.

The impact knocked us off our feet and tumbled great blocks of stone all about us. Dust and debris choked our lungs, and my ears rang from the unimaginable thunder-crack resulting from the horrendous crash. When I had gathered my wits, I pulled Queen Teldisforna from the rubble and bore her through rent corridors strewn with the bodies of her courtiers, knights, and domestic servants, and took her out onto the keep's lower battlement.

There we looked on high to discover that the colos-sal guns of the ancients had toppled from the wall, lying heaped and broken on the ground far below like a child's unwanted toys. But hope sprang in our breasts as we spied Lord Warquin descending the wall with his legendary rope and grapple, the massive sword with which he had slain the Dragon Snake of Vorna strapped to his back.

When the prince reached the base of the wall, knights poured from the citadel, surging and rallying around their lord as he strode bravely across the great plain, making directly for the steaming crater where lay embedded in the reddish dirt the glowing bolide. As the party neared the fallen stone, a terrifying bolt of lightning branched from the smoldering meteorite and the perfectly round sphere split open with a thunderous clap.

The queen and I gasped in dismay at the horror that emerged from the sky stone, but the knights of Yalura are stolid in their bravery. They gathered their courage and lined up before their lord, advancing upon the titanic, winged leviathan and her golden blade.

Would that they had turned and run. Tears flowed down my cheeks and those of my queen as the knights fell beneath the vengeance of the behemoth, their blades merely glancing off her gleaming violet armor. It seemed only moments before they were all gone, specters doomed to drift for all eternity across the great plain of the Citadel of Knives. That is, all but one, for the prince was still alive, and with him so too was hope.

There he stood, almost as tall as the terrible warrior who faced him. Valiant and grim was he, massive sword clutched in both hands, as he confronted the grinning, blood-streaked visage of the winged leviathan, her eyes burning from within like a crimson sunset.

But before the prince could even swing his blade, I saw the sword fly wildly from his hands and onto the dusty plain. I screamed in horror, or at least I think I did, for I was not in my right mind when the giant reached out a massive hand and clutched the top of Lord Warquin's head. Even at that great distance, I could see blood flowing down my lord's face as the leviathan's fingers dug into his skull and she forced him to his knees before her.

The winged woman's golden sword ignited with flame, arcing up high over her head. My queen and I watched as if we had turned to stone in our fright as a whitish mist phosphoresced from the prince and swirled upward to be drawn into the point of his opponent's sword.

The leviathan lifted her gaze from the bones and desiccated husk that were all that remained of the prince's corpse, until her burning eyes fell directly upon me and my queen, standing afar. Then the giant warrior spoke, her words amplified as if by magical means so that they somehow carried across the plain and came to our ears as if she stood but a mere stride before us.

"Do not lie to me or it will only go worse for you," came the booming, melodic voice, "for I know that she whom I seek has already come and gone from your world." The leviathan's eyes burned red like hot coals. "Tell me all you know of the one called Victory Harben."

—Chorelda Keem, Royal Scribe to
the Cloud Queen of Yalura

1

THE MISSING WAVE

I SUPPOSE I SHOULD BEGIN my story by telling you something about my lineage, as it might go a long way toward explaining how I got wrapped up in the extraordinary events I am about to relate. On my mother's side, I come from a family of intellectuals and adventurers, and by that I mean folks both too smart and too foolhardy for their own good, to such a degree that they tend to end up getting into a lot of trouble. I know enough about my own flaws to realize I belong to that same category. But at least we're an "interesting" family.

My grandfather, Dr. Karl von Harben, was for many years a German missionary in the Urambi region of central Africa, and he certainly saw his own fair share of misadventures, each of which could have easily sent him to an early interview with Saint Peter before the Pearly Gates. But he was a kind man who instilled in his children both compassion and a love of learning, and I miss him dearly.

Then there is my mother's brother, Erich von Harben, who graduated from university with honors at the age of nineteen, having pursued a course of study in the classics—namely, history, archaeology, and ancient languages. His "smarts" sent him on a reckless, solitary expedition to climb the forbidding Wiramwazi Mountains, where he nearly got himself killed half a dozen times after discovering the descendants of a lost Roman legion living deep in the remote jungle. And that was only his *first* adventure.

1

As for my mother, she was abducted at the age of twelve from my grandfather's mission by a band of frightful, bestial priests from the lost city of Opar—members of a species of archaic humans inhabiting an ancient colony purported to date back to the time of Atlantis. Yes, *that* Atlantis, the one that Plato wrote about, at least as far as anyone knows. Of course, none of that was her fault, and thankfully my grandfather was a good friend of Lord Greystoke—that is, Tarzan of the Apes—who extracted her from her dire predicament before she was fated to live out her years as a bloodthirsty high priestess of the Flaming God of Opar. But after she grew up, *her* "smarts" eventually got the better of her, too. During summer break before entering the graduate program in anthropology at Columbia University, my mother, Gretchen von Harben, got wind of a little secret—the existence of Pellucidar, the hollow world at the Earth's core—and wormed her way onto a hush-hush expedition via airship ferrying supplies to the inner world through the north polar opening. All well and good until her dirigible was attacked by flying pterosaurs—that is, winged lizards with razor-sharp teeth and claws—and she promptly fell off the ship during the conflict, only to parachute onto an island of sentient crab people and mind-controlling octopoids.

Now you know why I said we're an "interesting" family.

I guess I shouldn't complain. The latter escapade was how my mother met my father, after all, and without my mom's big brain leading her into danger, I wouldn't be here now telling you about all the trouble *I* ended up getting into myself.

You see, I was born in Pellucidar—a primordial land inhabited by dinosaurs and Stone Age tribes located, as I said, at the Earth's hollow core—in what would have been the year 1932 on the outer crust. It was there in Pellucidar that I spent the first twelve years of my life, in a world where time does not exist.

The idea that no time passes in Pellucidar isn't exactly

true, I'll grant you, but it sounds pretty romantic, doesn't it? Mr. Burroughs always did have a knack for such things, after all, and it's how he liked to explain the concept in his speculative romances about my friend David Innes.* But even as a little girl, I knew that was just a fanciful description. There *is* time at the Earth's core; it just *moves* funny. Believe me, I've done enough experiments to quantify it. I think it has something to do with the mass of the central sun that hangs eerily in the cavity of the hollow earth, but that's a differential equation I'm still working out.

In any case, as time moved funny during those first twelve years of my life, I had lived and breathed what my godfather told me equated to a lifetime of experience and a university education. From the age of five until I was almost twelve years old—that is, in terms of my biological age—I'd studied mathematics and engineering under the erudite and lovable old Abner Perry, who first came to Pellucidar along with David Innes in the "iron mole" prospector back in 1903. Together Abner and I pored over countless dusty, timeworn tablets salvaged from the ruined Mahar cities of Phutra and Kazra, which opened up a whole universe of advanced mathematics and physics for the impressionable young girl that I was. Not to mention we accidentally blew up a lot of things and caused general havoc among the locals of my home village of Sari, as we tried to invent and reinvent all sorts of new technological wonders (or "technological terrors," as David Innes was wont to call them) previously unknown to Pellucidar's inhabitants. That's why, when I first passed through the polar opening and crossed over its rim into the outer world—*your* world—on the occasion of my twelfth birthday, I was well ahead of the other kids my age in what would soon become my newly adopted home in Tarzana, California.

I won't lie. Being so book-smart caused me a lot of grief.

* See the novel *At the Earth's Core* by Edgar Rice Burroughs for the full account of David Innes' discovery of the inner world of Pellucidar.

Probably almost as much as those who were uncomfortable with the coppery brown skin and violet eyes I'd inherited from Nadok, my Voraki father. People of the outer world sometimes became uneasy around me. I could see them furrowing their brows and tilting their heads when they thought I wasn't looking, trying to figure me out and place my ethnicity within the comfort of their limited experience. Not to mention the stares I got whenever someone noticed the ritual tattoo on my right forearm that my father had given me as part of a tribal coming-of-age ritual when I was eleven. And those were the *best*-case scenarios. It didn't help any that the Second World War was raging and my mother was German. Maybe now you can see why I dropped the preposition "von" from my noble surname when I moved to the outer crust.

The truth is, I was from another world: I was Pellucidarian, a native-born Sarian at heart. But I'd also been raised by and around outerworlders. So the real truth is that I was . . . complicated.

When I was a young girl in Tarzana, I was taken in by the family of the captain of the O-220, the dirigible that had carried me to the outer world. Captain Heinrich Hines and his wife Anna, along with their boy Wolff, were a loving surrogate family for me, and my homelife with them was very happy. But my mysterious background and unconventional upbringing and education in Pellucidar, which I couldn't talk about to my schoolmates, made for a lot of unhappiness and angst during my first couple years on the outer crust. Eventually, under the encouragement of my math teacher, Miss Macrae, I tested out of high school and left the States to begin my undergraduate studies in England. I passed my Responsions at Oxford and, thanks to a little string-pulling by Lord and Lady Greystoke, I was able to skirt the age restrictions and enroll at—oh, let's call it Darkheath College. I pursued an accelerated track in Theoretical Physics and completed my undergraduate degree, and then went on to be granted my master's in the winter of '49. I returned to Chamston-Hedding in Yorkshire to stay with the Greystokes, who had taken me in during my breaks between terms at university, while I figured out what I wanted to do with my life.

That's where I was in the spring of 1950 when this whole business started, in my room at the manor scrawling down differential equations while I tried to figure out why, for the past two weeks, I could neither detect nor emit the Gridley Wave with the apparatus that had been installed at the estate.

I guess this would be a good time to explain exactly what the Gridley Wave is, or at least what it *does*, since there is still a lot my godfather and I don't understand about it. Without that singular "wave"—and there has been some debate over whether it is truly a wave or a particle, or both, but I'll get to that soon enough—there could be no radio contact between the Earth's outer crust and the inner world of Pellucidar. Nor could any practicable communication exist between Earth and the Red Planet of Barsoom, otherwise known as Mars. Only a handful of people on the outer crust knew of the reality of the Gridley Wave—myself; my godfather, Jason Gridley, who first discovered the wave; my uncle Erich; the Claytons; Captain Hines and his wife; and a select number of the Waziri tribespeople who had traveled via airship to the inner world; as well as Mr. Burroughs and *very* few others. We had each sworn an oath to suppress any knowledge or awareness of the phenomenon's existence, perpetuating the falsehood that, like Pellucidar and Barsoom, the Gridley Wave was but a fantasy of Mr. Burroughs' scientifiction. Thereby we hoped to protect those priceless worlds from interlopers who might seek to despoil and exploit them in the pursuit of profit.

And *that* was why I was so earnestly working on my equations. I had vowed not to rest until I determined why the Gridley Wave had, according to my detection equipment, disappeared from all creation as a principle of physics, as if it had never existed.

It was then, as I was absorbed in my work at the manor, that I heard something outside my window that resembled nothing so much as the buzzing of an oversized bumblebee. For some reason, it sounded eerily familiar, like something out of a dream shrouded deep in the haze of childhood. Moreover, I couldn't help but wonder what a bee was doing buzzing around out there in the cold, damp air of early spring.

I stood up and screeched open the window before my desk, ready to seek out the source of the infernal noise that had so rudely distracted me from my mental labors. But even as a gust of cool, damp spring air swept into the room, the clear soprano voice of Jane Porter Clayton, Lady Greystoke, carried up the winding stair.

"Victory, it's your godfather!" she cried. "He's come back from Pellucidar!"

Suddenly I knew where I had heard that whirring bumblebee noise before: it was the sound of the engines and propellers of the great O-220 dirigible—the very airship that, six years ago, had carried me from the hollow earth where I was born and out through the polar opening to my new life on the outer crust.

Now I had occasionally seen my godfather, Jason Gridley, in the intervening years since I had left Pellucidar, when he had visited the surface while ferrying cargo, supplies, and sometimes trusted passengers back and forth between the inner and outer worlds. Though I had kept in touch with him via the Gridley Wave set at Chamston-Hedding, we had seen each other only once since I had begun my studies at Darkheath. But that wasn't why I was so excited to see him. Well, it wasn't the *only* reason. I did dearly miss the "old man," as I liked to teasingly call him because of his apparent youth, which could be attributed only to the strange passage of time in Pellucidar. But what really got my heart racing was that I was certain he could be here for only one purpose, and it wasn't to go on holiday with his dearly missed goddaughter.

I practically flew down the stairs in a mad dash, passing a clearly bemused Jane Clayton at the bottom step. I crossed the spacious foyer and flung wide the great manor's towering doors, racing past the grand columns of the portico, down the steps, and out into the courtyard. Above loomed the mechanical behemoth, the O-220. Other than the *Favonia*, which had carried my mother to the Earth's core, it was the planet's sole vacuum airship, made possible only because its hull, frame, and vacuum tanks were constructed entirely of a rare metal known as Harbenite—as light as cork but stronger than steel—which my uncle, Erich, had discovered while exploring the remote Wiramwazi Mountains of central Africa.

As the massive airship descended upon the courtyard, Jane came out to join me, her long golden hair blowing freely in the harsh winds that buffeted us from the dirigible's mighty propellers. A moment later, the manor's elderly head steward appeared beside us, hand holding hat to his head against the fury of the artificial gale.

At last the six great wheels on the O-220's underbelly came to rest on the green sward before the manor, sinking several inches into the turf, for despite the Harbenite of which it was constructed, the fifteen-hundred-foot-long craft bore a sizable weight. The rumbling of the engines quieted with the artificial wind as the whirring propellers slowed and finally came to a stop.

Like a great tongue emerging from a giant's mouth, a ramp extended from an opening on the underside of the cabin. Within I could see some of the Pellucidarian crew tending their duty stations, all clad in animal skins—a remarkable contrast to the formal attire worn by the staff of the old English manor.

When I saw my godfather coming down the ramp, I didn't wait but ran forward to meet him halfway across the courtyard. We embraced in a grizzly bear of a hug, and when we pulled away, we were both wiping tears from our eyes.

Together we walked back toward the manor, arm in arm and beaming in each other's company.

"Where is your husband, Lady Jane?" Jason asked after exchanging a warm welcome with the mistress of the manor.

"He's off this morning hunting with Mr. Wood." Jane motioned in the direction of the thickly wooded forest that blanketed the northern portion of the estate. Stanley Wood, an American travel writer who had once played a role in one of Tarzan's African adventures, had been visiting Chamston-Hedding for the past week as Lord and Lady Greystoke's guest.

"We were up late last night in the great hall," I added, "as Tarzan and Mr. Wood enthralled us with their tale of the Gonfal of Kaji and the great emerald of the Zuli. If I hadn't been on the expedition to Yu-Praan when those Nazis tried to use a similar artifact to control people's minds, I'd have believed they were making it all up."

"You don't have to remind me, Victory," Jason said, "for I was there." Then the buoyant smile of our reunion faded from his handsome face. "Believe me, I would like nothing more than to spend a relaxing afternoon reminiscing with you and the Claytons over tea, but I have some sad and unsettling news. I've just come from Tyler Shipyards and Aeronautics in Santa Monica. I had hoped to consult with Mr. Burroughs in Tarzana about a serious problem I am attempting to solve. But I was too late. Have you heard? The Admiral has passed."

Jane placed a tender hand on Jason's shoulder. "Yes, we heard the sad news. It is a great blow to my husband and me, and to our entire family, for we loved him dearly."

"I'm sorry, Jason," I added, but the sentiment felt completely inadequate to the somber occasion. My godfather had been very close to Mr. Burroughs, whom he affectionately referred to as "the Admiral" because of an old yachting cap the esteemed author had taken to wearing at the beach many years ago. Jason often bounced ideas back and forth with

Mr. Burroughs about his scientific experiments, and I hazarded that my godfather had traveled to the outer crust to discuss the missing wave with his friend. Living in Tarzana in my youth, I had met Mr. Burroughs on several occasions, and once even gone on a little adventure of sorts with him and Inspector Muldoon of the LAPD. I liked Mr. Burroughs very much, for he was a man of sly wit and wisdom, but I was nowhere near as close to him as my godfather had been.

"I hope he is now traveling among the other planets," Jason said with a sad smile, "as he told me he hoped to do in the afterlife. But I've come to see you, Victory, for the same reason I wished to see Ed. I am on an urgent mission to—"

"To restore the Gridley Wave," I finished for him. "Yes, I know it's gone silent. I'm already working on the problem."

Joyfulness returned to Jason's smile. "Of course, I should have known."

I turned to the gray-haired steward standing prim and proper beside us. "Jervis, please get my bags ready for a long trip." The faithful old fellow bowed and turned to go back inside the mansion.

"Your bags?" Jason asked. "I figured I'd fly you over to the Clarendon Laboratory early this afternoon to run some preliminary experiments, and that we'd have you tucked into your bed at Chamston-Hedding by nine o'clock."

I dismissed the notion with a laugh. "Clarendon? That would be pointless, not to mention risky if someone at Oxford found out what we were up to. Professor Ralston already has reason enough to suspect I've been hiding something from him, what with the 'uncertainty apparatus' I told you I've been developing. He's sharp and wily enough to figure out we're working on a whole new principle of nonlocality." I looked up at the hulking frame of the O-220. "And who in their right mind wouldn't start asking inconvenient questions with that oversized albatross flying us around? No, not a good idea. It's just too dicey."

"Then what . . . and where?"

For a hair's breadth of a moment I considered my future: I'd been offered full scholarships to enter doctoral programs in Theoretical Physics at two prestigious universities, as well as an enticing opportunity to become part of the team that was attempting to set up a new cutting-edge particle physics lab at Geneva. After America had succeeded in splitting the atom at the end of the war, physicists had come into high demand the world over, a fact that had led to the accelerated track at Oxford that, along with my knack for science and math, had allowed me to earn my bachelor's and master's degrees in but a few short years. My future as a physicist looked bright indeed.

"I've been thinking," I said. "I remember seeing something carved into one of the ancient stone tablets in the Mahar city of Mintra when I was a little girl. It didn't make much sense to me then, but I now believe it may hold the key to how we can reinitiate the Gridley Wave." My dream of a rewarding career in the field of quantum mechanics faded into the dim recesses of my mind, replaced by visions of the alluring mysteries of the wondrous land of my birth.

"After all these years, you wish to return to Pellucidar?" Jason asked in astonishment.

"Yes," I said, finally knowing with utter certainty where I needed to be. "It's time."

2

A Primordial Homecoming

I **AWOKE IN UTTER DARKNESS** from the fog of strange dreams, unsure where I was. I rose from my soft bedding of what both felt and smelled like animal furs, and shook off the sluggish cocoon of sleep that had enveloped me. A thin crack of light peeked through the gloom. I staggered to the glowing vertical line and ran my hands over the edge of a hard, stout door, which creaked open on stiff wooden hinges when I pushed against it.

My eyes squinted involuntarily against the sun's harsh rays. I walked outside the hut and looked up at the great swollen orb of fire hanging precisely at zenith. It was no earthly sun that shone down upon me and warmed my bare arms and shoulders, or at least not the familiar sun known to the inhabitants of the Earth's surface. Pellucidar's sun appeared thrice the size of its counterpart in the outer world, looming in the turquoise heavens like the angry eye of a gargantuan cyclops glaring down in searing judgment upon the people of the inner world.

All around me rose the enormous bowl of the horizon. Imagine you are an insignificant flea standing on the inside of a globe so immense that its curving sides fade with distance into the vast interior of the hollow shell above and you'll have some idea of what I saw. It is a perspective, I am told, that is disconcerting to outerworlders, but for me it's always been just the opposite. While you might rightly question how gravity could possibly hold the people of Pellucidar to

11

the interior surface of a hollow sphere, a native of Pellucidar might ask what holds the people of the outer world to the exterior shell of a great ball of rock and dirt hurtling at terrifying speed through the immeasurable void of star-speckled space. Who could say which of the two scenarios was truly more implausible?

Well, I could, for one. I had a master's degree in physics, after all. But that was my mind speaking, not my heart. Living in the center of the hollow earth is as intuitive and natural for me as the odd phenomena of night and day are for you of the outer world, for I was born in Pellucidar. The massive curving bowl of the inner crust, the engorged flaming ball of the sun—they felt *right* in my hindbrain, even as a little alarm bell of warning rang softly and faintly in my forebrain. Of course, I knew the physics of the inner world made no sense. It was a problem that had long perplexed me, but for the moment it did not matter.

I was home.

The village of Sari was the same as I'd remembered it. Oh, there were little differences, such as the soaring radio tower topped by a parabolic dish of gleaming Harbenite rising from behind the little grouping of huts that served as Abner Perry's laboratory and workshops. Then there was the new fountain spouting proudly from the village's central plaza, a testament to Sari's wealth and status as capital of the Federated Kingdoms of Pellucidar, not to mention to the font's cast-iron plumbing. But the few strides of technological "progress" that David Innes and old Abner had introduced to Sari were countered by the locals' indifference to the passage of time in a primordial world of the Stone Age whose sun neither rose nor set. David and Abner had tried to introduce timepieces to the Sarians, for example, but watches simply unwound and were regarded as nothing more than pretty baubles and ornaments, and the water clock that Abner had installed in the village square was summarily ignored. And that magnificent fountain I mentioned? Right now I looked on as a warrior visiting the capital from the Lidi Plains tied his diplodocus to the plaque commemorating the gilaks'—that is, the humans'—victory over the dreaded Mahars, the intelligent winged reptiles who had once ruled over this region of Pellucidar. The great saurian mount's tiny head lowered on its elongated neck, and a long, thin tongue emerged from its mouth and began lapping up precious water from the fountain's sparkling basin. I would hate to see how the warrior would have shown his respect to a monument like the eternal flame of peace I once saw on a trip to Gettysburg. He probably would have roasted a *thag*[*] carcass over it.

The thought left me wondering how much I had changed since I had been away. For the past six years I had questioned my place in the outer world with each waking day, racked by the unmistakable feeling that I did not truly belong there, no matter how I excelled at my studies and felt fulfilled by the rewards of academic life. I had expected to be relieved to finally return home to the world of my birth, and in many ways I was. The warm breeze that blew over the valley was fresh and free of pollutants, carrying the fragrance of wildflowers. The distant roars of sabertooths and screeches of pterosaurs that rose from the lush scape of the surrounding jungle valley sent a tingle of excitement down my spine. And perhaps most importantly, there were none of the unceasing distractions of civilization; no one worried about the stock market, celebrity scandals, or the latest fashion trends from Paris. In Pellucidar, I felt truly *alive*.

But since I had returned to the Earth's core, I found myself thinking of little things I had taken for granted on the outer crust. I couldn't drift off to sleep listening to Nat King Cole or Frank Sinatra crooning from the speaker of my RCA Victor, for instance, and I felt a little groggy without my morning teatime curled up on a chaise longue with the latest

---

[*] The mighty aurochs of Pellucidar, equivalent to the extinct *Bos primigenius* of the outer crust.

Physical Review journal in my lap. And Abner's little workshop, despite his unceasing efforts, would never hold a candle to the Clarendon Laboratory at Oxford.

I imagined David and Abner must have felt much the same way when they first came to Pellucidar in the iron mole, that their urge to "modernize," "civilize," and "educate" the locals had resulted from their desire to rebuild around them the familiar things they missed from their everyday lives on the Earth's surface. Though my tutelage under Abner had cultivated my love of science, it had always been the thrill of discovery that had driven my desire to learn, not the desire for the familiar. But now, returning to Pellucidar after having lived in another world for so long, I wondered if I were guilty of looking through the same clouded lens as had David and Abner. Had I prejudiced myself to the free and simple primitive life of my fellow Pellucidarians? Had my years on the surface left me shackled by the so-called refinements of civilization? The last thing I wanted to experience when coming home was culture shock, and it left a bad taste in my mouth. If I didn't belong in Pellucidar or on the surface world, where *did* I belong?

But perhaps I was being too hard on myself. I had been home for only . . . well, I did not know precisely how long I had slept, what with the strange sense of timelessness in Pellucidar, but I felt that no more than fifteen hours could have passed since I had disembarked from the O-220. Besides, I had the mystery of the missing Gridley Wave before me, and if I feel at home anywhere in the universe, it is when I have a problem to solve.

It was with these disparate thoughts that I strode over to Abner's laboratory, hoping to find the old inventor hard at work on some new and implausible contraption. Abner had been my first mentor, and we had a special bond. When I was five years old, I decided I wanted to become a scientist and I had latched on to him, refusing to leave his side as he conducted his remarkable and often dangerous experiments.

My parents were terrified for my safety and forbade me to enter the lab without their supervision. Of course, I didn't listen to them. I was too mesmerized by the world of science that Abner had conjured to life for me. Before long, however, my parents relented. That may have had something do to with the fact that I had saved Abner's life on three separate occasions, when either his preposterous experiments or his habitual absentmindedness would have done him in. I had come to love the old fellow dearly, as much for his flaws as for his indefatigable genius, and there is nothing I wouldn't do for him.

My mind was so absorbed with these and other thoughts of my strange homecoming that, when I got to the lab and drew aside the animal-skin curtain that served as a door, I entered quite heedless of what I might find on the other side. Consequently, I ran headlong into what might have been a brick wall. As the transition between the brilliant sunlight outside and the relative dark of the lab's interior blinded me, I felt a strong hand grip my arm to keep me from losing my balance and being hurled to the dirt floor from the sudden, unexpected impact.

It was then that my eyes began to adjust and I realized I had collided not with a brick wall, but with a rather strapping young Stone Age man of about my own age. By the weak light of the room's single incandescent bulb, which I suspected was powered by a generator hooked up to the nearby water mill, I sized up the fellow. He wore nothing but an antelope-hide loincloth, a snakeskin headband tying back a shock of dark hair, and a belt about his waist from which hung a leather sheath holding a bone-handled stone knife. I studied the man's face and concluded that if it hadn't been for his great black forest of a beard, he might have been quite handsome.

"I am sorry!" the fellow exclaimed in the common tongue spoken in this region of Pellucidar. "Are you hurt, maiden?" Concern edged his voice and his brow was creased with worry.

"I'm fine," I said, clearing my throat and smacking imaginary dust off my khakis with my free hand, as if that might somehow reclaim my dignity. "Really, you can let me go now," I added, for the man was still clutching my arm. "I'm not going to fall over." I hoped only to find Abner as quickly as possible and put the embarrassing incident behind me.

The man loosened his grip hesitantly, as if testing whether I had truly regained my balance, before apparently judging that I had and releasing it altogether. Then his eyes grew wide and I heard a sharp intake of breath.

"Victory?" he exhaled. "Is that you?"

I tried to peer through that thick black beard. "Do I know you?"

"It's me. Don't you remember?"

I tried to recall every handsome young warrior I'd known before I'd left Pellucidar but came up short.

"You don't, do you? That's all right." He sounded a bit crestfallen, and I felt a bit guilty.

"I'm sorry . . ." I began, and then I heard a bark and what sounded like a dozen test tubes breaking on the floor from behind the thag-skin curtain that separated us from the adjoining room. An instant later, a great wolflike beast bounded through the curtain and into the room, barreling into me and knocking me to the floor. The brute proceeded to straddle me with its shaggy body and lick my face with its atrocious-smelling tongue. It was a *jalok*—a ferocious hyaenodon of the plains—but it acted like nothing so threatening as an overexcited puppy.

"Down, Rocky! Down!" the man cried. "Bad boy!" The warrior kneeled beside me, wrapped his muscular arms around the jalok, and lifted the heavy beast from my frame.

"Wait a minute," I said as I pulled myself up off the dirt floor. "This is Rocky? My old pet jalok?" Then my jaw hung open as the truth began to slowly dawn.

"*My* jalok," the man replied. And then, in English: "You gave him to me fair and square."

"Janson?" Again I squinted my eyes to peer through that beard. "You're Janson Gridley? Jason and Jana's boy?"

He smiled tentatively. "Uh . . . none other."

"I didn't recognize you behind that bushy beard!" I laughed, probably a bit too loudly. "I know Harbenite is scarce, but you really couldn't spare a sliver to make a straight razor?"

"I . . . uh . . . I'm sorry," Janson said, rubbing his hairy jaw. "I've been away on an expedition to the Terrible Mountains. I didn't have much of a chance to shave."

Again I laughed, but this time more gently. I'd only meant to jest about his beard, but my little quip seemed to have barbed him. "Janson, I'm *kidding.* That's what I do, remember? I'm so glad to see you!"

I opened both arms to embrace my old childhood friend, but Janson was already reaching out rather stiffly to shake my hand. I froze with both arms still outstretched and looked down at his extended hand. I should have just made a wise-crack like I always do and then hugged him anyway, but you know awkward moments. They creep up on you and turn your brain to mush. Even in the room's feeble lighting, I could see Janson's sun-bronzed face turning the color of pickled beets.

We were saved by Abner, who swept aside the curtain, strode into the room, and began cursing like a sailor. "Thirteen weeks of fermentation gone to waste!" he cried. "All because of that intolerable Baskerville hound of yours, Janson!" He again took up the cursing until his gray, be-spectacled eyes fell upon me. "Oh, forgive me, Victory," he said, as if I were still his eleven-year-old lab assistant and hadn't been away for six years. "I didn't see you here." And then he turned and went back into the next room, all the while muttering to himself something about the effects of the lack of cosmic rays in Pellucidar on his recipe for the perfect truffle sauce.

As Abner left, the lighting in the room grew suddenly

brighter and I turned to see a woman's silhouette framed in the doorway, the curtain pulled back as she peered inside.

"Victory?" came a familiar voice that brought a smile to my face.

"Yes, I'm in here, Mom." I looked back at Janson, who had taken hold of Rocky by his great scruffy mane and was endeavoring to keep the overenthusiastic jalok from bowling me over again. "Just catching up with Janson."

Janson lifted a thumb over his shoulder and jabbed it toward the door leading into the other room. "I'd . . . uh . . . better go help Abner clean up the mess Rocky made of the lab. Could you . . . uh . . . take Rocky outside and make sure he doesn't get into any more trouble?"

I slapped my thigh, then leaned forward and clicked my tongue at Rocky. "Come here, boy!" The great beast scrabbled forward with a puppylike squeal and began nuzzling his ferocious snout against my ankles.

"Janson, it's good to see you," I said, giving Rocky a good chin scratching. "Let's get together later and chat about old . . ." But when I looked up, I found Janson had already disappeared through the curtain without so much as a "see you later." I shrugged.

With a sharp tone I ordered Rocky to heel, which he did obediently, and thus escorted by my faithful old jalok, I walked outside to join my mother beneath the sweltering heat of Pellucidar's eternal noonday sun. I made up for the unfulfilled hug of a few moments before by embracing her for what must have been a full minute, if one could estimate time here, while she stroked my hair and rocked me back and forth like I was still a child, telling me how much she'd missed her little scientist. The feeling of motherly love that enveloped me was so heavenly that I didn't ever wish to let go, just as I'd felt when we first saw each other upon my arrival in Sari. When we finally pulled apart, there were tears of joy in our smiling eyes.

"I've missed my big scientist, too," I told her as we began

strolling leisurely across the grass beneath the brilliant azure sky. I've mentioned how Abner cultivated my love of science, but it was my mother who gave birth to it. She had been accepted into the esteemed graduate studies program in anthropology at Columbia University just before my family's aptitude for misadventure drew her to Pellucidar and diverted her from her chosen career in academia.* It was a decision she had told me she never regretted. The inner world, she had said, was a far grander ethnographic field school than any that a university of the outer crust could offer. She was right, of course.

"Now tell me about your reunion with Janson," she said, a sly smile on her lips.

"Well, let's just say 'awkward' has a new definition." I made a sour face. "You know me . . . always a little too quick with the jibes. And cut it out with that smirk, Momsy. He's not my type."

"You could do worse than Janson Gridley. He's smart, capable, handsome—"

I snorted just like I'd once done in class when Professor Ralston erroneously proclaimed he'd solved the Einstein–Podolsky–Rosen paradox. "Sorry, Janson was always a good kid, don't get me wrong," I told my mother, "but are we talking about the same trembling boy—two years older than me, I might add—who would still be stumbling around in the ruins of Mintra if I hadn't led him out? And I'm not sure that hideous beard qualifies as handsome." I shuddered visibly, and while I'm no Gaza de Lure, I think my performance was convincing. "Besides, I've got no room in my life for boys. As soon as Jason and I can restore the Gridley Wave's signal, I've got my PhD and a job offer in Geneva to think about."

"Believe me, I'm not trying to play matchmaker, Victory. Only you can chart your own destiny. But you're being unfair

---

* See the Edgar Rice Burroughs Universe comic-book miniseries *Pellucidar: Across Savage Seas* by Christopher Paul Carey and Mike Wolfer for the tale of Gretchen von Harben's first adventure at the Earth's core.

to Janson. He really is smart, just like your godfather. And that trembling little boy you once knew, I can assure you, has grown up to become a brave and honorable man."

"You wouldn't say that if you saw him a couple minutes ago."

My mother smiled knowingly. "Even the boldest warrior stumbles on the battlefield of the heart." She was quiet for a moment. "You know he asks about you often."

"Who? Janson? He *does*?"

I was trying to think of a clever retort to my mother's insinuation, but it was at that moment that Rocky began barking like a hound from Hell and then tore off across the green sward in the direction of Abner's lab. The jalok's gleeful bounds took him in a beeline for a tall figure making his way toward us, a jumble of scrolls sticking out from under the crook of an arm. It was Janson again.

"Oh, great."

My mother grinned and kissed my cheek. "I have to be running along, dear. Your father's in an especially good mood thanks to your visit and he's finally agreed to let me transcribe one of the secret oral myths of his tribe's Krataklak elders. Please come join us back at our hut—" she waved over my shoulder at the approaching Janson, who raised an arm to wave back, "as soon as you're done terrorizing your new fella." She winked at me and was gone before I could even utter a sarcastic "*Thank* you, Mother."

Rocky bounded back to me, huffing with joy. I picked up a stone and threw it across the meadow for the jalok to fetch while Janson approached. The great hyaenodon barked and tore off across the turf.

Janson stepped up with his armful of scrolls and greeted me with a flash of his strong, white teeth.

I smiled back, but said nothing. I was flustered by my mother's innuendo that Janson was sweet on me and, to be honest, still a little miffed that he'd had left me talking to myself back at the lab.

"My dad told me about the expedition to Mintra that you two are planning," he ventured after an awkward silence. "I would tag along, but he wants me to stay here and man the Gridley Wave station in case you're able to restore the signal."

"Good idea." I eyed the jumble of scrolls he was cradling.

Janson followed my gaze and looked down at the rolls of parchments and wax paper tucked under his arm, then almost dropped them all in a nervous jostle to extract one. With a lopsided grin peeking out from his bushy beard, he finally succeeded and held out the scroll to me.

"This is a rubbing I made from a tablet I found in the archives at Thotra."

I perked up at the name of the distant Mahar city and eagerly accepted the scroll, removing its leather tie and unfurling the thin, translucent paper beneath the brilliant light of the central sun. "You got this from Thotra?" Then it hit me. "That's why you traveled to the Terrible Mountains."

Janson nodded. "I'd been helping Abner catalog the tablets recovered from the subterranean libraries at Phutra and Kazra, when my father broke into the hut with grim news that the Gridley Wave had gone silent. I immediately thought of something I'd but recently read. Only ten or fifteen sleeps before, I'd come across a page of your notes. You must have written them right after we'd come back from Mintra when we were children. The paper was pressed between two sheets of rubbings from Phutra that referred to the writings of the great Mahar cosmologist Ral-nu-ka the Transcendent—at least I think it translates to 'cosmologist,' in the sense that Mahar cosmology encompasses the fourth-dimensional realm, not outer space like the cosmology of the outer crust. In any case, the tablet indicated that Ral-nu-ka's writings were housed in the library at Thotra, near what we now call the Terrible Mountains. Of course, the city was destroyed during the great uprising David Innes led against the Mahars, but due to Thotra's distance from Sari, Abner never got around to exploring its archives or even determining whether

they'd survived. But in your notes you pointed out a connection between what was said on the Phutran tablets about
the writings of Ral-nu-ka and something that Tu-al-sa, the
Mahar queen of Mintra, had shown you in her library when
we visited the city as children."

"I remember," I said. Why Tu-al-sa had felt compelled to
show me the records, I had never known, but I couldn't deny
the fact that if she hadn't, I might never have been motivated
to leave Pellucidar and travel to the outer crust to pursue an
education in math and physics.*

"You wrote in your notes," Janson went on, "that you
believed one of the tablets Tu-al-sa showed you referred to
the principle behind the phenomenon we call the Gridley
Wave. You wrote that the Mahars knew how to both 'turn on'
and 'turn off' that principle at will. Not the emission of the
wave, to be clear, but the very principle of physics itself."

I nodded, for that tablet was the very reason I planned
to return to Mintra. "And so you went to Thotra looking
for the writings of Ral-nu-ka," I said, finishing Janson's
thought, "to see what more you could learn about the Mahars'
knowledge of the Gridley Wave."

Janson nodded.

Recalling the Maharan I had learned as a child, I examined
the scroll, the original tablet of which I now realized must
have been etched by Ral-nu-ka the Transcendent herself. It
appeared as if the original tablet had been significantly
damaged, for only a few lines of the hieroglyphic script were
legible upon the wax paper.

"Is this all there is?" I asked.

"Unfortunately, yes," Janson replied. "The roof of the
niche where I found the tablet had caved in and smashed
most of the records to dust. I was lucky to have recovered
this much."

---

* See the Edgar Rice Burroughs Universe novel *Tarzan: Battle for Pellucidar*
by Win Scott Eckert for Victory Harben's encounter with Tu-al-sa, the
Mahar queen of Mintra.

My pulse began to race as I attempted to translate the remaining glyphs. "This is definitely about experimentations with the Gridley Wave. See here?" I pointed to a grouping of symbols. "It says something about . . . what's this? 'Hypergeometry'? I can't get the rest. Are you able to read it? My Maharan is a bit rusty after all these years."

Janson reached out for the scroll, which I handed back to him. I admit, I was a bit surprised as he ran a finger up a column of ancient glyphs and appeared to be silently mouthing what he read. It seemed my mother had been right about his smarts, after all.

I watched in anticipation as Janson's gray eyes roved over the relevant passage. "Part of the passage is missing, but it says something about 'experimentations with angular dimensionality' and 'the signal innovation making contact with the accessed hypergeometry.'"

"Well, ain't that keen?"

"Keen?"

"You know. Excellent? Superb? In a sarcastic way." I sighed as Janson's brow showed no sign of unfurrowing. "Never mind, it doesn't matter."

"The 'signal innovation' is obviously the Gridley Wave," Janson went on, "but do you know what Ral-nu-ka means by 'angular dimensionality' or 'the accessed hypergeometry'? Your notes mention that Tu-al-sa told you something about 'the angles.' What was that all about?"

"I don't exactly know," I admitted. "But Tu-al-sa had said the Mahars learned how to communicate with the so-called lower orders—and by that she meant gilaks—by beings that taught her kind how to 'access new angles.'"

"Beings?" Janson asked. "What kind of beings?"

"Again, I'm not sure," I said. "But she called them the Numinous Ones, and also referred to them as Those from Above."

From what I had gathered from Tu-al-sa at the time, the Mahars believed they had detected other orders of reality at different geometrical angles from our own, by which I could only imagine she meant other dimensions. I had done a lot of thinking about the subject and concluded, just as the ancient Mahar scholars had, that the existence of an infinity of alternative realms of existence lying invisibly alongside our own could be the answer to one of the biggest mysteries in my field of study: that is, what goes on under the hood, so to speak, in quantum mechanics— namely, why a photon or an electron can express itself as either a particle or a wave, depending on how one looks at it. Niels Bohr and his colleagues at Copenhagen would have thought the idea amounted to bupkis; they didn't believe it was practical to ask or even possible to know why. And that was the prevailing belief in quantum mechanics. But the Mahars clearly believed they knew why, and the reason was "the angles."*

Janson made a face like he'd accidentally swallowed a frog but was too afraid to admit it and spit it out.

"Okay, give it up, Nature Boy," I said, though the look on his face told me he didn't get the song reference. "What's on your mind?"

"It's just that . . . do you think it's safe?" He tapped a finger on the scroll. "You know, experimenting with ancient Mahar science without having the full picture? Maybe you and my father could bring back rubbings from the tablets you find in the library at Mintra. Then we can reconvene after you return to Sari and we can study your findings and decide what to do. Abner will want to examine—"

I raised a finger. "I don't disagree. I'm all for taking it slow and following the scientific method, but I don't think that's going to fly with your old man. I've never seen him so anxious, have you?"

Janson sighed heavily. "You're right. I guess that's what

---

* Clearly, the Mahars anticipated the many-worlds interpretation of quantum mechanics long before it was proposed on the outer crust by Hugh Everett in 1957.

happens when you get a wave named after you and then said wave disappears. But you'll promise me you'll be careful?"

"I'm always careful."

Janson's lopsided grin reappeared. "Just like when you led us straight into a Mahar den when we were kids, no doubt."

I laughed, pleased that this conversation was turning out better than our last. "*Exactly.* We came out of that just fine, right?"

Rocky loped up to me and dropped the stone he'd fetched at my feet.

"And look, we even got a faithful pet jalok out of the deal." I picked up the stone and tossed it again. Rocky craned his neck to watch as the stone made a wide arc in the air and landed in the grass right before the doorway leading into the lab. He bolted to retrieve the stone.

Janson turned to follow Rocky back to the lab, but before he had a chance to pull his disappearing act again, I called out his name.

He turned, his eyebrows raised.

"It really *is* good to see you again after all these years," I said.

He nodded with a smile and headed back for the lab.

3
THE MIND VAULTS OF MINTRA

AFTER BEING PRESENTED as honored guests at a great bonfire celebration attended by David Innes, the emperor of Pellucidar, and Dian the Beautiful, his empress, Jason Gridley and I made final preparations for our journey to distant Mintra. I had hoped to see Janson again before we left, but when I asked his father where he was, he said his boy was back at Abner's lab with his nose stuck in a tablet. And so I bade an emotional good-bye to my parents, and then boarded the main cabin of the great O-220 airship with my godfather, feeling a little nervous thrill in my stomach as Captain Hines gave the order to cast off and engage the engines.

As we rose into the air I looked down at the village of my birth and watched it grow smaller below. Then I spied a tiny figure emerge from Abner's lab and jog over to stand beside my parents. It was Janson, and he was waving good-bye.

My godfather, waving down at his son, saw me smiling and elbowed me. "Congratulations," he said, grinning slyly.

"For what?" I asked.

"For managing to get his nose out of his tablets," he replied.

"Me?" I exclaimed, confused. Then I began to sense a conspiracy. "Wait a minute," I said sharply. "Have you been talking to my mother?"

Jason began to whistle innocently and examine the blue sky through the window of the cabin.

"Uh-huh," I said, rolling my eyes. "I thought as much." I felt the sudden urge to run to my cabin and stick my own nose in one of the physics books I had brought with me from the outer crust, but I didn't want to give my godfather the satisfaction, and so I stood my ground, gazing down at the stunning vista of the Pellucidarian landscape below.

And thus we embarked upon the first leg of our travels aboard the O-220, which soon carried us far out over the rolling aquamarine waters of the Lural Az toward that great peninsular continent that ranges far to the east of Sari.

If it is a strange experience to find oneself within the inner crust of Pellucidar, looking up at the great bowl of land and sea that rises precipitously on all sides, it is odder still to view the breathtaking sight from the vantage point of an airship. Often we flew low over the water, the tall windows of the main cabin allowing us to gaze down in wonderment as gargantuan saurians of the deeps broke the sea's surface in enormous briny swells that rained down like waterfalls from the monsters' dark, glistening hides. Seabirds and winged reptiles roved the skies in flocks so vast they temporarily darkened Pellucidar's eternal noonday sun, casting massive shadows over the ocean's glittering surface. But at last we left the savage seas behind and reached the distant coast, passing over the Valley of the Jukans and its strange, half-mad inhabitants, and thence made our way across a great stretch of jungles, mountains, and rivers, until finally we reached the cliffside village of Lo-har. Here we moored our ship and disembarked along with all of our equipment. We were to proceed on foot for the remainder of our journey, for the O-220 was needed to deliver crucial supplies elsewhere in the empire.

In Lo-har we were greeted by Wilhelm von Horst, or Von as he is known to the locals. Von Horst had accompanied Jason and Tarzan on their first expedition through the polar opening to Pellucidar, and after a series of hair-raising adventures, he had taken La-ja, daughter of the former chief, as his mate and become chief of Lo-har himself.* The Lo-harans furnished us with supplies and everything we needed for the overland journey that lay ahead of us, including a diplodocus (or *lidi* in the language of Pellucidar) with which to draw the cart that carried our portable Gridley Wave radio tower and its transmitter-receiver apparatus.

And so it was that after many sleeps we came to the green meadow beneath which lay the ruins of the subterranean Mahar city of Mintra. The only discernible evidence of the city's existence was two colossal towers rising to either side of a yawning opening in the ground, one of the monoliths lying cracked and toppled. I had often wondered what dire event had determined the sorry fate of Mintra. The city was located in a land far away from the Federated Kingdoms, and so it had not fallen at the hands of the great revolt led by David Innes, but rather as a result of some unknown cataclysm of the distant past.

When I was eleven years old, I had been intensely curious about the Mahars and their ancient civilization, so much so that I had run away from home, following the trail of an army from Sari that I had heard was headed for a newly discovered Mahar settlement said to be in league with interlopers from the outer crust. I had never seen a Mahar, but I had read much about them in their own words from the stone and clay tablets and cured scrolls recovered from the Mahar cities of Phutra and Kazra after their destruction by the armies of David Innes.

Before David led his revolt, the Mahars were the all-powerful masters of Pellucidar. They are great winged reptiles, their outward appearance being identical in everything but size to the genus of flying pterosaurs of the Jurassic known as *Rhamphorhynchus*. Whereas the largest specimen of *Rhamphorhynchus* found on the outer crust is not much larger than a goose, the Mahars range from six to eight feet

---

* See the novels *Tarzan at the Earth's Core* and *Back to the Stone Age* by Edgar Rice Burroughs.

in length. Their heads are long and narrow, and equipped with penetrating round eyes. Razor-sharp fangs line their beaklike mouths, and their membranous wings, when extended, can span from twelve to twenty feet depending on the size of the individual.

Though the Mahars may look like small-brained pterosaurs, they are a sentient species with a capacity for intelligence equal to or even surpassing our own. They communicate not through sound, as we do, but by some means we cannot even fathom that is akin to, though not the same as, telepathy; I had some ideas about that, which I was hoping I might confirm with a further study of the records at Mintra. Their race is all-female, having in the remote past disposed of sexual reproduction in favor of a heavily guarded means of artificial fertilization, which they refer to as the Great Secret. Moreover, the Mahars are the inheritors of an advanced civilization. Though not equipped with dexterous hands and fingers like humans, they nonetheless build great subterranean metropolises by employing their servants, the Sagoths, the sentient gorilloids of Pellucidar, who also serve as their army and protectors.

For all these reasons, I became fascinated by the Mahars at a young age, but I would be lying by omission if I didn't mention another reason. Long after the gilaks under David Innes drove them from the Federated Kingdoms, the Mahars attempted an incursion into the borders of the empire. It was upon the eve of a great battle between the armies of gilaks and the forces of the Mahars and their Sagoth legions that I was born. My mother had told me I was named after a barbaric warrior queen who had appeared to her in a dream vision and told her that my birth presaged victory in the coming battle—a victory that indeed came to pass. When the gilak troops heard of the omen, my name became their rallying cry in a violent clash in which every last Mahar among the enemy forces was wiped out.

Now my very nature causes me to question everything,

and so I'm not one to be naïve. I understand all too well that there are circumstances in which one must defend oneself against aggressors, whether they are schoolyard bullies or opponents in battle. I had lived on the outer crust through much of the Second World War, after all, and I have certainly faced my share of tormentors in high school and even at university. But to have one's name appropriated as a battle cry that contributed to the slaughter of hundreds of members of a sentient race is not an easy thing to live with. I thought about it often as a child, and, well, it left its mark on me. What if the conflict between the Mahars and the gilaks had come about because of a cultural misunderstanding and could have been prevented? Our races were so alien to one another: we did not understand much about the Mahars, and I had a hunch the Mahars did not truly understand much about us.

Even as a little girl, I felt the same way, and that is why I ran away from home and trailed the gilak army, intent on seeing the Mahars with my own eyes so that I might better understand them. I've mentioned that I like solving problems, and I tend to go straight to the source to get my answers, even if it causes me a great deal of trouble. You know, that family trait again. Eventually I was detected and caught by the gilak warriors I was following, but I managed to slip away again when we came to ruined Mintra. Down into the dank depths I went. Perhaps I *was* somewhat naïve then, but all the same I was not wrong, for in the bowels of the dead city I encountered my first Mahar—a wise old matriarch known as Tu-al-sa—and it was from her that I learned her kind were much more than just bloodthirsty reptiles who consumed the flesh of gilaks in ghastly rituals.

Tu-al-sa was said to be one of the most ancient individuals of her entire race. Moreover, she was the same Mahar whom the villainous Hooja the Sly One had cleverly placed on board the iron mole excavator in the place of Dian the Beautiful without David Innes' knowledge when he had returned to the outer crust after his initial adventures in Pellucidar.* Tu-al-sa had been to the surface of the Earth and seen what no other Mahar could even imagine: that the only world her kind had ever known since the dawn of their species was but the interior of an insignificant, hollowed-out ball of rock and dirt hurtling through an infinite cosmos.

Having been born at the Earth's core myself, I know firsthand what it is like to look up for the first time at the black void of the heavens, filled with burning stars and with nebulae and galaxies so distant they are but smudges of light glimmering against the stygian sky, and to see the glittering jewels that are the other planets turning ever so slowly on the ecliptic against the backdrop of the Milky Way. It is a sight at once wondrous and disconcerting for an inhabitant of Pellucidar—wondrous because it opens up an immeasurably vast universe of limitless possibilities, and disconcerting for the very same reason, for such an infinity can make one seem very small and insignificant. But for the curious mind, it is wonder that dominates the spirit, and when I met Tu-al-sa, I knew that it was wonder we both shared. In Tu-al-sa I felt a kinship. She even roused a form of envy in me, for I had lived my whole brief life within the inner world and had never gazed up at the stars—and yet Tu-al-sa had escaped Pellucidar, at least for a time, and done just that. In that way she was superior to me, and in what must have been only a few scant hours that I spent with her, I came to regard the queen of dead Mintra even as one might a mentor.

The secrets that Tu-al-sa showed me in the archives of Mintra—what she called the "mind vaults"— forever changed the course of my life. There I learned that the Mahars had focused their intellects not solely on the biological sciences and architectural engineering, as Abner Perry had been led to believe after examining the archives in the library at Phutra, but also on advanced mathematics and physics.

---

* See the novels *At the Earth's Core* and *Pellucidar* by Edgar Rice Burroughs for more on Tu-al-sa's unanticipated journey to the outer crust.

These branches of knowledge, she had told me, were inextricably woven into the very fabric of existence itself, of all living things. When I left Tu-al-sa and Mintra behind, my desire to know more about these disciplines was practically bursting at the seams, and my craving to see the stars with my own eyes burned as hot and bright as Pellucidar's eternal noonday sun. And so I begged my parents to allow me to travel to the outer crust and pursue an education in math and physics, a plan to which they had reluctantly agreed.

Now here I was, six years later, on the doorstep to the mind vaults of that same dead city of the Mahars, intent on solving the mystery of the silenced Gridley Wave. Recent reconnaissance of the area by agents of the emperor of the Federated Kingdoms had reported that Mintra was now abandoned, that even its last known inhabitant, the matriarch Tu-al-sa, had at last abdicated her throne and departed the ruins, and may even have departed the world of the living.

I did not know it at the time, but I was about to find out just how wrong those agents of the emperor were.

4

THROUGH THE LOOKING GLASS

HAVE IT!" I cried out in joy.

"Good, because *I've* had it with this suffocating tomb," Jason Gridley said. "Every time I hear an echo of our own movements down here, my hair stands up on end."

We were deep in the archives of Mintra, having descended the stairway leading down from the dark maw that yawned between the two colossal stone towers on the surface. Openings in the ceiling of the vast subterranean chamber cast down slanting beams of sunlight upon the city's cyclopean architecture—great buildings and soaring towers that rose amid wide plazas, paved avenues, and bridges spanning precipitous chasms. For a while we had become lost in the maze of interconnected structures, but at last I found what I had remembered from my previous visit so many years before: the odd grouping of buildings ornamented with domes and turrets and archways that hid the entrance to the winding tunnels leading down into the bowels of the underground city, and ultimately to the mind vaults, where Tu-al-sa had shown me the massive library of clay and stone tablets and manuscripts of cured animal hide.

Rows upon rows of niches set in the forty-foot-high stone walls of the great chamber surrounded us, each alcove filled with dozens of tablets covered in the hieroglyphic language of the Mahars. Jason stood over me as I kneeled on the floor before one of the niches, shining the beam of his flashlight on the tablet in front of me so I could see what I was doing.

33

"This is the tablet I remember reading during my visit here as a little girl," I said in wonder. "And I'm pretty sure I got it right back then. The author of the tablet is discussing an effect whereby a wave function can pass through a barrier without the need for potential energy. This has to be referring to the Gridley Wave."

"You're talking about quantum mechanical tunneling."

I grinned. My godfather was no slouch. He had graduated with honors from Stanford, and was the discoverer of the Gridley Wave and inventor of its transmitting-receiving apparatus. I knew he kept up as best he could with the latest developments in theoretical physics on the outer crust. That didn't mean I didn't like to tease him good-naturedly about being out of touch with modern science, just to keep up our old routine, but right now I was too excited by what I'd found to needle him.

"You got it," I said. "The tablet's explaining how the Gridley Wave can pass through radio interference, no matter how severe. Or any barrier, for that matter, including lead plating. I've conducted further testing at Clarendon that I need to show you. I think you could detonate an atom bomb and transmit a Gridley Wave signal straight through the mushroom cloud with absolutely no degradation."

The beam illuminating the tablet I was reading grew unsteady as Jason cranked the little handle that powered the dynamo to recharge the flashlight's waning battery.

"Hey, can you hold that thing still?" I asked, anxious to glean more secrets from the ancient tablet.

"I could simply let the battery drain out," Jason replied, "and then we'll find out how well you see in the dark."

I turned and shot a guilty smile back at my godfather. "Sorry. Point taken. I just want to pour all the knowledge from these archives straight into my brain as quickly as possible!"

"Aren't you taking the phrase 'mind vaults' a bit too literally?" Jason said, grinning. I groaned and, smiling back at him, rolled my eyes. "Well," he continued, "how about we put what you deem to be the most essential tablets in our packs, and we carry them up to the surface to examine in the sunlight? I don't know about you, but I'm starving."

My stomach growled at the suggestion. "We have been down here a long time, haven't we?" It was a very "outer crust" thing to say, using the philosophical concept of time so casually in conversation, and suddenly it dawned on me just how infected I'd become by the surface world during my long sojourn there.

I made a final inventory of the tablets nested in the niche and concluded that only three of them had anything to do with the phenomenon we called the Gridley Wave. I slipped one of the tablets into my backpack, Jason took custody of the other two, and then we began the long ascent back to the surface.

As we passed back along the dark, winding tunnel, I called for my godfather to stop.

"Did you hear that?" I whispered, looking back down the tunnel the way we had come.

He stood stock-still and cocked an ear. "No," he said finally. "Nothing. What did it sound like?"

"Like a gust of wind." Or the whoosh of air beneath great wings, I thought, but I felt it must be my ears playing tricks on me and I did not voice my fears. "Probably just our own echo. Let's keep going."

Jason said nothing, but he had taken a spear along as a precaution, and I saw his grip on the weapon's shaft tighten. We passed out of the tunnel without incident, however, and made our way through the cyclopean city and up the steep stairs carved out of the side of the cavern, the stone doubtless worn smooth by the feet of countless generations of Sagoths and their gilak slaves.

When we finally emerged from the underground complex, we were both famished. We raided the supplies that we had left in the cart near where was tied our lidi, whom I had

named Frankie due to his tendency to make crooning vocalizations. After wolfing down a bellyful of antelope jerky,
I crossed the meadow and flopped down on my stomach
with a bowl of wild berries to munch on while I studied the
tablets we had laid out in the grass. On the other side of the
meadow rose the forty-foot-tall, latticework radio tower we
had assembled at the site, at its pinnacle a sleek parabolic
antenna. Near the tower, we had set up our portable Gridley
Wave transmitter-receiver, which was connected to a bank
of powerful batteries we had brought with us from the outer
crust. I looked up and saw Jason, finished with his meal,
running a series of checks on the apparatus.

As I returned to translating the hieroglyphics on one of
the tablets, I got to wondering. If the Mahars knew so much
about science, what might they understand about the strange
physics of the inner world and its central sun?

I rose and stretched. If I were back at Oxford, I would
have gone to the pub and sat alone in a dark corner, sipping
on an ice-cold root beer float to stimulate my thinking. I
wasn't, so I made do by pacing back and forth on the green
sward, absorbed in my thoughts, until finally my gaze fell
upon my canvas pack, which lay in the grass where I had
left it. I picked up the bag and took out the leather belt and
holster that held the pistol-shaped device I had been developing in secret at the Clarendon Laboratory. I jokingly
called it an "uncertainty gun," in part because Heisenberg's
principle had inspired its design, but also because I had
little idea what effect it might generate when activated. And,
of course, because it happened to look like a gun.

But it really wasn't a gun. Rather, it was a device designed
to intertwine subatomic quanta and direct them along a
barrel-shaped waveguide in much the same manner as a cord
connected to a radio set acts as a transmission line for elec-
tromagnetic energy. Only Jason knew I had been working
on the device, and he had cautioned me against discharging
it without further testing. In point of fact, I had been running

a number of tests in the little lab I had set up at Chamston-Hedding on the same day I noticed that the Gridley Wave apparatus there had failed. Curiously, from that day on, I had been unable to get my equipment to detect that singular effect on subatomic particles—what the physicist Erwin Schrödinger had called *Verschränkung*, or entanglement—that the device should have generated. It certainly could have been that my lab equipment, which is highly sensitive and hence extremely finicky, was not working properly. But I wondered. Could there be a connection between the sudden inability to transmit or receive the Gridley Wave and the lack of functionality of the device? It made a kind of sense, after all, even if I didn't understand the specifics, as the Gridley Wave and my "gun" both operated on the principles of entanglement and nonlocality. And so I had brought the device along with me when I left Chamston-Hedding for the inner world, on the off chance that it might somehow prove useful in our quest to once again detect the now-silent Gridley Wave.

I strapped the belt holding the uncertainty gun around my waist, thinking that if we were able to restore the Gridley Wave using the information from the clay tablets, I could then test the device to see if it had regained its ability to generate its subatomic entanglement effect. I had added a component to the gun that would trigger a sound much like that of the whine of a photoelectric cell if its entanglement effect was primed and working, without actually discharging said effect along the waveguide. If I pressed the priming button and heard the whine after we'd restored the Gridley Wave, then we might establish definitively that there was a correlation between the gun's principle and that of the wave.

I walked across the meadow to where Jason was tinkering with the machinery. Planting my hands on my hips, I gazed up at Pellucidar's eternal noonday sun. "You know, this world is impossible."

Jason stopped his tinkering. "And yet you were born here," he said. "Does that make *you* impossible?"

I flashed him a smile at the allusion. He knew of my fondness for Lewis Carroll's tales of Alice in Wonderland, which he had read to me when I was a child. "Only before breakfast," I replied, paraphrasing the Queen's response to Alice.

"We're missing something," I went on. "I know it. For millennia, the people of the outer world believed the Sun, the Moon, and the stars revolved around the flat disk of the Earth, that the seas poured off the world's edge in an unimaginably titanic waterfall that fell into oblivion. It took just one person to change our viewpoint and allow us to understand what was really going on. I think it will be the same with Pellucidar."

I wondered what the ancient Mahar scholars had known about the uncanny force that held the central sun in place. Abner's hypothesis was that molten matter and gases had congealed due to centrifugal force during the Earth's formation, leaving behind a luminous core held in abeyance at the exact center of the hollow globe by the equal attraction of the gravity of the solid crust in all directions. But that was poppycock. Any freshman physics student at university could disprove that proposition with the most basic equation. And yet what alternative explanation could there be? Maybe a clue lay in the tablets we had recovered from the buried city, for I had noticed while we were down in the subterranean archives that one of them made reference to the sun.

I strode back across the meadow, kneeled down in the grass before the tablet I had last been reading, and returned to translating the strange glyphs. Jason followed and I could sense him standing over me.

"There, I was right!" I exclaimed, coming across a passage I had remembered reading six years before.

"You can read Mahar that easily?" Jason asked.

"Learned at the knee of Abner Perry himself." I didn't tell him that I had become rusty and had spent the majority of our journey aboard the O-220 in my cabin brushing up on the Mahars' hieroglyphics using a primer that Abner had loaned me.

I continued to translate the columns of glyphs etched into the clay, my pulse beating faster as long-forgotten secrets revealed themselves. It was all laid out so clearly in what I read, and there could be no mistaking that we had found the right tablet. "The ancient Mahars *did* know about the Gridley Wave," I said. "And apparently it failed in the past, for they knew how to restart it, too. Here's the frequency we need."

"How could they know about the Gridley Wave?" Jason asked. "They don't even have machines."

I stood up and walked over to the transmitter-receiver apparatus. Jason followed, and together we gazed up at the radio tower.

"I've been thinking about Abner's theory," I said. "He believes the Mahars project their thoughts into the fourth dimension, where they can access the thoughts of a fellow conversant via a sixth sense. What if scientific understanding isn't always limited to being able to build machines and fancy apparatus, that sometimes it's the result of simple biology? The Mahars have abilities we humans haven't evolved, and apparently one of them is a faculty that allows them to 'hear' oscillations in the frequencies of energy and subatomic particles. Of course, I don't really mean they hear them, since Mahars don't have ears."

I returned my attention to the transmitter-receiver. On our climb up from the mind vaults, we had discussed my cursory examination of the tablets and my memory of the knowledge they contained. There was every reason to believe we had uncovered the Mahar's precise instructions on how to reinitiate the Gridley Wave, which Jason and I hoped we could achieve by employing the apparatus we had transported from Sari.

Well, I thought, there's no time like the present, especially in timeless Pellucidar, and so I began to turn the apparatus' frequency dial to match the numerical value I'd translated from the Mahar tablet.

Jason's face suddenly looked strained. "Victory, I know we both agreed to do this, but I'm having second thoughts."

"Don't worry," I said. "Like I told you, I think you're right. It's only a simple matter of tuning the transmitter just right to fish the signal out of the higher frequencies and restore the wave." Jason had been on edge ever since our return to the inner world, and I thought a little reassurance might put him at ease. "Here . . . this should do it, according to the tablet." I fine-tuned my adjustment by inching the dial forward just a hair, causing the indicator needle to creep up into the meter's red "warning" area. The latter was an artificial threshold that Jason and I had added to the meter out of an overabundance of caution, simply because we had never dialed up the frequency quite that high before. All the same, there was no good reason to think it would be any more harmful than adjusting the tuning dial on a common household radio set.

The Gridley Wave apparatus began to hum serenely. I took in my godfather's exasperated look and smiled. "Like we were just saying, for all these years we've been stuck on Niels Bohr when we should have been reading Dyson and Feynman. No wonder we haven't been able to figure out why the Gridley Wave's stopped working."

I stood up. "It's like my uncertainty gun prototype. I wouldn't have been able to develop it if I hadn't been thinking outside the lines." I drew the uncertainty apparatus from its holster, its copper and gold fittings glittering in the brilliant sunshine.

Jason eyed the device warily. "You're eighteen years old. Shouldn't you be at the prom or something instead of making guns? Put that thing away until we've tested it. For all you know, it might blast a hole in the wall of our universe."

"And shouldn't you be in a rocking chair?" I quipped back. "You're what . . . a hundred and *two*?" Jason must have truly been on edge, for he looked hurt despite the fact that I was just engaging in our usual playful razzing, so I softened my tone and placed a hand on his shoulder. "But thanks to Pellucidar's timelessness," I said, "not a gray hair on your head and as scandalously handsome as ever." Jason gave me a sad little smile, and suddenly I thought about the great loss in my godfather's life and how it must have affected him.

"I was sorry to hear about Mr. Burroughs," I said, again knowing the words were completely inadequate. "I know you two were close."

Jason's look grew distant, and I knew half a dozen life moments he had shared with his friend must be playing out on the screen of his memory. Jason had been devastated by Mr. Burroughs' death, for the two had been good friends for many years. Mr. Burroughs had been right there when my godfather first established contact via Gridley Wave with David Innes in Pellucidar, and had in fact been monitoring the apparatus when, shortly thereafter, while Jason was away on his initial voyage to the inner world, the first transmissions were exchanged between Earth and Barsoom.

"Thank you," he said at last. "Things just aren't the same without him."

I had been about to ask Jason about the last time he had spoken with Mr. Burroughs, when suddenly the apparatus beside us let loose with a shrill, ear-piercing whine that made the hair on the back of my neck stand erect. A strange radiance fell upon us from above as a beam of white-violet light, spiraling with interlocking sine waves, shot straight up out of the parabolic dish on top of the radio tower. The intense helix of light beamed up into the sky toward the central sun, which it hit dead-on.

The sight was an impossibility. The Gridley Wave is an invisible emanation, passing unseen through void, energy, and matter all the same. Or at least so it had always been in our experience. But then, we had never before set the frequency into the range delineated in the hieroglyphics of the ancient Mahar tablet.

I did not have much time to think about it, for within the barest of moments after being struck by the inexplicable beam, the eternal noonday sun of Pellucidar turned as pitch black as a solar eclipse viewed from the surface world. But no heavenly body had drifted in front of the inner sun. No, the great shining orb had simply gone dark, as if the searing flames radiating from its surface had been suddenly extinguished. Around the darkened disk phosphoresced an eerie corona of crimson-tinged violet, casting a dim and surreal luminance upon the landscape.

I cannot describe the absolute horror that threatened to suffocate me at seeing Pellucidar's perpetual sun go dark. It imparted a feeling so disconcerting that I could not form a coherent thought or even utter a sound. And as words were taken from me, so too did the vocalizations seem to have been taken from all life in the inner world. A hush fell over all.

For a moment, it seemed as if the unnerving silence would go on for all eternity. But then, as the terror mounted in my own breast, so too did it overtake all animal life surrounding us. As if every creature in the inner world had suddenly awakened at the same instant, a great communal cry of primal fear arose from all directions. The deafening roars, shrieks, yells, and screeches resounded in our ears. Then the earth beneath us began to shake with the thunderous pounding of the hoofs and feet of the great saurian and mammalian beasts of Pellucidar.

I looked to Jason, whose gaze of apprehension momentarily met my own before I was almost raked beneath a fury of razor-sharp talons. A fleet-footed dromaeosaurid had emerged from the jungle's edge and raced in mindless terror directly through the meadow where lay our campsite, barely missing me in its mad rush to escape that which neither it nor we could understand.

I attempted to collect my scattered wits, casting about in search of a refuge against the furious exodus of primordial life.

Then came a whooshing sound and a flutter of great wings behind me.

I spun around, as did Jason beside me, to face a sight that sent a shiver down my spine.

It was a Mahar. Her magnificent wings arched and menacing, she stood before the yawning opening that led down into dead Mintra, flanked by the dark outlines of the two colossal stone monoliths that rose up out of the earth.

I whipped the uncertainty gun from the holster at my hip. The act was a testament to how rattled I was. After all, the device was not truly a gun, and I could not anticipate the effect it would discharge should I pull the trigger. Most likely, it would emit a harmless subatomic particle or simply do nothing at all. But the Mahar would surely believe the apparatus to be a gun, one of the deadly new weapons that had been used to cut down her people during the gilak revolution led by David Innes. For all I knew, my rash act could trigger a war, but even in my apprehension I had the sense not to point it at our unexpected visitor.

But Jason was not so circumspect. He leaped for his spear, which lay between us and the Mahar, and yanked it from the ground where he had thrust it after we had ascended from the subterranean city. Now he menaced the great lizard with its sharpened flint point.

"Don't hurt her!" I cried, lowering my gun. "We don't know what she wants."

"It's a *Mahar*, Victory," Jason retorted. "It wants to enslave humanity."

"That's an assumption. The Mahars think differently from us."

But my godfather would have none of it. "It's not an assumption," he said. "It's demonstrable history."

I made a noise of dissatisfaction. "History is written by the victors. Our two races have *never* understood one another."

"They've never given us a chance to understand them." He shook his head. "You and Abner. Always inventing things like uncertainty guns and cannons, only then to act as gentle-hearted as swans."

"A swan will bite your fingers off," I said tersely.

I was angry at my godfather, who carried the prejudice of every gilak of the inner world I had ever known. I am not naïve. I understood all too well the horrors that had been thrust upon the human race during their subjugation and slavery to the Mahars. Had I lived in those dark times, I too would have fought for freedom until I had breathed my last breath. But that was the past, and sometimes there are better ways than fighting. Smarter ways. The Mahars had long regarded us as we do cattle, and they had had little evidence to believe otherwise. When David Innes had united the gilaks of the region to rise up against their reptilian overlords and the Mahars had realized their mistake, it was too late for thoughts of peace between the two species. David had stolen the Mahars' very secret of reproduction, without which their entire race was doomed to extinction. Was it any wonder they wanted to exterminate us? Would not the gilaks have done the same were they forced into a similar predicament? In the intervening time since that first war with the Mahars, why had no one even *tried* to bridge the gap between our peoples?

Even as I chided Jason, an unsettling sense of familiarity began to creep over me and I gasped.

"What is it?" he asked.

"I can't explain how I know," I replied, "but I've met this Mahar queen before. I just *feel* it's her. The Sagoths call her Tu-al-sa, one of the most ancient Mahars—and the very same whom David Innes once carried to the surface in his iron mole and later returned safely to Pellucidar. When I was eleven years old and first came to Mintra, she and I had a . . . conversation. It's what made me want go to the surface world and study math and physics."

"You're scaring me, Victory," he said. "This is starting to sound like a setup."

I shushed him, for a voice that was not a voice sounded in my mind. Imagine an idea has been beamed directly into your cranium and your brain proceeds to lag a fraction of a second behind as it seeks to translate the wordless concept into your native tongue and you will have the barest notion of what I experienced. It is an inadequate description of Maharan communication, but until you have had the disconcerting experience of being "spoken to" by a Mahar yourself, it will have to suffice.

"Little gilak, rein in this animal's flapping orifice."

"She thinks we're rude for chattering in front of her," I told my godfather. "Well, for moving our lips, anyway . . . But she knows we're communicating between ourselves."

"Your limited mind conceives not that your fluilation teteculates with another angle."

Somehow I knew those new "words" were meant for Jason, but old Tu-al-sa must have wanted me to "hear" them, for they formed in my mind as well. Another shiver went down my spine at the words "fluilation" and "teteculates." Though the terms were not in my vocabulary and I did not know their meaning, Tu-al-sa had conveyed them to me when I had met her as a child in the buried halls of dead Mintra. I had asked her how she could communicate with gilaks, as at one time it was believed that Mahars could not use their telepathy-like ability to exchange ideas with "lower orders" such as gilaks. Tu-al-sa had replied that the Mahars had learned new techniques of communication from "Those from Above." The Mahar queen of Mintra had then gone on with her unfathomable explanation: *It was the Numinous Ones who taught us how to access new angles and teteculate with the fluilations of the lower orders. This is but one of several things that Those from Above have taught us."* Who or what the Numinous Ones or the Ones from Above were, I had no idea.

Jason's eyes narrowed. "My *fluilation . . . teteculates?*" he said questioningly. "I'm sorry, I don't know those words."

"Just as you are oblivious, perhaps all within Pellucidar must soon pass into oblivion . . . and so, too, all who lie at the angles beyond."

I tensed as the word "angles" formed in my mind. She was clearly referring to the hypergeometries discussed by Ral-nu-ka the Transcendent in the tablets that Janson Gridley had uncovered in the archives at Thotra. The same "angles" that Tu-al-sa had told me about when I was eleven years old—the "angles" that the enigmatic Numinous Ones, Those from Above, had taught the Mahars how to access.

My godfather was right: it had to be a setup. But if that were true, Tu-al-sa was playing a very long game. Could Tu-al-sa really have begun laying the groundwork for her machinations when I had met her when I was but a child? It seemed impossible. But then, Mahars did not concern themselves with the past or the future like humans of the outer crust. They existed in the perpetual now, and thought only in a single tense: the present. It is a concept hard for the human mind to grasp.

"Lying at angles beyond?" Jason pointed down at the ground. "You mean those inhabiting the surface of the sphere of dirt and rock that surrounds Pellucidar? The people of the outer crust?"

"This communication becomes ineffective."

As the sting and frustration of Tu-al-sa's psychic utterance rang in my mind, she raised one of her wings as if she meant to whirl about and take flight back down into the dank depths of her moldering city.

But I could not let her escape so soon. Without the radiance of its sun, Pellucidar and all of the bountiful life that it supported would perish. Too much was at stake to let the differences of our species separate us. I had to understand what had happened to the sun.

"Wait!" Spreading my arms and bowing my head to appease her species' innate sense of superiority, I went down on one knee before the dread matriarch of Mintra, bathed in the dim, reddish-violet light cast down from the darkened orb. "Hear my thoughts, O Mighty and Sagacious Queen! We are not your enemy."

Tu-al-sa lowered her wing and looked down on me with her beady reptilian eyes as if I were but a small rodent that had caught her fancy. I hoped she wouldn't play out that metaphor any further, as I knew Mahars had a taste for mammalian flesh.

Gathering my courage, I went on. "Your people have essential knowledge about the principle with which we . . . *teteculate* . . . with those beyond Pellucidar. We seek your help! Why has the principle failed? And what have our adjustments to our transmitter using the ancient tablet done to Pellucidar's sun?"

"I remember you, daughter of Nadok the Voraki," the queen said in my mind. *"'Victory' . . . a repellent appellation signifying the Sarians' triumph over and mass slaughter of my people."*

She'd struck a sensitive nerve with me, for truly did I feel some guilt over the origin of my name, but one can either become a victim of what has been or the succor of what is to come. I preferred the latter, so I pushed back, though I made sure to do so gently. "I didn't get to choose my name or what happened between our peoples in the past," I said. "But together we can choose our future. Let's put our differences behind us and work together in peace. Will you help us?"

Jason made a step forward with his spear. "Don't trust it, Victory!" he cried.

I waved at Jason to stand down. "Put down your spear. If we can't show a little trust, we'll never get anywhere."

Jason did not relinquish his weapon, but neither did he advance further.

For her part, Tu-al-sa seemed unfazed. Instead, she leaned forward and loomed over me, turning her head to one side and craning it down on her thin reptilian neck. One of her small dark eyes regarded the tattoo on my outstretched right arm.

"Your flesh is marked, Victory Harben."

"My tattoo?" I said. "I got it as a little girl. It was decreed by the Krataklak elders who guide the Voraki, my father's tribe. A sort of coming-of-age ritual."

"So Nadok tells you."

I wanted to protest the implication that my father had misled me about the tattoo. My father was no liar. The Krataklaks were the crab-people who lived in symbiosis with the Voraki, and their elders served as spiritual guides to my father's people. He said they had sent him the symbols in a dream-vision and instructed him to inscribe them on my forearm, strange characters they said would one day help me on my life's journey.

But Tu-al-sa gave me no opportunity to object. The great matriarch beat her regal wings and took flight, sailing through the air and just barely missing our heads as we ducked to get out of her way. She alighted on the other side of the meadow before the control box of our Gridley Wave set.

My godfather and I stood in disbelief as the wizened old reptile placed one of her scaly, clawed appendages on the frequency dial of the apparatus.

"I now reveal to you its true meaning . . . and help you, as you request."

What did she mean by "its true meaning"? Surely not the meaning of my tattoo . . .

But before I could voice my question, the Mahar ran her talon over the dial, turning it until the indicator needle on the gauge above moved into the red warning area—the extreme "danger" zone.

The apparatus began to screech violently like a raging, out-of-control siren. Simultaneously, the oscillating sine wave emanating from the parabolic dish atop the Gridley Wave tower intensified until it transformed into a beam of solid white light, blinding in its intensity. At the point where the beam intersected with the disk of the darkened sun, a second beam mirrored slantingly down toward the surface of the inner world.

Feeling a great heat at my back, I turned my head to look behind. I gasped in fear and startlement. Only a few feet to my rear, the beam of blinding white light reflecting from the darkened orb of the sun terminated in the form of a whirling maelstrom of energy. Within moments, the lateral tornado of light grew larger, its swirling whirlpool maw irising open until it encompassed a diameter twice my height. I braced my legs in a low stance to keep the furious gale generated by the maelstrom from blowing me off my feet.

I locked gazes with my godfather and saw my own shock and desperation reflected back at me on his strained features.

Then the impossible happened. The raging tempest lifted me off my feet and into the air. I felt myself swept backward. The uncertainty gun flew from my grasp.

I was too stunned to scream as swirling tendrils of white and violet energy surrounded me and the maelstrom swallowed me whole.

5

A Bridge too Far

I DON'T KNOW HOW LONG I was engulfed within that whirlwind of violently churning energy, but I experienced a dreamlike sensation of my entire essence being impossibly long and flat, and of being sucked through an infinitely long soda straw. Then, suddenly, I was no longer in the tempest and was again standing on firm ground.

I felt the hot wind of Pellucidar against my back gusting out of Tu-al-sa's maelstrom, from which I had just emerged. When the wind suddenly ceased, I turned to look behind. For a split second I saw a diminutive version of the cyclone of whirling energy shrinking as it irised closed. And then the maelstrom was gone as if it had never existed.

Above me in the crystal-clear night sky, a wide planetary ring arced across a backdrop of nebulae and stars more brilliant than any visible from Earth on the clearest desert night. I stood upon a spire of orangish rock speckled with patches of a strange teal growth that resembled moss. Below me, a little stream cut through the craggy terrain.

A creature unlike any I had encountered before watered at the stream. Its body and legs were shaped like a giraffe's, but its neck was a long and flexible snakelike tube. Two serpentine ancillary appendages with mouths at the ends emerged from the creature's forebody, snaking downward and lapping up water with their narrow tongues.

The thing must have heard my sharp intake of breath, for it whipped its neck around and glared at me with its single eye, which resided at the end of the stalk. One of its two ophidian appendages turned toward me, its lips pulled back to reveal sharp, triangular teeth.

I heard a gentle wafting sound. I looked up to see a horse-sized creature in the sky, its body and wings as thin and translucent as wax paper. It phosphoresced with a soft green luminescence as it fluttered across the cosmic tapestry above.

A little thrill that was part fear and part exhilaration ran through my entire frame.

"Well," I said aloud, "Earth *was* getting a little boring . . ." My voice sounded hollow, as if the air were thinner than that of Pellucidar.

I could not deny that I was on another world and that the maelstrom had carried me here. But how could that be? How had Tu-al-sa accomplished it? And why?

As the immediate shock of my unexpected and unwilling transit began to wear off, two things occurred to me. First, I realized I was cold. The temperature must have been about fifty degrees Fahrenheit, a marked contrast to balmy Pellucidar. I was still wearing the clothes I'd had on when I had left the inner world: knee-high leather boots, khaki pants, and a button-down shirt, the hem of which I had pulled up and tied around my upper waist, the short sleeves rolled up to my shoulders. It was nighttime on the world upon which I found myself, and so there was no sun to warm me, if indeed a sun ever rose and set upon this world. I didn't even know if I was on a planet or a moon, or maybe even an asteroid.

My second realization was that my whole body, from my head to my toes, was tingling as if it were bathed in a strong field of static electricity. I wondered if the prickling sensation might be a side effect of passing through the maelstrom. I rubbed my hands against my arms, torso, and legs, and yet the effect persisted.

Whatever the cause of the tingling and the explanation for my transference to this new and completely unfamiliar environment, it was clear that any wild conjecturing about such matters, however important and stimulating it might be, must for the moment take a back seat to what was now my highest priority: survival in what was in all likelihood a hostile extraterrestrial world. If I could not stay alive here, then I would never be able to return to Pellucidar and help my godfather restore the extinguished sun that threatened all life within the inner world.

I was convinced I was on an alien world not only due to the exotic environment all around me, but because every Pellucidarian is born with a homing instinct like that of a carrier pigeon, which indicates the precise direction of the place of one's birth regardless of where one might be in the inner world. Now my homing instinct cried out to me that my home village of Sari lay at an exacting though inscrutable pinpoint in the heavens located just below the arc of the planetary ring. This surprised me, for I had never been able to sense the direction of my homeland when I resided on the Earth's outer crust, a fact I had always found most disconcerting. But now was not the time to tackle that mystery.

My first course of action was to find a way down from the craggy spire of orangish rock upon which I found myself. While I'd been assessing my new situation and surroundings, I had been observing the bizarre creature below. The thing, though it looked utterly alien, seemed to exhibit the casual demeanor of a grazing antelope, a species with which I was quite familiar thanks to my upbringing in untamed Pellucidar. Even now the creature was reaching up with one of its appendages to nibble on some of the teal moss that grew in a dark area between the crags of my spire.

I got down on my hands and knees and proceeded to crawl down from the summit. As I descended, I scraped my palms more than once on the sharp, uneven edges of the rocky tower. But I have always enjoyed a good rock climb, and I felt invigorated by the fact I was taking assertive action in the face of the completely unknown and unnerving circumstances in which I found myself.

When I was about halfway down the spire I stopped at one of the mossy patches, which glowed softly beneath the brilliant starlight. Though I wasn't hungry, having but recently taken my fill of dried antelope jerky and wild berries just prior to Tu-al-sa's startling arrival in our camp at Mintra, I scooped up some of the teal growth and stuffed it into my pockets. Who knew how long it would be before I encountered another source of nourishment on this world, if indeed the moss was edible to humans? I would be foolish if I didn't start planning for a long stay here.

I sized up the creature with the snakelike neck and appendages and looked around the unearthly landscape for what might serve as a weapon. I don't find pleasure in depriving any creature of its life, and I would first attempt to subsist on the moss indefinitely if I could. But I would do what I must to survive. Though I was out of practice after my six-year hiatus on the outer crust, I knew how to track, kill, and skin an animal, as well as how to prepare and cook my catch in the wilderness, having been instructed by both my father and one of the best hunters in Sari, Tanar, the son of Ghak the Hairy One. Of course, that was in Pellucidar, where, from what I could tell after scanning my current surroundings, the natural resources were quite literally of a different world from this one. In these extraordinary surroundings, would I be able to find good stone capable of knapping into a spearpoint, or a means to light a fire and the fuel to keep it going so that I might cook my meal in the wilds of this wholly unknown and unexplored planetary body?

When at last I reached the base of the spire, the foraging creature fixed its eyestalk on me and began to move away slowly toward an adjoining outcrop. That was fine with me, as I didn't relish the idea of killing the animal, which had done nothing to harm me. Nor did I wish to be killed by it. Though the creature appeared to be docile, I was in a strange environment and could not afford to make any rash assumptions. For all I knew, the thing might charge me down and rake me to death with the razor-sharp teeth at the ends of its appendages, or spit lethal poison at me from its two mouths.

Now that I was a bit closer, I could see that it was truly a magnificent creature. I wondered what outlandish idiosyncrasies of extraterrestrial natural selection had caused it to evolve its unique form, what with its feeding orifices at the ends of its tentacular arms and its single fist-sized eyeball blinking at me with such curiosity, wonder, and doubtless fear at the end of its tubular neck. About the size of a Shetland pony, the animal appeared so meek and harmless that I began to wonder if I might not make friends with it. And I could certainly use a friend on this alien world.

Slowly, so as not to startle the beast, I reached into my pocket and withdrew some of the teal moss I had seen it champing on earlier and held it out on my open palm.

"Hey, there, big guy," I said in a soothing tone, as if I were merely coaxing Freckles, my neighbor's skittish cat back in Oxford, with a saucer of milk instead of trying to entice a shockingly bizarre and unearthly life form to eat out of the palm of my hand. "I've got some nice yummy moss for you."

The creature's eyestalk instantly jutted up stiff and straight, its single orb now wide and unblinking. Suddenly I realized I was breaking my own resolution not to take any rash actions, and I fought to remain calm. What was I thinking, trying to feed and make friends with this strange wild beast?

But then, much to my relief, the animal's eyestalk relaxed and the orb resumed its incurious blinking. Simultaneously, a low, faint trilling arose from the thing's mouths, a sound that I could only interpret as an expression of contentment and trust. The creature took a tentative step toward me, and when I continued my attempt to entice it with reassuring sweet talk, it padded forward timidly until it was close enough to extend a timorous appendage. With cowlike lips, it grasped a few pinches of the bluish-green moss from my palm and began chewing it with an unusual grating motion of its triangular teeth.

It was all I could do to keep myself from bursting out with a little laugh of joy, thereby releasing the nervous tension that had been building in me since the incident at Mintra. Perhaps this new world wasn't so bad after all. If I could make a friend here this easily and quickly, then maybe—

A shadow darkened the brilliant starlight cast down from the glittering heavens, accompanied by a whoosh from above. I ducked instinctively as a blur of thin translucent wings and a long spiny body and tapering tail swooped down only inches above my head.

Then came the unholy screaming. I felt something warm and wet spray across my face.

The shadow lifted almost as soon as it had come. In the gentle light of the scintillating stars and shimmering interstellar gas clouds, I saw a sight that left my heart pounding out of control against my rib cage.

The animal I had been feeding lay flailing on the ground, its tubular neck sliced off and spouting alien lifeblood. The hideous screams were coming from the two mouths on the ends of its writhing appendages. My newfound friend was dying.

I was in shock. All time seemed to flee existence. But then, timelessness is the natural state in the inner world of my birth, and one does not survive long in my homeland of Sari if she freezes in her tracks at the first sight of unforeseen peril. My Pellucidarian reflexes kicked in swiftly, and it was a good thing they did. I looked skyward just in time to see our ruthless assailant swooping back down at us from the heavens. It looked vaguely akin to a colossal brine shrimp with the wings of an enormous firefly, so wax-paper thin I could see the stars shining through them. Its perfectly round, many-fanged mouth was gulping down what was left of my doomed friend's eyestalk.

The injured creature was no longer screaming. It was now moaning softly and pitifully as it lay on its side against the orange rocks. My heart ached for it, but I had no time for compassion.

Without hesitation I snatched up a stone—roughly the size and shape of a baseball, though it was much weightier—from the edge of the stream. The winged monster was almost upon me, its gaping maw filled with sharp and deadly teeth that gleamed like polished crystals. I took a deep breath and grasped the heavy stone tightly in my fist, winding my arm like Hal Newhouser to gain momentum.

The attacker from the sky hissed as it swooped down, its spiny torso casting a shadow over me. I felt a gentle gust of air waft from beneath the monster's wings. At the last moment possible, I released my projectile with all the force I could muster, both centrifugal and muscular.

The stone flew true, straight into the flying terror's gullet. Startled by what was doubtless an unexpected act of resistance, the monstrous firefly crashed to the ground just beyond the now-still form of my moss-eating friend. My downed assailant began rasping for breath in a most unsettling fashion as it choked on the stone that was now lodged deep in its throat. But the dreadful noise did not last long. After only a few hair-raising moments as it thrashed and gagged, the monster lay dead.

My heart still galloping, I kneeled beside the docile creature that had been attacked by the vicious flying thing. Its ophidian appendages, once writhing with life and energy, were now limp and unmoving.

I arose from the animal's lifeless corpse and scanned the heavens. I spied a number of small specks against the pale yellow-and-orange band of the planetary ring, near where it met the horizon. The specks were slowly growing larger.

My heart sank. It could only be more of the monstrous fireflies. I waited only long enough to confirm my fear that they were headed in my direction. And much to my dismay, it soon became evident they were approaching rapidly, as if hellbent on investigating the murder of their fellow.

I began running. I followed the stream, which ran in the opposite direction from the wide arc of the planetary ring. I knew enough about astronomy to guess I was probably heading either north or south from this world's equator. But I didn't care where I was going, as long as it was away from the ravening death dealers from the sky.

I don't know how long I ran before I came to a horrifying realization: the warm and wet spray on my face was the moss-eating creature's blood. I stopped long enough to wash off the gruesome stuff in the stream. This was not just for decorum; I feared the fireflies might be able to smell the scent of their prey's blood. In fact, for all I knew that was how the companions of the specimen I had killed had known to head straight for the scene of the disturbance.

I continued running, positioning myself behind the plentiful outcroppings and rocky spires where possible, in such a way as to keep them between me and where I had last spied the flying monstrosities. Eventually, when I judged I had put a safe distance between myself and my pursuers, I slowed to a walk.

Once, I encountered a group of the docile animals belonging to the same species as my unfortunate friend, as they watered at the stream and grazed on the teal moss. This time, I did not stop and try to tame the creatures. If they were a food source for the terrors from the sky, I did not want to be anywhere near them, and so I left them behind as swiftly as I could.

When I became thirsty, I stopped and tested the stream's water. Before swallowing it, I cupped a little in my hand and dipped my tongue into it. The water tasted clean, though it carried a slight metallic tang. Tentatively, I swallowed a mouthful and waited a couple minutes. I felt fine, so I had my fill from the stream until I had slaked my thirst. Thereafter, I stopped to drink as needed. I could not afford to become dehydrated on my long march to wherever it was that I was going.

I also knew I could not afford to grow weak. When I found my stomach growling after what I judged to be two or three hours of travel, I attempted a similar experiment with the moss as I had with the water. The stuff was stringy and made for a lot of chewing, but its taste, which vaguely resembled that of black licorice, was not unpleasant.

As I walked on, I replayed over and over in my mind the incident with Tu-al-sa at the ruins of Mintra. I tried to recall everything she had communicated to my godfather and me. Jason had said the Mahar queen's sudden appearance felt like a setup, and I couldn't deny it, especially now.

I proceeded to retrace the events that had led me here, trying to make sense of it all: The disappearance of the Gridley Wave to all of our detection apparatus. The ancient tablet of the Mahars bearing instructions related to activating and reactivating the Gridley Wave principle. The beam that had shot forth from the radio tower when my godfather and I had applied the frequency detailed in the tablet. The darkening of Pellucidar's inner sun. Tu-al-sa's inference that she would reveal my tattoo's meaning just before she manipulated the controls of the radio set and thereby summoned the cyclone of energy that had swallowed me whole. My sudden appearance on this alien world.

My physicist's mind went into overdrive. Was it possible that by dialing up the Gridley Wave apparatus to its highest frequencies, Tu-al-sa had somehow managed to generate an Einstein-Rosen bridge? Also known as a one-dimensional tube, this was a theoretical construct that tunneled through the fabric of spacetime and could allow for matter to pass through, depositing it at different spacial and temporal coordinates. Theoretically speaking, there was no reason an Einstein-Rosen bridge that had one end located in Pellucidar couldn't connect via its other end to another world located light-years across the galaxy or even further.

But such a bridge was just a hypothetical model, one that seemed unlikely given the astronomical amount of energy that would be required to pry open a hole in spacetime and keep it stable long enough for something to pass through from one side to the other.

Could that be why Tu-al-sa had beamed the high-frequency Gridley Wave at Pellucidar's sun? Had she somehow tapped the sun's energy, using it to pry open a one-dimensional tube and keep it from collapsing while I passed through?

I made a quick mental calculation and knew that could not be the answer, or at least not the whole answer. Even the Earth's sun, let alone Pellucidar's relatively puny counterpart, could not account for the energy needed to generate a stable Einstein-Rosen bridge. Accomplishing such a feat would require an amount of energy so enormous it could be produced only by another theoretical construct known as a dark star—that is, a region of spacetime whose gravity is so strong that even light cannot escape it—and no one even knew if dark stars existed, for no astronomer had yet been able to observe one. And yet I could not otherwise explain the phenomenon that had transported me instantaneously across the cosmos to this strange and unearthly world.

I circled back to Tu-al-sa's mention of my tattoo. How was sending me through an Einstein-Rosen bridge to a distant alien world a revelation of my tattoo's true meaning? And she had said she would help me, as I had requested. But in what way had she helped me? Had she restored the sun of the inner world to its normal radiance? There was no way for me to know the answers to any of these questions. And if there's one thing that rankles me most, it's when I don't know the answers.

What bothered me even more was that I was clueless as to the fate of my godfather. I had left him behind in Pellucidar with the strange emission still beaming at the central sun from our Gridley Wave tower, in the company of perhaps the most cunning Mahar alive. Moreover, I couldn't shake the memory of the expression on Jason's face as he saw me being pulled into the raging maelstrom—a look of utter fear for my well-being. Even if he were safe and Tu-al-sa had somehow managed to restore Pellucidar's sun, I knew he would be racked with worry over my safety. Even worse, he might believe I was dead. I could only hope that Tu-al-sa had provided him with an explanation for her actions, that she had told him she had sent me through the funnel to another world. At least that would give him hope.

I didn't even want to think about how my parents would react to the news of my disappearance. I knew they would not blame my godfather. They knew he loved me like a daughter and would have done everything in his power to protect me. But they would be anguished.

Thoughts of my loved ones and their concern for my fate bolstered my determination. I would learn to survive on this world and, by hook or by crook, find my way back home. Exactly how, I did not know. But I have always liked a challenge. And this time it looked like I'd found myself a real doozy.

I continued along the streambed of my newfound world, keeping an ever-watchful eye on the heavens. I dared not stray from the little winding creek, for I knew it was possible the maelstrom could reappear where it had formed before. At some point I would retrace my steps, and if the maelstrom appeared there again I would enter it and hope that it would lead me home. I would have remained near the area where I had emerged from the whirling portal but for the deadly terrors from the sky. I would just have to find a way to deal with them later.

After some time, the landscape began to descend with the course of the stream until it emptied into a vast and glittering sea. I gasped at the beauty of the sight before me. From the shoreline out to the distant horizon, the sea glowed with a strikingly orange luminescence. Gentle waves rolled over the black sand of the beach, which sparkled beneath the light cast down from the planetary ring and the blazing stars beyond it.

Unlike an earthly sea, the water did not smell brackish, nor did I taste the metallic tang of the stream water when I tested it with my tongue. When I scooped up some of the seawater in my cupped hands, I found it to be warmer than the surrounding air, which itself had increased a few degrees in temperature as I neared the shore. The water tasted fresh and clean, though I refrained from drinking it as I did not know the origin of the sea's orange glow. The latter could have been the result of bioluminescence from bacteria or even a toxic chemical reaction. Until I could determine the source of the radiance, I would stick with quenching my thirst from the nearby stream.

For no good reason other than I had to choose one way or another, I began walking along the leftward shore. Though I had grown tired as I had descended along the little streambed, the fresh, clean sea breeze and the sight of the vast glimmering ocean reinvigorated me. It can certainly be terrifying to find oneself inexplicably transported to an unknown world, but it can also be an experience of jaw-dropping wonder. And so it was for me as I walked along an alien shoreline and gazed out over the alien sea.

My wonder only increased after I nearly tripped over a large stone jutting from beneath the ebony sand. As it was the first such rock I had encountered along the shore, I kneeled in the wet sand and ran my hands over the exposed face of the cold stone. It was neither wholly rough nor wholly smooth but a combination of both, and a little thrill ran through me when I realized it was embossed in bas-relief with regular but curved lines of grooved bumps, like the characters of a written script. Energized by the discovery, I fell to digging out the stone with great vigor. Before long

I had outlined a much larger surface than I had at first anticipated, so large that I could not hope to uncover it all, especially as the tide was coming in—the latter being evidence, I speculated, that this world had a moon.

As I fought against the recurrent collapse of sand from the ceaseless waves, I managed to clear off a two-foot-by-two-foot section of the stone's face. This was squared off on the two ends that emerged from the sand and slanted down at a low angle to hint at a presumably larger portion that lay who knew how deeply in the sand. I stood up and admired my handiwork, the monolith's bared face glistening with wetness beneath the refracted light of the broad heavenly ring.

On the face of the stone, encircled by three rings of the strange and unfamiliar script, was a large symbol. At its center was an upraised semispherical disk surrounded by a thin ring bisected by eleven smaller and equidistantly spaced disks. The steeples of a large eleven-pointed star speared each of the smaller disks.

Upon gazing down at the symbol I felt a strong sense of déjà vu—the kind that's so intense you can almost hear that Looney Tunes sound effect of a spring boinging back and forth as your vision goes in and out of focus. At least that's what it felt like to me. And yet with my rational mind I knew I had never seen the symbol before.

Was this all a dream? It sure seemed like it as I stood there gazing down at an ancient extraterrestrial artifact half buried in the wet sand, basking in the glow of a planetary ring, interstellar nebulae, and strange constellations on the shore of a shimmering tangerine sea.

As if triggered by the sight of the weird, familiar-but-not-familiar symbol, the tingling sensation that had accompanied me since my arrival on this alien world intensified. I felt the hairs on the back of my arms and neck stand erect as a prickle of static electricity swept over my whole body.

I heard a loud crack, like the snapping of a steel wire.

Whether the sound issued from without or within me, I could not say. Then came utter cold and complete darkness, and the icy, measureless void rushed past me at dizzying speed.

6

FUGUE FOR A CHESHIRE CAT

WHEN I OPENED MY EYES and my senses returned to me, I discovered I had left behind the ringed planet and stood upon yet another alien world.

I could go on at length to describe my new surroundings, but there would be little point, as I did not stay there long. Suffice it to say that it was a world very different from the previous one, inhabited by a race of humanoids who, like on our own world, were made up of groups and individuals prompted to do good or evil, or to act with indifference, based on their own life experiences, insights, prejudices, compassion, and self-interest.

After about an earthly week on that world, I again felt the peculiar electrical tingling course through my body, followed by a sound like that of a steel wire snapping and the rush of the cold void as I hurled though endless space. And then there I was upon yet a third strange world.

I would like to tell you that was the end of my travels, but it was not. The uncanny effect seized me dozens, or maybe hundreds, of times, and upon each instance I found myself transported to a new place or time. Sometimes I remained on a particular world for what seemed weeks or months; other times a seemingly infinite array of worlds flickered past me in but an instant. Soon I lost count of the worlds I had visited, for I had no way to record their number.

Each time I manifested on the new world, I was always as naked as the day of my birth. Now I'm not by nature or upbringing overly modest. I had been raised in Pellucidar, after all, where clothing is practical and often at a minimum thanks to the radiant warmth of the eternal noonday sun. But I had resided on the outer crust for the past six years and had grown used to its customs. Moreover, the sentient locals among whom I manifested—some of weird physical makeup by earthly standards but often looking as human as you or I—were seldom as open-minded in regard to the lack of clothing as were the inhabitants of Pellucidar. As such, I often landed, as they say, in hot water. Therefore, I was forced by circumstance to become resourceful, and soon I developed a knack for assessing my environment at but a moment's glance and attiring myself as adequately as possible with whatever resources were immediately at hand.

Though many times I experimented with attempting to carry material objects with me on my unbidden transits, I always found myself empty-handed when I emerged from the void into my new circumstances. As disconcerting as this development was, another was even more so: in no way could I control when the transit effect would take hold of me and, by extension, the duration of my stay upon a particular world. I forged as many friendships as I made enemies during my world-hopping travels, so that in equal measure I felt as if I were either departing too soon from those with whom I had developed a bond or vanishing just in the nick of time from those who sought to kill me, imprison me, or worse.

On rare occasions I found myself back on the comfortable soil of the good old green grassy planet Earth, but never in a time or a place with which I was familiar. Always I appeared in the past from the vantage point of 1950, when I had left Chamston-Hedding for Pellucidar aboard the O-220, except for the one time I traveled to the distant future. But never did I manifest within the timeline of my life.

On one of my transits I materialized in ancient Britain and narrowly escaped beheading by a wolf's-head-helmeted grandson of Cingetorix. In another I hopped the freights

and made my way across the western United States in a
boxcar of hoboes in the 1910s, transiting on to the next
world with a feeling of frustration, as I'd had no time to
make contact with anyone I had known on Earth who might
have then been alive, such as a middle-aged version of my
grandfather or Mr. Burroughs, or my mother, uncle, or
godfather as a child.

Curiously, I did have a compelling reason to wish to
contact Mr. Burroughs. When I was a child on the outer
crust, being privy to the truth of the existence of Barsoom,
I had read with great interest a number of his tales about
that deathless Virginian, John Carter, and his adventures on
the Red Planet. My godfather had even once allowed me to
speak via Gridley Wave radio to a Barsoomian scientist in
the employ of Dejah Thoris, Princess of Helium, though I
had long puzzled over the fact that our earthly telescopes
could detect no life on Mars. But more to the point, one of
the things I remembered from the accounts of John Carter,
which Mr. Burroughs had published under the guise of
fiction, was the means by which the former had transported
himself back and forth between Earth and Mars. Always had
his transits been preceded by a sound like that of a steel wire
snapping, followed by the sensation of careening at great
speed through the cold, trackless immensity of space—
precisely like my own transits from world to world.

I knew this could not be a coincidence. The effect that
had seized me must be akin to the same method employed
by John Carter to travel between Earth and Mars—a method
that, if I recalled correctly from the tales I had read as a
youth, John Carter had perfected with the help of a unique
individual known as Kar Komak, the Bowman of Lothar.
This Kar Komak was a sort of Pinocchioesque "thought-
being" who had been generated from the mind of a member
of an ancient Barsoomian race, and who later, through
sheer force of will, manifested as a very real physical entity
of flesh and blood. But of more interest to me in my current

circumstances, this strange Barsoomian had instructed John
Carter in a method by which he could bring physical objects
and adornments with him when he traversed the void.

Time and time again I racked my brain, trying to recall
any hint recorded by Mr. Burroughs in his novels about the
particulars of Kar Komak's method. Each time I failed.

One day I shall record for posterity all of the marvelous
and fantastical worlds to which I was hurled by the strange
force, but there are too many speak of on this occasion, when
I fear the signal with which I am communicating to you
may go out of phase at any moment, and that I shall leave
you before I have a chance to finish relating the larger story
of my adventures, which, from your expression, I can tell
you are eager to see through to the end.

Be that as it may, on two previous occasions I have transmitted to you accounts of my travels through the cosmos
that are of particular relevance to the story at hand. These
I shall summarize for you momentarily in order to refresh
your memory, for I had good reason to recount them to an
amazing individual who was to aid me greatly as I hurtled
headlong through spacetime toward an uncertain fate.

7
A Cold Welcome

GAIN I FELT THE COLD rush of space that spanned the transition between worlds. With all my willpower I sought to perceive my surroundings, using each of the five senses known to earthly life. But again, as was typical of the fifty or a hundred or a thousand transits through the cosmos that preceded this one, I could sense nothing but utter coldness and a feeling of plunging at great speed through an infinite immensity.

When my senses returned, I found myself standing outside the massive walls of an enormous city, whose soaring spires and grand architectural features glittered with scarlet scintillations in the light of a small, low-hanging sun. One great stately tower rose above the rest, proud and majestic, like a crimson spear skewering the cerulean heavens, where tiny pinpoints of light glimmered faintly like distant jewels. I spied half a dozen small, sleek craft darting through the air above the city like tiny fireflies, one alighting upon a flat-topped roof that extended high atop a turret. I stood in the center of a paved roadway that ran straight up to a gargantuan gate, the towering doors of which, carven with ornate designs and studded with countless sparkling jewels, were closed.

I breathed in the cool, thin air of this new, unknown world—unknown to me, in any case—and felt a little thrill of exhilaration run through my frame. What would I find upon this spin of the spacetime roulette wheel? Would it be hostility and violence, as seemed to exist on so many of the worlds I had visited? Or peace and repose, which I found to be much rarer, though I was heartened to have encountered many individuals and groups who sought to bring the latter to their strife-torn cultures and heart-rending situations?

I was not to wait long before I found out, for behind me came the sound of great wheels rolling upon the pavement. Before I knew what was happening, I was forced to hurl myself onto the hard ground in a wild leap to get out of the way of what was barreling directly for me at great speed. As I stood up again, dusting off both my naked form and my bruised ego while I checked for injuries, a cacophony of cruel laughs rose from the vehicle that had nearly ended forever my fantastical travels: a colossal chariot drawn by a many-legged beast that stood ten feet at the shoulder, with a hairless, slate gray hide, and yellow-hued, hoofless, and nailess feet padding silently on the roadway. I barely had time to take in the towering, green-skinned, six-limbed creatures standing in the chariot at the creature's reins before another beast-drawn vehicle sped past me, occupied by the same breed of fiendish jockeys and laden with an abundance of exotic furs and silks.

Prompted by what had now become instinct upon transiting to a new world, and also to take some fair compensation for having my dignity so dishonored by the hit-and-run fiends, I reached out and snatched a bolt of gauzy silk hanging over the chariot's side. Just as quickly, I unfurled the little roll of gossamer fabric and wrapped it around myself rather neatly, tying it off at one shoulder with a smile of satisfaction and a sense of accomplishment.

But my good mood was not to last long. The chariot from which I had taken my bounty, having just passed me by, screeched to a sudden halt. One of the green jockeys leaped from the vehicle's open back end, at first shambling rapidly toward me on four limbs as it used its intermediary pair as legs, and then standing solely on its two lower limbs as it rose to its full, terrifying height of twelve feet. I made to assume a defensive jujitsu stance I had learned from my friend Tarzan, but I was not quick enough for the green terror that towered over me. One of the thing's intermediary limbs swung out and backhanded me in the face with a stone-hard fist.

All sense left me, and the next thing I knew I was sitting on the cold pavement. I drew back my hand from my stinging cheek and gazed wonderingly at the blood on my palm. Where was I? Where had the blood come from? Just now, it was hard to remember.

I felt warmth on my face and suddenly knew the blood was flowing out of my own nose. With the realization, my wits came back to me.

I leaped to my feet just as the shadow of the pale olive behemoth fell over me. Or I should say, I tried to leap to my feet. Instead, I flew into the air, propelled by the lesser gravity of whatever world I had landed on, and came crashing down some half a dozen yards distant on my hands and knees, skinning them in the process. The giant threw back its head and cackled with the most spine-shivering laugh I had ever heard, seeming to take demented pleasure in both the injury it had inflicted upon me and the ludicrous spectacle I had made with my ungainly leap.

The creature was at the same time distinctly alien and familiar. Its eyes, set back from its temples and bearing crimson irises in the otherwise all-white orbs, protruded in a peculiar manner from the opposite sides of its head. At first, both eyes were turned toward me, but when one of the creature's fellows shouted out an exclamation, one of its eyes rolled backward independently of the other, and then just as quickly returned its furious gaze to me. Two cup-shaped antennae—or were they ears?—rose from its head and gave the thing a vaguely insectoid appearance. Curving up from a mouth of china-white teeth were two enormous tusks that reached past the height of its eyes and almost to the bases of its antenna-ears. Other than ornaments of shining white metal studded here and there with precious stones of various colors, it was entirely naked, though the adornments were abundant enough to prevent me from determining its sex, if indeed their lack would have revealed it.

You might ask why such a frightful creature was as familiar as it was strange, but it would have been so to anyone who had read Mr. Burroughs' tales of John Carter. Instantly I knew that I was looking upon what the great author had termed a "green Martian" and, by extension, that I could be standing upon only one planet in the known universe—Barsoom!

If this was a real-life green Martian warrior, then I was in a real pickle indeed and could expect no mercy, assuming the tales I had read as a child depicted with any accuracy the members of the ferocious hordes who roamed the Red Planet's dead sea bottoms. The thing would doubtless wish to torture me to death. Or perhaps it would drag me back from whence it came and imprison me down in the dark, forbidding pits that lay beneath one of the ruined and abandoned cities of the ancients, driven mad by my blindness as a thousand cold and sinuous bodies creeped and crawled over my frame. According to the accounts of John Carter, such were the fates in store for those unfortunate enough to fall into the hands of the green Martian hordes.

Once again I rose to my feet, clenching my pitifully small fists and preparing to give as good an accounting of myself as I was able before I suffered such a grim and forlorn destiny. But now a much larger specimen of the same race as my foe emerged from behind the halted chariot. Its skin was of a darker olive hue than the other, and it must have stood fully sixteen feet in height. The thing drew a great longsword from a scabbard that hung from its trappings, its red eyes blazing with fury as they locked upon me.

Suddenly, I realized that my initial tormentor was likely a female of the species. Doubtless it was a male that now confronted me, and he had had enough of the disturbance to his caravan and meant to put an end to it personally. That is, he meant to put an end to *me*.

As I prepared to make a desperate leap in the lesser gravity and thus hope to avoid being cut in twain, a cry—quite human, though in a language I did not recognize—rang out from the direction of the gate. I looked beyond my aggressor to see the great towering doors swing open, and from between them marched a group of twenty or so black-haired men whose complexions bore a deep reddish-copper hue. They wore harnesses from which depended the accoutrements of war, and otherwise were adorned with little else. Longswords, shortswords, daggers, and mean-looking pistols dangled from their hips. A warrior at their fore, wearing a thin fillet from which sprouted three vibrantly colored feathers, was obviously their leader.

The great hulking brute of flesh and bone and tusk turned as the party approached. He sheathed his sword as the warrior in the lead strode up to stand directly before him, and then grabbed me roughly by the arm and dragged me forward. The two leaders exchanged harsh words before the copper-hued man coolly drew his longsword from its scabbard in a clear challenge. The towering green monster shoved me at his female companion, who grabbed me by the arm in such a viselike grip that it was all I could do not to cry out in pain. Again, the great male drew his own longsword, his snowy white teeth gleaming in a mirthless grin. Clearly the giant thought he would make short work of his much smaller, two-armed challenger.

"Wait!" I cried in English as I strained against the woman's grasp. Then I uttered the only word I knew in the common tongue of Barsoom—a term of greeting—hoping it would ease the rapidly escalating situation, and continued in English: "Kaor! Kaor! Please, there's no need to fight over me!" I tugged at the gauzy fabric I had wrapped around myself, looking up at the giant, four-armed warrior. "I meant no offense by snatching this out of your chariot, mister, though I admit I didn't take too kindly to being nearly run over, either." I began to untie the knot that secured my makeshift clothing, but the leader of the red warriors, upon seeing this, held up a hand for me to stop and proceeded to exchange another series of firm words with his would-be opponent. Twice I heard the name "John Carter" spoken in the verbal volleys, first by the red Martian leader, and then by the green man.

Silence reigned for what seemed an eternity, as the two leaders stared metaphorical daggers at one another, each gauging whether the other would be the first to strike with his weapon.

Then, much to my surprise and immense relief, the green man returned his sword to its scabbard and barked an order at the woman holding me. My captor uttered what I took for a Martian curse and then shoved me roughly at the leader of the red men.

I smiled at her as widely as I could with my teeth, only because I knew it would annoy her, and she grinned back at me in kind. Only later was it explained to me what smiling means to a green Martian, and that my action could very well have precipitated the two parties into violence, for among the people of the hordes, a smile is an expression reserved to convey sentiments of the utmost disdain and cruelty. I guess I should have paid closer attention when reading the tales of John Carter as a child, but how could I have known then that I would one day cross the icy void to Barsoom?

The warrior who had intervened on my behalf smiled reassuringly at me—for among the red Martians, a smile is but a smile—and then barked an order at his men, who fell in about me and their leader with military efficiency and proceeded to escort us through the great gate and onto a wide boulevard that ran into the gleaming city. As we proceeded on I saw many pedestrians crowding the street, both male and female, and of the same handsome race as my escort. We walked a short distance along the thoroughfare before proceeding down a ramp that led beneath the buildings that rose upon one side of the street. Here the warrior and I left behind our escort and entered a tube-shaped car, the door of which opened before us automatically and, after a number of people left the car and others entered from the street, closed behind us just the same.

Inside, the car was outfitted with comfortable seating and illuminated by lamps that emitted a soft glow that was much more pleasant than the harsher electric lighting with which I was familiar on Earth. I sat down next to a young, strikingly gorgeous woman, who was attired in golden, jewel-studded armlets, bracelets, and other ornaments, including a dagger sheathed in an intricately decorated scabbard made out of some bright whitish metal and trimmed with gold. She smiled pleasantly at me, though she tilted her head in a questioning manner as her gaze took me in, as if she had never in all her life seen a more curious creature than myself. The woman said something to me in her native tongue. I could only smile back and shrug. The warrior I was with uttered some unintelligible words to her, which resulted in what I took to be a little gasp of astonished comprehension from the woman, as if my companion's words explained everything. Then, apparently satisfied, she settled back in her seat, her eyes going droopy with that bored look that is apparently common to commuters everywhere, regardless of the planet on which they engage in public transit. Within moments, we were speeding along beneath the city toward an unknown destination.

The car stopped twice to off-load passengers and allow new ones to file in from the street. Then my escort and I were disembarking ourselves into a great chamber of marble walls decorated with colorful murals of complex geometrical designs. We climbed a spiraling ramp that led to another grand hall, where I was motioned by the warrior to sit and wait on a stone bench that sat against one side of the massive room, at one end of which towered an arched doorway limned with gold and studded with precious jewels. Four warriors, armed to the hilt with longswords, shortswords, daggers, and pistols, stood guard on either side of the doors. Meanwhile, my guide opened a smaller door, also flanked by guards, that stood in the wall opposite the bench. The two men stood at attention, their countenances stony, as they let him pass, making it clear to me that my escort was a person of importance in the palace, for such I had decided was where I had been brought.

The man emerged a few moments later and motioned me to enter the doorway through which he had just come. I rose and did as he indicated. As I entered the room ahead, I heard the door close behind me. The man had not followed me in.

8

IN THE PALACE OF THE PRINCESS

I FOUND MYSELF in a lavishly decorated chamber, its ceiling high and vaulted. In one portion of the room, artful murals adorned the walls on either side of a long table carved out of a quartzlike stone, giving the impression of a conference hall where a minister and his cabinet might discuss the affairs of state. Adjoining this more open space, the ceiling lowered into a restful salon filled with inviting divans and chaise longues.

"Do not be alarmed," intoned a clear and even female voice in perfect, though faintly accented, English from somewhere deeper in the chamber. "Kantos Kan must return to assuage the wounded feelings of the Thurd delegation. I understand your unexpected appearance at the gate caused quite a stir. The Thurds are a proud people, and your theft of silk from their caravan did indeed upset one of their women, but it has hardly shredded our budding treaty with them."

A curtain drew aside across the room and I gasped at the stunning beauty of the woman who stood before me. She had all the looks of a Hedy Lamarr or a Gene Tierney, enhanced by a symmetry of features whose geometry lay not in any earthly ratio but rather in that of an alien world. Her trappings wrapped around her slender frame in an artful manner, adorned with an abundance of many-faceted rubies and emeralds that sparkled in the soft glow of the room's artificial lighting, which was emitted from bulbs like those

I had seen on the train. A length of crimson silk, not dissimilar from that which I had pilfered from the chariot of the green Martians, wound around her perfect figure and complemented the clever twinings of her trappings.

The woman exuded a kind of natural magnetism that was in no way lurid or unseemly, but was instead regal and dignified and pure. All the same, I thought instantly of that timeless line from Marlowe's tragedy that I'd read in my British literature class—"Was this the face that launched a thousand ships / And burnt the topless towers of Ilium?"— and wondered a little sadly at what challenges confronted this Barsoomian Helen on a daily basis. I did not fail to notice the dagger at her hip, like the one worn by the woman on the train but more ornate, and considered that it might be more practical than perfunctory in this warlike culture.

If this woman was who I thought she was, perhaps one of my analogies wasn't too far off the mark; while studying physics at Darkheath, I had read a declassified report indicating that Hedy Lamarr had as much brains as she did beauty, and that she'd helped develop a radio navigation system for Allied torpedoes during the war. If I was correct, the woman before me, like Miss Lamarr and myself, held an interest in science, as well.

"Welcome, Victory Harben, to the palace of Dejah Thoris," the woman said, confirming my suspicions as to her identity, and then she crossed the chamber to me. She placed her hand upon my shoulder in what seemed a gesture of greeting, and I reciprocated. "You are to be my guest here in Helium," she said, her tone kind and heartening, "where you will be safer than any other place upon Barsoom."

So this, then, was the incomparable Dejah Thoris, Princess of Helium and wife of John Carter, Warlord of Barsoom! But how could she possibly know my name? And by what bizarre quirk of cosmic coincidence had I been led straight into the palace of the mate of John Carter of Mars?

"How . . . ?" I began, but Dejah Thoris simply smiled

and motioned me to be seated upon a richly embroidered divan.

"I know you must have a thousand questions," she said, taking a seat upon a divan adjoining mine. "As do I. But know from the outset that I am aware of at least the beginnings of your journey, for your friend—is the word 'godfather' correct?—Jason Gridley has, like you, been drawn to this world not long ago and told his story to my husband, John Carter."

I leaped up from the divan. "My godfather is here? Take me to him!"

"Sit, young Victory," Dejah Thoris said, and I reluctantly obeyed, though my heart was beating fast and hard at the thought of Jason being so close at hand and that I might at last be reunited with him. After I'd settled back in my seat, the lips of my host curled into a smile, and she continued. "You remind me of Tara, my daughter. She is as brash as she is beautiful, and also gifted with a sharp intellect."

"Princess, forgive me for being so abrupt," I said, "but you must understand that I have been hurled unwillingly upon a horrendous odyssey and am fearful as to the fate of my godfather, Jason Gridley. It has been long since I have seen him. Please tell me, is he safe and unharmed?" During my cosmic travels, I had once transited to an underwater world where I met a man whom I overheard speak my godfather's name. Thus had I learned that Jason Gridley had indeed followed me into Tu-al-sa's maelstrom. But my transit had been brief and I had been swept away to the next world before learning anything more as to my godfather's fate.*

"That I do not know," replied the Princess of Helium, "for he disappeared under mysterious circumstances while providing invaluable assistance to John Carter in grave matters that threatened all life on Barsoom. Those matters

---

* See the Edgar Rice Burroughs Universe novel *Carson of Venus: The Edge of All Worlds* by Matt Betts for Victory's brief visit with the Earthman Carson Napier on the planet Amtor.

have been resolved, but my husband tells me he can only assume that Jason Gridley has also been unwillingly transported to yet another world, a phenomenon with which it seems you are familiar."

"I must speak with John Carter immediately," I said. "I must know what my godfather has told him of the events that have transpired since I left Pellucidar."

"Alas, John Carter is not in Helium. He is away dealing with the aftermath of the Oolscar affair."* She must have seen how crestfallen I was, for she rose from her divan to sit beside me and placed her hand reassuringly on my own. "But my husband has told me in detail of the time he spent with Jason Gridley. You will be pleased to know that both the Gridley Wave and Pellucidar's sun were restored shortly after you departed Jasoom's inner world. Moreover, it seems that your godfather followed you into the strange cyclone generated by the creature named Tu-al-sa. Jason Gridley said he believed the cyclone was something the scientists of Jasoom have theorized about called . . ." She closed her eyes a moment as if searching her memory for the term. "Something they called an *Einstein-Rosen bridge*."

"He figured it out, too!" I exclaimed. I could have jumped for joy, so elated was I to finally have some concrete knowledge of my godfather's existence since I had left him behind in Pellucidar on my seemingly unending ride on the currents of spacetime. I was equally elated to hear about the restoration of the Gridley Wave, and even more so Pellucidar's sun, for I had been agonizing over the fate of the inner world's inhabitants since the outset of my cosmic journey.

"But then a strange effect seized your godfather," the princess continued, "and proceeded to hurl him one world to another, even one time to another. He is searching for you, Victory, but he is not in control of the phenomenon that effects his transits from world to world, or time to time.

---

* See the Edgar Rice Burroughs Universe novel *John Carter of Mars: Gods of the Forgotten* by Geary Gravel.

And I suspect, from your sudden appearance outside the gates of Helium, that you too have been seized by the strange phenomenon. Am I correct?"

"On the nose," I said. "As far as I can tell, there seems to be no rhyme or reason to it."

"I would not be so sure."

A sense of foreboding fell over me. "What do you mean?"

"I do not know precisely," Dejah Thoris said. "But there is something John Carter related to me that makes me wonder if there is not indeed a common thread that runs through your unbidden travels across the cosmos. He told me that while he and Jason Gridley were in the subterranean 'Perfect World' of the Oolscar, they spied in an enclosure meant for the display of animals a strange being whose form did not resemble that of any known form of life on Barsoom—a sentient quadruped that bore a human face, a child of its own kind strapped to its back. When my husband went to seek sustenance for the famished creatures, Jason Gridley felt the electric tingle that typically precedes his transits—"

"I've got that too!" I interjected.

Dejah Thoris smiled and nodded. "And then, after the prickling of energy ran through him," she continued, "your godfather watched as the two beings appeared to vanish into thin air before his very eyes. He could only wonder whether they had been carried to Barsoom by the phenomenon that had transported him there, and if that same phenomenon had snatched them away."

"Wait!" I exclaimed. "I have encountered just such a creature and her child. Her name is Ren-ah-ree of the land of Va-nah, and her child's name is Da-va-ro!"

I explained that on one of my transits I had found myself in a hollow world called Va-nah, much like Pellucidar, but pierced by massive holes called Hoos that led to the outer crust. There I had met Ren-ah-ree, a member of a coarse, bellicose race of quadrupedal warriors called Va-gas.

But beneath Ren-ah-ree's belligerent demeanor I had found a warm and courageous heart—a mother who would do anything to protect her young child, Da-va-ro. Pitted against a common enemy, we became at first reluctant allies, and then at last friends.

But most importantly, I told Dejah Thoris, Ren-ah-ree had said that when I first appeared in Va-nah, she could perceive a "purple wind" swirling around me. "Moreover," I went on, "she and I could somehow communicate, though we had never learned each other's languages. Later, she explained that she had been away from her tribe gathering fruits when an ebon-winged warrior woman had appeared in the sky surrounded by a purple glow. The winged woman had no sooner materialized than she vanished, but when she disappeared, a current of the purple wind that had been surrounding her swept out and seized Ren-ah-ree and her young son, Da-va-ro, who was strapped to her back. The next thing the Va-gas knew, she and her son were in a strange place deep underground—not a hollow world like Va-nah, but a cavernous one that sounds a lot like your Oolscar's 'Perfect World'—where they saw other two-legged people like myself."

"It was Jason Gridley and John Carter that she saw!" Dejah Thoris exclaimed.

"That's my guess too," I replied, "now that you've supplied the missing pieces of the puzzle. Or at least some of the missing pieces. In any case, Ren-ah-ree and Da-va-ro were in the cavernous realm for an indeterminate length of time before they again found themselves back in their homeworld of Va-nah. Shortly thereafter, I was hurled to Va-nah and met them there."

Here I had to back up and recount another of my transits to Dejah Thoris, for I too had encountered the same ebon-winged warrior witnessed by Ren-ah-ree.

On an earlier occasion, I explained, I had visited what I had initially thought was a dinosaur-infested world called

Caspak, but which I later came to believe was but a remote island located in the middle of one of Earth's oceans—but Earth from a couple of decades before I was born. There I had met a young woman named See-ta, who befriended me and helped me survive the terrors of her primitive land. But then we were captured by a ghoulish race of winged humanoid creatures called Wieroos. But before the Wieroos could sacrifice us to their god Luata, a thunderclap ripped through the air and a strange being appeared out of nowhere. Lahvoh of the Zarafim, she had called herself. She was a giant, towering even over our daunting Wieroo captors. Ebon wings sprouted from her back, and iridescent violet armor encased her formidable frame. She wielded a golden sword, the blade of which burst into flame when the Wieroos attempted to attack her, and with which she appeared to drain the very soul out of one of her slain victims.

"More importantly," I went on, "she said she had detected me moving through 'the angles'—that is, what I believe to be other dimensions in spacetime. Let's just say this Lahvoh wasn't exactly happy about my jaunts through the universe. When she noticed my tattoo"—I held out my right forearm so that Dejah Thoris might examine the ritual marking my father had inscribed in my flesh—"she seemed to recognize the symbols and became agitated. I asked her what the symbols said, for I myself didn't, and still don't, know. My father said he'd received them in a dream from his tribe's elders, but he never told me their meaning other than to imply they were part of a coming-of-age ritual before I was to leave for the outer crust. Be that as it may, Lahvoh refused to tell me anything about the symbols, saying that surely I must know their meaning. I reaffirmed that I did not and she became irate, saying she would take me back to be interrogated by her masters, whoever or wherever *they* were. Then, when I made my move to escape, she flipped her wig." Dejah Thoris raised a perfect eyebrow.

"Well, if you want to be accurate," I admitted, "she tried to *murder* me."

I shook my head in bafflement. "What could it all mean? It can't be a coincidence that Jason and I both encountered the Va-gas. Nor can it be a coincidence that the winged warrior woman was involved in both incidents."*

"It is curious," Dejah Thoris said, furrowing her brow. "There are certain instances in my husband's life wherein he has experienced coincidences that are beyond any rational explanation. You also seem to be bound up in such a panoply of absurd quirks of fate. Why, for instance, should you arrive here, outside my very gates, instead of, say, in Zodanga, faraway Gathol, or, even more likely, upon one of the un-inhabited dead sea bottoms of my cherished but dying world? And why Barsoom at all? Why not on Cosoom or Sasoom or even tiny Rasoom hurtling so close to the face of the Sun? No, it cannot be mere chance that brings you to my palace. But if it is not chance, is it then fate? This I doubt as well. No, I believe it is *you* who have drawn yourself here, though for what purpose I cannot fathom. You are unknowingly guiding your fate, drawing yourself ever close to your destiny with each leap through space and time."

It was an interesting theory, and one to which I had given some thought. I went on to try my best to explain to Dejah Thoris the phenomenon that Schrödinger had called *Verschränkung*, or entanglement—the idea that one subatomic particle could somehow be bound up with the essence of another subatomic particle, as if a characteristic had been instantaneously transferred from one particle to the other without regard to distance or time. Einstein didn't

---

* See the bonus novelette "Victory Harben: Prisoners of Caspak" by Mike Wolfer in the back pages of *Tarzan: Battle for Pellucidar* by Win Scott Eckert (Edgar Rice Burroughs, Inc., 2020) for Victory's encounter with the winged warrior Lahvoh, and the bonus novelette "Victory Harben: Stormwinds of Va-nah" by Ann Tonsor Zeddies in *John Carter of Mars: Gods of the Forgotten* by Geary Gravel (Edgar Rice Burroughs, Inc., 2021) for Victory's adventure in Va-nah with Ren-ah-ree and Da-va-ro.

believe in such seemingly fantastical action at a distance. But there were other reputable physicists who did. Had Tu-al-sa's maelstrom somehow imposed an entanglement effect on Jason and me, binding us in some manner with each other and also with some other destiny of which we were unaware? Was that what had drawn us both along the axis of space to Barsoom, though we were still out of sync on the axis of time?

Dejah Thoris remained quiet as I spoke, and for some time afterward she seemed to be ruminating on my words. "From what you have told me," she said at last, "I do not believe that the *jeddara* of the creatures you call the Mahars meant to do you harm. On the contrary, she seemed to wish to help you. Moreover, the effect that has seized hold of you seems uncannily similar to the method by which my husband himself has learned to traverse the void, a technique he has refined with instruction from our friend Kar Komak, the Bowman of Lothar. The people of the ancient city of Lothar have a saying: 'All is mind.' According to the Lotharians, reality is not what it seems. Matter, they say, is subservient to thought. This is part of the method that Kar Komak has taught to John Carter, allowing him not only to traverse the void at will if certain circumstances are present, but also to carry physical objects along with him during his translocations.* It would seem that such a talent would be useful to yourself, would it not?"

I smoothed down an unseemly ruffle in my gossamer attire. "Well, it certainly would have saved me from some embarrassing episodes, that's for sure. But more importantly, if I could control my transits through the void, I could return home to Pellucidar."

For the next couple hours—or a little less than a "zode," as I learned the equivalent span of time was called on

---

* See Edgar Rice Burroughs' novels *Thuvia, Maid of Mars* for more on the philosophies and mental abilities of the Lotharians, and *The Chessmen of Mars* for John Carter's account of learning a new means of traversing the void from Kar Komak, the Bowman of Lothar.

Barsoom—Dejah Thoris and I discussed my predicament. The princess maintained that my best hope in gaining control over my transits lay in learning the mental techniques practiced on Barsoom by the ancient Lotharians. As she had upon many occasions discussed the topic with her husband, she shared with me all that she knew, and together we even practiced an exercise that John Carter had told her was particularly helpful in mastering the art of traversing the void.

Eventually our conversation returned to the topic of what it all could mean—Tu-la-sa's shrouded machinations, the maelstrom, the angel with the flaming sword, the latter's interest in my tattoo and the Mahars, and precisely who her soul-hungry masters could be. For me, my singular story always returned to Tu-la-sa, for she had been the one who had set everything in motion when I was yet a young girl of eleven years of age.

"You make a good case that Tu-al-sa didn't mean to harm me," I told Dejah Thoris, "but you might imagine I've got a few bones to pick with her. I mean, with all the times that I've nearly gotten myself killed, you can hardly say that she's—"

I stopped in midsentence, my heart plummeting into the pit of my stomach.

Dejah Thoris, taking notice of my distress, asked, "What is wrong, Victory Harben?"

"I have a feeling we're going to have to make some quick good-byes." I stood up suddenly. "I just felt an electric tingle run through me. You know, like the kind of sensation that always heralds my imminent departure from one world and my advent on the next."

A peculiar look came over my host's exquisite features. "I feel it too," Dejah Thoris said, also rising to her feet.

"You *do*?" I thought of what my friend Ren-ah-ree had told me about getting caught in the winged warrior's wake—her "purple wind"—and being suddenly transported to another world. Not that I wouldn't want the company, but the last thing I wanted to do was to carry an unwilling Dejah Thoris along with me on my next transit, or even worse, to hurl her to some other far-flung world without me. "Wait, that's *not* good. Not good at all."

I had only just spoken the words when a thunderous crack reverberated throughout the chamber. A queasy feeling overcame me, so extreme that I staggered. Dejah Thoris seemed similarly affected, for I saw her grip the arm of her divan to brace herself. For a moment my vision grew blurry, as if a giant spectral hand had wiped itself in a swirling motion over my field of sight and smeared reality before my very eyes. A strong gust of wind buffeted me, blowing back my unruly hair from my face. When my vision cleared, I saw that Dejah Thoris and I were no longer alone.

A giant female warrior glided down on wings as black as sin from the high vaulted ceiling and alighted on the floor, a golden sword glittering in her hand. She was arrayed in gleaming armor of shimmering violet and a helm reminiscent of ancient Greek design, including a golden plume that crested from front to back down the center of the head. Her armor-plated boots and gauntlets were the pitch black of a furnace, as was the silken hair that flowed down over her shoulders from beneath her helmet. The colossal woman towered over us—seven feet tall if she were an inch. Coal-black eyes set in a ghastly white face peered out through the T-shaped opening in her helmet, settling first on the princess, and then drifting with glacial sangfroid to rest upon me.

It was Lahvoh.

"What were you just saying about entanglement?" I said to Dejah Thoris, whose eyes grew wide in a look of astonished acknowledgment.

"At last I have found thee, Viktree," the winged woman said in English, or at least so the words translated in my mind, for I wondered if Dejah Thoris heard our uninvited guest speak in the common tongue of Barsoom. "Is that not the name the little savage from the land of Caspak called you?"

"Well," I replied, wincing, "let's just say we're going to have to work a little on your diction. Maybe if you took off that cast-iron oven of a helmet, it might be easier for you to enunciate properly."

"You will accompany me to the domain of my masters," the giant said icily, ignoring my razzing, "where you will explain the markings on your body and why the little savage from Caspak spoke to you of the Mahars of Pellucidar. Or . . . you will die in this very chamber."

I raised my hands in a placatory gesture. "Now listen, lady, don't snap your cap. I realize we got off to a bad start when we first met. Let's just slow down a minute and go back to the beginning. Now *why* exactly are we in a rhubarb over my tattoo?"

I was hoping my well-reasoned, if a little brazen, speech might get some answers out of this muliebrous Bredbeddle, but at that very moment a warrior in the guard of the princess appeared in a doorway adjacent to the black-winged giant. Assessing the situation in but a glance, he flung his longsword from its scabbard and ran forth to put himself between the colossal woman and his princess.

"No!" I cried out to the man. "Don't provoke her!"

But I was too late. Lahvoh's black lips grinned devilishly as the length of her golden sword burst into flame. Her blade swung down as the faithful guard attempted to parry the blow with his own sword, only to cry out in horror as his weapon shattered into half a dozen pieces. Lahvoh's smirk deepened. She reached out a black gauntleted hand and throttled the man, lifting the poor fellow off the ground even as she plunged the blade deep into his midsection.

Dejah Thoris whipped the bejeweled dagger from her hip and made to leap upon the winged warrior like an angry tigress, but I blocked her advance with a firm arm. I knew what would come next, as I had seen it once before, and I could not allow the Princess of Helium to fall victim to it.

We both looked on in wide-eyed horror as Lahvoh dropped the lifeless corpse of the guard with a heavy thud onto the crimson carpet. Then she raised her flaming sword above her head and parallel to the floor in what was clearly a practiced, ritual motion. A mist as white as alabaster arose from the body of the dead man, the vapor glowing and swirling as it was drawn up into the tip of the flaming sword. I saw a flicker of orange in the woman's eyes that, disconcertingly, I didn't think could be attributed to a reflection from her fiery blade.

"An appetizer for my hungry gods," she crooned. Ecstasy laced Lahvoh's words as the mist flowing into the sword diffused into thin wisps and then disappeared entirely. Then she fastened her dark eyes upon the princess. "I see the barest teteculatory impression surrounding you that does not match that of your friend here. Could it be that you are bound to another who has made a habit of traversing the angles? Ah, I see the answer in your eyes. Yes, you will make a fine main course for my masters."

"Run, Victory Harben," Dejah Thoris ordered. "I shall try to delay her while you escape."

"Uh-huh," I said. "Not gonna happen."

I knew there was no physical defense either of us could mount against the violet-armored behemoth that confronted us. She was just too powerful. But if I could not defeat our opponent by physical means, then perhaps I could try something altogether different. What was it the ancient Lotharians had said? All is mind? Well, then, I would give Lahvoh a piece of my mind.

I stepped between Dejah Thoris and the giant armored warrior. Then, in the desperation of the moment, I put into practice the exercise the princess had but just taught me, concentrating every ounce of my attention, every fiber of my being, on Lahvoh, willing her to travel through the angles back to from wherever she had come.

On she came toward me, her sword flaming brightly as its heat radiated upon my face, her once-black eyes now lit from within as by orange fires. I wondered if I were throwing my life away on a foolish notion, but I concentrated still harder, conjuring in my thoughts the trackless void with which I had become so familiar. I pictured Lahvoh hurtling through the cold reaches of space.

Suddenly I felt a presence alongside my own consciousness, and somehow I knew that it was Dejah Thoris, steeling her own mind and yearning with her utmost willpower to imagine Lahvoh into the oblivion of nonbeing.

The world began to blur before my eyes. There was a sound like the snapping of a steel wire, followed by an ear-splitting crack that was louder than any terrestrial thunder. Then I was hurtling through the icy void.

But this time I was not alone.

9
FIERY ANGEL

WHEN I TRANSITIONED FROM THE VOID, cold air buffeted me. The little I could make out amid the darkness that surrounded me—tiny, distant lights, far to one side beneath me, like those of a city seen from an airplane—told me I was plunging through the night sky toward the ground far below.

I was in free fall!

Terror seized me, but I had enough sense to spread out my arms and legs to create as much wind resistance as I could to slow my fall. Not that it would matter much. When I hit the ground, my body would still be flattened to a bloody pulp. But as my mother always told me, you do the best you can with what you've got.

I craned my neck against the force of the wind, looking up to see a tiny, winged humanoid form silhouetted against the eerie violet glow of the atmosphere above.

Lahvoh. She had come with me through the void. Or I with her. I did not know which.

All that mattered now was that her small form was growing larger as she swooped down at me through the dark heavens, her great wings drawn back to give her speed.

For a moment, my heart leaped with hope. Hope that my enemy was diving through the sky to save me from certain death. Hope that, whatever I represented to her, I held something of value in her mind that she did not wish to see perish as a heap of broken flesh and bone squashed flat against the surface of an alien world. Though I didn't particularly relish the thought of becoming Lahvoh's captive, I would take it any day over the alternative. If I managed to survive my present predicament, at least it would buy me some time to think my way out of the next one.

But my hope didn't last long. Three dark, sleek saucer-shaped objects shot from somewhere out of the edges of the night sky and surrounded Lahvoh in a triangular formation. Her dive toward me stopped with a sudden, violent jerk to her frame as a brilliant beam of light radiated from each of the three craft and illuminated her form. There she hung suspended in midair, as if the beams of light somehow held her in abeyance, while I continued to hurtle toward certain death upon the surface of the dark world below.

Out of nowhere, blinding light surrounded me. I felt a powerful jolt. No longer did I feel the cold winds rushing past. I squinted against the intense radiance and realized I was surrounded by three points of light spaced equidistantly. Whatever the craft were that had surrounded Lahvoh and halted her in mid-dive, it appeared that three of the things had similarly encircled me and put an end to my free fall. I too hung in midair, miraculously suspended by beams of light.

Suddenly, the wind against my body told me I was moving again, though this time not in free fall but in a controlled and much slower descent. The three craft maintained their formation around me, continuing to rake me with their intense beams.

I looked back to where I had seen Lahvoh. She was much closer now, perhaps only two hundred yards away, making furious struggling motions in the air. She seemed to be trying to break free of the grasp of whatever force held her in place. Then the sword in her hand burst into flame as I had seen it do twice before, once on Caspak and again in the palace of Dejah Thoris on Barsoom. She proceeded to raise the sword, pointing it upward over her head, and the flames blazing across its blade seemed to run off the shaft and shoot straight up into the heavens.

Far above, a wide section of the atmosphere at which she had directed her sword seemed to catch fire, raging like an unholy inferno.

As if in response to Lavhoh's action, the three craft surrounding her extinguished their lights and shot off like bullets toward the patch of flaming sky. Lahvoh, now free of the restricting beams, arched back her wings and resumed her dive in my direction.

Meanwhile, the three craft surrounding me continued their descent, carrying me along with them. Gradually, the ground grew nearer and immense hills of purple sand came into focus. As I neared the ground, the craft carrying me downward slowed, so that when at last I alighted on the plum sands, I was set down as gently as a leaf on Earth falls onto the floor of a grassy meadow on a windless day.

The instant that my feet touched the ground, the craft surrounding me also touched down and their beams went dark. I could see the gloomy, saucer-shaped forms resting where they had landed a hundred yards away to my left, right, and rear, respectively.

I had been set down in the middle of a vast bed of sand, upon the opposite side of which I saw Lahvoh winging down to earth directly in front of me. When she alighted, she began striding purposefully in my direction, her sword still blazing.

I held my ground, the strong, cool desert wind blowing in my hair and fluttering my gossamer attire.

My gossamer attire! I had somehow managed to bring it with me through the void! Dejah Thoris had been right about the mental powers and techniques of Kar Komak and the ancient Lotharians.

When Lahvoh came within ten feet of me, she stopped. The light cast by her fiery sword upon her pale face, gleaming armor, and great arching wings made her look like a devil out of some old master's painting.

"You surprise me, human," the giant woman said, disdain edging her melodious voice. "Who would think that one of the lower orders would have the strength to carry me with her through the angles? All the more reason to end you now on this insignificant world before you pose a threat to my divine masters."

"Look, lady," I replied. "I don't know wherein your problem with me lies, but it's not like I'm in control of this Cheshire cat routine. So you don't like me traveling through the angles? Well, neither do I. Kindly direct me back to Pellucidar and I'll get out of your hair, and that of your 'divine masters,' too."

"Pellucidar . . ." the woman rasped. "Is that from where you hail? It is surprising, for the humanoid species in that world has barely advanced beyond intelligence of the most primitive apes. But it does explain your knowledge of the Mahars, of which my masters will wish to know all the details. Perhaps I shall spare you after all." She extended her free hand toward me, around which faint wisps of purple mist formed and began to swirl.

I recalled what Ren-ah-ree of Va-nah had told me about her and her child being swept up in "purple winds" that had surrounded a winged woman, a phenomenon that had carried them all away to another world. I had assumed that something about the eyes of a Va-gas could perceive a part of the spectrum that human eyes could not, as Ren-ah-ree had said she could see traces of a violet aura surrounding me after my own transit through the void, but now I questioned this, for I too could see the violet aura surrounding the winged woman quite clearly. But that was something to puzzle out at a later time. Right now I had more important things to worry about, for I could only conclude that Lahvoh meant to transport me through the angles to the realm where her masters abided, wherever that might be. And it didn't take much thought to convince me that was a very, *very* bad idea.

I steeled my mind, remembering the mental techniques that Dejah Thoris had taught me during our brief time together. As she had instructed, I sought a point of focus deep within my mind and heart. Then, with all my will, I imagined the winged woman was no longer standing before me, that she had gone back to from wherever she had come.

Nothing happened. I tried once more, deepening my focus. Again, nothing. Without Dejah Thoris to assist me in my mental efforts, I might as well have been daydreaming.

"Do not resist me, Victory Harben," Lahvoh said. "That is what the red woman called you, is it not?"

"Yeah, you got it, lady. And since we're now getting to know each other and become friends, what's your moniker again? Miss Lahvoh, was it?"

The woman sneered. "Just 'Lahvoh,'" she said, and I saw orange light flicker in her narrowing eyes. I grinned, taking some satisfaction at having gotten under her skin. And why stop now? I thought.

"That's kind of a self-righteous appellation, isn't it? '*Just* Lahvoh'? I thought angels were supposed to be above the vainglorious thing."

In response, the winged woman raised her flaming sword above her head and then held it parallel to the ground in the same practiced motion I had observed her perform back on Barsoom. I recalled my godfather's customary admonition that one day my sharp tongue was going to get me into a lot of trouble, and that when that day came I'd learn an important lesson. Well, it looked like he was right and I was about to gain some precious wisdom for the few remaining seconds I had left before I shuffled off this mortal coil.

Suddenly I felt extremely weak and tired, as if I'd gone sleepless for several nights straight and run a marathon on an empty stomach. A mist appeared before my eyes. Not a glowing purple mist like the one that had formed around Lahvoh's hand when she tried to pull me with her through the angles. No, it was the same ghastly alabaster mist that she had drawn from the corpse of the warrior she had slain on Barsoom. Except, this time the mist was coming from *me*.

My knees buckled and I fell upon them in the sand. I felt nauseated. I attempted to rise and get back on my feet, but the very effort spent what little energy I had remaining and I fell forward face-first upon the desert floor. Even as I fought to keep my eyes open, I sensed Lahvoh looming over me. She was draining the very life force from my body, siphoning it into her fiery sword.

I guess this was it. The end of the very short life of the little Pellucidarian girl born as Victory von Harben. For some reason, as I breathed my last few breaths, I thought of Janson Gridley. It puzzled me. Why Janson? Briefly, I felt a pang of regret that I'd not gotten to know him better, and then the thought drifted away on the same breeze as did the remainder of my vitality.

As my awareness faded, I heard a hissing sound, like that caused by a pneumatic door opening. No, it was three hissing sounds, coming from the direction of each of the craft that surrounded us. In the dustup with Lahvoh, I had forgotten about them. Funny how being confronted by a winged behemoth from another dimension and her flaming sword will do that to you.

I used my remaining strength to lift my head. Through blurry eyes I perceived a human-shaped figure emerging from an opening in the craft on my left. In its hands it held an orb of glowing yellow. I turned to my right and saw a second humanoid form carrying an identical orb. If I'd had the strength to look behind me, I guessed I would have seen a third.

From somewhere so close it sounded like it was inside my own head, I heard a steel wire snapping. Then a thunderclap tore through the world and all went dark.

10

AMONG THE THIRD CONTEMPLATION

WHEN MY SENSES RETURNED, I wondered for a moment if I had died and awoken in heaven. I lay supine upon a soft bed beneath silken sheets of the purest white. I propped myself up on my elbows to gaze upon a spacious, high-ceilinged room with pearly white walls and open, arched doorways leading out into wide hallways. Through the doorway on my left came a pleasant breeze laced with the fragrance of wildflowers. Beside my bed was a small round table upon which rested a clear glass filled with a pinkish liquid that, just to look at it, might have been a strawberry milkshake. The room was lit with a general ambient glow, the origin of which, strangely, I could not pinpoint. A small oval table, before which sat two comfortable-looking chairs of sleek design, stood near one of the walls. On the opposite side of the chamber, a little artificial waterfall burbled down the face of the wall into a marble basin, producing a pleasant trickling sound that helped ease the anxiety I might otherwise have had at waking up in a strange environment. Intricate mosaic tilework, whose geometric designs created the illusion of slowly shifting patterns, covered the floor of the entire room, as well as that leading out beneath the three arched doorways.

I threw off the sheet covering me to discover I was garbed in a slipover gown of a white silken fabric. I sat up and slid my legs over the edge of the bed, feeling weak and shaky. A yawn seized me and I stretched away the drowsiness and fatigue from my weary frame. Tentatively, I touched my feet to the cool, tiled floor and stood up. Though I felt a bit unsteady, I was strong enough to walk across the room to the nearest archway, determined to track down those who had brought me here and discover their intentions.

When I came to the doorway, I stopped. It was not that I wished to stop; rather, I simply could not bring myself to continue forward and walk beneath the arch. To be clear, no thought or emotion, such as fear or wariness, prevented me from passing through the doorway. On the contrary, I very much wanted to leave the room and explore what lay beyond. It was just that I could not. Any mental order that I gave myself to proceed was met with a complete lack of response by body, nerve, and muscle, as if the thought directive simply could not reach its destination and went unheeded.

I repeated my attempt to leave the room at the two other doorways, but each time I was met with the same inability to pass beneath the arch.

I hoped only that I had not suffered permanent brain damage when Lahvoh had tried to siphon away my soul stuff with her flaming sword, and that any impairment she might have inflicted upon my mental functions would at some point be healed with the passage of time.

Puzzled and discouraged by my powerlessness to pass beyond the chamber, I walked back to the bedside table and lifted the glass of pinkish liquid to my nose. The glass was cool to the touch, and its contents smelled faintly of sweet fruit, though of a variety I could not place.

A male voice came from the nearest entrance, and I turned suddenly, still holding the glass, to gaze upon a man standing in the archway. He appeared to be in his mid-thirties by earthly reckoning and was attired in a black formfitting jumpsuit with turquoise-sequined stripes running down the arms, legs, and sides. His features were regular and handsome, his skin tone a shade darker than my own and his figure fit and well-proportioned. He smiled and repeated the words he had spoken but a moment before, which were in a language I did not know or recognize. Simultaneously, he mimed drinking from a glass.

I looked at the glass in my hand, then tilted my head and gave him a dubious look. He laughed and proceeded to cross the room in a nonthreatening manner, take the glass from my hand, and imbibe a deep draft of the pinkish liquid. Still smiling, he licked the foamy residue from his lips with apparent pleasure, and returned the glass to me. Again, he motioned for me to drink.

I shrugged and obeyed, taking in a mouthful of the viscous concoction, which tasted somewhat like a mix of vanilla and coconut with a faint chalky aftertaste. I felt a little surge of energy pass through me, and my companion urged me to down the remainder, which I did, for the stuff tasted even more divine than the strawberry milkshake I had at first imagined it to be. Another surge of energy coursed through my frame, greater than the last. I no longer felt even the barest trace of fatigue. In fact, I felt better than I had ever remembered, and not just physically. It seemed as if my mind, emotions, and body were in complete harmony with my entire being.

When I set down the glass, my companion raised a finger and spoke more in the strange language. Then he left the room, returning but a few moments later carrying a small case, which he set at the foot of the bed. He extended a hand to indicate the case, and then promptly departed from the room once again.

I set the case on the bed and pressed a button on one side that opened the latch securing it. Inside, I found a black formfitting uniform much like the one my host had been wearing, though with purple-sequined stripes running down the shoulders, arms, legs, and sides, and smaller stripes crisscrossing the breast, in place of the turquoise stripes that decorated his attire; the stripes, I learned later, could be made to generate a faint radiance with a simple press of a button on my belt, the charge for which was renewed by a combination of energy converted from body movement and exposure to light, whether natural or artificial. Also in the case were knee-high boots, similar to those worn by the man. These were made out of an extremely lightweight silver metal that reminded me of Harbenite, the extraordinarily durable substance discovered by my uncle Erich in the Wiramwazi Mountains of Africa back on Earth. Underclothes and thick socks completed the raiment in the case.

Apparently the man wished me to change into the clothing he had provided, and seeing no reason not to, I proceeded to slip out of the silken garment I was wearing and don my new uniform. The clothing and footwear fit to a T, as if it had been custom-made for me, and I wondered if perhaps it had. When I had completed my task and was fully appareled, I felt like a woman reborn.

My host returned a few minutes later, nodding and smiling with approval at my new getup. I smiled back my appreciation, and he motioned me to take a seat in one of the sleek, cushioned chairs at the little oval table. I did so, and he sat down as well.

Now he proceeded to talk my ears off, apparently oblivious to the fact that I failed to understand a single word he uttered. Eventually, he stopped speaking and waved his hand as if it were my turn to babble on. Who was I to argue? The man had treated me with kindness and respect, after all, and so I spoke back to him in a flood of English, which I knew must have been as unintelligible to him as his language was to me. All the while, he sat with his ear cocked, as if he were soaking up every meaningless syllable for its pure aesthetics alone.

After I had gone on thus for a long while, recounting pointless trivia such as my love for the music of crooners like Frank Sinatra and Nat King Cole, and even at one point reciting the complete lyrics to "Way Back Home," which had been a little hit for Bing Crosby with Fred

Waring and His Pennsylvanians not long before I'd left the outer crust for Pellucidar, my companion raised a hand and beckoned me to stop speaking. Then he resumed his own pointless babbling for about a minute before again motioning me to speak.

We continued in this manner for what must have been half an hour, when, just as I was about bored to tears, a single word in his otherwise incoherent diatribe suddenly made sense to me. I interrupted him and repeated the word.

"*Kjarna*," I said. "It means 'Mercury,' doesn't it? Like the planet, I mean, not the fleet-footed god of the ancient Greeks. 'Kjarna' means 'Mercury,' the first planet from the Sun." I didn't know how I understood the word, but somehow I knew its meaning with certainty.

The man smiled and nodded vigorously, and then continued speaking. After a few more minutes of speaking to one another in our native tongues, the meaning of a second word became clear to me, and then a third and a fourth. At that point, the linguistic floodgates opened, and I began to understand at first whole phrases, and then entire sentences spoken by my companion. And soon it became apparent that he had begun to understand me, as well. Before long, I lost track as to whether I was speaking to him in my tongue or his own, but one thing was for certain: we were communicating with one another with a crystal clarity of meaning and understanding. I asked him how this could be, but he only replied that our minds were now in mental sympathy, as if that explained everything.

My host told me his name was Maksata Tul ko Ragi ro Njorath ro Volstari, which loosely translated to "The Two Hundred and Third Idea of the Third Contemplation of the Thought Lords." He instructed me to refer to him as Maksata Tul henceforth, explaining that this was the "familiar" aspect of his name used by friends and family. He said I was on the planet Kjarna, or, as I have indicated, Mercury. What power had brought me here was as yet unclear to his people, though they had had forewarning that travelers from beyond were about to enter their world. My arrival, he said, as well as that of my fellow traveler, was a rare event, for normally Kjarna was sealed off from such incursions by the powerful minds of the Volstari, or Thought Lords.

When he mentioned the fellow traveler who had accompanied me to Kjarna, Maksata Tul saw me flinch. "Do not worry, Victory Harben," he said. "We have sent her away from Kjarna and she cannot reenter our world without the consent of the Volstari, who are not inclined to let such a horror back into our precious domain."

"The people who came out of those flying saucers," I said. "The ones with the glowing orbs. They sent her away?"

"Indeed," said Maksata Tul. "I was one of them. As a psychophysicist of the Third Contemplation, I had been among those who detected the pending disruption in—what was the term you used?—the 'angles'? It is an appropriate term, though we might say 'dimensions' or 'hyperrealities' if we spoke your tongue in its native form. Be that as it may, after detecting the future incursion of our world, I was tasked with intercepting you and your friend—"

"Believe me," I interjected, "she's *not* a friend."

Maksata Tul smiled. "I gathered as much. There are still nuances to our language, such as sarcasm, that upon occasion do not properly connote. In any case, I was tasked with leading the team to confront you and the other being. You were forecast to penetrate our world by the Volstari. We were to contain you both and then interrogate you as to your origins and your purpose for encroaching upon Kjarna. As for the glowing orbs, they are but mental foci that allow the bearer to channel the will of the Volstari."

"Now hold on a minute," I said. "You've said a bundle already, and I do want to dig into that, but right now let's go back to the beginning. You said we're on Mercury. Now that's impossible. First of all, there's the gravity. It feels about the same as on Earth, a planet with much more mass than Mercury.

But more importantly, Mercury's the closest planet to the Sun. It's only about thirty-six million miles from dear old Sol. We'd be burned to a crisp if we were on its surface."

"So we would," replied Maksata Tul, "had the Volstari not intertwined Kjarna's Ninth Planetary Ray with the Ninth Solar Ray, thus mitigating the harmful radiation of the Sun. Even so, we must abide on Kjarna's dark side. As for the gravity, it is a combination of the will of the Volstari and the fact that Kjarna is mostly composed of a massive iron core. At one time our world had an outer crust like that of the third planet." Maksata Tul paused as a sad look crossed his handsome features. "But in ancient times a great catastrophe ripped it away."

My heart began racing upon hearing my companion's explanation. "Wait a minute. Planetary and solar rays? Like in Mr. Burroughs' Martian tales?"

Maksata Tul's mood brightened and he shook his head. "I have no idea who 'Mis-tur Buros' is, though I feel I should like to hear his tales of the fourth planet. Djanthrel bears many interesting, though distastefully bellicose, people. We have even detected a few great minds there observing us through their powerful telescopes."

"Never mind about Mr. B.," I said. "But I do wish to learn more about the solar and planetary rays. I am a physicist on my world, but we have not yet detected such phenomena."

My host raised an eyebrow. "Curious. You are a physicist and you could not detect them? How could you even study gravity without understanding how it is affected by the planetary and solar rays?"

"Well, if you'd like to know the truth," I said, "the people of my planet are a little on the bellicose side ourselves sometimes, and that tends to get in the way of progress. We're working on it, climbing up out of the muck of our last world war and trying to look on the brighter side of things. Don't count us out yet."

"Kjarna has observed the third planet as well," Maksata

Tul said. "We are aware of the war, but I did not realize it had ended." He looked at me strangely and added, "Yes, curious indeed," and I could almost hear the cogs in his mind turning.

"You say we're on Kjarna's dark side," I continued, "and that we must remain here if we are to survive the intense radiation from the Sun. How does that work? Do you pick up all your belongings and move to a new city on the other side of the planet every day to avoid the daylight?"

"There is no need," my host explained, "for all of our metropolises move upon a great track that encircles the whole of Kjarna, moving across its surface at a rate that will keep them forever on the planet's dark side."

"You mean we're moving on such a track right now? I don't hear or feel a thing."

Maksata Tul gave me a patient smile. "Suffice it to say it is not like the physical train tracks of Tjephra." Tjephra was the Kjarnan name for Earth. "Kjarna rotates on its axis precisely three times for every two revolutions it makes around the Sun. Therefore, a Kjarnan day is equivalent to about fifty-nine Tjephran days, give or take. Thus, our cities travel a little more than one hundred and sixty miles across the face of Kjarna in a Tjephran day." Of course, Maksata Tul did not use the term miles nor did he state the number fifty-nine or one hundred and sixty, but those were the translations that I garnered from our mental sympathy.

"Perhaps you will enlighten me about these nonphysical 'tracks' upon which your cities move," I suggested.

"Indeed," Maksata Tul said. "All in good time."

"Well, speaking of things I don't understand," I said, "how is it that I can't leave this room no matter how much I try? Am I a prisoner?"

"May I ask you if you are a prisoner of the effect that has seized you and hurled you through the angles? If the answer is yes, then perhaps you will come to regard your stay on Kjarna as a respite from imprisonment."

"You're good with words, Maksata Tul," I replied. "No doubt about that. But a prisoner is a prisoner. And at some unknown point, my next transit will come and I will leave not only this room, but Kjarna itself."

"Ah, there you are wrong, Victory Harben. For you have been summoned to testify about your appearance on Kjarna in the Hall of the Volstari in a quarter of a year."

"A quarter of a year!" I laughed. "Surely I will have gone on to the next world before then."

Again came that patient smile. Or was it a patronizing smile? I was starting to wonder.

Then it dawned on me. I did the quick math based on the information Maksata Tul had given me and determined that a quarter of a Kjarnan year would be the equivalent of only about twenty-two Earth days. Still, there was no way of knowing when the transit effect would take hold of me and carry me away. I told my host—or my keeper—as much.

"Just as the powerful minds of the Volstari prevent the being you call Lahvoh from entering our world," he replied, "so too do their minds prevent the transit effect from seizing you. You *will* appear in the Hall of the Thought Lords within a quarter of a year."

Suddenly, Maksata Tul cocked his head to one side as if he were listening to something I could neither hear nor otherwise perceive. Then he returned to his normal deportment and smiled once again.

"I am delighted to inform you that the Volstari have decreed you are to be honored as a guest until your appearance before their court. You are to have free reign of the Third Contemplation's facilities and will stay here at my family's apartments."

"Wait, you were just speaking with the Volstari?" I asked.

"Indeed," replied Maksata Tul.

"I would like to speak with them as well. Is that possible?"

"Alas, you must wait until your summons in a quarter of a year," said Maksata Tul. "But until then, there is much you may learn here among the Third Contemplation that I believe you will find to be of great value in your travels. You have a sharp and inquiring mind, Victory Harben, and you are uniquely positioned because of the effect that has seized you to understand much about the cosmos. I believe you will find the wait most stimulating and rewarding. But for now, I suggest that you rest."

With Maksata Tul's last words, a wave of torpor swept over me, and I wondered if his suggestion that I rest had somehow implanted the notion of fatigue in my mind, much in the same manner as a hypnotist can implant a subliminal suggestion in the mind of his subject.

"I shall let you sleep off your weariness," he said, rising from his chair. "But when you wake, you will feel refreshed and find that you are no longer bound to this room, but rather have free reign of the premises and my family's house-hold and laboratories. Simply call out and a servant will come and provide for your needs. My wife and I would be honored if you would break your fast with us and our young daughter. But for now, sleep."

And with that, Maksata Tul left the room, and I, despite the many questions whirling in my mind, proceeded to crawl back into bed and fall into a delightful slumber.

11
A NEW SCIENCE OF MIND

WHEN I AWOKE, I felt both rested and refreshed. I called out as Maksata Tul had instructed me to do and was greeted by a young woman dressed in an outfit similar to my own, although her sequined stripes were of glittering orange, not purple. She told me her name was Taldala Ren and that she was in the employ of the Maksata family and would see to my needs for as long as I resided there.

The woman instructed me to follow her, which I did, and though I hesitated before the doorway leading out of the room because of my previous experiences, I found that this time I was able to pass over its threshold with no trouble whatsoever. Apparently, as Maksata Tul had stated, the mysterious Volstari had indeed lifted the mental restriction preventing me from leaving the room. Or perhaps Maksata Tul had done so himself, for as I have mentioned, I had not failed to notice that the manner in which he had last spoken to me resembled that of an earthly hypnotist.

I was led only a brief distance down the hallway into another tiled chamber, this one equipped with a pool of steaming water set in the floor. Taldala Ren pointed out a small lavatory adjoining the chamber where she said I would find soap, towels, and other toiletries for my bath. She told me I would not require a change of clothes, as my outfit was "self-cleaning." Though I did not question her about this at the time, I later learned that Kjarnan clothing is subjected to a permanent subatomic field that swiftly disintegrates any

106

accumulation of grime, thoroughly cleansing it in a matter of minutes. I thought about the years I'd wasted washing my clothes when I might have been doing something more worthwhile—like reconciling the Standard Model with general relativity, for one—and I resolved that one day I would introduce this Kjarnan innovation to Earth. Even if I didn't earn a Nobel Prize in Physics, it would surely win me an award in humanitarianism.

My stay with the Maksata family over the next few weeks was among the most interesting, intellectually rewarding, and happy times in recent memory, especially since I no longer had to worry about being tossed from world to world with no forewarning. Maksata Tul and his wife, Maksata Sol, were the most gracious of hosts, treating me as if I were their long-lost daughter. And as for their real-life daughter, Maksata Dor, I felt as if I had gained a younger sister, even if she was something of a smarty-pants.

I found that I was in an enormous complex in the city of Korelj, where resided the class of Kjarnan society known as the Third Contemplation, which, if I understood correctly, was made up of people who were said to have been spawned from the thoughts of the Volstari. At first I did not know whether this was a belief of religion, an abstraction of philosophy, or a hypothesis of science. I was reminded of Kar Komak and the Lotharians of Barsoom, whom I had recently discussed with Dejah Thoris. Among the Lotharians were said to be two factions, the realists and the etherealists. Both groups believed in what they called the Great Truth, the belief that "all is mind." But they differed in that the realists believed they themselves were real but the etherealists were but figments of the realists' imaginations, generated by their thoughts; whereas the etherealists believed even the realists were imaginary—that there was no such thing as matter and all was truly composed of thought and thought alone.

When I told Maksata Tul about the Great Truth of the Lotharians, he replied that, although the realists and the etherealists seemed to have a primitive conception of the makeup of reality and to understand very little about the science of mind and matter, their notion was essentially correct. "This you have verified yourself by your transits through the cosmos, as well as your ability to bring with you to Kjarna the apparel you wore while on Djanthrel. You achieved this by the power of your mind alone, just as the Volstari maintain the city of Korelj where we now find ourselves. Mind is indeed all."

When I asked Maksata Tul if he could teach me more about the science of mind and matter, he said he would be pleased to do so, but that I would gain a better understanding if I would first learn the rudiments of Kjarnan psychophysics at an elementary level. This, he told me, would best be achieved by studying alongside his own young daughter, whose knowledge and understanding would be closer to my aptitude, and by this I took him to mean my primitive earthly intelligence.

Of course, I resented the implication. I was an Oxford-educated physicist, after all, and here I was being told that I must be tutored by the man's twelve-year-old daughter! But then again, had I not faced such prejudices because of my age while in school? Because of my youth in Pellucidar, where the strange sense of timelessness allowed me to pack a lifetime of learning into what were but a few short years on the outer crust, I had known much that even university scholars didn't know by the tender age of eleven. Who was I to judge the smarts of a Kjarnan adolescent?

"Maksata Dor will also be able to help you reconstruct the 'uncertainty apparatus' prototype of which you have told me," Maksata Tul went on. "It should be but a simple matter and perhaps a good school project for my young daughter."

I bit my tongue, resisting the urge to tell my host that the invention of the uncertainty gun was the end result of ten thousand years of earthly civilization, not a schoolgirl's extra-credit assignment. But I had a suspicion it would only make me look even more like a novice in his eyes.

Thus it was that I began my study of Kjarnan psychophysics alongside Maksata Dor in the Maksata family laboratories in the halls of the Third Contemplation of the Volstari. Maksata Dor looked to all appearances like an earthly girl of her stated age of twelve, this being a translation to Earth years via our mental sympathy, which I had attained with the remaining two members of the Maksata family after engaging with each of them in a babble-filled conversation similar to that I had had with Maksata Tul. Following the path of her parents, Maksata Dor was in training to become a psychophysicist, though she would emigrate from the Third Contemplation and join the Fourth upon her seniority, at which point she would be considered the fourth-generation progeny of the Volstari's thoughts.

Maksata Dor and I began, as her father had suggested, by attempting to reconstruct my uncertainty gun prototype. I had thought the Clarendon Laboratory at Oxford to be the most cutting-edge experimental facility in existence, but soon I learned just how wrong I was. No matter the resource I asked for, it was provided, almost as if Maksata Dor had materialized it out of thin air, and knowing the mental abilities of the Kjarnans, perhaps she had. In fact, by the time we had replicated my work back on Earth and had a fully functioning mechanism, I was confident that the new apparatus was in many ways superior to my previous prototype.

One innovation was the interface of a scintillating aquamarine crystal with the device's induction coil, which Maksata Dor told me served as both a focus and filter for the reception of the various cosmic rays that primed the quantum particle receptacle (or "probability chamber," as I had dubbed it) housed within the gun's cylinder. We had even employed the Kjarnan equivalent of Harbenite in the device's construction, a substance my companion told me was known on Kjarna as *toralj*, and to the scientists of Barsoom under the name *forandus*, and which, as I had suspected, had been used in the manufacture of my lightweight metallic boots. This not only made the apparatus more durable; it also broadened the types of subatomic quanta that could be contained within its probability chamber and projected along its waveguide, or, to put it in a layperson's terminology, shot down the gun's barrel. This, Maksata Dor explained to me, would allow for an increased range of functionality for the gun. "Not only can this new version of your 'uncertainty gun' discharge a semirandom *janvik* effect, what you have told me you call a 'probability field'; it can also be equipped to certain specific functions, such as replicating, storing, and interacting with other *zuvans*." When I asked her what she meant, a conspiratorial twinkle danced in her eyes and she motioned for me to come closer.

"My father has forbidden me from speaking to you of the other being who entered our world with you," she whispered into my ear, exhibiting all the excitement of a child confiding to a sibling that she was going sneak out of her bedroom and open her presents before Christmas day. "But he has told me that he and the others of his party detected several zuvans of differing purposes—auras, you might call them in the crude language of Tjephra—surrounding the one you call Lahvoh. You may have noticed the violet glow emanating from her, an aura made visible by the mental foci employed by my father's party. A simple modification to your uncertainty apparatus prototype will allow you to identify and replicate such auras, and then impose them each in turn upon the object or being of your choice."

My pulse quickened. "What do you mean by 'zuvans of differing purposes'?"

"You know how your uncertainty apparatus works, do you not?" replied Maksata Dor.

"Well, not exactly," I admitted. "I mean, in principle, it generates a subatomic entanglement effect, a resonance of sorts between quanta. The local quanta become entangled with . . . well, I am not actually sure. If my godfather's and my experiments with the Gridley Wave are correct, the quanta resonate with identical quanta at different points in space, and potentially also at different points in time. That's why we believe the Gridley Wave functions irrespective of background interference—the Gridley Wave doesn't pass *through* the space between the quanta; it just instantaneously connects the quanta, transmitting information between two points without regard for distance in the continuum of spacetime. Though the Gridley Wave is exactly that—a wave—in one respect, it's also a resonance between particles across spacetime. Any background interference is simply bypassed because the communication is nonlocalized; it's just two particles doing the same happy dance together across the room from one another, so to speak. And theoretically, the Gridley Wave can communicate not only over the limitless distances of space, but also across time itself. But I digress. My point is that the uncertainty apparatus is based on the same resonance principle as a Gridley Wave transmitter-receiver. The quanta emitted from the uncertainty apparatus interact with 'like particles' at a subatomic level, and I believe that when they do, they trigger the generation of what I call a probability field, which will produce what would appear to be a random effect. I admit that I never actually had a chance to fully test my old uncertainty apparatus back on Earth."

Maksata Dor let out a little sigh, presumably at my ignorance, and I felt my cheeks begin to warm. "First of all," she said, "the apparatus entangles with the *volatra*—that is, the life force, the conscious and subconscious mind or spirit—of its user. So the effect it produces isn't random but semirandom. It won't violate your will, for instance. Well, that is not exactly true in all cases, since you can't actually *will* the apparatus to produce a precise effect. How can I put it so that even a Tjephran can understand?" Maybe a little less condescendingly, I wanted to reply, but I was too excited by what I was hearing to let my damaged pride get in the way. "The semirandom effect entangles with the essence of who you are," she continued. "It will never violate your conscience. And the more you use the apparatus, the more entangled it will become with you. If you use it frequently enough, it will cease to function for other would-be users."

"You're telling me that if I pull the trigger of the gun, it will pull a semirandom effect out of my pretty little brain and impose it on its target? So if I'm full of ice cream and butterflies and love, it won't hurt the target. But if deep down I have murder in my heart, it could very well kill that target I'm aiming at? And if I use the gun frequently enough, it will become useless for anyone else and won't even discharge?"

"I don't know what 'ice cream' and 'butterflies' are, but I believe that is what I just said."

Suddenly I wondered, with some desperation, what had become of the uncertainty apparatus prototype I had left behind in Pellucidar. I could only hope that it had not fallen into nefarious hands. Further, I wondered why the prototype had stopped functioning at the same time the Gridley Wave went silent, and I asked the question of Maksata Dor.

"You told me you had been running tests on the wave when you were constructing the apparatus, no?" she said. "Clearly, the wave became entangled with the device, and when the former disappeared, the latter simply ceased to function."

"Clearly," I said with a grin, as if the answer to my question had been obvious. "I have a another question for you. You mentioned 'zuvans of differing purposes.' That is, auras that surrounded the one called Lahvoh. Could you tell me more about them?" I wondered if the "purple wind" that my friend Ren-ah-ree of Va-nah had seen swirling around Lahvoh could have been such an aura. Moreover, I had witnessed wisps of violet energy churning around Lahvoh's hand when I had faced off against her on the blue sands of Kjarna. Had the winged behemoth activated a type of zuvan that she meant to hurl against me as a weapon?

"The zuvans," Maksata Dor replied, "consist of different combinations and frequencies of planetary and solar rays that have been harnessed in such a way that they create a localized concretion, a kind of aura, as I have said, or what physicists on Tjephra might call a 'quantum entanglement field.' My father says his party detected several different zuvans swirling about her. They managed to copy an impression of only one of these, a zuvan allowing for the translation of language, much like the mental sympathy generated by the Volstari that is allowing us to communicate right now, but a field that would produce such an effect without the need for a facilitator such as the Volstari. Another zuvan, they believe, is responsible for the being's ability to traverse what you have told me you call 'the angles.' But that field they were not able to copy and store. Doing so takes time."

"How much time?"

"A few minutes with the proper device."

I held up the uncertainty gun admiringly. "And this new prototype? Would it be able to copy and store such a zuvan as the one that allows Lahvoh to traverse the angles at will, and then impose it on a target?"

"With a few simple modifications, yes."

I saw my big grin reflected back at me on Maksata Dor's pretty little face.

"Then what are we waiting for?" I said. "Let's get to work."

I paused and wiped a trickle of sweat from my brow, then noticed that Maksata Dor's face appeared flushed.

"Is it getting hot in here or is it just me?" I asked.

"The being named Lahvoh," replied Maksata Dor, "managed to damage the protective shell of planetary and solar rays that surrounds Kjarna."

"That sounds serious. Should I be worried?"

Maksata Dor made a dismissive sound. "The powerful First Contemplation is deep in meditation, repairing the damage with the will of their minds. Let us get on with our work."

As Maksata Dor and I proceeded in secret upon our little project to equip the uncertainty gun with technology that would allow it to detect, replicate, and store zuvans, I contemplated my good fortune at having arrived on a world that was host to precisely the technology I needed to capture for myself Lahvoh's ability to traverse the angles in a controlled fashion. I reflected on how Dejah Thoris had told me she believed that the destinations of my transits were not, in fact, random, but rather that I was carrying myself closer and closer to—what exactly? I was not sure, but in light of the staggering coincidences—which the princess had said her husband, who had also sought to master the art of interplanetary transits, had similarly experienced during his many adventures—it was hard to argue against her thesis.

In any case, with such a field as the one possessed by Lahvoh at my disposal, it was fully possible that I would be able to direct myself through the void to the time and place of my choosing—in this case, Pellucidar in the year 1950. And if I found, as I suspected, that my godfather had followed me through the maelstrom, then perhaps I could use my newfound ability to track him down and bring him back to Pellucidar, as well.

There was only one little hitch—to capture the translocation field for myself would require another confrontation with Lahvoh. And who knew the functions of those several different other auras that Maksata Tul and his team had detected around her, and whether any among them might serve as formidable weaponry? Not to mention the fact that I was not eager to again face the prospect of having my soul leeched out of my body by her flaming sword. Only the intervention of the powerful Third Contemplation, channeling the power of the mighty Volstari, had prevented my swift demise upon my last encounter with the violet-armored warrior. I knew I couldn't count on assistance from my Kjarnan friends in any future confrontation with Lahvoh that might occur upon some remote world.

At last came the day when little Maksata Dor announced that we had achieved our goal and the necessary adjustments and modifications to the uncertainty apparatus were complete. Now, she said, it was time to test the gun's functionality by imposing the "translation" aura upon a test subject, and by that she meant on me. My young companion first showed me the appropriate settings among the gun's copper and gold fittings needed to select the effect we wished to impose, further instructing me on the proper dials to fine-tune in order to capture and store a zuvan and the button to press to complete the process. I made her show me this process twice, after which I repeated it myself to ensure that I understood it perfectly and would be able to repeat the procedure if or when the time came.

When we had both assured ourselves that I had thoroughly absorbed the lesson, Maksata Dor said, "Now I shall temporarily remove myself from our mental sympathy. Then try speaking to me in a language with which I am completely unfamiliar." The girl closed her eyes for a moment and then began speaking in what was, to me, gibberish. Apparently she had done as she had indicated and somehow ended our mental sympathy.

The girl proceeded to motion me to stand several feet away from her, then aimed the barrel-shaped waveguide of the uncertainty gun at me and pulled the trigger.

At first I was convinced that the apparatus had failed. Other than the photoelectric whine signaling that device's entanglement effect was primed and ready and the sound of the gun's trigger clicking, there was nothing to indicate that anything had discharged from its barrel. Of course, I was not sure why I expected bells and whistles in the first place. Many zuvans, Maksata Dor had assured me, were invisible to the naked eye.

"Did it work?" I asked in English, with a tone of skepticism. Maksata Dor made to speak, but I cut her off. "Wait! Before you reply, I want to put our little experiment to a real test."

Maksata Dor smiled and nodded for me to proceed. It was an indication that she could already understand me, but

I wanted to be sure the zuvan imposed on me could translate even the most obscure language.

"Kreeg-ah po histah eta-nala-den yo," I said in the low guttural tones of the frightful priests of Opar, whose language I had first learned from my mother. The root forms of that speech I later discovered were also common to the languages of the Mangani, or great apes, of Africa and the Sagoths of Pellucidar.

"There is little native grass on Kjarna," Maksata Dor replied in words I could perfectly understand, "other than that created by the minds of the Volstari, so why, my friend, should I beware of snakes in the grass?"

"Well, Dory," I said, using my nickname for little Maksata Dor, "it looks like you're going to get an A-plus this semester, after all," for indeed she had garnered the precise meaning of my words.

"Oh, by the way," said Maksata Dor as if it were but an afterthought. "I made a little adjustment to the translation zuvan. I don't have complete confidence that it will work, but with any luck I have bound your clothing and the un-certainty apparatus to a tight radius around your volatra. If by any chance the Volstari release your physical form from their mental hold and the transit effect again seizes you, the gun and your clothing will accompany you."

"Well, aren't you a peach!" I exclaimed, for I can't begin to convey how tiresome it had become to alight upon some alien world in my birthday suit, not to mention that time I materialized without habiliment at the height of a raging battle in Roman Britain.

It was at that very moment that Maksata Dor stood up as straight and stiff as a board, a startled look on her face.

"What is it, Dory?" I asked. "Is there something wrong?"

"It is the Volstari," she said with urgency. "It is time for your hearing before the Thought Lords."

12

IN THE HALL OF THE THOUGHT LORDS

BARELY HAD TIME to register Maksata Dor's pronouncement before the world faded into darkness around me, as if a black velvet curtain had dropped before my eyes. When the curtain of obscurity raised but a moment later, I found myself standing in the center of a great rotunda of polished amaranthine stone, the ceiling of which faded from my vision in a ring of blinding radiances some hundred feet above. I counted eleven equidistantly spaced lights, which were of such brilliance that I was forced to direct my gaze away from the harsh glare and down at the floor, where my eyes met a sight that left me both startled and full of inquiring wonder.

There, set into the marble tilework, was a symbol that I had seen only once before, half buried in the sandy beach on that first, nameless world I had visited upon being ejected from Tu-al-sa's maelstrom: a convex disk surrounded by a thin ring that was bisected by eleven smaller disks, which were in turn speared by the steeples of a large eleven-pointed star. I was, in fact, standing upon the very center of the convex disk, which was approximately six feet in diameter.

Whatever could it mean? Moreover, where was I? Only moments before I had been standing with Maksata Dor in one of her family's laboratories in the facilities of the Third Contemplation; now I was here in the Hall of the Thought Lords of Kjarna. Was either place a truly real, physical location, or was I merely hallucinating all that appeared to register

117

upon my consciousness through my senses? I did not have long to contemplate any of these questions, for only moments after I had arrived in the chamber, a man's deep, reverberating voice rang out from somewhere amid the blinding lights above, so loud and abrupt that I started.

"*Victory Harben!*" came the voice. "*You have been summoned to the Hall of the Volstari to stand trial for your unlawful entry into the domain of Kjarna. How do you plead?*"

"Uh, how about innocent?" I realized my pronouncement was not very assertive, so I began again. "What I mean to say is that I didn't intend to come here to Kjarna, most honorable Volstari, if that is who you are. I have been seized by a force I don't understand, one that's thrown me willy-nilly from one world to the next. I have no control over the phenomenon. But I have learned much during my stay here with the Maksata family, who have treated me with nothing but kindness and hospitality. Moreover, I believe the knowledge I have gained on Kjarna may eventually lead me to the answers I seek, and hopefully also to the ability to control the phenomenon that has seized me."

"*Victory Harben!*" thundered a second voice, this one female. "*Do you admit, then, that you are guilty of not being in charge of the course of your own destiny? Such is a grave violation among the laws of our kind.*"

"Well, first of all," I replied, "that's a little unfair, isn't it? I'm not exactly sure anyone is in control of her own destiny. After all, how *could* one be? There's a lot being thrown at us in the course of our lives, much of it random or from our environment, and people generally respond as best they can. Do we make mistakes? Sure, but that's how a human being learns and grows and hopefully finds her place in the world. Or worlds, as the case may be. Second, I am new to Kjarna, and I didn't come here of my own accord. How can I be bound by your laws when I am ignorant of them? I'm not saying I wouldn't respect your laws if I knew them. But I don't know them. When two cultures meet, allowances must be made—"

"*Silence!*" rang out a third voice, this one, as far as I could tell, being devoid of gender. "*You know well that you have drawn yourself here. Otherwise, why do you bear* hulavaluhomsko *inscribed upon your flesh?*"

"Hoola *what?*" I held out my forearm and pulled down the elastic sleeve of my jumpsuit to reveal my tattoo. "You mean this? You can actually read it?" I was astonished, for as I have mentioned before, I myself did not know the meaning of the symbols that my father, Nadok, had inked into my skin. And yet my winged nemesis Lahvoh had seemed to recognize the symbols when I first encountered her in the land of Caspak. And now, so too did the Volstari of Kjarna.

The male voice spoke again. "*You have told Maksata Tul the theory of a woman from Djanthrel—that you drew yourself to the worlds to which you transited. I tell you now, that woman was correct. Therefore, I ask you, why have you come to Kjarna, Victory Harben?*"

"Most honorable Volstari," I proclaimed, "I tell *you* in all honesty that I don't know what drew me here. But something strange is going on indeed, for I do recognize this—" I pointed at the star-shaped symbol of interlocking disks set into the floor upon which I stood, "though I don't understand its significance. I saw this same symbol on a rock buried in the sand of a far-flung world, the first world upon which I found myself after leaving Pellucidar."

The blinding lights high above me flickered as if in agitation.

"*She in earnest does not know why she is here,*" said a fourth disembodied voice. "*Nor does she understand the significance of the symbols on her flesh and the representation on the floor of this chamber that memorializes the Great Experiment, so that we shall never forget.*"

"It is no longer to be called such," chided a fifth voice. *"It is the Great Failure."*

A murmuring of *"Ayes"* spoken by perhaps ten or twelve distinctive voices echoed among the bright lights above, clearly agreeing with the sentiment of the fifth speaker.

"Why would she be drawn to the Great Failure," said the third voice, *"unless she is a portent of doom for Kjarna! Her volatra has become knotted and entwined with our shameful mistake. We must not allow her to leave our world or she will surely draw calamity with her wherever she goes."*

"It is so," said the first voice. *"Are all in agreement?"*

Again came the chorus of *"Ayes."*

"Victory Harben," said the first voice, *"you are hereby sentenced to remain on Kjarna for the remainder of your mortal existence."*

"That's just not gonna fly," I said. "You don't have the right to do that. You're going to punish me because of *your* Great Failure? What kind of justice is that?"

"Show her the Great Failure!" came a voice.

A clamor of voices followed the imperative: *"Yes, show her!" "Show her, yes, yes!" "Show her!" "We must show her!" "Show her the Great Failure!" "Show her both the Primal Failure and the Great Failure!" "Show her!"*

Again the veil of black velvet dropped before my eyes, and then lifted upon a scene of the dark void filled with burning stars. A planet swung into my field of vision, one bearing blue seas, and continents of brown and green, and drifting white clouds.

"This," said a voice, *"was Kjarna eons ago when the solar system was young. In our brashness, we, the Volstari, sought to alter the Sun and the planets to our own liking, changing not only their form and shape but also their relation to one another. We desired to remake the natural world in the mold of our own thoughts and to create a new system in accord with our own powerful minds. But then, amid our hubris, disaster struck and we nearly destroyed our homeworld of Kjarna."*

A second planet swung into my field of vision, colliding in a hellish conflagration with the beautiful world of Kjarna, the horrendous impact tearing away both its atmosphere and outer crust and flinging them into the void, even as the planet itself shot off at a sickly angle through outer space.

"This we call the Primal Failure. Only by the power of our minds were we able to prevent Kjarna from tumbling into the Sun, stabilizing it in its present orbit and bending the planetary and solar rays about it to generate and protect its new atmosphere."

I saw a wide view from space of Kjarna as it exists today, its surface scarred by deep canyons and craters and marked by barren mountains and bleak deserts.

"But though we nearly destroyed our world," the voice continued, *"we did not acknowledge our hubris. Instead, we moved our endeavor into deep space, many light-years away from our solar system, where we could inflict no harm upon Kjarna. With our minds, we learned to open up rifts in the dimensions that lie between space and time, so to more easily travel back and forth between Kjarna and our new project. And it was there, in that remote region of the void, that a misguided faction arose among us who precipitated the Great Failure, and it was there, because of the severity of our errors, that the remainder of our people decided to withdraw back to Kjarna, retreating to the self-imposed isolation of our own minds so that we might never again in our arrogance unleash the unforeseen and wreak havoc upon—"*

With no warning, the image of the planet Kjarna suspended in the star-spotted void of space dropped away and again I found myself in the blinding hall of the Volstari. Again the glaring lights flickered as if in agitation and a susurrus of voices whispered all about me. Something was clearly wrong.

"What is it?" I exclaimed.

"The unthinkable has happened," said a small voice at my side.

I looked over to find little Maksata Dor standing beside me, as if she had materialized out of thin air. I took note that she had the uncertainty gun we had built together holstered on a belt fastened about her narrow waist.

"The un*thinkable*?" I asked. Being that we stood in the hall of the *Thought* Lords, that didn't sound good.

"The powerful First Contemplation has failed," said Maksata Dor. "They are unable to repair the damage to the protective atmospheric rays that surround Kjarna. Our planet is swiftly dying."

"How long do we have?"

"Not long if the Volstari cannot repair the concretion of rays."

The susurrus of voices had become eerily silent.

"Can they?" I asked.

"It remains to be seen," replied the girl. "They are trying now, even as we speak."

For how long we waited there, I do not know, for in the hall of the Volstari, as in my homeworld of Pellucidar, time did not seem to pass with the measured regularity that it did on the outer crust of Earth. But at last, the disembodied male voice that had first spoken broke the silence, sounding forlorn and defeated.

"*We have failed. All life upon Kjarna shall perish in only five jolars.*"

The blinding lights above grew dim. Five jolars were the equivalent of an earthly day.

"Wait, there is yet hope." It was the voice of Maksata Dor beside me.

"*Share your thoughts with the Council, Maksata Dor.*"

"Perhaps there is a reason after all," the girl went on, "why Victory Harben has been drawn to Kjarna. For without her arrival here, she and I would not have produced that which is potentially the salvation of our world."

"*Do not speak in riddles, young one. If she and the one*

pursuing her had not trespassed upon our world, there would be no threat to Kjarna."

"That is not for me to judge, Honored One," Maksata Dor said, "and who knows what is the cause and what the effect when time and space are but constructs of the mind? What I do know is that, despite the monumental power of their thoughts, neither the First Contemplation nor the Volstari themselves have the capacity to repair the damage rendered by the intruder. Never have we of Kjarna needed physical apparatus to detect and transmit zuvans, as we have always relied upon the minds of you, the Volstari, and your powerful Contemplations for such purposes. But together, Victory Harben and I have constructed a physical device powered not by the minds of the Volstari or your Contemplations, but by the fabric of the void itself. With a simple adjustment, the device we have built may be tuned to a frequency in resonance with the original state of the atmospheric shield. If brought within close proximity to the nexus of the failing rays, the apparatus may be discharged directly upon the area of weakness, repairing it instantly."

Now the lights above grew suddenly brighter.

"There is only one problem." Maksata Dor gazed up at me with great sadness in her eyes. "For such a device to function, it must lie within the radius of its user's zuvan. Therefore, the user must discharge the apparatus in direct proximity to the area of weakness. The odds that the user will survive the intense heat of the atmosphere are slim to none. Already has the device bonded with Victory Harben. No other may use it, for it is not in resonance with any but her, nor have we enough time to construct another apparatus before the calamity falls upon us and destroys all life upon Kjarna."

I smiled down at Maksata Dor. Leaning over, I unbuckled the belt holding the uncertainty gun from around the hips of the young girl and secured it around my own waist.

"I'll take those odds," I said. "But only if the Volstari agree to let me go on my way if I survive."

The lights flickered amid a murmuring of disembodied voices.

"So it shall be, Victory Harben," came the ethereal male voice that I had come to guess belonged to the leader of the Volstari. *"Maksata Tul will teach you how to control and navigate a flier. Go now. There is not much time left."*

Suddenly the black velvet curtain again fell before my eyes. When it lifted, I was back in my apartments in the Maksata residence of the Third Contemplation in the city of Korelj. Maksata Tul was standing before me. In his hands he held what appeared to be a wide ring cast out of toralj, the Kjarnan equivalent of Harbenite. This, looking like nothing so much as the neckpiece of Captain Nemo's diving helmet, he fitted over my head and positioned on my shoulders. Maksata Tul proceeded to instruct me in the operation and meaning of the buttons and glowing circles of light that were set into the metallic ring, demonstrating their various functions, the primary one, he said, being the activation of a bubble of glowing energy that surrounded the head and would sustain the wearer in hostile environments. This would be necessary, he explained, when I neared the area of weakness in the upper atmosphere that I sought to mend. He also gave me a metallic belt equipped with assorted compartments and utilities, which he told me might come in handy should I manage to survive my daunting task. These, along with the belt from which depended the uncertainty gun, completed my uniform.

Over the next few hours, Maksata Tul took me up for practice runs in one of the Kjarnan fliers—the sleek, black saucer-shaped craft that had rescued me from my free fall through the night skies of Mercury upon my arrival. The controlling mechanism of the craft was exceptionally simple in both design and execution, having been developed by a people whose technology was based on their advanced psionic mental abilities. Of course, I had no such talents, but soon I learned that the machinery made up for any such deficits on my part.

The engine of the Kjarnan flier operates much after the design of its Barsoomian equivalent when in the atmosphere, propelled as it is by the Eighth Planetary Ray of Kjarna, though certain innovations of the Volstari and their Contemplations have enhanced the Mercurian ships' speed and navigational precision over that of their neighbors on the Red Planet. The planetary rays are specific to the particular world; thus the Eighth Ray of Barsoom is different in essence from the Eighth Ray of Kjarna (though at the time I was still at a loss to understand why such ray phenomena had not been detected on Earth). When passing beyond the atmosphere into outer space, as I was told the flier was equipped to do, the craft utilizes a combination of the Eighth Solar Ray and various Eighth Planetary Rays—or, when coming into the proximity of planetary satellites, Eighth Lunar Rays—receiving the particular ray from the approaching body and expelling it from one of the multiple exhaust separators to propel the ship on its way, thus overcoming the pull of unwanted masses and moving toward desirable ones.

Though I had only a few short hours before my flight, I took the time to study the flier further, and was informed that one of its components draws energy via a matrix of solar rays to run the various instruments and other functionality on board the craft. This included an auxiliary engine that powered a series of propellers designed to deploy from the ship's hull in the event of a catastrophic loss of the main engine. Though the craft's power source is unlike any known on Earth, the design of its auxiliary motor is not dissimilar to that of the turbines that drive the props of an ordinary terrestrial airplane or helicopter. Though I did not know it at the time, the knowledge I had managed to glean from my brief study of this Kjarnan innovation would one day prove to be invaluable.

When Maksata Tul was satisfied with my ability to handle the craft, we returned to the landing tower in Korelj from which we had departed. There we were met by Maksata Sol and Maksata Dor, who brought us refreshments and a small meal, upon which we picnicked right there upon a little bench on the edge of the landing pad before disembarking on our grave mission. The Maksatas feigned as much good cheer as they could to buoy my spirits, but I caught the furtive glances they exchanged among each other when they thought I wasn't looking.

When we were finished with our repast, I hugged little Maksata Dor and thanked her for all she had taught me about Kjarnan physics. "You are a fine teacher, Dory," I told her, "and there's no doubt in my mind that when you immigrate to the Fourth Contemplation, it will shine as the brightest progeny of the Volstari's thoughts." Dory tried to maintain her usual demeanor of haughty superiority, but then at last the façade broke and tears came to her eyes, and she proceeded to sob softly against my shoulder as we hugged good-bye. I cried a little too, touched by the revelation that the aloof little show-off cared for me after all.

After bidding adieu to Maksata Sol, and allowing her and her husband to spend a private moment together, I took Maksata Tul aside and addressed him solemnly. "I have a cautionary tale to tell you," I said, "one that you and the Volstari would do well to consider in earnest before it is too late."

"I am listening," replied the psychophysicist. "But we have little time to spare before we must depart."

"Don't worry," I said. "This won't take long, and I'll get straight to the point." Maksata Tul smiled and nodded for me to proceed, so I didn't shilly-shally. "When I was a little girl back on my world of Earth—Tjephra, as you call it—an aggressor arose who took advantage of many other nations' meekness and desire for peace. Those nations stood back and allowed that aggressor to violently seize its neighbors' territory, and to murder and subjugate many of their citizens. Now it seems to me that your people have sealed themselves off here on Kjarna, thinking you'll keep the rest of the universe at bay as you sit back in repose, indulging yourselves in your worthy thoughts—and they are indeed worthy from what I've had a chance to observe during my stay here. But there's a big universe out there, and you're a part of it, no matter what you choose to believe. I get it. You're embarrassed because you made some mistakes in the past. You've imagined it's some kind of act of penance to hole yourself up on this sunbaked rock that you call home, hiding behind your planetary zuvan fields to keep out 'intruders' from both this reality and an infinity of hyperrealities. But we all make mistakes. We have to get back up and get to the stuff of life, not cower in the shadows. It's how we grow, become better, stronger people. But hiding in the shadows is neither living nor dying, and unfortunately it's the approach many on Earth took for far too long. Now I don't know who or what you Kjarnans are hiding from, and I'm the first person to say that diplomacy is always the best option if the parties at odds are willing to tango. But I also know that withdrawing from the world in the face of a bully cost my world dearly. More than eighty million souls by one reckoning—so many that it's hard to know for sure. And it was almost too late by the time my people showed some moxie and fought back. Don't make that same mistake. It could very well make your people's Great Failure look like a bed of roses. That's my advice. Take it or leave it." I clapped a somber and contemplative Maksata Tul on the shoulder and grinned. "Lecture over, mister."

The temperature had risen swiftly while we were on the landing tower and the psychophysicist wiped a trail of sweat from a heat-flushed cheek. "I shall consider your words in earnest, Victory Harben. Now let *us* not hesitate before it is too late to save *my* world."

"Hi-de-ho, let's go!" I exclaimed, using an expression frequented by Poppy Pickerall, my roommate during my first semester at Darkheath, whenever I had my nose in a textbook and she wanted to go out on the town, which pretty much summed up our perpetual state of existence back then.

Maksata Tul grinned back at me. "Moxie indeed," he said, and then he shook my hand in the American fashion as I had once instructed him. "Good luck, Victory Harben. Regardless of the outcome of your mission, the deepest thoughts of the Volstari are indebted to you for your compassion and self-sacrifice."

"Hey, I'm just looking to get off this baking brick and find my way home. And if we sit around and do nothing, we're all going to bake, anyway. If I bake up there—" I pointed up into the black, star-filled sky, "at least I died trying to do something."

The psychophysicist pursed his lips and looked as if he were thinking, which I suppose was a given being that he was a corporeal expression of a contemplation of the so-called Thought Lords. Then my companion brightened and said, "Let's take a powder."

"Hey!" I exclaimed approvingly. "I'm proud of you, Max. You're getting the lingo down."

Without further ado, we strode across the platform and boarded our respective ships via the beams of their ethereal Eighth Ray "elevators," which lifted us up into hatches set in the bellies of the hovering craft. The plan was for me to follow Maksata Tul's saucer to the area of weakness in the upper atmosphere, at which point my friend would break off and observe from a lower altitude as I flew into the firestorm and worked my magic.

As I strapped myself into my seat and activated the dome of force that sealed me within the saucer's cockpit, I breathed a prayer to St. Christopher. My mother told me he was said to protect travelers from sudden death, and I certainly thought that applied under the circumstances. I also opened my heart to the Kratalak elders of the Voraki, the spiritual leaders of my father's tribe, asking for strength. I didn't know if I believed in either ritual, but I figured it couldn't hurt to hedge my bets, and it comforted me to think of my parents before departing on a mission that would, in all likelihood, result in my untimely demise.

An eerie whirring sounded in the cockpit as I engaged my ship's engines, increasing in intensity as I took to the air and followed Maksata Tul's craft up into the dark skies of Mercury. Within moments we had left behind the lower atmosphere layer and were soaring through the Kjarnan equivalent of the Earth's stratosphere, barreling at breakneck speed toward the upper layers. Already I could see above me the great borealis of orange and crimson that Maksata Tul had told me indicated the outer shell of the rapidly deteriorating atmosphere.

As I neared the damaged layer of the heavens, the temperature control system that had kept the cabin cool and comfortable during the outset of my flight began to fail. The cold air blowing out of the vents became at first lukewarm, and then finally hot and dry.

Maksata Tul signaled me over the radio that the time had come for him to cease his ascent and for me to continue on my own. Then his craft veered sharply to one side and my own ship shot past his into the fiery borealis.

Flames raged over the dome of force that protected the main cabin, and my craft bucked wildly like an enraged bronco. Holding on fiercely to the steering mechanism with one hand, I pressed a control on my neckpiece with my other and a glowing field of energy bubbled around my head as my suit's life-sustaining system activated. I felt a momentary sensation of relief as blessedly cool air filled the cavity of my helmet and the cooling fibers of my suit switched on and lowered my body temperature. Before takeoff I had already adjusted the setting on my suit that extended its protective, elastic fabric down my arms and around my hands and fingers in the manner of thin, formfitting gloves. If I hadn't done so, my exposed skin would have become scalded when I reached my destination and I would have been unable to manipulate the controls of the uncertainty apparatus.

I reached for the gun at my hip and drew it from its holster, almost dropping the device like a hot potato as it burned my hand despite the protective fabric. Wincing with pain, I adjusted the setting that would allow the gun to discharge the necessary zuvan field to resonate with the damaged atmosphere and restore it to its former condition before Lahvoh had committed her spiteful atrocity. Maksata Dor had attuned this zuvan field to the device while her father and I were taking practice runs in the flier. I pressed the uncertainty gun's priming button, and the ensuing photoelectric whine told me the device was charged and ready. Locked and loaded, as my godfather liked to say when he cocked his twin forty-fives.

The dome of force above me darkened automatically to compensate for the blinding flames that were searing the ship's hull, casting the interior of the cabin in a sickly crimson light. Suddenly I was fighting for each breath and I felt my consciousness dimming.

I tried pulling the trigger to discharge the gun, but now I was weak . . . so weak that my hand did not respond to my mental command. I tried again, but to no avail.

I was too late! I had waited too long to activate the gun and discharge it! Now an entire world would die because of my failing . . .

As my awareness faded, I wondered if the pain and guilt I now experienced was equivalent to that which the Volstari bore because of their Great Failure. If theirs was even a fraction of what I felt, I could only empathize with them, and for the first time I understood the terrible shame that must have made them hide themselves away in the blinding glare of the sun on their little world of rock and iron.

All went dark around me and I knew that I was losing

the battle against Morpheus, that inexorable wooer of sleep and unconsciousness. I tried to sense my hand and feel my finger on the trigger of the gun, but I could not. Even so, in my desperation, I imagined that I could, and with all of my being I willed myself to pull the trigger.

I heard a click, and then, without knowing whether the gun had discharged and I had succeeded in my mission, I was rushing headlong at furious speed through the cold void of space.

13
CHIVALRY IS DEAD

A SUCCESSION OF WORLDS flitted past my field of vision, as rapid and dizzying as a roulette wheel in a Las Vegas casino. It was almost too much for my mind and my consciousness to register. Then all went black.

When I came to my senses, the aroma of sweet, fresh grass filled my nostrils and the chirping of birds sounded pleasantly in my ears. The songs of very earthly birds, I noted—robins and starlings and marsh warblers. I rose up on my elbows, my unruly hair falling down around the silvery metallic neckpiece affixed to my Kjarnan jumpsuit. Gripped in my right hand and pressed against the wild green grass that grew beneath me was the uncertainty gun, my finger still on the trigger.

Wherever I was, I had brought both the gun and my attire with me through the void. I could come to only one conclusion: the zuvan that Maksata Dor had imposed on me seemed to have stuck and her modification had succeeded.

The thought of little Dory brought back the sting of my anxiety for the welfare of all Kjarna and its inhabitants. Had I succeeded in pulling the trigger, causing the uncertainty apparatus to emit the zuvan field and repair the atmosphere? I examined the gun and pressed the priming button. Again came the familiar whine of a photoelectric cell as the gun charged to readiness. Though I didn't know how traveling through the void might have affected the gun's charge, I let out a little sigh of relief. If the gun had not discharged, the indicative whine would not have sounded, as the apparatus would already have been primed. Unless the gun had discharged while I was still in the Kjarnan atmosphere or depleted itself at some point in the unknown span of time during which I had crossed the void, I must have succeeded in my mission. That, at least, imparted a tentative solace.

I rose to my feet and gasped in astonishment and joy at the sight that met me. A radiant yellow sun of middling size cast its warm light down upon my smiling face, while white puffy clouds floated languidly in the powder blue sky. Verdant hills, fields, and valleys surrounded me on all sides. And through a rift between hillocks about a mile from where I stood, I espied the towers of an old castle encircled by a bone-dry moat.

I was on Earth. I could *feel* it. And not just Earth. This was England. I didn't need to be standing in the center of London with Westminster Abbey towering over me to confirm it. All I had to do was look at the sparrows and blackbirds and blue tits, to smell the wild lavender and clover and the fresh breeze of springtime, to feel the pull of earthly gravity upon my frame.

Moreover, I could no longer sense my Pellucidarian homing instinct pointing me in the direction of Sari, the village of my birth. When I had immigrated to the outer crust upon the occasion of my twelfth birthday, I had discovered that my homing instinct had ceased to function when I was on the surface world. I had discussed this unsettling fact with my godfather's wife, Jana, the Red Flower of Zoram, and discovered that she, too, had lost the ability to detect the direction of her homeland when she had resided on the surface. At the time, Jason Gridley had speculated that it was simply the thickness of the Earth's crust that blocked the ability of Pellucidarian natives to sense their birthplaces when in the outer world. But since I had entered Tu-al-sa's maelstrom and departed Pellucidar, I had experienced the incontestable homing instinct time and time

again upon whatever world I manifested, except for the rare
few occasions when I had returned to the Earth of another
time or epoch. It was a mystery that had left me puzzled
and disconcerted, while at the same time I was ever thankful
for the tantalizing reminder of my home as I traveled unbidden and alone throughout the cosmos. As yet I had come
up with no theory to explain the perplexing phenomenon,
but now once again the lack of answers troubled me.

In any case, I was back in England's green and pleasant
land! And if my guess was right, based on my familiarity
with the local geography, I was somewhere to the north of
London, perhaps in Derbyshire. I scanned the skies and
listened intently, searching for the sight of an airplane or
the rumbling buzz of its engines, but I could detect no evidence of either. Ever the optimist, I told myself a plane
would come along soon enough and began hoofing it through
the tall grass, heading down toward the little vale in which
the castle resided. There I hoped to find someone who would
allow me to use a telephone or might drive me to the nearest
town, where I could hitch a ride to Oxford or maybe all the
way to the Greystoke estate in Yorkshire.

I had walked perhaps a quarter of a mile when I came
upon a dirt road. It was then that my buoyant spirits
promptly evaporated and my heart took a sickening plunge
into the pit of my stomach, for down the lane came a figure
on horseback fully clad in mail armor, visor and bracers
and all—a real live knight if I had ever seen one, which I
hadn't outside of a historical reenactment to which Poppy
Pickerall had once dragged me kicking and screaming.
Behind the knight and his horse loped a small pony that
carried a boy of about ten to twelve years of age wearing a
plain brown tunic that fell to his knees. Presumably he was
the knight's squire.

Well, there was no use keeping my eyes peeled and my
ears open for any airplanes now. I was on Earth, all right.

The Earth of medieval England. I knew I should have paid more attention in that Chaucer seminar.

I considered running down the hill to avoid what would surely be an awkward encounter, but I quickly thought the better of it. The knight and his boy were mounted and could easily chase me down before I could make it to the nearest tree line and hope to escape. Well, I would just have to talk my way out of the situation, then.

But when the man approached and began shouting down at me from his horse through his raised visor, I swiftly recalled why I had hated that Chaucer class so much, for I understood not a single word he said. The man's speech was so archaic that it was all gibberish to me. Regardless, I began speaking to him as if I were carrying on a perfectly reasonable conversation, hoping this would give my translation aura a chance to resonate in mental sympathy with the knight, in much the same way that Maksata Tul and I had bantered on meaninglessly to one another before our minds ultimately connected and communication became possible.

Fortunately, understanding kicked in sooner rather than later, and I began to pick out a word here and a word there, and then to understand phrases and ultimately complete sentences.

"From where dost thou hail, woman?" the man said. "And in what infernal garmenture art thou attired? Art thou the witch reputed to live at Castle Torn yonder?" He pointed down the hill toward the old fortress. Disapproval and scorn, thick and bitter as blackstrap molasses, ladened his words.

"Nay," I replied, hoping my feeble attempt to sound old-fashioned would lend assistance to my translation aura. "I am thus attired, Sir Knight," I continued, thinking on my feet to explain my outlandish clothing, "for I am on my way to a costume ball at the castle of Sir Ellington."

"Sir Ellington?"

I pshawed. "Surely thou knowest Sir Ellington, Duke of

Harlem? I must be on my way, for I am his ward, and surely he and his lady art missing me."

"What is thy name, woman?"

"I am Lady von Harben," I said, "but who art thou who so accosts a gentle lady without making introductions?"

"Von Harben? Dost thou hail from Allemagne?"

"Nay. My mother hails from Allemagne, but I wast born in the village of Sari." Then, tiring of the man's rude inter-rogation, I added, "Whence dost *thou* hail, O Nameless Knight of Endless Questions?"

"Quiet thy tongue, wench!" Suddenly the man's eyes locked on my Kjarnan neckpiece and they fairly bulged from their sockets. I heard a soft beeping and realized one of the buttons on the neckpiece was blinking with a reddish luminance.

"I knew it upon first giving sight to thee!" cried the knight. "Thou art a witch indeed!" And with his last state-ment, he whipped his gleaming and very sharp-looking longsword from its scabbard.

"Oh *brother*." I sighed. "Listen, it's just part of my getup, mister," I said, momentarily forgetting to maintain my archaic speech. I was too concerned with the meaning of that little red light turning on, for if I was correct, it was a warning signal that something *very bad* was about to happen. "I mean . . ." I continued, "the light that dost shine from my garmenture, Sir Knight, is but the trick of a cunning artifice consisting of a burning candle housed within a cleverly designed—"

But there my little fib ended, for the man advanced swiftly upon his mounted horse, the pointy end of his sword lunging at my breast. I leaped backward to avoid being skewered, but he charged me down like a mad thag and I fell upon my backside as his mount reared and whinnied, the beast's heavy hooves stomping down all too close to my recumbent form.

"What is that witching device upon thine ham, sorceress?" The tip of the knight's blade hovered but an inch before my nose before swaying down to clink upon the uncertainty apparatus that I had returned to the holster belted around my waist.

"Nothin' doin', Sir Knight," I said, swatting away the blade with the back of my hand. "I've got plans for that 'witching device,' and they don't involve you, pal."

"Ah, so thou admittest thy demonic heritage, witch?" cried the knight. "That is enough for me! I shalt sever thy foul head from thine unhallowed shoulders!"

As he swung back his sword arm and I prepared to meet my maker, something large and looming blocked out the sun behind the knight, and a dark shadow fell over us both. Then my eyes adjusted to the gloom and I gasped, for I had perceived that which had cast the stygian umbrage upon us.

"Uh . . . Sir Knight," came my faltering response. "I know we've had our differences, you and I, but I don't want to see you die. Run, and run fast, mister!"

But my admonishment was to no avail, for a behemoth clad in iridescent violet armor unlike that worn by any chevalier who walked the Middle Ages rose up behind the unsuspecting knight. The poor fellow, who had been about to behead me, bellowed a gruff cry of utter surprise as a massive gauntlet throttled him from behind and pulled him roughly from his horse. Suddenly I saw the two great arching wings like those of a giant bat that had cast the shadow over us, and the being to which they were attached.

It was Lahvoh. She had managed to track me through the angles once again.

The knight's steed whinnied in terror and bolted down the hill toward the old castle at full gallop, while to the man's rear the youthful squire's pony did the same, knocking the boy who had been holding the animal's reins to his knees. The squire stumbled back up to his feet, sputtering meaningless syllables of utter fear, and proceeded to run at breakneck speed for the nearest hedgerow with nary a glance back at his noble lord.

As for the knight, he didn't stand a chance. He met the same grim fate at Lahvoh's hands as had that brave member of the Heliumetic guard who had given his life in the defense of Dejah Thoris during my brief advent on Barsoom. Before I could even get back to my feet, faint wisps of alabaster mist—all that remained of the knight's life force—were siphoning into the ravening tip of Lahvoh's flaming sword.

While Lahvoh was thus occupied, I adjusted a couple of dials on my uncertainty gun, raised a little wire antenna from a curving crevice set into its side, and confirmed that the apparatus was still primed. Then I slipped the gun back into its holster and picked up the knight's longsword, which he had dropped in the grass when Lahvoh had so rudely interrupted his plans to murder me. The blade was heavy and unwieldy in my hands.

By this time, Lahvoh had completed her task. She dropped the withered husk of the knight to the ground, his suit of full plate clattering onto the field like a sack of tin cans being tossed into a trash dump. Then she locked her dark eyes on me, malice writ clear on her features.

"What's your beef with me, lady?" I said. "You wake up without your morning coffee or something? Let's cut to the chase and do without the mystery nonsense. Why are you following me?"

The furious glare that seared out at me from behind the shimmering visor was as blistering as the sun. "At first my masters thought you were but a curiosity, Victory Harben. A lone soul who somehow discovered the secret of traveling through the angles. Such a curiosity was but an insect to be squashed. But now I have learned the truth, from your very own words, and from the one who followed you from Pellucidar."

A bolt of fear shot through me. "My godfather . . . you've . . . encountered him?"

Lahvoh grinned—a smirk without an ounce of humor. "I did not need your godfather to discover the true purpose of your excursions into the void. You revealed it to me yourself when you spoke of Pellucidar. You are but a pawn of the Mahars, who seek to wield you as a weapon against my celestial masters. But the Mahars are weak and short-sighted. They are as blind as they are deaf, having no conception of what lies waiting for them out in the infinite reaches of the angles."

"You're wrong," I said. "I don't work for the Mahars. They're the hereditary enemy of my people." But I wondered if there might be some truth to Lahvoh's accusation. I still did not know why Tu-al-sa had thrust me into the maelstrom that had ushered me upon my unbidden odyssey through spacetime.

"And *you* are wrong when you state that I followed you through the angles. I did not follow you; not this time. No, I merely laid a trap, and you stepped right into it. It is your teteculatory apparatus that betrayed you."

I released one hand from the hilt of the knight's sword and fondled the grip of my gun in its holster. "You mean my uncertainty apparatus?"

"Ah, is that what you call it?" She laughed. "It is an apt name. Go ahead. Draw it. It is but a harmless bauble. A primitive tool crafted by a primitive mind."

I left my gun holstered and reasserted my grip on the sword. "Watch it with the barbs, lady. I'm a Stone Age girl at heart. Trust me. You don't want to make a savage like me angry."

"Were you not but a primitive savage, you would have figured out by now how to use your trinket to lead you directly to my masters. That is doubtless what the old Mahar queen wished you to do. But she overestimated you and you have failed. Now you will spend the last few moments of your life regretting your decision to ally yourself with the enemies of the divine Harods."

"I'm not allied with anyone, let alone the Mahars. I'm just trying to find my way home. If you want to know the truth, I've never even heard of the Harods, miss, divine or otherwise. Unless you mean the department store in Knightsbridge. It's a little too rich for my blood, but one time Lady Greystoke got it in her head to take me there and play dress up. You should have seen how ridiculous I looked all gussied up like one of the Queen's china dolls. And then who should walk into the store and see me but Professor Ralston! My cheeks never burned so hot, let me tell you."

I was stalling for time. Unbeknownst to Lahvoh, when I had adjusted the settings on my uncertainty gun and raised the tiny wire antenna, I had triggered little Maksata Dor's innovation. With each second that passed, my gun was busy making an imprint of one of Lahvoh's zuvan fields—in this case, the one that permitted her translocation through the angles—and transferring it to a storage repository built into the apparatus.

"You have spirit, little savage," Lahvoh said, advancing with her flaming sword. "A spirit that will be most savory to my divine masters and their bottomless appetites."

The angel swung her fiery blade at me with the force of a locomotive at full steam. If I had met the blow with my own strength, I would have died then and there. But I had more sense than that. Employing a move that David Innes had drilled into me during spear training when I was a little girl, I fell low upon my knees and dug my sword's tip into the ground, steepling it at an angle so that the earth took the full force of Lahvoh's strike.

"Do you really think so?" I rose, my two-handed grasp firm on the dead knight's blade. "I've always thought I was rather quite bland, really. In fact, the very same Professor Ralston I ran into at Harrods—one of my favorite mentors, you know, even though we don't always get along so well— has even called me 'tasteless' on quite a few occasions. Now you wouldn't want to disappoint your masters' heavenly palates by having them choke down little old flavorless me, would you?"

Again she swung her sword, lazily this time, as if she were but playing with me. I leaped out of the way, though I cannot truly say I did so gracefully.

"Your godfather's pneuma satisfied them well enough."

Suddenly a little lump constricted my throat and I staggered as if I had been dealt a physical blow. My penchant for small talk had evaporated.

"What . . . what did you say?"

Again Lahvoh met me with that humorless smirk, her fiery blade crackling in the spring breeze. "You heard me well enough, Victory Harben."

"I don't believe you!" I gritted my teeth and lashed out with a reckless swing of my longsword. Lahvoh simply caught the breeze under her great wings and floated up and backward into the air, avoiding my rash blow. "You're lying! You used one of your quantum-field tricks to pluck my memories of my godfather out of my mind, didn't you?"

"Ah, you know of the zuvans," Lahvoh crooned. "You have learned more than I reckoned on Kjarna. Did you learn also of the Volstari's Great Failure? Did they tell you how many died as a result of their 'Great Experiment'? And the great injustice it imposed upon those who survived? Perhaps I shall bring you back to my masters, where you will learn the truth and come to serve the deific will of the holy Harods."

"Not a chance!" I cried, and then leaped forth and slashed with my weapon, this time scoring a hit and raking the razorsharp blade across the angelic warrior's glistening faulds. Though I had struck with great force, the blade left not even a scratch. Even so, Lahvoh's features twisted in rage beneath the visor of her shining helm and her eyes flamed to orangered as if backlit with a furious and very real hellfire.

"I know you're lying about my godfather," I taunted. "I bet you don't even know his name."

"You may believe that if it makes you feel better, young human," replied the towering angel. "But it does not change the fact that my sword has reaped your friend's soul and his bones lie bleaching on some forgotten world in an inaccessible angle. Now, meet your doom, Victory Harben! The Numinous Ones cannot save you, as they could not save your godfather . . . Jason Gridley."

A faint beeping sounded at my hip. I flung my sword to the ground and whipped my gun from its holster, smacking down the button on the frame of the apparatus that completed the transference of Lahvoh's teleportation aura.

"Got it!" I exclaimed. "You really do need to stop running off at the mouth, Lahvoh. It'll be your undoing. Well, actually it already was." I raised the uncertainty gun. "Take the 'A' train, sister!"

Then I fired point-blank at the confused and surprised angel—or whatever she or it was. The pull of the trigger was followed by an earsplitting roar like that of a hundred thousand surfs crashing upon the shores of a hundred thousand worlds.

From the muzzle of the gun poured what I can only describe as the fabric of the cosmos rippling open like dozens of swiftly expanding bubbles, each of which was composed of a universe in itself filled with endless stars and galaxies and unimaginably beautiful nebulae in an infinite array of shapes, colors, and configurations. The blast of bubbling realities struck Lahvoh head-on, enveloping her and sweeping her away until she grew smaller and smaller in the limitless depths of the universes into which she fell. Perhaps you won't judge me too harshly if I say I gained not a little satisfaction from seeing the expression of shock and fear that racked her angelic countenance as she spiraled away and ultimately disappeared into the boundless void.

As the void shrank toward nothingness, I was about to congratulate myself on overcoming my tenacious nemesis, and thinking about walking down and quenching my thirst at the little brook near the old castle in the valley below. But just then a tentacle of the cosmic rift swept out of the diminishing void where I had last seen Lahvoh. Like a hellish whip flung at me out of spite by that fallen angel, it lashed around my form and dragged me inexorably after her into that ineffable realm between realities, where I hurled in mute terror through the yawning abyss of timeless and formless eternity.

14
ROUND AND ROUND SHE GOES

GRAY MIST AND IMPENETRABLE CLOUDS shrouded the world to which the void flung me. I could see only half a dozen feet through the ashen pall, though nearby I heard the sound of waves crashing against rocks. I shall never know the name of that cloud-blanketed world nor of its people, if it had any, for I did not remain there long. But unlike upon the occasion of my previous transits, I was not to be cast to the next world unbidden.

I kneeled down upon the bed of pale lavender moss and examined the uncertainty gun, which I had held fast in my hand as I was hurled through the trackless immensity of space. Lahvoh was nowhere to be seen, but that didn't mean she was not out there somewhere lurking out of sight behind the gray veil that surrounded me. I needed to move quickly.

I lifted a small panel on the side of the gun that encased a series of tiny gauges, which Maksata Dor and I had installed to indicate the storage capacity of captured zuvan fields. The needle on the first dial rested at the highest tick mark, signifying that its corresponding receptacle had been filled to capacity. I grinned. Lahvoh's transit aura, which allowed her to move at will through the angles, had been replicated and stored safely within the gun!

The calm and reassuring words of Dejah Thoris sounded in my mind. She had suggested that the mysterious force that had repeatedly seized me was hurling me through the void toward some ultimate destination, one to which I was

144

unwittingly drawing myself. Moreover, the leader of the Volstari had affirmed the same sentiment with what seemed great authority. And now I held in my hand the key to unlocking the ability to traverse the void at will.

As I studied the apparatus, tears began to well in my eyes as I recalled Lahvoh's claim that she had murdered my godfather and fed his soul to her ravenous masters. I did not want to believe her. I *could* not believe her. Not if I wanted to continue functioning.

My despair turned to anger until at last a great rage consumed me. I had to get off this cosmic merry-go-round of horror as swiftly as possible. The cost of doing so did not matter.

It was then that I made my decision. I would turn the gun on my own body and pull the trigger, imposing the teleportation aura on myself. Then I would repeat the procedure as many times as was necessary, until I slowly but inexorably drew myself to the final destination for which I was fated. If I arrived at death, so be it. It was better than being cast about like a leaf on the wind, with no control whatsoever over my own destiny.

With grim determination I flipped the switch on the apparatus that overrode the probability field generator and activated the primary zuvan field repository. I pressed the priming button on the side of the apparatus and heard the familiar high-pitched photoelectric whine. Then I positioned the gun in my hands so that the barrel-shaped waveguide was aimed squarely at my breast, locked my thumbs together on the trigger, and pulled without a moment's hesitation.

As it had before, the fabric of the cosmos rippled forth from the gun's muzzle, but this time it hit me head-on and I experienced all the terror that Lahvoh must have felt when I had blasted her back on medieval Earth. Suddenly I found myself hurtling through the cold void of space as I had upon uncounted instances before, but now there was one important difference—I had entered the immeasurable abyss of my own choosing.

Within mere moments—or perhaps it was an eternity, for time flows strangely when one traverses the void—I found myself upon a world of solid crystal, inhabited by revolting crimson worms that burrowed only inches under the translucent material beneath my feet. After but a few seconds' pause, I turned the uncertainty gun upon myself once again and pulled the trigger.

Again came the void. Again I arrived upon a strange world. And again I turned the apparatus upon myself and fired.

I proceeded to repeat the process ad nauseum, and with each instance the immortal words of Ted Mack on *The Original Amateur Hour* echoed through the caverns of my mind: "Round and round she goes! Where she stops, nobody knows!"

Sometimes I came to a world in the midst of a situation from which I could not immediately extract myself, preventing me from imposing the zuvan field upon myself and being whisked away to some other bizarre and distant world. Upon such rare occasions, I remained only as long as either circumstances or good conscience required, and then once more I was on my way, spinning the cosmic roulette wheel with a squeeze of the uncertainty gun's trigger.

Occasionally during these rare stopovers I heard tales of a towering winged warrioress who had preceded me. Sometimes she left behind dark threats to the locals; other times promises of bountiful reward. But the sentiment was always the same: she wanted the inhabitants of the worlds I visited to restrain and imprison me until the time came that she could return and take custody of me herself.

Upon other occasions I took an hour or two to gather my thoughts and review all the strange and harrowing experiences that had confronted me since leaving Pellucidar. I tried to make sense of it all, to put the splintered pieces of what seemed to be a shattered puzzle back together.

During our last encounter, Lahvoh had taunted me, saying that even the Numinous Ones could not help me. I did not know who or what the Numinous Ones were, but I had heard of them once before. That had been in the ruins of Mintra when I had been but a child. Upon that occasion, Tu-al-sa had told me the Numinous Ones had taught the Mahars how to access "the angles," and also how to communicate with the "lower" orders, such as the gilaks, or humans, of Pellucidar. And now here were the Numinous Ones again! Clearly Lahvoh believed that I was in league with both the Mahars and the Numinous Ones, but as to what sort of game we were all supposed to be playing together, I had no clue. Lahvoh had also proclaimed that I was but a pawn of the Mahars, who sought to wield me against her celestial masters.

Here at last I had Lahvoh's motive for pursuing me. She believed I was a threat to her masters, whom she called the divine Harods. Could she have been telling the truth? Had the Mahars somehow come under the scrutiny of the otherworldly Harods and made enemies of them? Had Tu-al-sa come to believe that throwing me into the cogs of the Harods' machinations might somehow foul up the works and neutralize a lethal threat? I did not know, but I felt I was inching closer and closer to unwinding the mystery of why Tu-al-sa had swept me up in her maelstrom and hurled me upon this weird and terrifying odyssey.

It was in such a manner that between my transits I sometimes took the time to cogitate upon the enigma of my situation. But more often than not, I simply pulled the trigger of the uncertainty gun as soon as I arrived upon a new world, discharging the transit aura upon myself and hurtling through the void to my next destination. Rinse and repeat, as my old chem lab teacher used to say.

I do not know how many spins of the cosmic roulette wheel I took. Soon they all became a blur and my mind became muddled, so that sometimes I even forgot why I was pulling the trigger—or lost all sense of where or even who I was. I existed solely to drive myself forward through the cold, infinite void—onward, ever onward toward the unknown.

Until at last, upon arriving on yet another fantastic new world, I pulled the trigger . . . and nothing happened.

15

HUCKLEBUCK

ABOVE ME IN THE TWILIT SKIES arced a procession of four heavenly bodies. I guessed that all of them would have been about equal size had it not been for their perspective, the nearest appearing a little larger than the Earth's moon when viewed from the surface of that planet. But the geography of the world upon which I now gazed was not a bleak, colorless landscape of mares and craters, but rather one girdled by vast oceans whose azure waters washed up against mauve and heliotrope continents, all of which peeked through a miasma of swirling clouds. The four worlds were set within a narrow band of haze that bisected the darkening amber heavens, as if they might have shared an orbit in a curving cylinder of atmosphere that ran through outer space. I had never seen anything quite like it in all the spectacular worlds I had visited.

I was standing in an open meadow surrounded by a lush forest whose foliage consisted of a myriad of stunning hues: turquoises and yellows, oranges and lavenders, as well as other colors that seemed alien to the earthly spectrum. Mushrooms and other fungi large and small, consisting of uncounted shapes and colors, abounded in the sylvan environs, some standing taller than my own height, and a soft velvety moss of brilliant lime green ran from the meadow to the forest's edge. A pleasant chittering of insects arose from all around, while from somewhere deeper within the wood came an owllike cooing, long and low and sad.

I inhaled deeply of the cool breeze, which carried scents suggestive of raspberries and pine.

I took a moment to examine the uncertainty apparatus. Once again I turned it upon myself and pulled the trigger, but as before I was rewarded only with a metallic click. I flipped open the panel on the gun's side, discovering as I had feared that the needle on the zuvan field's repository gauge rested at "zero," indicating that the transit aura had been depleted. The gun was empty. Kaput.

"Well, that's just dandy," I said aloud. I closed the panel on the apparatus and returned the gun to the holster at my hip.

It was then that I experienced the unmistakable feeling that I was being watched. I turned around to see an unassuming little creature crouched on a decaying log observing me with its tiny coal-black eyes. I could discern no other features upon the animal's face or head other than two pointy black nubs of ears positioned above the dark orbs—essentially the thing was a white furball about the size of half a loaf of bread, with a strangely spotted tail that twitched back and forth in a manner reminiscent of a cat's when the feline has been entranced by the sight of a bird. I breathed a sigh of relief upon realizing that my watcher did not seem to be anything menacing—at least not that I believed, although I had learned during my far-ranging travels that appearances could be deceiving.

"Hey, little guy," I said softly as I lowered myself slowly to my knees on the soft bed of verdant moss. "Come on over here and let's get to know one another." I extended my arm in a leisurely manner, inviting the animal to sniff the back of my limp hand and determine that I was not a threat. The animal responded with an exuberant trill that sounded like nothing so much as a mallet running rapidly across the keys of a xylophone, and then proceeded to scurry toward me along the log with what seemed great eagerness.

A commotion arose suddenly from deeper in the forest

and the animal stopped in its tracks, jerking its furry head in the direction of the disturbance. Something was moving through the brush. A moment later voices broke forth from the trees, though not in any language I could understand—at least not until I was in proximity of the newcomers long enough for the translation aura Maksata Dor had imposed on me to take effect.

At the sound of the voices, the little furball of an animal made another trill, this time one of unmistakable alarm, and then bolted off into the woods, leaving me to face the new-comers alone. Though I hadn't expected the tiny animal to lend any support should the strangers prove to be a danger, all the same I could not fail to observe that I felt strangely abandoned by its abrupt exit.

Swiftly the voices and the stirring of brush from within the woods grew louder until momentarily a group of about twenty men and women of a race I had never before en-countered broke through the forest's edge and marched into the meadow.

In terms of overall form, they were every bit as human as you or I. Their skins, however, were of burnt orange and they were covered from head to toe in both black and cerulean blue tattoos of great artistry and complexity. Regardless of the age or sex of the individual, the heads of the strangers were covered in great bushes of white hair that fell about the shoulders. The men wore nothing but scanty loincloths that appeared to be made from the scaly hide of some unknown animal that caught the dying sun-light like tiny mirrors, whereas the women were somewhat more modestly covered in sashes composed of the same glimmering material.

With the party was a man whose brown skin and black hair contrasted sharply with the orange complexions of the others. Clearly he was their prisoner, for his wrists were bound before him by hide strips and two guards armed with crystal-tipped spears walked at his rear. He regarded me with obvious interest as he spied me when he emerged from the forest, and perhaps with no less curiosity than his captors, for as I stood there I must have been quite the strange spectacle for them all, what with my Kjarnan jumpsuit and its purple sequined stripes running up and down my sides, arms, and legs, and my boots and wide neckpiece of gleaming toralj.

But they were stunned by my appearance for only a moment before a tall, middle-aged man pointed his elaborately carven bone scepter at me and shouted angrily.

"No need to get huffy, mister," I said. "If you don't mind, I'll just be on my way."

My words seemed to have no effect other than to cause the man with the wand, who seemed to be the group's leader, to shout even more vociferously at me. Instantly two women with intimidating spears advanced upon me, menacing me with the crystal tips of their weapons.

"Hey, hey—*hey*!" I exclaimed, waving them back with one hand and drawing my uncertainty gun with the other. "Put those things away. You don't want to see what will happen when I pull the trigger of this thing." I kept the barrel of the gun angled up and away from the two warriors in case they knew what a gun was and might think I was eager to fire it at them. It was all a bluff, anyhow. I didn't even know if the gun was operational after having spent its zuvan repository on my wild ride on the cosmic wheel of fortune. And even if it was working, triggering its main functionality would result only in the generation of a semi-random effect that, as Maksata Dor had once explained to me, was somehow tied to my own conscience. Now did not seem like the best time to perform such a potentially hazardous gamble with the apparatus.

The newcomers' prisoner had shown surprise upon first seeing me, but upon hearing me speak his eyes grew wide. Then he surprised me in equal measure by speaking in perfect English—and by that I mean that I understood him word for word without the aid of my translation aura, which had yet to kick in.

"The Nuvors mean business," said the man, and color me a liar if his accent wasn't American. "Gun or no gun, they outnumber you. Better do as they say unless you want to end up shish-kebabbed on the end of one of their spears. Just be glad we're not in the hands of the Keelars or you already would be." When I stared at him in a shocked stupor, he smiled and added, "You can explain to me later how you know how to speak English."

Reluctantly, I lowered my uncertainty gun with slow deliberation and, crouching low, set it upon the meadow's mossy floor. Instantly the two spearwomen shoved me to the ground and tied my hands with leather thongs, grinning like devils all the while. Meanwhile, the leader of the Nuvors snatched up the uncertainty apparatus and deposited it in a sack of scaly hide that was slung around his shoulder.

"Okay, mister," I said to my fellow prisoner, "but I'd better not regret this."

"Be thankful you're alive to regret anything," he replied, but the Nuvors' leader apparently didn't like his prisoners to chitchat among themselves, for he strode up to the man and struck him a fierce blow across the face with his bone scepter. Blood began flowing from the nose of the black-haired man, but he merely grinned in defiance at the leader. My newfound acquaintance was evidently a personification of unwavering courage. Good, I thought. Maybe I could trust him after all. If I were going to get out of this situation, I would need a friend of stern mettle.

Without further ceremony, the chief of the Nuvors waved his wand and his people resumed their march through the forest, leaving the peaceful meadow behind and prodding my fellow prisoner and me along at spearpoint down an overgrown and tangled trail that wound through the maze of trees and giant mushrooms.

We continued along thus for some time as the amber sky

darkened to a rich navy and then finally to black. Above us
the four heavenly bodies shone brightly in their U-shaped
arc, casting sufficient light upon the forest trail to allow us
to continue. Soon the demeanor of our jailors took on an
air of sullen drudgery as we proceeded, and I decided to risk
a whisper to my comrade in captivity.

"My name is Victory Harben," I said softly. "What's
yours?"

"Tangor," the man replied. "At least, that is how I am
known on Zandar and the other worlds of the Omos system."
He gazed up at the procession of radiant planets in the
heavens.

"Zandar," I whispered. "I am on Zandar."

"Yes," said the man. "Are you from Earth?"

I smiled in the refracted light of the alien worlds above.
"Yes, I'm from Earth," I said. "Well, Pellucidar, actually, but
that's a long story."

"I am also from Earth," the man replied. But then one of
our guards overheard us whispering and shouted at us to be
quiet. By this time, my translation aura had achieved mental
sympathy with our captors and I understood the Nuvor
guard perfectly. We both obeyed his order, but eventually
the grind and graft of our march took hold once again and
our guards grew droopy-eyed and uncaring as we trudged
along the twisting trail.

"The Nuvors are taking us to their village," Tangor ventured quietly when he finally judged it was safe. "There they
mean to sentence us after a mock trial and execute us as
sorcerers."

I sighed. "It's always the witch thing, isn't it?"

My companion grinned. "You've been through something
like this before, then. Good. That means we can count on
each other when the time comes."

I returned his grin with a plucky smile. "You got it, mister."

"I have been marooned here on Zandar for a great while,"
Tangor continued. "Years, in fact. The power station that

transmits the energy required to run my ship's engines went silent long ago. The amplifier was on Poloda, a planet located almost directly on the opposite side of the solar system from Zandar. Without the signal, my radius ship is useless. Even should I modify its engines to be powered by a fuel source such as petroleum, it would not be sufficient to carry me through the atmospheric belt even to Wunos or Uvala. They are the worlds that adjoin Zandar. Poloda is much farther away."

So I had been right. The planets of this solar system shared an orbit that was occupied by a vast cylindrical channel of atmosphere that connected them all. I didn't even want to think about how that was possible. The physics of such an arrangement gave me a headache, but then again, I had learned on Kjarna that forces of nature existed, such as the solar and planetary rays, that were unaccounted for on Earth. It was my belief that such forces explained the impossible physics of Pellucidar's eternal noonday sun and its low-hanging geostationary moon, so why then should I be surprised to discover that other celestial enigmas such as the Omos system's atmospheric belt might be similarly explained?

"I was able to evade most of the belligerent locals," Tangor went on, "all the time I was stranded on Zandar, but recently the Nuvors found where I had hidden my ship and were picking it apart when I intervened." He sighed heavily. "Alas, without the plane, I shall never be able to get back to Yamoda."

"I thought you said you came from Poloda," I said.

"I did." Tangor smiled sheepishly. "Yamoda isn't a planet. It's . . . she's . . . a friend."

I smiled knowingly upon hearing the tender tone in the man's voice and decided to change the subject. "Okay, so just how did you get here from Earth?" I asked.

"I died and woke up on Poloda," he said with an admirable deadpan. "And you?"

"Uh . . ." I stuttered. "I didn't die. At least I don't think so."

Tangor shot me an eager look beneath the planet-light, as if the fate of the whole universe hinged upon my words, but at that very moment we broke into a little clearing and the chief of the Nuvors raised his baton high in the air, shouting out an order for our party to halt its march. "Actually, it's complicated," I said. "And it looks like we're making camp. A story for another time?"

Tangor nodded.

Soon we were put under the watchful eye of a burly, ill-tempered giant of a Nuvor. When Tangor and I attempted to speak to one another, he scowled and smacked us each hard on the shoulder with the large, flat head of his crystal-tipped spear. We got the idea and promptly clammed up, sitting down with our backs against the long hollow bole of a fallen tree as we watched the members of the party busy themselves with their duties.

About half the group was occupied with gathering dry branches from the forest's edge and assembling them in the center of the meadow. It was evident they were making a bonfire, which one of the Nuvors lit soon enough by striking a piece of flint against what appeared to be a thin strip of carbonized iron over some kindling. The steel was the first evidence I had seen of metallurgy among the Nuvors, for their belts were either simply tied or held fast by a wooden buckle and, as I have mentioned, their spearheads were made of hard, translucent crystal. They wore no ornamentation other than interwoven thongs of black leather knotted around their wrists and ankles, while on their backs were slung packs made of the same scaly, reflective material that composed their loincloths and sashes.

While the fire was being made, the other half of the group was engaged in preparing some sort of concoction beside the small stream that ran through the camp. I watched as they gathered up a particular variety of magenta-hued mushroom that grew along the streambank, sliced the fungi into pieces using small sharpened slivers of crystal, and deposited their spoils in an earthenware pot, which one of the members of the party had been carrying in his pack.

At one point our guard stood up from where he had been sitting and, glowering at us, told us to stay put. Then he walked over to a woman who was helping to prepare the concoction. His scowl promptly disappeared, and though I could not hear what he said, he was undoubtedly trying to impress the woman with his small talk. She continued to go about her business, either uninterested in the man's advances or playing hard to get, though her grimace gave evidence toward the former.

While our guard was thus occupied, I turned to my companion. "Should we make a break for it?"

Tangor shook his head of black hair. "The Nuvors are expert spear throwers. One of us may make it into the forest, but the other would surely die beneath that fellow's crystal spear. For now, we wait."

I sighed. I was willing to take my chances right then and there, but the man was probably right, and if I lived and he died, I wouldn't feel too good about it. And even more so the other way around.

"What are they doing?" I asked, nodding in the direction of the men and women engaged in their task beside the stream.

"Preparing spirits for tonight's revelry. When they get the fire going, they'll add stream water to the pot and boil the mushrooms, which will release a sweet-tasting intoxicant into the water. *Yerstal*, they call it. Think of it as mushroom beer. Tastes a lot like root beer, actually, but a small cup carries the punch of a fifth of bourbon."

Suddenly I became exceedingly thirsty. "Yerstal, eh? I don't suppose they have a nonalcoholic variety and a mushroom that tastes like vanilla ice cream. I sure could go for a root beer float right about now."

"Well, actually . . ." Tangor began, but then he noticed that our guard was turning away from the object of his tender attentions. The burly fellow walked over to us and proceeded to smack us on our shoulders with the flat and unyielding crystal head of his spear.

"Hey!" I exclaimed with all the indignation I could muster. "What was *that* for?" The man had been so preoccupied with the woman that I did not believe he could have heard us talking among ourselves. But my impudent question only yielded me another smack on the arm by that painful crystal spearhead.

Tangor began to rise to defend me, but I motioned him to sit back down. I didn't want him to get speared to death on my account. Besides, if I played it cool and bided my time, maybe I could get my sweet revenge later.

"Okay, mister, you win," I said to the guard as I rubbed my stinging arm. "I'll shut my trap. But I don't think your actions are helping you make any headway with your lady friend." I pointed to the woman over by the stream, who was glaring at the man. Clearly she had witnessed his unprovoked bullying and did not approve.

The burly guard spat a word under his breath that my translation aura confirmed was a vulgar curse, but the man sat down sullen-faced and thereafter left us alone. I guess I had gotten my revenge a little quicker than I'd anticipated.

As the evening settled in, the Nuvors gathered about the great bonfire they had made and proceeded to imbibe deeply of the yerstal. Apparently they were celebrating our capture and the great honor that it would bring their chief when they returned to their village. Soon the party became inebriated, breaking into laughter and song and telling crass jokes. Our guard watched the merrymakers with a deepening scowl on his face. Eventually, he wandered over to the others and asked to partake of the drink, but the chief of the band only glared at him and pointed his bone scepter back in our direction. Slack-shouldered and glowering, the guard returned to his duties watching over us.

Tangor and I decided it would be best to take turns sleeping while the other remained on watch, as we did not desire to become victims of the drunken revelers should they get rowdy and out of hand, nor did we trust that our belligerent guard wouldn't take out his frustrations on his defenseless prisoners. Thus it was that Tangor volunteered to take the first watch and I drifted off to sleep, falling into a strange dream in which Janson Gridley was crossing a vast storm-racked ocean in a tiny boat in search of me, as colossal saurians rose up out of the depths and attempted to snatch him from the deck and swallow him down gullets the size of five-story buildings. I awoke with a start just as one of the behemoths was about to clamp its enormous toothy jaws on Janson.

Disturbed by the nightmare and unable to get back to sleep, I pushed myself up from the ground with my bound hands and examined my surroundings. Someone was watching me, but it wasn't our ill-tempered guard, who, judging from the empty cup that lay beside him, had somehow managed to get ahold of some of the potent spirits after all and lay facedown on the carpet of moss some dozen feet away, snoring. No, my watcher was none other than the little furball of an animal whom I had encountered when I first arrived upon the world of Zandar. He was sitting up on top of the hollow log near where I had been sleeping and peering at me with his two tiny black eyes.

"You again," I whispered. "Shoo! These Nuvors look like they're the kind of people who'll roast you on a spit for breakfast."

But the little guy wouldn't budge. On the contrary, he stood up on his hind legs and began to do a ludicrous little dance, gyrating his hips and wagging his posterior in a comical way that reminded me of a dance that had been all the rage when I'd left Earth. "Okay, Hucklebuck," I said, referring to the dance and the song of the same name that had inspired it. "I get it. You're happy to see me. But I don't want you to get killed like these guys are going to do to me."

As if reacting to my words, the little creature instantly ceased his silly dance, stood up stiff and straight, and let out

a series of ear-piercing shrieks filled with alarm. The hellacious screeching sounded like a demented musician playing
scales *prestissimo* on a broken xylophone.

"Shush, you little furball!" I remonstrated. "Didn't I tell
you? I don't want to see you get roasted on a spit!"

Tangor, who had been watching the entire exchange
between me and the animal, rose to his feet. Looking distressed at the development, he raised his bound hands and
put a finger to his lips.

But it was too late. The guard had stopped his snoring
and was now rolling over and sitting up, turning his big ugly
mug in the direction of the distressed animal. By this time,
however, my newfound friend had shot off into the night
like a streak of white lighting and was nowhere to be seen,
leaving the guard to fix his eyes on little old me.

The giant grabbed his spear and stomped across the short
distance that separated us until he loomed over me.

"The Chief does not wish me to kill you," he said, "for
he seeks that honor for himself in the temple of Zorval.
But Great Zorval is known for His impatience and He will
surely reward me if I feed your spirit to Him now." He
raised his spear to thrust it into my breast, even as Tangor
launched himself at the man, knowing full well he would
die in my place.

But quicker than Tangor was the massive freight train of
white fur and razor-sharp ivory tusks that barreled into the
attacking guard and hurled him fully twenty feet into the
air. The guard came down on the bed of moss with a heavy
thunk and lay there unmoving.

I gazed open-mouthed at our unexpected champion and,
I expected, soon-to-be executioner. The beast stood as tall
as an adult male African bush elephant, and its girth was
nearly as great, although it was hard to estimate the latter
due to the monster's shaggy coat of snow-white fur. Its eyes
were large black round orbs that were vaguely reminiscent
of a rabbit's, although they seemed menacing as they glowed

orange in the reflected light of the dying bonfire. Atop its head were two long black pointy ears, and from its rear grew a great feline tail spotted with strange ringlike markings.

An intense wave of déjà vu swept over me. I knew I had seen this creature before . . . but where?

Then, suddenly, as I peered up into those dark round eyes, it dawned on me.

"Hucklebuck?" I said in astonishment. For the beast that stood before me was truly a colossal, though much fiercer-looking, doppelganger of my little furball friend. But somehow, although I understood neither how it was possible nor the certitude of my conviction, I knew that the beast was not just a larger version of the smaller animal's species. No, the monstrous beast and my rodent-sized friend *were the exact same animal.* Somehow, the smaller creature had transformed and become big. Very big.

"Well, aren't you a little Jekyll and Hyde?" I exclaimed with laughter. The monster responded with the same exuberant xylophone-scale trill as it had when I'd first met his tiny version and he had seemed so happy to see me. The strange thing was, the trill now sounded different to my inner ear, as if it carried a wordless undercurrent of meaning: *Intense love, combined with a dash of mocking annoyance at my slow-witted human mind.* Could it be that my translation aura had kicked in and was interpreting the creature's melodic cry? It was an intriguing thought, but this was not the time or place for analysis.

By now the entire party was waking up and the drunken warriors were all scrambling to grab their crystal-headed spears.

I eyed the giant Hucklebuck's razor-edged tusks, which gleamed like fine white china in the brilliant light of the planets overhead. "I don't think you mean my friend and me harm, do you, little-big guy?" I said. "We've got to exeunt stage left in a jiffy. Here, can you set me free?" I raised my bound hands, and without so much as a moment's hesitation, the creature lowered himself down on his great haunches and slid one of his tusks beneath the leather thongs that tied together my wrists. With a jerk of the beast's head, the tusks cut through the cords and I was free of my bonds.

"Him too," I said, pointing at Tangor, and a moment later Tangor also stood free.

I ran to Hucklebuck's side, reached up as high as I could to grasp on to a thick wad of his fur, and then pulled myself up until I had saddled my legs around his neck.

"What on earth are you doing?" Tangor cried.

"We're not on Earth," I said, grinning, "so why play by Earth rules?" Tangor shot me an exasperated look. "Don't worry, it's as easy as riding a lidi. Come on!"

Tangor let out a deep sigh and nodded, though he looked troubled. "I don't know what a lidi is, but I'll take your word for it."

"Hucklebuck, down, boy!" The towering animal crouched at my command and allowed Tangor to climb up his fur and mount him behind me.

When we were all settled in, Tangor said, "Now let's get out of here!"

"Not quite yet," I rejoined. "I've got to get my gun back from the chief."

"That's a bad idea," he said. "A *very* bad idea."

"Maybe." I eyed a group of angry-looking Nuvors who were running straight at us with spears. "But it's too important to leave behind with these poor sots." I leaned forward and rubbed our furry mount behind the ears. "Hucklebuck, I need to get my weapon back from the chief. The one with the bone stick. And don't kill anyone, if you can help it, okay?" I hoped my translation aura was working both ways and Hucklebuck would get the gist of my instructions. If not, well . . . I got the feeling we were going for a wild ride one way or the other. "Now go get him, boy!"

Instantly Hucklebuck leaped forward, charging directly at the group of advancing warriors. When they saw the great monster barreling at them, they broke to either side and fled into the forest. I spied the Nuvor chief standing beside the smoldering remains of the bonfire and pointed at him. "There he is!" I cried, and with both hands held on to Hucklebuck's fur for dear life as he veered and bounded off straight for the chief, who, seeing what was coming for him, scrambled to put the remains of the fire between him and the mountain of muscle and white fur that was running him down.

"Victory!" Tangor cried behind me. "Stop your furry friend before he—"

But it was too late for me to do anything, even if I could have. Hucklebuck leaped directly into the smoldering fire, flinging hot embers high into the dark morning sky as burning branches and wood flew every which way. When we burst out the other side of the burning remains, Hucklebuck extended his clawed front feet, digging them into the mossy turf and tearing up the soft ground as he brought his great bulk to a halt only half a dozen feet before the terrified chief.

The leader of the Nuvors had dropped his bone scepter, but in his shaking hands he held my uncertainty apparatus, its barrel-shaped waveguide pointed at us.

Apparently he did know what a gun was after all, for he cried, "Great Zorval, protect me!" and pulled the trigger. Nothing happened except for the hollow click of the trigger mechanism. Even had he known how to prime the apparatus, the gun would not have fired for him, for long ago it had become attuned to my unique volatra, or life force, and so would have discharged only for me.

"Turns out Great Zorval is a friend of mine," I called down to him, "and He's not too happy with you. Now give me the gun and I'll put in a good word with Him for you and your people. Otherwise, Hucklebuck here is going to toss you up into the air like he did your warrior over there." I motioned across camp to where our surly former guard still lay facedown in a bed of moss.

"Forgive me, O Emissary of Great Zorval!" the chief said between sobs.

"Don't sweat it, mister," I said. "Now give me the gun."

He did as I ordered and tossed the gun to me, which I managed to catch by the grip. I breathed a sigh of relief and secured the apparatus in its holster.

"Much obliged," I said. "Now be sure you don't follow us, and while you're at it, stay far away from the great flying ship that you desecrated. It was a gift to my friend here from Zorval Himself so that it might carry us to His heavenly domain."

The chief's countenance suddenly darkened. "Blasphemy!" he cried, snatching up his bone scepter and shaking it at me. "Slay the enemies of the Great Zorval!" he cried to his warriors. The latter, who had been cautiously peering out from their temporary refuge in the forest, now began running toward us.

I turned to Tangor behind me. "What did I say wrong?"

"The Great Zorval," he replied, not without a trace of humor, "is a giant fish. His archenemy, Darvod, is a gargantuan bird whose realm resides in the sky."

"Me and my big mouth," I said. "All right, Hucklebuck, giddyap!" I kicked my legs against the sides of our colossal mount, who responded instantly by leaping clear over the chief's head in a single bound. Spears flew at us, but quicker than the spears was Hucklebuck, who artfully dodged the crystal-tipped missiles while Tangor and I did our best to hold on to the beast's shaggy white fur.

Before I knew it, we were deep in the tangled reaches of the Zandarian forest and had left the camp of the angry Nuvors far behind.

16

A TONE PARALLEL TO SARI

WHEN IT BECAME APPARENT that we were not being pursued, I asked Tangor if he knew the way back to his ship. He cocked back his head and squinted up through an opening in the forest's canopy. By now, the dark heavens had begun to lighten, but the procession of planets and a million scintillating stars still shone down brightly out of the predawn sky.

Tangor pointed off to our left. "A march of about three days, at our current pace."

I leaned forward and rubbed Hucklebuck warmly behind the ears. "Can you take us thataway, boy?" I intoned encouragingly as I motioned to the left. At once, our great white shaggy mount responded, bounding off in the direction I had indicated.

"Do you know this creature?" Tangor asked me, laughing in the exhilaration of the moment as the alien trees and gargantuan fungi sped past us in the dim morning light.

I shook my head and spoke over my shoulder. "Never seen him before in my life. At least not that I can recall. But I admit, he seems strangely familiar, and when he came out of the forest this morning, I experienced the strongest feeling of déjà vu." I failed to mention my belief that Hucklebuck had first appeared to me in a much smaller form, as I didn't want my new friend to think I was crazy. "Another thing I can't figure: when I first met him, he seemed to understand

me straightway, before my translation aura even had a chance
to take effect."

"Translation aura? Is that how you were able to speak the
language of the Nuvors?"

"Yes," I said, "but I'll explain later, along with a lot of
other things. Sounds like we'll have plenty of time to talk
as we make our way to your ship."

At the break of dawn, we emerged from the woods onto
a gently curving shoreline that outlined the roiling expanse
of a vast aquamarine sea. Hucklebuck seemed overjoyed by
the development, and he bounded across the orange sands
and ran down into the waves, the action of which sprayed
Tangor and me in a cool, pleasant mist. I cried out in laughter,
and soon Tangor joined me, while our playful mount pulled
back from the water and fell into an easy trot as he padded
his huge clawed, catlike paws across the wet sands.

I asked my companion if we were in any danger of being
spotted by the Nuvors or some other enemy as we proceeded
in the open in such a manner.

"No, not by the Nuvors, in any case," he replied behind
me. "Their major settlements are located far to the south.
The party that imprisoned us originated from a small village,
a recent incursion in these parts. My ship remained unmo-
lested for as long as it lay there, until Chief Oranza and his
people moved into the area not long ago and stumbled across
it during an exploratory jaunt."

As we traveled along the shoreline over the course of the
next three days, stopping every so often to gather the bountiful fruits, berries, and mushrooms along the forest's edge, I
filled Tangor in on my story. He listened with apparent
earnestness as I related my bizarre and fantastical tale, which,
upon my telling it, seemed unbelievable even to me, despite
the fact that I had lived through it. But Tangor did not
render judgment, at least not in words, though I didn't know
what he was thinking. Occasionally, he asked for clarification
on this point or another, especially when I spoke of Pellucidar

and the state of things on Earth's outer crust when I had left it. But otherwise he remained silent, as if digesting my words.

During the morning of the last day of our journey, Tangor indicated that we should leave the aquamarine sea behind and cut back into the forest via a trail for which he had been on the lookout. We continued on through the trees and giant mushrooms for a few hours before the forest began to thin and then at last fell away entirely to an expansive plain of emerald moss. This we crossed, making for a mountain range that loomed darkly in the distance, until by late afternoon we arrived at our destination, which lay nestled on the edge of the foothills.

Here two spurs of the mountain range formed a small valley that opened onto the mossy plain. Tangor told me he had dragged his flying ship to the deepest point of the V-shaped dell with the help of a team of bison-like beasts he had gone to great lengths to acquire and tame, though he had released the animals into the wild when they had completed their task. Then he had camouflaged the plane by covering it with piles of leaves and branches he had gathered in the foothills.

When we arrived at the site, the great ship stood exposed, having been recently found by the Nuvors and uncovered as Tangor had returned from a journey far to the south in search of supplies to repair his plane. That trip, he explained, had been partially successful, in that he had returned with large spools of copper and steel wire he had obtained after much trouble from a belligerent though more technologically advanced race than the Nuvors. He planned to use these materials to create an antenna in the hopes of picking up an energy signal from the planet Poloda so that he might power his plane's radius engine.

The ship itself looked like a cross between one of the most advanced fighter jets of the U.S. Air Force back on Earth and something straight out of the pages of *Amazing Stories*. Its sleek, aerodynamic design gave it an otherworldly and—from my viewpoint as an Earthling of the mid-twentieth century—futuristic appearance, as did the strange material from which it was cast, which Tangor explained to me was a rigid plastic that was virtually indestructible and bore many similarities to metal. It was the strength of this plastic that allowed Polodian engineers to withdraw air from the hollow spaces within the fuselage and wings, creating a vacuum that gives the ship considerable lifting power and maneuverability, thus reducing the need for a lengthy airstrip on takeoff and landing.

By the time we arrived at Tangor's camp, evening was settling in and we were tired and hungry from our expeditious flight through the Zandarian forest. Tangor lit a little fire and we sat around it, warming ourselves and enjoying a repast that consisted of a sort of crunchy and not unpleasant-tasting bread made from a local plant that my companion had recovered from the food stores he had buried at the site.

Hucklebuck was grooming himself just beyond where Tangor and I sat around the fire, when suddenly he let out a cavernous yawn. I turned and grinned at the great beast, without whom we both would still be captives of the Nuvors, if not speared to death by them. Over the past three days of travel I had come to learn that Hucklebuck and I shared a special bond. Though Tangor was in proximity of the range of my translation aura, which should have affected him with the same facility for understanding foreign tongues as it did me, only I seemed to be able to gain any sense of understanding of our furry friend's xylophonic vocalizations. Moreover, Hucklebuck treated me with the same affection that a pet does its owner, snuggling his great bulk up against me when we camped in the wilds during our journey, and nuzzling me warmly with his furry snout as he trilled contentedly. All the same, I sensed that he was not a pet, but rather an intelligent being with his own ideas about what was right and wrong, and possessing his own sense of agency.

Hucklebuck was one big question mark to us both, and what we witnessed next only deepened the mystery surrounding him, for as we sat around the campfire, his great bulk began to shrink quite rapidly before our very eyes.

Tangor and I both stood up, shocked and somewhat distressed, for it was the first time we had witnessed such a transformation of our friend, though it would not be the last. At the time we had no conception that he might not keep on shrinking until there was nothing left of him. Within moments, however, the process stopped, though it was a very different Hucklebuck who stood before us when it did.

Now he again resembled the little furball of a creature I had first encountered upon my arrival on Zandar, though even smaller than the half a bread box he had been at that time. His beady black eyes drooped as if he were sleepy, and he crawled over to me, whereupon I scooped him up in my hands and he proceeded to curl up into a tiny ball and fall asleep within moments, snoring with a faint trill as he snoozed contentedly in my open palms.

"Amazing!" I whispered, not wanting to wake up him. "He's become the same little critter that he was when I first ran into him! It doesn't make sense. A transformation like the one we have just witnessed would seem to break the law of the conservation of matter. His mass must go *somewhere*, but where, I don't know. You're sure you have heard of no such creature as this on Zandar or Poloda, or any of the other worlds to which you've traveled?"

"No," replied Tangor, shaking his head in disbelief at what he had just seen. "Hucklebuck is unique in my experience."

I sat back down beside the crackling fire, cradling the tiny Hucklebuck in my arms as he continued his snoring.

"You'd better hope he doesn't get big all of the sudden," Tangor said, "or he'll crush you under the weight of several tons."

"Awwww," I replied, "Hucklebuck wouldn't do that to me, would you, little-big guy?" I kissed the little snoring furball on the head and couldn't help but grin at how adorable he looked.

We sat there in silence for some time before I got to wondering about another mystery.

"So you've heard my story, Tangor," I said. "It's a strange one, I admit, but now the time has come for you to tell me your tale. How did an Earthman come to find himself in the Omos system, which you have told me lies some 450,000 light-years from our home planet?"

Tangor smiled. "My tale is as outlandish as yours, and I am afraid just as inexplicable. It all began in September 1939. I was an American attached to the U.S. Army Air Corps, and my squadron was flying a bombing run behind the German lines when my plane was attacked by three Messerschmitts. I managed to shoot down two of the planes before the third raked me with its guns and a bullet found its way into my heart, at which point my plane nose-dived and began its death spiral to the Rhine Valley below. I knew with utter conviction that it was the end for me, but God or fate decreed otherwise, for the next thing I knew I was standing stark naked upon another world, my head still whirling from the tailspin. At first I thought I had awakened in Heaven, or perhaps even that other place, but soon I discovered that I was upon a world as real and tangible as the Earth from which I had come, and one populated by people just as fallible or ingenious, slothful or industrious, forlorn or hopeful. It became apparent right away that I was not in Heaven, in any case, for the world upon which I found myself, which was called Poloda, was racked with total war. I fell in among the people of a nation called Unis, and soon I came to love and respect them, for they were as proud and good as the citizens of my own beloved country back on Earth, and they were up against odds that were just as grim. I quickly enlisted in the war effort, and I was eventually granted the right to join the flying corps. But I am getting ahead of myself.

"One day, several weeks after my advent on Poloda, I began to have strange dreams of Earth, as if I were a spirit drifting listlessly across its surface. This occurred over a period of days, as I seemed to witness events transpiring on Earth in real time. With great consternation, I watched my family go on in the face of my death, and I experienced great pain to see my mother sitting alone in our family manor for hours on end gazing teary-eyed at a framed portrait of me upon the mantel. I wanted to give her some sign that I was still alive, but I found much to my frustration that I was only a mute, formless spirit. Even so, during repeated visitations in my dreams, I strained with every fiber of my being to reach out and nudge the portrait of myself at which she ceaselessly stared, until at last I succeeded and knocked my picture from the mantel. I saw my mother give a start and stand up, a shocked look upon her face, and then I felt a rushing sensation and I awoke again on Poloda.

"Thereafter, when I dreamed, I found that I could no longer return to those whom I had loved and who mourned my death. Instead, I saw endless miles of ocean racing beneath me, until at last I found myself in the study of a man at his typewriter in the evening hours. Though my efforts to speak with him did not succeed in eliciting a response, I recalled the incident with the portrait, which convinced me I still had some physical connection to the world I had left behind. Therefore, I strained my will to the utmost and, reaching around the man, tapped my fingers on the keyboard of his typewriter and began to tell the story of my life on Poloda. I continued this in the weeks and months that followed, up until the night before I took off in my plane for Tonos. Since that time, I have not been able to make contact with either the man at the typewriter on that tropical island or Earth itself in any manner."

Tangor's remarkable story left me astounded. There were details of his account, such as awakening stark naked upon an alien world, that were eerily reminiscent of my own experiences, but it was at that moment in the telling of his tale that I decided to set the snoring little Hucklebuck gently on the ground beside me and Tangor just happened to take notice of the tattoo on my forearm.

A look of surprise mixed with suspicion crossed the man's face. "You have not been telling me everything, have you, Victory?" he said. "Otherwise, you would have explained to me why the tattoo on your arm spells out the characters 'H-A-L-O-S' in the Unisan script of Poloda."

I stood up, stunned. "What in all the worlds do you mean?" I exclaimed. "This tattoo was given to me by my father, a tribesman of Pellucidar, the primitive inner world that resides at the Earth's core, as I have explained to you. He did so under the direction of his tribe's Krataklak elders, who instructed him during a dream vision. Neither my father nor the Krataklaks know anything of the planet Poloda, let alone the nation of Unis, of which I have just learned for the first time as you related your tale."

Tangor stood up and rubbed his chin as if he were thinking deeply. "Then this is indeed a strange development, one worthy of the grand cosmic coincidences of which you have told me your friend Dejah Thoris spoke."

I stood there in mute stupefaction, my mind racing but coming up with no explanation other than that I had somehow been drawn to this very place and this very moment by some mysterious and inexorable force that was guiding my fate.

"You have no idea, then, what the name Halos signifies?" Tangor asked, and it seemed that the dumbfounded look upon my face had at last convinced him that I was telling the truth as I knew it and was withholding no information from him.

"None whatsoever," I replied.

Tangor knitted his brows. "It is curious . . ."

"Yes?" I said in an effort to prompt him to go on, for it was clear that he was thinking hard about something.

"The characters of the Unisan language," he replied, "are said to be derived from the ancient liturgical script of the planet Uvala. In fact, I have heard it said that the symbols have survived more or less unchanged for centuries, and maybe even millennia."

"Uvala," I repeated. "That's the planet you said is one of the two worlds that are next to this one along the atmospheric belt."

"Yes." Tangor pursed his lips as if something had occurred to him that left him uneasy. "I once rescued the life of a woman on the planet Yonda who claimed to have visited Uvala."

"Go on," I said, for Tangor had become suddenly quiet.

"Now this interested me greatly," he continued finally, "for during my residence on Poloda, I had learned that in the era before the war with the Kapars, the people of Unis practiced a religion that had since been set aside and forgotten during the long years of fighting for their survival. This faith taught that those who died on their world moved on to Uvala, the planet that lies upon the opposite side of the star Omos from the vantage of Poloda. The woman told me she was a member of some society or sect that she called the Numinous Ones, whose temple was to be found on Uvala. I told her I would very much be interested in visiting this temple, but she warned me that visitors to Uvala were forbidden, for it was what she called 'the Gateway to Halos.' When I asked her what Halos was, she replied that it was there that my pneuma had been destined to travel before it was deflected to Poloda. I asked her to explain, but she told me she had already said too much. Nonetheless, I was intrigued, and I determined that one day I would travel through the atmospheric belt to Uvala to unlock its secrets. But I have been stranded on this world for years now, trying to find a way off. My plane has received no signal from any of the Unisan power stations on Poloda in all the time I have been on Zandar, and thus my ship cannot fly. But now here you are, having materialized out of nowhere and bearing a tattoo that spells out the name Halos in the Unisan script. Moreover, you have told me of these same Numinous Ones, who were referred to in vague and mysterious terms by both the Mahar queen Tu-la-sa and the winged terror who is hunting you called Lahvoh. Curious indeed, is it not?"

I was speechless. There was but one conclusion I could make from Tangor's remarkable story, which was that Dejah Thoris had been utterly correct in her conviction that I was being drawn through the void toward a certain purpose via some inescapable principle of quantum entanglement. And another thing became clear: we must repair Tangor's ship and fly it through the atmospheric belt to Uvala at all costs. Only there would I find my answers.

I told Tangor as much and he agreed. "If you can help me repair my ship and get it flying again, I would be happy to take you to Uvala. But therein lies the challenge."

I grinned. "I was made for challenges."

"Listening to your own tale, my friend," Tangor said, "I can verily believe that you were," and he laughed.

"Well, I've been listening closely to your tale," I said, "and I was wondering if you could back up to something you said at the beginning so I can see if I heard you right. You said you are an American but you were flying a U.S. bombing raid over Germany in September 1939. That doesn't make sense. The United States didn't enter the Second World War until after the Japanese attacked Pearl Harbor in December 1941."

Tangor gave me an odd look. "What is the Second World War?" he asked. "Surely you mean the Great War, which began in 1914 and was still raging when I died in 1939. Has there been another Great War since that time, one that you now refer to as the Second World War?"

"Wait a minute," I said, my mind whirling. "Are you telling me that where you came from the Japanese attack on Pearl Harbor didn't draw the United States into the war?"

Tangor made an intonation of puzzlement. "Oh, there

were occasional armistices during the Great War. But essentially the United States was never *not* at war with Germany. Not since 1914, in any case. I presume we still are, if both sides haven't annihilated themselves by now."

"It can't be . . ." I said, stunned, as the truth began to dawn on me. "You aren't from my world after all. You are from *another Earth!*"

I stood up as I made my incredible pronouncement, the very ground feeling unsteady beneath my feet as I realized that even now I might not be in the same universe as that of Earth. My whole perspective of reality seemed to shift with the thought, which within but a fraction of a second spurred a dozen other wild speculations within my mind.

"It seems absurd," I said to my companion, "but the idea that we are from different iterations of Earth—different *universes*, plural—may actually be the key to a series of mysteries that have baffled me since I was a little girl. When I left Earth in 1950, what astronomers knew about Mars didn't jibe with what Mr. Burroughs and my friends and I knew to be the truth about Barsoom. But now I understand: Mars and Barsoom aren't the same place! Upon all those occasions when I looked up at Mars from the Earth's outer crust, I wasn't looking at Barsoom, with its vibrant cities and lush farmlands along its expansive canal network. No, I was looking at a dead planet. Barsoom and Mars are not the same! At least, my Earth's Mars is different from Barsoom. But it would seem that your Mars and Barsoom are the same planet. And what if . . ."

Tears began to well in my eyes as the staggering revelation came into focus, and little Hucklebuck woke up and, making his soft, xylophonic trilling noise, tried to wrap his tiny arms around one of my ankles, as if to try to reassure me and make me feel better.

"And what if," I finally managed to continue, "it's the same with Kjarna and worlds such as Cosoom and Barsoom, all of which were said by Mr. Burroughs to harbor intelligent life?

They aren't Mercury or Venus or Mars. Or they are, but they're *your* Earth's Mercury, Venus, and Mars, not *my* Earth's. And what about . . . what about Pellucidar, where I'm from? We've suspected for a while now that there was something strange about the polar opening to the inner world. Occasionally those entering and leaving would see a strange auroral phenomenon. Other times, those searching for the polar opening were never able to find it. What if it's not just instrument failure or miscalculation? What if the opening is really not there? What if there's a *gateway* at the pole? One that opens sometimes, but not others. A gateway to another universe, perhaps to the hollow core of *your* Earth, where the very laws of physics are different. That's why a tiny sun can hang in the middle of a hollow world—it's held in place by the solar and planetary rays! That's why we've never detected the rays on the outer crust. They don't *exist* in our universe—they exist in *your* universe. Maybe the aurora at the North Pole is a manifestation of some kind of field, one that reaches down into the crust and rings it like a subterranean shell. So that when David Innes and Abner Perry dug down into the Earth's crust in their iron mole, they passed through the field into the other universe!"

I removed a charred twig from the fire and, after perching Hucklebuck on my shoulder, strode across the camp to the side of Tangor's plane. There, using the charcoal on the end of the stick after the manner of the tip of a pencil, I drew a crude diagram on the fuselage.

"Looks like you've got it all worked out," Tangor said approvingly, after examining my handiwork.

"Not entirely, I'm sure," I said. "I think this is a good general working hypothesis, but what are the specifics? For example, is there another Victory Harben in your world, similar to me but with a different life history? Or was a version of me ever even born on your world, being that events unfolded differently there? And at what point did the two Earths diverge? You said your Great War began in 1914,

INTER-ANGULAR RELATIONSHIP
BETWEEN EARTH AND JASOOM

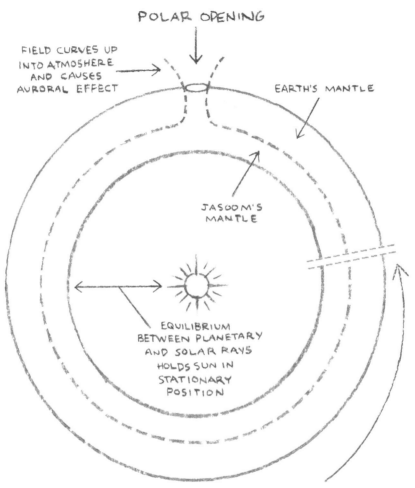

POLAR OPENING

FIELD CURVES UP
INTO ATMOSHERE
AND CAUSES
AURORAL EFFECT

EARTH'S MANTLE

JASOOM'S
MANTLE

EQUILIBRIUM
BETWEEN PLANETARY
AND SOLAR RAYS
HOLDS SUN IN
STATIONARY
POSITION

FIELD IS ERRATIC,
SOMETIMES ALLOWING
TRAVELERS TO PASS
THROUGH, SOMETIMES NOT

IRON MOLE PASSED
THROUGH FIELD, TRAVELING
FROM EARTH'S OUTER
CRUST TO JASOOM'S
INNER CORE

WORKING HYPOTHESIS ONLY — MUST VERIFY THE MATH!

though it continued more or less uninterrupted until at least 1939, when you died upon your world. My world also had a Great War that started in 1914, but it was finished and done with by November 1918."

"My Great War had a brief armistice in 1918," Tangor interjected, "but the fighting resumed shortly thereafter."

"So perhaps that is the point of the divergence," I said, "though I suppose it would take a detailed analysis by the historians of both Earths to know for sure. In any case, to avoid confusion, from now on let us refer to your Earth as 'Jasoom,' the Barsoomian name for the third planet in orbit around Sol. Your Sol, that is." I thought for a moment. "It is strange, is it not, that Mr. Burroughs, who came from my Earth, knew and wrote tales concerning multiple worlds that exist in your universe? It is almost as if he had a special connection to your universe. Now that I think of it, I recall that in one of his stories he said that his family owned a string of general stores in Virginia, but as far as I am aware, Mr. Burroughs' lineage was from the Northeast and the Midwest, not the South. Could it be that he had access to the biography—or maybe even some kind of more direct contact—of an alternate version of himself, one who hailed from 'Jasoom,' and that he sometimes wrote about that alternative Edgar Rice Burroughs in his novels?"

"I do not know," said Tangor, "but now I am left wondering about the identity of the writer to whose side my spirit drifted after my advent on Poloda. Could it have been this same Mr. Burroughs of whom you speak? And if so, in which universe did he reside?"

"It is an intriguing thought," I said. "But I don't think my mind can handle any further speculations tonight. This evening has ushered in enough revelations to last me a lifetime! If only I could speak to my godfather about them . . ."

During my travels through the void, I had once before jury-rigged a Gridley Wave device, although I'd had to leave it behind upon the world where I had created it before I could manage to establish direct communication with my friends on Earth and in Pellucidar. Now, upon hearing about Polodian radius technology, I wondered if I might somehow adapt it to re-create a device powerful enough to send a signal across 450,000 light-years to the Gridley Wave station in Sari, Pellucidar. Thanks to my Pellucidarian homing instinct, which was still somehow bizarrely in effect, I could pinpoint the exact direction in the sky to which to transmit a signal. Perhaps I could make contact with Abner Perry, and then at least let my friends and family know that I was still alive. If the Earth existed in a universe parallel to Pellucidar, then my godfather had already proven that a Gridley Wave signal could be transmitted between the two universes. And so even if I currently resided in a different universe from my friends, I might still be able to make contact with them.

It was with these thoughts swirling in my head, along with the evening's many other staggering revelations, that I finally drifted off to sleep beside the warmth of the campfire, while Hucklebuck trilled contentedly in my arms.

17
CONTACT

OVER THE NEXT FEW WEEKS I divided my time between two tasks: first, my study of the Polodian radius technology, a subject on which Tangor proved to be an apt and able teacher; and second, my efforts to build a Gridley Wave apparatus using the radio and spare parts and other materials from the *Starduster*, the name I had given Tangor's flying ship after he told me its Unisan Air Corps designation amounted to a jumble of random letters and numbers. If I could manage to contact Abner Perry in Pellucidar, I believed there was a very real possibility that he and I might devise a way of getting me home, and also develop a means to track down my godfather, wherever he lay in the infinite angles of reality, for I refused to believe he had perished as Lahvoh had taunted.

Abner was a scientific prodigy, and even if nine out of ten of his harebrained inventions ended in disaster, the tenth was often of such brilliance that it would have turned science on its head had it become known to researchers on the outer crust. But Abner's indefatigable genius, should I manage to contact him—as well as the skill I had developed as his young mentor in Pellucidar at keeping him on track when his erudite mind would otherwise amble into the ethereal realms of impracticability—was but one tool in my arsenal.

I also had another secret weapon to assail the problem of getting me home, and that was my knowledge of Kjarnan science—in particular, what I had studied about zuvans at

180

the side of that little genius, Maksata Dor. Moreover, I had in my possession a unique piece of technology equipped with innovations developed directly from Kjarnan science: my uncertainty apparatus. This, I was convinced, would be the key to establishing communication with my faraway friends, for I had not forgotten the fact that the gun's entanglement effect had ceased operating on the very same day that the Gridley Wave had gone silent in the spring of 1950. I had known for some time now that there was a correlation between the principle of the uncertainty gun and that of the Gridley Wave itself. Thus, I had already developed a hypothesis as to how I might adapt the gun to transmit and receive Gridley Wave signals, and I was eager to put it to the test. What is more, my uncertainty gun was already adapted with a zuvan field repository. If I could but find a way to refill the exhausted transit field chamber, I might also discover a means to control the destination of the translocation effect and be able to send myself home.

I had but recently come up with an analogy that I believed came close to describing the nature of the transit effect that Tu-al-sa must have somehow imposed on me via the Einstein-Rosen bridge she had generated. It was as if I had been hurled into a great funnel, the top of which is wider than its lower, narrower spout. When I was first thrust into the funnel, I had bounced around wildly, chaotically, and less frequently against the wide, upper walls of the funnel. However, as time went on, gravity—and by that, I mean gravity in the Einsteinian sense; that is, the curvature of spacetime—pulled me down into the lower, more narrow spout of the funnel, at which point I naturally began to bounce more rapidly against the funnel's walls. In my metaphor, the increasing number of impacts I experienced as I passed down the funnel's narrowing spout was symbolic of the increasing number of coincidences I had experienced during my cosmic jaunt through the angles of hyperreality—the very same coincidences that Dejah Thoris had first proposed to me on Barsoom, and that the Volstari had reaffirmed during my audience with them in the Hall of the Thought Lords back on Kjarna. That is, I was knocking myself more rapidly against the narrowing spout of my metaphor, and with each bounce I was getting closer and closer to the goal that must lie in wait for me when, ultimately, I would be expelled from the other end of the funnel. I had speeded up my slide down the funnel's narrow spout by artificially imposing the translocation zuvan on myself in a rapid-fire fashion via my uncertainty gun. Thus it was that I had eventually come out the other end of the funnel and been deposited on the planet Zandar in the Omos system. There at last my cosmic travels had come to a stop, as there was nowhere left for me to fall. I had followed the curvature of spacetime to the point of ultimate entropy, and the translocation effect would carry me no farther.

Tu-al-sa had sent me on my way to where she had believed I needed to be, and now I was here, on Zandar. The final "coincidence" on my journey—and by coincidence, I mean "entanglement event"—had been meeting Tangor, who just happened to be the one person in the entire Omos system who could make clear for me the significance of my ritual tattoo. Otherwise, I would have never known that the characters of my tattoo spelled out the name "Halos." And if I had not met Tangor, I would have never learned of the connection between the mysterious "Gateway to Halos" and the planet Uvala. The funnel had deposited me precisely where I needed to be so that I would have the means at my disposal—that is, Tangor's ship—to cross the Omos system and find my way to Uvala, the Gateway of Halos. There, I knew, lay my destiny, and the ultimate reason Tu-al-sa had swept me up in her spacetime maelstrom. Though I was determined to find a way back home at all costs, I knew that I must first confront what lay waiting for me on Uvala. And that meant repairing the *Starduster* and finding a way to power it so that we might leave Zandar behind and fly through the atmospheric belt to neighboring Uvala.

And so it was with a fury that I attacked the two-pronged problem of repairing the flying ship and constructing a Gridley Wave device with which I might contact Abner Perry in Pellucidar. It was upon one evening about three Zandarian weeks into my stay at Tangor's camp that I at last reached a crucial stage in achieving the latter of my two goals. I had woven together a wide canopy of the copper wire that Tangor had acquired, and tied it high above in the branches of the trees that overlooked our little camp. I proceeded to connect the canopy to the metallic dish from Tangor's plane that was responsible for receiving the radius signal from the power station on Poloda. My intent was for the canopy to serve as an antenna array, which I would then use to transmit and receive a localized Gridley Wave radio signal. All that remained was to construct a functional Gridley Wave apparatus, which I at last achieved by connecting Tangor's shipboard radio speaker and microphone to my uncertainty gun.

My godfather and I had long ago surmised that the Gridley Wave acted on a hypothetical process that physicists back on Earth called quantum mechanical tunneling, the very same principle upon which my uncertainty gun operated. I shall not bore you with the details of this principle other than to use the same words I employed to describe it when I explained the phenomenon to Maksata Dor back on Kjarna. And that is to say that Gridley Wave communication is essentially just two "like" particles doing the same happy dance together across the room from one another, or in this case, across the gulf of 450,000 light-years that separates the Omos system from Earth. I had come to believe that the idea of distance was irrelevant, especially if my hypothesis was correct that reality was actually made up of a spectrum of "universes," a sort of Swiss cheese maze of alternate realities. Remember how I said that the Gridley Wave was both a particle and a wave? Well, what I meant by that was that in order to send a Gridley Wave signal between, say, Earth and Pellucidar, all one needs to do is to resonate a specific particle in one universe with a "like" particle in another universe. And it was the same here in the Omos system: I just needed to tunnel through spacetime and resonate a particular particle located at our camp here on Zandar with a "like" particle in Sari, Pellucidar. As long as the two quantum particles were in resonance, it didn't matter how far away the two points were, or even if they existed in different universes.

Still, though I believed my hypothesis was sound, I received nothing but static when I adjusted the radio dish so that it pointed directly to the point in the starry night sky above where my Pellucidarian homing instinct told me my home village of Sari lay. Though I sat there for hours making tiny adjustments to the radio dish, nothing but whistles and pops came from the speaker beside me as I spoke repeatedly into the microphone. Soon, my own voice addressing the empty static started to feel like a mockery.

Frustrated and dejected, I was about to shut off the radio and give up for the night when I heard what sounded like the faintest of voices speaking behind the thick wall of static.

"... *is that you ... Janson ... Where ... you?*"

When I grabbed the microphone and spoke into it, I was trembling with excitement. It was hard to tell through the static, but surely the voice I had heard was that of Janson Gridley!

"Speak louder, please!" I said. "I can barely hear you. Did you say *Janson*? Janson Gridley?" Again, nothing but static from the speaker, so I continued in the vain hope that my godfather's son could hear my transmission. "Janson, you have to listen to me. I've figured it out! There are worlds upon worlds, Janson—ours is not the only universe! You have to tell Abner to direct the Gridley Wave antenna at Sari Station toward the globular cluster NGC 7006. Tell him to open the band wide and adjust the frequency to

85.609238. That will put our signals in resonance so we can establish a fixed connection." I paused, listening for a reply, but none came, so I went on. "I have to tell you what I have discovered, as I believe it's of great pertinence to what's happened to me. Tell Abner that the old Mahar Queen Tu-al-sa somehow used Pellucidar's sun to generate an Einstein-Rosen bridge. He'll know what I mean. Anyway, it swallowed me and somehow imposed a quantum translocation effect on me. I've been bouncing around willy-nilly from world to world. But that's only the beginning of it! Tu-al-sa must have known that Pellucidar and Earth don't exist in the same universe. There is a field surrounding the Earth's upper mantle, one that serves as a portal between universes when traveling between the outer crust and Pellucidar. The field is what causes the aurora effect at the North Pole. I'm guessing the iron mole also passed through a field that joins the two universes. It's incredible to believe, I know, but all of God's creation consists of multiple realities! That must be what the Mahar tablets from Thotra meant when they referred to hypergeometries!"

I knew I was rambling, but it was the best I could do under the circumstances, as excited and jolted as I was to have received Janson's signal. My heart pounded in my chest as I strained my ears for the barest whisper of a reply. I waited so long that I almost fell over when the voice of Janson Gridley rang out loud and clear from the speaker: "*Victory! Are you with my father? Tell me how to find you!*"

"No, I'm not with your father. Listen to me! Localize my signal by adjusting the dial on your Gridley Wave set to 85.609238. Once we're in resonance, Abner will know how to trace the signal back to my location and establish a permanent connection." Only more static from the speaker. Why static, I thought? If the Gridley Wave operated by means of quantum mechanical tunneling, there should be absolutely no degradation of the signal.

"Janson, do you hear me? Janson!"

But I had lost the signal. Try though I might, I could not seem to reestablish the connection.

Finally, after several minutes of failed attempts to lock on to Janson's frequency, I stood up from the radio set, my whole body shaking with a bad case of nerves. "Holy mackerel!" I exclaimed to Tangor, who had been woken up by all the commotion and walked over to see what all the excitement was about. Hucklebuck, still in his small form, was also awake now, perched up on his hind legs on the mossy ground and fixing me with his beady black eyes in a look of intense curiosity.

When I explained what had happened, Tangor and Hucklebuck stayed up with me all night as the planets arced high above our heads in the starry heavens and I attempted to reestablish Janson Gridley's signal. At last, as the great sun Omos brightened the morning sky and then rose upon the horizon, I drifted off into a restless sleep with the microphone still in my hand and my ear pressed up against the speaker.

18
LOYALTY AND SACRIFICE

THE TRANSMISSION FROM JANSON GRIDLEY changed everything. Someone from back home knew that I was alive, even if he had heard only a few words that I had broadcast. Somehow that made all the difference. Though I was thousands of light-years from home, I was no longer alone. There were people back in Sari thinking of me. Janson would tell Abner and my parents, and they would know that I hadn't perished, that there was still hope of finding me. And I knew they would be looking for me, trying everything they could think of to get me back to them. No longer did I need to shoulder the burden alone. Until I had heard Janson's voice, I don't think I realized just how truly lonely I had become, thrust from world to world with nothing but my wits and my agility to keep me alive.

Now I threw myself into my task of adapting the *Starduster* to a new energy source with single-minded determination. I must get to Uvala and solve the mystery so I could end this business and get back home. And within two short weeks I had my breakthrough.

The answer to adapting the plane was deceptively simple for anyone with a working knowledge of Kjarnan aerospace engineering, which I had taken a crash course in while preparing for my mission to mend the Kjarnan atmosphere. I had learned that Kjarnan fliers were outfitted with an apparatus that draws energy via a matrix of solar rays in order to power the craft's instrumentation. As a fail-safe, this apparatus was also equipped to power an auxiliary engine should the ship suffer a catastrophic loss of the main engine while flying in Kjarna's atmosphere. That engine was no different in any meaningful way from the turbine engine of Tangor's plane. Fortunately, the apparatus that received the energy signal from Poloda to power the radius ship was similar enough to the Kjarnan apparatus that it was but a simple matter for me to adapt the receiver so that it might be adjusted to the "frequencies" of the solar rays emanating from Omos, the sun of this unique solar system, thereby establishing the necessary matrix of rays to power the craft. A craft with an engine fueled directly by the solar rays in such a manner—rather than indirectly via a power station that stored such rays and transmitted their converted energy via a signal, such as had been developed by scientists on Poloda—would be able to traverse the entire atmospheric belt that connects the eleven planets of the system, since the ship would always be in direct proximity to Omos and thus have continuous access to a perpetual fuel source.

After I divulged the good news to my companions, we had a brief celebratory meal before we got to work once again. Tangor informed me that the trip through the atmospheric belt would require between thirty-five and forty days of uninterrupted travel. Therefore, we would need to gather enough rations and supplies to survive the duration. There would be no rest stops. If the engine failed, we would be suspended in midair within the confines of the atmospheric belt until we died of thirst or starvation, and there our corpses would remain, encased in the coffin of our ship, until they eventually decomposed. If for any reason the trip took too much longer than expected, we would die just the same, for there was only so much room on board the plane for food and water storage. But Tangor had made the interplanetary jump on several occasions, and he seemed confident that we could make the flight just as safely as he had previously, though he cautioned that the passage between worlds should not be taken lightly.

"Nor," Tangor added, "should you take lightly the wild *frozahs* or colossal *zuduvahs* that sometimes range into these foothills out of their stomping grounds to the north. If you see one, run away as fast as you can and find someplace to hide. Preferably block yourself in a cave if it is a frozah, for they are as comfortable in the trees as on the ground. And if it is a zuduvah? Well, let's just hope you don't run into one, for I don't have any advice for you there."

"This isn't my first walk around the park," I assured him. "I was born in Pellucidar, after all. Hucklebuck and I can take care of ourselves, can't we, buddy?"

The little furball let out a vicious but all-too-cute trill and then jumped into my arms for an evening snuggle.

I grinned widely. "See?"

Tangor grunted dubiously and went back to finishing his dinner.

And so it was decided. In the effort to gather foodstuffs so that we might survive the journey through the atmospheric belt, Hucklebuck and I would forage for wild nuts, berries, fruits, mushrooms, and tubers in the nearby foothills, while Tangor remained to keep vigil over the radius ship in case the Nuvors decided to return, as he predicted they would. We awoke and departed camp each morning before the crack of dawn so that we might cover as much ground as possible and still have time to return to our base before nightfall. Hucklebuck proved to be a valuable companion on our excursions, carrying his weight by climbing up high into the trees and shaking down fruit by jumping up and down on the branches with his pudgy little body, or burrowing beneath the soft, moss-covered soil with his tiny clawed hands and digging up delicious roots and tubers.

One afternoon we had ranged about as far from camp as I felt comfortable, when a storm blew up suddenly out of the northwest. First came a frigid wind as the sky on the horizon darkened in a mix of deep indigo blue clouds shot with traces of sickly mauve. Upon seeing the billowing tempest headed our way, Hucklebuck let out the most disconcerting trill of unease. Suddenly all the fur on his body bristled and he arched his back, looking like a frightened cat. But a cat he was not, and I watched as he grew into his titanic form before my very eyes. Now once again the size and girth of an African bush elephant, he communicated to me in his wordless musical language, telling me we must return to camp as swiftly as possible, for it was clear he regarded the coming storm as a grave threat to our safety.

I was just about to climb up his fur and onto his back when out of the clear stretch of sky that lay in advance of the squall shot a bright white bolt of lightning—striking Hucklebuck squarely on the back!

"Hucklebuck!" I screamed hoarsely in unrestrained panic, for truly I believed the strike must be fatal.

If my bestial companion had bristled before upon glimpsing the storm, now every hair on his body shot up so stiff and straight that he might have been a cartoon character sticking his finger into an electrical outlet. His great dark eyes grew wide and protruding, and his tusked mouth gaped open and let out the most heart-wrenching moan I had ever heard uttered by either human or beast. Though he still stood upright upon his four massively muscled legs, Hucklebuck had dug his claws deep into the mossy turf. Now he shook his enormous head as if trying to wake up from his stupefaction, and his whole body shuddered and trembled.

It was then that I noticed a whitish-yellow energy coursing faintly over his frame, like a lingering echo of the phenomenon that had struck him. But within a few moments, as his hair lay back down and returned to its normal shaggy coat of white that accompanied his titanic form, the flashes of light vanished.

Hucklebuck sat down on his haunches for a moment as if to rest from his trials, while I threw my arms around his great bushy neck and stroked his fur reassuringly, tears of relief in my eyes. He proceeded to nuzzle me with his snout, and a burst of musical notes erupted from deep in his throat, reassuring me that he was all right and just needed a moment's rest. He was going to live!

As the gale increased about us and my furry friend took his repose, I thought back to what had just happened. In the instant terror of the moment, I had believed the bolt that had struck Hucklebuck to have been lightning, but now I reflected that it had looked more like a straight beam of intense white energy than a jagged firebolt. Had what stuck him been a natural phenomenon? It was impossible to say, for I knew so very little about Zandar's environment and virtually nothing about its meteorology.

After only a minute or two, Hucklebuck lifted up his immense frame and shook himself like a wet dog. Then he urged me with wordless melodic tones to climb up on his back so that we might be on our way in the face of the storm that was barreling down upon us. Reluctantly, I complied, and soon the mossy hills were rushing past in a blur as my Brobdingnagian mount carried us forth, the raging tempest at our heels.

It was not long before the storm overtook us. It began first as an ice-cold downpour, the enormous raindrops stinging our backs like lead balls from a pellet gun. Then began the driving sleet, which swiftly transformed into hail—first the size of golf balls, and then as large as my fist. Hucklebuck took partial cover behind a hillock that shielded a portion of his bulk from the slanting trajectory of the hail. I covered my head with my arms to prevent my skull from being cracked open while I slid down the wet, matted fur that now hung from Hucklebuck's neck. As soon as I reached the ground, a shaggy claw swiped out at me and drew me under the warm furry belly of my selfless and heroic friend.

"Keep your head low, buddy!" I cried. "You've got a thick skull, but trust me—the physics of a baseball hitting your noggin from the height of those clouds will crack it right open!"

But somehow we both survived the quarter of an hour during which the hailstorm beat down upon us in its relentless fury. Then resumed the frigid rain, and again I shivered in the agonizing cold, my limbs and face growing numb as my misery only continued to increase. Hucklebuck, sensing my distress, gently lowered his warm belly down upon me, careful not to crush me beneath his six-ton frame. I continued to shudder in the cold, but soon I began to regain sensation in my hands and face, and eventually I again felt the blood pounding through my tortured limbs. If not for Hucklebuck, I knew I would have died there in those mossy foothills. For a second time, he had saved my life.

Whether an hour or six had passed since the storm first struck, I knew not, but finally it abated into a light rain, and at last I succumbed to sleep. I dreamed what seemed endless hours, or even days, of restless dreams. Many of these revolved around Janson Gridley, who had leaped into the void upon a surfboard, but instead of riding upon an ocean wave, he rode upon a beam of light that pierced the stygian abyss of space. Often I would see him streak past me, reaching out a hand to grab my own as I too hurtled at the speed of light through the void. But never did we make contact, for too fast did we fly through the trackless infinity of black nothingness.

"Victory, wake up! I'm right here!"

Suddenly I awoke with a start, convinced beyond a shadow of a doubt that I had heard Janson's voice whispering forcefully into my left ear. I turned in that direction, only to find that my left ear had been pressed directly against Hucklebuck's shaggy white cheek. Illuminated in the soft glow of the morning light, he lifted his head at my motion and nosed my own cheek with his fluffy snout, which seemed to have dried out and was now soft and warm.

I smiled and scratched the fleecy scruff under his chin. "We made it, buddy!" I exclaimed. "We survived!"

Hucklebuck trilled contentedly. I reached into the sack that was slung over my shoulder and removed one of the apple-like fruits we had gathered on our excursion. "Eat up, Hucklebuck!" I commanded, holding the fruit up to his snout. With a snap of his large, sharp teeth, he snatched up the fruit and then wolfed it down, after which he emitted another melodic trill of happiness.

I gave him another fruit to gobble down and then fished in the bag for one of my own. The early morning light of Omos was shining from beneath the eastern hills, casting the sky in a beauteous array of yellow-orange hues. I chomped down on my breakfast bounty only to look up and find Hucklebuck staring at me with a look I had never seen before on his both adorable and frightful countenance.

"What is it, buddy?" I asked. "Is everything okay?"

He trilled, and his wordless statement left me baffled and wondering if my translation aura was malfunctioning. He had communicated in essence that I was a sight for sore eyes, and that he had experienced a profound sorrow during my long absence.

"I guess I was asleep for a lot longer than I thought," I replied. "But there's no need to miss me, little-big guy. I'm right here." And I threw my arms around his shaggy neck while he made a noise that was a cross between a xylophonic trill and a cat's purring. This was not a vocalization that my translation aura could interpret, but I didn't need the latter to know that it meant he was happy.

Hucklebuck got up, stretched like a cat, and let out a cavernous, though melodic, yawn. With a tuneful utterance, he indicated that I should climb up onto his back and that we should be on our way. I didn't hesitate, for Hucklebuck appeared to be fully recovered from the trials of the storm, and I knew Tangor would be worried sick that we had not returned to the camp before the previous nightfall. Even now, he might be setting out in search of us.

We had proceeded perhaps half a mile from the sheltering

hillock where we had taken refuge when a frightful moan rang out from the forested hills that surrounded us. Hucklebuck got low to the ground and his tail shot out straight behind him in what I took to be an expression of apprehension and defensive readiness.

"Uh . . . Come on, boy," I said. "I'm thinking we should take Tangor's advice and get away from whatever made that noise as fast as we can."

But it was too late. Already could I see the treetops swaying up high above as something large—no, *gargantuan*—was moving through the woods in our direction. Within moments the trees parted and I stood frozen in shock and disbelief at the behemoth that stood before us. Surely this was the colossal zuduvah of which Tangor had warned.

When it reared up on its powerful, stocky hind legs, as it did when it emerged from the forest, the creature stood nearly thirty feet high. Its face resembled your worst imagining of a demon's skull, colored a dull yellow-brown, with long, dreadful horns of deep crimson curving from the temples, as if they had been washed in blood. The monster's torso was vaguely humanoid in form and muscled like a gorilla, but there the comparison ended. Ropy, vertebrae-like structures forming intricate symmetrical patterns snaked around the areas of its body that were not covered in mossy green fur, providing a sort of ribbed armor plating. Its writhing arms were segmented like the body of a centipede, at the ends of which were three razor-sharp claws.

"Hucklebuck, run!" I cried, but my faithful companion only put himself between me and the terrifying behemoth, digging his own long claws into the dirt and snarling with a fierce atonal trill.

"No, boy! *No!*"

My heart plummeted into my stomach when the thing looked past Hucklebuck, locking its three fiendish azure eyes upon me. The creature fell forward upon its arms, which immediately grew rigid to support its massive weight. Then it charged directly at me.

Rather I should say it tried to charge at me, for I screamed in horror and futility as Hucklebuck, less than half the devilish monster's size, launched himself in the air straight for the thing's ropy, muscular throat, goring it with his sharp ivory tusks. The creature released a hellish roar and fell back to one side, distracted from its previous intention to kill me.

Though Hucklebuck's attack had caught the creature by surprise, so fixated had its primitive brain been on me, now it again stood up on its squat, tree-trunk legs, thus unburdening its arms, which instantly lost their rigidity and wrapped around Hucklebuck's torso like twin boa constrictors. With all its might the creature squeezed with its bony, segmented limbs.

A scream of terror cut off in my throat as Hucklebuck trilled in atonal agony and his beautiful black eyes glazed over as they protruded from their sockets. A trickle of blood the color of blackberry wine began running from Hucklebuck's mouth, staining his pure white fur.

I had to do something. Instinctively, I reached for my uncertainty gun. But its charge was sapped, a consequence of my recent efforts to use it as a Gridley Wave interface in hopes of contacting with my friends in Pellucidar. What else could I—?

I opened a panel in my utility belt that revealed a series of buttons and switches used to control various functions built into my Kjarnan attire. My fingers faltered as Hucklebuck let out another pitiful trill. Then, at last, I found the button I was looking for and snapped it down.

Instantly, the large light positioned squarely in the front center of my neckpiece began to strobe with a blinding white light, accompanied by a piercing electronic alarm klaxon. I ran up directly under the towering fiend and waved my arms, shouting over the screeching noise emanating from my neckpiece: "Hey, you ugly troll! I'm far tastier than my friend! Come an' get me!"

But I need have said nothing, for the demonic giant's three eyes had locked on to my flashing, clamoring neckpiece the instant I had pressed the button to activate it. Casting Hucklebuck aside like an unwanted plaything, it dropped down on its now-rigid forelimbs with an earthshaking boom. I heard Hucklebuck's great bulk crash into the trees and brush at the forest's edge, and I cringed.

But I had no time to check on Hucklebuck's condition, no matter how badly wounded he might be. Already I was running up the slope for the trees that edged the opposite side of the hillock, knowing there was little chance I might survive the onslaught of the hideous behemoth that wanted me dead.

A whoosh of stinking wind came from behind and I turned to see the thing only twenty feet to my rear, its revolting skull-like maw wide open, a long thin tongue lashing out in anticipation of its meal. It was over. This was to be the end of my long journey through time and space, and I would never know the answers to the mystery that had drawn me here to my death on distant Zandar.

Suddenly the monster let out a tortured, earsplitting roar. I looked behind in astonishment. Hucklebuck was now mounted on the behemoth's back, sinking his bladelike tusks deep into his antagonist's neck. Though the zuduvah writhed and thrashed with a violence like nothing I had ever seen, Hucklebuck clung on with tenacious determination, stabbing, ever stabbing with his razor-sharp tusks. Though the thing tried to reach its assailant with its centipede-like arms, the appendages apparently could not bend backward with the same flexibility with which they writhed out from the creature's forefront. Never could they land upon its attacker and drag him off. Meanwhile, the great white fury that was Hucklebuck continued to gore his long tusks into the base of the monster's skull, over and over, as rivers of thick bluish blood seeped down the creature's torso in a gruesome shower. The monster let loose one last bloodcurdling screech and then heaved over with a great crash. There it lay, and it moved no more.

I raced back down the hill as quickly as my feet would carry me to find Hucklebuck lying on his side next to the corpse of his kill. Hucklebuck's lungs wheezed and labored, and blackberry blood still trickled from the corner of his mouth out onto his once snow-white fur. I knew it in my heart: my faithful and loyal friend was dying.

I threw my arms about his great neck, heedless of the blood, and, sobbing, told him what a good boy he was, and how we were going to have a thousand wonderful adventures together. He trilled softly back at me, melodic and sorrowful, and my translation aura sounded a single word in my mind—*love*.

I am not embarrassed to say that I wept uncontrollably. It is neither a sin nor a weakness to grieve. For without grief, we would not be human or have any moral compass by which to judge that which is precious in life. I had only just come to know Hucklebuck, but I felt like we had been together my whole life. I could not conceive how I would manage to go on without him. But I would stay at his side until he heaved the last breath from his mighty chest. I owed him that much, and so very much more.

As I embraced my dying friend, an electric shock jolted me. I pulled back to see the same faint whitish-yellow energy coursing over his frame as I had witnessed when he had been struck by the strange bolt from the sky just prior to the arrival of the storm. Within seconds, as I sat there upon the ground beside my friend, watching stupefied, the eerie glow intensified, until I was forced to shield my eyes against the blinding radiance.

I don't know exactly what happened next, for the light was too dazzling for me to see anything through the intense luminosity, but then the light died as suddenly as it had come. When my eyes adjusted to the relatively fainter light of the ordinary Zandarian morning, I saw lying before me on the lime green moss the tiny form of Hucklebuck. He was curled up into a little ball of fur, snoring away with a faint trill just as he had when I had first seen him reduce in size. My heart leaped with hope—he was recharging in his natural hibernation state! He was healing himself!

But what of the strange electrical phenomenon that I had just witnessed run across his frame, which I thought could only be connected to his encounter with the firebolt that had struck him before the storm had hit? I stood up, my eye drawn to another faintly radiating figure that lay some half dozen feet away.

I gasped as I looked down upon a man's supine form. It was none other than—Janson Gridley.

19

REUNION, DEATH, AND ESCAPE

ANSON!" I CRIED, throwing myself upon my knees before his outstretched body. He wore only an antelope-skin loincloth and thag-hide sandals, just as he had when I had last seen him so long ago in Pellucidar, but now his face was clean-shaven, revealing features even more handsome than those of his father. He groaned and turned his head, gazing up at me as his drowsy-looking eyes widened in recognition.

"How—?" I exclaimed. "How is this possible?"

Janson gave me a weak smile and said, "You can blame Abner. He . . ."

"This was Abner's doing?" I felt guilty pressing him while he lay in such a weakened state, but I needed to know. Now. And desperately.

"Got your signal . . . faint . . . but Abner . . . transmitted a Gridley Wave signal back along the coordinates . . . converted me to energy . . . managed to send me with it along a carrier wave."

"Abner did *what*?" I howled. "He sent you along a *carrier wave*? That's not possible. Not even *remotely* possible."

Janson smiled again. "Get used to it. There are people smarter than you." I let out a chirp of laughter and he went on. "Of course, in this case . . . it was Mahars. Abner got the idea from a tablet we pulled out of old Mintra . . . A forbidden method . . . perhaps we should have listened . . . That, plus an idea from Moritz . . . that is, before he bumped

199

his head and lost much of his memory . . . Of course, their theory . . . didn't work out that well for me . . . Seems I got entangled in your big furry friend." He turned his head and regarded Hucklebuck snoring away on the bed of moss. "Or little friend . . ."

"You were *in* Hucklebuck?"

"*Verschränkung* . . . that's what Abner calls it . . . *entanglement.*"

"Yes, I know." I smiled and touched Janson's cheek tenderly. "That degree in theoretical physics from Oxford and all."

"Show-off." Janson grinned with his eyes. "Anyway . . . a *verschränkung* effect . . . it was the only way to convert me back into matter . . . a congealing force, Abner called it . . . It caused my essence to, well . . . merge with his." He extended a limp index finger in the direction of the snoozing Hucklebuck. "In any case, Abner said the Mahars found a safer, if less precise, way to travel through the angles . . . but beyond our capacity to create . . . something called . . . a Rosenberg tunnel?"

"An Einstein-Rosen bridge," I said, "but close enough." All about us birds chirped and cooed in the Zandarian forest. I felt like I was living in a dream. How could this be real? Was I really talking with Janson Gridley?

I examined his outstretched form and noted that the flashes of light that skimmed across his body were increasing in intensity.

Janson seemed to notice too. "I'm slipping," he said, his voice weakening even further. "I can feel it . . . I'm slipping away . . ."

I reached out and grabbed his hand tightly, felt an electrical tingle. "Janson, no." I said firmly. "You're *not* slipping away. You're going to stay right here with me, okay?"

"I'm not going to make it . . ." he croaked out of a dry throat. "But it was worth it."

When I spoke, my voice quavered with emotion. "It wasn't worth it, Janson. It wasn't worth it at *all.*" I choked on a sob.

Now the radiant halo surrounding Janson's entire form increased to a blinding intensity.

"Janson!" I yelled. "No! Stay here with me! Please! *Janson!*"

Abruptly the light was gone, and so too was Janson Gridley, as if he had never been.

I looked down at my hand, clutched into a fist, my nails digging into my palms. In those final moments, I had tried to hold on to Janson's hand with all my strength, to make him stay. But all my strength was not enough. He had slipped away all the same.

Remember what I said about grief? Well, it turns out that was an understatement. I scooped up the tiny form of Hucklebuck in my arms and began running in a daze through the forest in the direction of our camp. I don't remember much about the journey, for the trauma of the past several hours had done its damage and blotted out great stretches of my memory. I suppose that is nature's kindness. I didn't want to remember. I wanted to erase it all.

When finally I staggered back into camp, I knew something was wrong. The engines of the plane had been fired up, and Tangor was closing up the compartment on the undercarriage that held the food stores. When he saw me, he rushed forward and grabbed me by the shoulders.

"Are you okay?" he exclaimed. "What's happened? You look terrible. I was about to take the ship out and search for you."

Before I could reply, clamorous shouts and a burst of hellacious, otherworldly barking erupted from the south-eastern foothills.

Tangor's face grew grim. "The Nuvors are coming," he said. "And they've got a pack of ravenous frozahs with them."

"Let's get out of here," I said.

"Hucklebuck," Tangor said, pointing to the bundle of fur cradled in my arms. "What's wrong with him?"

"He'll be okay," I replied. "We just had a little tangle with a zuduvah."

"A zuduvah!" Tangor exclaimed. "And you're *alive*? Well, I'm glad to hear it, but he can't come with us. Say your good-byes, and quickly. There's no more time."

"Are you out of your mind?" I cried. "Hucklebuck saved my life—not once, but three times. He comes with us. No discussion."

"What if he decides to grow big while we're halfway through the atmospheric belt?" Tangor objected. "He'll rip the ship apart!"

"He would never do that," I said decisively, then poked Hucklebuck in his furry little stomach. "You'd never do that, buddy, right? *Right?*"

The little guy continued to saw away with his faint trilling snore.

We were climbing into our respective cockpits just as a band of Nuvor warriors emerged from the tree line, Chief Oranza in the lead. The transparent bulletproof plastic of the canopies closed down over our heads just as the first volley of spears clanked against the fuselage.

"Uvala or bust!" I shouted into the microphone that permitted communication between the two cockpit compartments.

"Aye, aye, Captain!" Tangor yelled back as the vertical exhaust ports fired and the *Starduster* lifted up slowly into the air, leaving Chief Oranza and his warriors shaking their fists at us amid a furiously swirling cloud of dust and leaves.

20
THE GUARDIANS

I HAD EXPECTED THE TRIP through the atmospheric belt to be long and boring, like a nonstop flight between New York and London. It was anything but monotonous, however, and that was a very good thing, for it took my mind off the painful experience I had endured on Zandar. I didn't want to think about the latter. I *couldn't* think about it. It was one thing to have lost Janson so swiftly after our reunion. It was another to realize that he had cast himself across the cold light-years of space on the mistaken idea that he was rescuing me, based on the even more mistaken notion that he loved me. I could not bear it. I needed time to sort through my feelings, but my feelings were the last thing I wanted to experience right now.

I shall not tax your patience by giving you a detailed account of all the wonders and terrors that Tangor and I witnessed during our thirty-six-day journey, for our passage through the 7,200-mile-diameter channel of atmosphere that rings the Omos system and connects its eleven planets has little bearing on the account at hand. Suffice it to say that I had little expected our crossing between worlds to include perilous encounters with gargantuan winged terrors; flying "snakes" whose lighter-than-air bodies resembled writhing, mile-long gasbags; and even an irregularly shaped hunk of rock about three miles in diameter that hung suspended in our path in the exact center of the atmospheric belt. Upon the surface of the latter, before our ship soared

onward and the planetoid passed beyond our sight, I thought
I had glimpsed a shining monolith encircled by a plaza filled
with a throng of tiny humanoid figures, though Tangor had
failed to see the megalith and its teeming congregants, so I
could have been mistaken so quickly did it pass by. Neither
did I expect that our ship would be rocked with great frequency by harrowing regions of turbulence, which I hypoth-
esized were caused by whatever unknown law of physics held
the atmospheric belt in place and gave it its perfect tubular
form, a field I believed acted as a sort of magnifying lens
through which light from the star Omos heated up vast
patches of air. It was a novel theory, though as a physicist,
albeit one from another universe where the laws of physics
varied considerably from those found in this one, I knew I
must caution myself against drawing any decisive conclusions
without concrete evidence.

At long last we left behind the mysteries of the atmospheric
belt and felt the gravitic pull of the planet Uvala. Tangor
knew precisely when to right the ship so that we would not
barrel like a bullet straight into Uvala's surface, executing
the maneuver with considerable skill, as he had made the
crossing between worlds on a number of occasions prior to
being marooned on Zandar.

From a high altitude, Uvala, where it peeked out from
behind great banks of billowing white clouds, appeared to
be a planet of two massive continents bisected by a vast
world-ringing ocean. The landmasses exhibited a range of
purple and taupe hues, whereas its great annular sea was a
rolling expanse of dark blue-black over whose churning
surface we skimmed after we had made our descent. Tangor
made for the coast of a great peninsula of the southern
continent that jutted out into the sea toward a similar head-
land to the northwest, the latter belonging to the continent
on the opposite side of the channel. I had spied the two
peninsulas while we were still high above the planet and,
after a quick mental calculation in which I took the seven-

thousand-mile-diameter of the planet as my baseline (that being the diameter Tangor informed me was common to all worlds in this singular planetary system), I reckoned that the channel between the two capes consisted of a span of perhaps six hundred miles or more.

When we approached land, a small cove came into view, on the flat plain beyond which clustered what appeared to be an assemblage of enormous longhouses bordered on the south by a forest of massive, towering mushrooms, the tallest of which must have soared nearly a mile into the heavens. I guessed that it was the profusion of these mulberry- and amethyst-hued fungi that gave the landmasses their dark purple aspect from high above Uvala, a color that had been discernible even from the surface of neighboring Zandar.

Hucklebuck, who had slept in his hibernating state through most of our voyage to Uvala, woke up upon hearing the change in the sound of the engines as Tangor brought the ship down on the edge of the village. After wriggling out of the sack in which he had slumbered during our planetary transit, my furry little companion crawled up onto my shoulder and peered through the transparency of the canopy, gazing out in wonder with his beady black eyes at the new sights before him.

The vacuum within the hollow spaces of the *Starduster's* fuselage and wings provided considerable lift, allowing for us to make a gentle, almost vertical landing, so that as we touched down we were able to take in our surroundings with ease and clarity. My eyes widened and Hucklebuck let out a xylophonic trill of excitement when a group of the settlement's inhabitants emerged from the village gate and began approaching our plane, for the towering, lanky, plum-skinned giants must have stood fully twenty feet tall.

"We've made a big mistake," Tangor said through the intercom upon seeing the imposing size of the villagers. "Stay strapped in and get ready for takeoff!"

"I don't see any weapons on them," I countered, trying to remain level-headed. "They seem peaceful. Look at their bearing. It's slow, plodding, nonthreatening." And it was true. Though a group of about a dozen giants was headed our way, the gait of their long, gangly legs was ponderous and unhurried, the expressions on their elongated, almost rectangular faces relaxed and indifferent.

"A single one of those monsters," Tangor replied, "could pry open our canopies like the lid on a can of sardines."

I couldn't argue with Tangor's assessment, but I had come too far to let a case of the jitters stop me from pursuing the mystery that had drawn me to this world. "Now let's not get off on the wrong foot," I said, and before Tangor could object, I had hit the switch that raised the canopy over my head and was already crawling down the small ladder affixed to the fuselage outside my cockpit, Hucklebuck clinging to my hair and still perched on my shoulder. Though a small room where I could stand up and stretch adjoined the cockpit in which I had been confined during much of our interplanetary journey, I had begun to feel like one of the canned sardines from Tangor's metaphor. Thus it was that when I jumped down from the ladder onto terra firma and took in a deep breath of the fresh sea breeze, a wave of blessed relief swept over me. Instinctively, I pulled my arms behind my head and stretched, releasing more than a month's worth of tension from my weary frame.

Just as I was in the act of doing so, the giant in the lead of the group stopped about half a dozen yards away and pointed at my upraised right forearm. Turning to another giant at his side, he croaked the word "Halos," his voice deep and gravelly, his tone one of awe. The other giant nodded gravely.

By this time, Tangor had climbed down out of his cockpit. When he heard the name the giant had spoken, his hand dropped down to rest upon his holstered sidearm, a Polodian military-issue pistol.

"Don't," I said to him, while still beaming a smile at the giants. "We've obviously come to the right place."

"Why do I get the creepy feeling they were waiting for us?" Tangor asked.

"Just don't do anything threatening," I said. "At least until my translation aura has a chance to take effect and we find out what their intentions are."

I pointed to my tattoo and nodded rapidly while continuing to smile. "Halos," I said, with as much cheer as I could muster.

The leader of the giants nodded slowly in return, and what I took to be a forced smile formed upon his lips. A rather terrifying smile, I might add, since his mouth was full of gleaming, needlelike teeth. Still, my impression was that he was offering a well-intended overture, and so I stepped forward until I stood directly beneath the colossal, plum-skinned man. The top of my head barely came up to his knees, so that I had to crane my neck all the way back to look up at his face.

Now that I was closer to the giants, I was able to discern more details of their features and habiliments. Long, straight black hair fell down about their oblong faces, and oval disks that might have been made from either bone or ivory pierced their elongated earlobes. Thin black lines were inked into their dark purple skin in complex and interlocking geo-metrical designs. A cottony cloth garment that appeared to be stained with indigo dye crossed their chests. The four males of the group wore loincloths of the same material that hung to their knees, while the others of the party wore knee-length kilts, four of whom I took to be females due to their wider hips and more gracile facial features, and four others for whom I could discern no visible signs of gender. The heads, shoulders, chests, waists, hips, and limbs of all members of the party were narrower in proportion than those of humans, giving their forms a gangly and awkward appearance, but I was later to learn that the giants were anything but cumbrous or feeble. Inches-thick calluses grew upon the soles of their bare feet. Their noses were flat, with straight, horizontal slits for nostrils, their eyes dark orbs with large black pupils surrounded by irises of deep purple that showed no whites. Their mouths were wide, their lips thin, and their teeth, as I have mentioned, were long, fine, shiny needles that gave them a ghastly demeanor when they smiled. But the practice of grinning, I would discover, was not a common expression among their kind, for they habitually expressed their emotions solely with their eyes.

The leader of the giants spoke a word I did not understand, and then as one the long-limbed goliaths turned their backs on us and began loping toward their village.

"I think they want us to follow them," I said to Tangor, who seemed to have relaxed somewhat after witnessing the giants' peaceable reception.

With a grin, he bowed lightheartedly and flourished a hand in the direction of the retreating giants. "Lead on, McDuff," he said, misquoting Shakespeare, unless the bard of Avon had penned the line differently on his Earth.

The giants led us into their village down a boulevard of well-trodden dirt that ended at a tall and impressive long-house, the entrance of which towered more than forty feet above our heads. As we passed inside, a delicious aroma wafted into my nostrils and made my stomach growl audibly, for the food stores on the *Starduster* had grown bland and uninteresting to my palate during our lengthy interplanetary journey. Before us stretched an impossibly long wooden table sized for the giants, with tall benches on either side that ran beyond our field of vision. Tangor and I did not resist when one of the giants lifted us up like toy dolls and set us down upon the nearest bench, for it was too high for us to climb up on ourselves. Even so, to reach the tabletop, upon which at each of our places was set an oversized plate, bowl, and spoon, we had to stand up on the bench, and I, being shorter than Tangor, was forced to stretch up on my tiptoes. The dozen or so other giants who had accompanied us from the ship sat down and took their own places, the leader sitting directly across from us. Soon a giant entered from a kitchen upon the other end of the hall, carrying a great tray piled high with warm aromatic bread, which he placed on our plates. Next came another giant who dished out a mouth-watering soup into our bowls from an enormous ceramic pot he carried. Our meal turned out to be a delicious bisque filled with succulent mushrooms and assorted vegetables with which I was unfamiliar. A ravenous Hucklebuck, who had eaten little upon our journey on the *Starduster*, jumped up on the table and made for my bowl. I shooed him away and then, gaining the attention of the leader, pointed at my bowl and then at Hucklebuck. The leader said something to one of the servants, who entered the kitchen and returned moments later with a small bowl for my furry companion. Hucklebuck was elated, and even well mannered enough to fish out choice tenders from his bowl using a tiny spoon that was provided him.

Over the course of our meal, my translation aura took hold and we proceeded to converse pleasantly with our gargantuan hosts. It seemed that the race of giants was known as the Davrohendur, which meant the Guardians. We were in the village of Ohm, upon a continent called Ufrahoodrosin, which translated to "The Bowl of the World." The leader of this clan of the Davrohendur, who sat across from us, was named Kloovos. I asked him what he knew of Halos, but he shook his head and said he was forbidden from talking about it by the Ones Who Know. I asked if he could take me to the Ones Who Know, and he replied, "Why should I take you when you already know the way?" When I told him I most certainly did not know the way, he regarded me for nearly a full minute with his dark, inscrutable eyes. "Why do you not fly to the Ones Who Know in your dead bird?" he asked. I gathered that "dead bird" was the Davrohendur rendering of "flying machine."

"We would if we could," I maintained, "but as I said, we don't know the way. Would you take us?"

"It is a long voyage across the Strait of Delirium to the Bay of Mind." Again he regarded me from out of the abyssal depths of his impenetrable eyes. "Long and treacherous is the Path of Memory up which you must climb to the Temple of Flesh and Bone." He lifted a long, crooked finger and pointed it at Tangor. "He may accompany you to the Bay of Mind, but he cannot ascend the Path of Memory and enter the temple, for he has never been there before and has not the permission of the Ones Who Know. You two," he pointed to Hucklebuck and then to me, "will be welcome to return to the temple."

"I assure you I have never been to the temple," I said. "None of us has." A xylophonic chirp burst from Hucklebuck, which my aura translated as a wordless tone of dispute. I cocked my head questioningly at my furry companion, who mimicked my gesture back at me with comical precision. I laughed and exclaimed, "What's gotten into you, buddy?"

"He remembers," said Kloovos, and Hucklebuck seemed to puff up with pride. "But it matters not. I shall take you as far as the Bay of Mind. From there, you must proceed on your own. We shall depart in the morning."

And with that, Kloovos rose from the table along with the other giants who had been seated with us, whom I took to be either his counsel or perhaps his honor guard. One of the giants who had served us proceeded to escort us from the central longhouse to a smaller hut along the village's periphery, where we found bedding already prepared for us. There we slept piled beneath blankets that I later learned were woven from mycelium, which kept us warm during the cold, damp seaside night that soon settled over the village.

We were awakened early the next morning by the sound of a giant in the village center blowing into a conch shell, as the sun crept up from beneath the eastern expanse of the great mushroom forest. We were provided breakfast in the central longhouse, and then escorted to the cove, where three massive ships lay at anchor upon the placid waters. According to Kloovos, the ships were organic in nature, having been grown from giant fungi and molded during cultivation into the form of seaworthy vessels by a process that, when described to me, seemed similar to the method by which a bonsai tree is artfully pruned. When the proper shape is arrived at, a singular strain of slime mold is grafted onto the body of fungus. This grows over the hull of the entire vessel, interacting with the base fungus beneath, both hardening and waterproofing it. The masts, yards, and rudder of the ship are grown and prepared in this same manner, and vast sails of woven mycelium complete the design.

One giant picked up Tangor and another did the same to me, depositing us in large sacks slung over their backs. They then proceeded to wade out into the sea, the water coming up to their waists as they made their way toward the anchored ships. Hucklebuck trilled at me as the giants carried us like children strapped to their mothers' backs, expressing a wordless sentiment that I translated nonetheless as *"See? This is what it's like for me when you stick* me *in your bag!"*

Gently, the giants set us down upon the deck of one of the ships, nearly capsizing the craft and knocking us into the sea as they pulled themselves over the stern and boarded with their prodigious weight. The sheer size of the ships was staggering, as of necessity they must be constructed with such great girths that they can carry the weight of a working crew of twenty-foot-tall Brobdingnagians. Despite their substantial size, the ships were in actuality but modest boats to the Davrohendur, for they were crewed by a complement of only six colossal sailors, which was all the vessels could carry and still remain seaworthy.

Tangor nearly threw a fit when he discovered that the giants had taken his plane from where we had landed it outside the village and carried it to the ship on which we now found ourselves. They had lashed the *Starduster* to the deck with cables of mycelium as thick as a muscular man's arms, making it snug and secure. Tangor and I walked all around the plane, looking for signs of damage, but we found none. When Tangor asked why they wished to bring the plane along with us, Kloovos replied, "Because it is the will of Those Who Know." Tangor looked like he was going to blow a gasket, but then he cooled down and said he guessed it was better than leaving it behind unattended on another continent. "I only hope that Those Who Know have some answers for us when we get to where we're going," he added under his breath, "because I'm getting a little tired of being one of Those Who Don't Know."

The crossing of the Strait of Delirium from the village of Ohm to the Bay of Mind is a voyage of some six or seven hundred miles. Fortunately, the Davrohendur are expert sailors, having developed the fore-and-aft sail, which allows them to sail against the wind. On the first quarter of our journey, the waters were calm and smooth. But as soon as we passed that point a heavy crosswind swept in from the northwest. The giants manning the three ships of our little flotilla pivoted their sails into the wind and our speed increased. At first I was glad of this, but then I noticed the giants casting fearful looks at the heavens. Suddenly, a giant on one of the adjoining vessels pointed to the sky, and I saw a batlike creature winging its way beneath the gray clouds. A tubelike structure projected from the center of the thing's beaked head, and when I strained my eyes I perceived a mist of dark material spouting from the protuberance.

One of the sailors on our ship handed Tangor and me damp cloths, which she instructed us to place over our mouths and noses. When I asked what was happening, she replied, "The *krulek* is under the control of the Understory and is spreading its mind spores. If you breathe in too many of the spores, they will drive you mad."

That didn't sound good. I immediately picked up Hucklebuck and put him in my shoulder bag. "I know you're not going to like it," I told him, "but you're going to have to stay in here for a while."

I looked up at the giant sailor. "What happens if you breathe in just a few of the spores?"

"You will fall into a dream," she said, "from which you may or may not wake up."

"Just great," I said, and then I remembered no more.

When I awoke, Tangor was hovering over me, looking like his best friend had just died. "Can you understand me?" he asked worriedly.

"Clear as a bell," I said, but I felt light-headed. I looked up to see a steepled ceiling spinning dizzyingly above me. "Where am I? Am I on the ship?"

"No," Tangor said. "You breathed in some of the spores and lost consciousness. The Davrohendur weren't sure you'd wake up. *Tuvrahovek*, they call it. The Sleeping Dead. You're in a longhouse on the plateau that lies atop the cliffs far above the Bay of Mind."

"Hucklebuck?"

"He's right here," Tangor said, picking up the little furball from beside him and passing him to me. "He never left your side." I took hold of Hucklebuck and held him up to my cheek while he trilled contentedly.

I saw an oblong purple face somewhere high up above, spinning sickeningly along with the steepled ceiling.

"You will be well more swiftly than you think, Victory Harben," said the giant, whom I now recognized as Kloovos. "You just need food and fresh air. Then you will be ready to make the climb to the courtyard of the Star Tree and tread the Path of Memory." I saw him extend an infinitely long arm, and then a bowl of mushroom soup was being lowered to me.

I set Hucklebuck down and sat up on an elbow. For a moment the room seemed to spin out of control.

"Slowly," the giant intoned. *"Slooowlyyyy . . ."*

Shakily, I took hold of the bowl that had been proffered me and, tipping the edge, slurped down a mouthful of broth. Already, I felt a little better. The world was no longer turning so sickeningly. I picked up the wooden spoon in the bowl, fished out a mushroom, and chewed it down. It was the most delicious thing I had ever tasted. Suddenly I realized I was ravenous, and before I knew it, I had downed the whole bowl.

"Good," said Kloovos. *"Goooood."*

Warily, I rose to my feet. The giant lifted a gangly arm and indicated the nearby door, which I had only just noticed. I picked up Hucklebuck and perched him on my shoulder. Then, on unsteady feet, I made my way outside.

We were high on a cliff above the sea, a fresh ocean breeze blowing over me. The *Starduster* had somehow been transported from the deck of our ship, carried up the sheer cliff face, and deposited here on the plateau, where it lay at rest upon a violet sward speckled with beautiful white wildflowers. To my right, four rows of colossal longhouses stretched across the arcing crown of the tableland.

A long shadow fell over me from behind.

"It is time," said the gravelly voice of Kloovos.

I turned to face the giant, and as I did so I saw beyond him another span of precipitous cliffs rising high above the plateau.

Kloovos raised a lanky arm and pointed to the cliff top.

"The Numinous Ones await you," he said, and a chill ran down my spine.

21

THE PATH OF MEMORY

OGETHER KLOOVOS AND I walked to the foot of the soaring cliffs. The giant Davrohendur kneeled so that I might again climb into the sack that was slung over his back, and when I had done so, he rose and began to scale the nearly vertical rock face. At first I marveled that his large hands and feet could find purchase on the steep, smooth granite, but soon I noticed that a ladder of zigzagging hand- and footholds had been cleverly carved into the stone in such a manner that they were virtually invisible to anyone standing at the base of the cliffs.

At last we reached the summit and Kloovos pulled his great frame up onto the plateau. Again the giant kneeled, and I extracted myself from the carrying sack and took in our new surroundings. We stood on what amounted to a second tier of tableland that rose above the Bay of Mind, the first tier being the arcing tract of land upon which were built the longhouses of the Davrohendur and from which we had just ascended. Before us lay a courtyard, perhaps the size of a football field, across which curved a narrow stone path. In the exact center of the courtyard grew what appeared to be a remarkable tree. Its branches and leaves glistened like white crystal in the silvery rays of sunlight that pierced the gray clouds and shafted through the gentle mist hanging over the plateau. Beyond the tree lay a small forest tangled with vines and undergrowth growing all along the steep crag that soared into the clouds. As the billowing haze drifted across the pinnacle above, I could occasionally catch glimpses of what appeared to be the spires and minarets of a large stone structure emerge from behind the grayness.

"Aye," said the deep, gravelly voice of Kloovos when he saw where my gaze had settled. "The Temple of Flesh and Bone."

I pointed to the crystal tree in the middle of the courtyard. "And what's that?"

"That is the Star Tree, which looks forward and backward and in between."

"You don't say?" I grinned, but I don't think old Kloovos found the humor in my retort. Still, the sight unsettled me. My friend Tarzan had once told me of an extraordinary tree he had encountered long ago that bore an uncanny resemblance to this one—a tree that held mysterious powers over time and space.*

"Come," said Kloovos, and we stepped onto the stone path and began walking across the courtyard.

The path brought us nearer to the Star Tree and I stopped and gazed up at it. It rose nearly fifty feet into the air, with a multitude of branches covered in shimmering leaves that tinkled in the breeze like a vast wind chime made of glass. When I scrutinized the tree more closely, I thought I saw something moving beneath the surfaces of the sparkling trunk and branches, like small schools of fish swimming through a clear syrupy liquid. I also noticed an oval opening of crude stonework that lay at the foot of the tree, leading down into the earth beneath the great crystal bole. I made to walk over to the tree for a closer look, but Kloovos leaned down and gently placed a couple of giant fingers on my shoulder.

"That would be unwise, Victory Harben," he said. "Come." He motioned for me to continue down the path.

Just then, out of the corner of my eye, I thought I saw a tiny flash in an opening in the clouds to the west. I looked

---

* See the Edgar Rice Burroughs Universe novel *Tarzan and the Dark Heart of Time* by Philip José Farmer.

again at the patch of sky and this time there could be no mistaking it—I saw three more sparkling flashes against the lavender heavens.

"Did you see that?" I asked.

Kloovos made a noise deep in his throat. "It is the Zarafim attempting to enter our world. But do not fear. The will of the Numinous Ones is strong."

I suddenly felt cold all over. The winged warrior Lahvoh had said she was of the Zarafim. Were the Numinous Ones preventing her kind from transiting to Uvala just as the Volstari had used the power of their minds to stop Lahvoh from entering Kjarna's atmosphere when she had been attempting to track me down and kill me?

"Is there any chance they'll succeed?"

"Though they have tried for some time now," Kloovos said, "never has a Zarafim entered our world. But the heralds of the infernal Harods are devious."

We continued down the stone path.

"Is this the Path of Memory you told me about?" I asked, indicating the walkway down which we trod.

"No," Kloovos replied. "*That* is." He pointed ahead to a dark opening in the forest where the stone path ended. "Here I must leave you, but not before giving you a gift." He removed from a sheath strapped to his lower left leg a slim knife fashioned from a single piece of bone. "This was carved from my father's shinbone. The Path of Memory ascends to the Temple of Flesh and Bone, where you will find those whom you seek. But the path is not an easy one to tread. See that you are not ensnared in the tangled web of reminiscence or you will fall into the turbulent pools within your own mind, never again to emerge." He leaned his lanky frame forward and extended the bone knife on an open palm. "If your own reflections seek to strangle you, do not hesitate: cut them away before it is too late."

I took the knife and slid it beneath my belt. "Thank you," I said, and recalling the etiquette of the hunters of Pellucidar,

I added, "I am honored to carry the knife of the father of Kloovos."

The giant Davrohendur bowed somberly. Then he turned his back on me and with a slow, loping gait began making his way back down the stone path that led to the precipice overlooking the bay.

Before I could stop him, Hucklebuck jumped from my shoulder and scampered down the stone path. "Hey, buddy!" I cried after him, but already he had disappeared up the trail that led into the shadowy wood.

I suddenly felt very alone. Moreover, I didn't like the thought of Hucklebuck running off by his lonesome into the gloomy forest. Everything about this place gave me the creeps.

I stepped forward and stood before the dark opening in the trees. A few feet into the tangled foliage I could see nothing but pitch black. A shiver ran through my frame. Suddenly I realized the temperature had dropped several degrees, and I looked up to find the gray clouds had completely obscured the lavender sky. I pressed a button on my neckpiece to trigger the heating mechanism in my Kjarnan jumpsuit, but somehow even the resulting warmth that spread over my limbs and torso failed to assuage the relentless chill that cut through the air.

I felt foolish just standing there looking into the blackness, so there was nothing for it but to set my jaw and proceed forward into the dark and misshapen forest.

Where the stone pathway ended at the entrance to the gloomy wood, a dirt trail began. Roots of all sizes and shapes crossed the narrow footpath, my way ahead illuminated dimly by the lights on my suit's neckpiece as well as the faint violet radiance of its sequined stripes. While I was thankful for the light my suit shed on the path, it did nothing to quell the eerie ambiance of the sullen trail, but rather only intensified it.

The knotted, crisscrossing roots made for difficult walking as the path wound its way upward at an increasingly steep angle. Several times I tripped and stumbled, ending up on my hands and knees. This was an unusual experience for me, for I normally enjoy a good climb and I have never lost the nimble reflexes I developed as a youth in the wilds of Pellucidar. Never, that is, until now, when I found myself faltering and sprawling with disconcerting frequency. Soon I began to grow tired and frustrated. Perhaps if I just sat down for a moment and collected myself I could attack the trail with renewed vigor. I had just been through a trying experience, after all, having undergone *tuvrahovek* at the mercy of the mind spores that had fallen over me while crossing the Strait of Delirium. That must be it. I just needed to rest.

And so I sat down in the middle of the trail, my feet stretched before me, my arms leaning back to buttress me up. I would sit here for only a minute or two and then resume my way. But as I rested, a wave of weariness swept over me and I felt my eyes drooping. Maybe if I closed my eyes for half a minute I would regain my strength. Ah, yes! That felt blissful. Just a minute more. Maybe two . . .

. . . What am I doing back at Darkheath? Haven't I graduated? Have I decided to come back to Oxford and pursue my doctorate, after all? No, there is Edward Kennington sitting beside me, looking as handsome and dreamy as ever, and I am back in my first seminar with Professor Ralston. We have just been dismissed and I ask Edward if he would go with me to the winter ball. He laughs at me and tells me he doesn't go on dates with walking differential equations that don't know their place. I want to answer in kind but all the air seems to have been sucked out of the room. I could scream right then and there, but instead I bottle it up and in miserable silence walk back to Steadford House . . .

. . . I am in high school in Southern California. I am in trouble. Again. That afternoon I was tormented by a bully and ended

up breaking his nose. I don't regret a thing, but I tell the principal how so very sorry I am. Mrs. Hines comes to get me and brings me home to our Spanish American–style ranch house in Tarzana. I open the door to my room so I can throw myself down on my bed and sulk, and plan for the future. I have been talking with Mrs. Macrae, my math teacher, and she says she has been speaking with Lord and Lady Greystoke about the possibility of me testing out of high school and going to study in England "at an institution that is more appropriate for a young lady of your extraordinary aptitude." When I enter my room I see Chauncie, my beloved tuxedo cat who has loved me as no one else since I left the inner world, lying dead on the carpet. I pick him up and hold him. His body is still warm. I take him out into the backyard without telling anyone, find a shovel in the shed behind the house, and bury him deep in the ground . . .

. . . I am nine years old and I am in Abner Perry's laboratory. He has just turned around and knocked over an entire row of test tubes, the contents of which have spilled onto a beautifully embroidered antelope skin. The latter was a gift from Lorana the Fair to Abner in gratitude for a concoction he brewed in his lab that had saved the life of her elderly mother when a deadly flu recently swept through Sari. Abner has feelings for Lorana, but he's too flustered around her to do anything about it. He's also so oblivious he doesn't immediately realize he has utterly annihilated Lorana's cherished gift. When he finally does discover the ruined skin, he pins the blame on me and chews me out in a less-than-holy tirade. I can't keep from laughing and I take full responsibility for the calamity. Other than my parents and my godfather, I love Abner more than anyone in the world, inner or outer . . .

. . . "Eat your dinner, dear," my mother says, placing an earthenware bowl in front of me at supper time. We are in our family hut in Sari. My father is there as well, making affectionate eyes at my mom. The two are clearly, embarrassingly, in love. I look

down at my bowl and find that instead of holding thag stew, it's swirling with stars and nebulae and galaxies against the backdrop of the pitch-black void of space. I stick my index finger in the bowl and churn the contents, watching mesmerized as two galaxies merge. "Don't play with your spacetime, Victory," my mother chides. "That never ends well." . . .

Wait. That never happened. What's going on?

. . . I am a newborn in my mother's arms. I am lifted away from that comfort and warmth and protection by other hands. I am taken outside into the dark. The Dead World, the inner world's pendent moon, blocks out the eternal noonday sun of Pellucidar. I am carried far away by whoever holds me. We come to a great gathering of warriors where burning torches have been staked into the ground. I am lifted up on high like an offering to the gods of war while the warriors begin to chant in a frenzy of bloodlust and savage passion: "Death to the Mahars! Victory! Victory! Victory!" . . .

I am suffocating. I gasp for air but none comes. My neck is sore. Where am I? I feel something gripped in my hand. It is smooth and sleek. Why am I asleep? I should be climbing the Path of Memory. Memory . . . Wasn't I supposed to remember something? What is in my hand? Is that what I must recall?

And then I remembered! It was a knife that I gripped so tightly, made from the shinbone of Kloovos' father. What was it Kloovos had said? *"See that you are not ensnared in the tangled web of reminiscence or you will fall into the turbulent pools within your own mind, never again to emerge."*

I struggled to open my eyes but they seemed to be glued shut. I reached my free hand to my throat. I felt thick, ropy cords beneath my fingers, wrapping around my windpipe and suffocating me. No, not cords! Roots! The tangled, crisscrossing roots that lay across the Path of Memory were strangling the life from me! *"If you find yourself strangled by your own reflections,"* I heard Kloovos say in my mind, *"cut them away before it is too late."*

The knife! I brought the bone blade to my neck and pried it beneath the roots that were choking me as effectively as any garotte. I cut one root, then another and yet another. With each root that I severed, I found myself gaining more energy, until at last I was able to pry open my eyes. In utter horror, I looked upon a mass of roots, illuminated in the dim light cast by my Kjarnan suit, writhing of their own volition as they attempted to asphyxiate me. But what horrified me even more was the fact that some of the roots glistened like crystals. Were they the roots of the Star Tree? Was the tree trying to murder me? Or had its crystal roots merely been responsible for my trip down memory lane? Had touching them somehow transported me through time and space to different periods of my life, as Tarzan had once told me contact with the crystal tree he encountered in Africa had done to him?

Unless I freed myself, none of the questions mattered. And so with every ounce of strength and determination that remained to me, I cut and slashed, hacked and sawed. Finally, I could breathe again. I severed the last root, slipped the bone knife into my belt, and tore away the bundle of writhing creepers that covered my neck. Then I rose to my feet and ran up the steep incline as fast as my feet would carry me.

Ahead in the surrounding dark I saw an oval of light. It drove me on, spurring me wildly up the suffocating path that closed about me like the gorge of some dreadful leviathan that had swallowed me, until at last I was passing through a narrow archway of twisted vines and branches. I emerged from the foul forest onto a small walkway of white stone that snaked up a gentle rise amid the surrounding mists.

After I was about a dozen yards beyond the forest I stopped to catch my breath. The mists cleared as if in response to my arrival, and before me at the top of the incline stretched a wide plaza, behind which rose a massive temple complex composed of dark gray stone, its imposing towers soaring into the lavender heavens. The architecture evoked that of a Tibetan monastery or perhaps the mythical Shangri-La, with minarets and spires sprouting from an array of granite edifices of assorted shapes and sizes. Here at last must be the Temple of Flesh and Bone.

In the center of the plaza a lone figure wearing a dark hooded robe sat cross-legged, hands nested together in its lap as if meditating. I continued climbing the walkway until I stood before the figure on the plaza's edge. I smiled and raised a hand in greeting.

The figure drew back its hood, revealing the face of a man who appeared to be about thirty years old by earthly reckoning. His face was handsome though stern, with sharp features that evoked a sinister demeanor. Black, intricately braided hair framed his pale angular face, and dark eyes peered at me from beneath arched brows.

"She who flees the Path of Memory," he said, "does not truly enter the Temple of Flesh and Bone." His tone did not hide his scorn.

But I'd had enough. "Listen, mister," I said, "I didn't come all this way, across the angles of time and space, chased by a vindictive angel with a flaming sword, and through *that* in particular"—I pointed back at the tangled forest— "only to be turned away by mumbo jumbo I might find in a fortune cookie."

The man's face pruned. "You should thank me, girl, for turning you away, for you will find your soul leeched from your mortal shell before you can take one step into the realm of the—"

"Enough, Salokin!" The scolding voice rang out from the great archway leading into the temple, where stood an older woman, her long snow-white hair wisping from beneath the hood of her black robes. "She has proved herself to be worthy of entering the Temple of Flesh and Bone by treading the

Path of Memory and emerging whole of spirit. Moreover, she is under the protection of Altovos and the Numinous Ones themselves."

"One may emerge from the Path and still not be whole," retorted the man.

"Do not bicker with me, Salokin," the woman said firmly, "or I shall have you sweeping the floors of the entire temple like I did when you were an ill-tempered brat of a child. Do not think for a moment I merely jest. As for the girl, it is not your place to judge her spirit. Do not suppose yourself to be a lion, when you are but a mouse, adept." The old woman spoke the language of the Davrohendur, and while she did not really say "lion" or "mouse," that is how my translation aura sounded the words in my mind.

The man jumped up in anger and glared at me. Then he strode across the plaza, the fringes of his dark robes swishing over the tiles, and passed through a smaller doorway in the temple's granite face.

"Thank you," I called to the woman, who motioned me to join her beneath the crown of the imposing archway. When I had crossed the plaza and stood before her, I asked, "What did I do to upset him?"

"Absolutely nothing," the old woman said, "except step in the way of one who expected to be rewarded for his idleness. Now he must work, and he resents you for it."

"I don't understand," I said.

"Do not concern yourself with Salokin," said the woman. "You have more important things to worry about."

"Speaking of . . . did you happen to see a furry little guy about so big"—I cradled my hands to indicate the size of Hucklebuck in his small form—"come scampering out of the forest? He's in my care and I'm responsible for his safety."

The woman smiled. "He is with the adepts in the Amaranthine Court."

"Is he safe? He'll be okay? I was worried about him when he escaped from me and ran up the path."

"I think you will find he has a mind of his own," she said. "He is safe. But we have tarried long enough. The Numinous Ones await."

We passed inside the archway and I proceeded to follow the woman down a series of austere granite corridors, appointed at intervals with wall sconces bearing guttering candles. We turned often from passageways, at times climbing winding spiral staircases and at others descending them, or passing through shafts so narrow that our shoulders rubbed against the rough stone walls. Twice we passed rooms filled with robed figures. In one chamber the occupants sat cross-legged on the hard stone floor as if in meditation. In another, adepts worked at long wooden tables, dipping pens into ink bottles and hand-lettering scrolls in a fine calligraphic script. Finally we came to a star-shaped room in the center of which was yet another spiral staircase. This one, however, cork-screwed down and down and still farther down, deep beneath the temple, terminating in what appeared to be a small rectangular waiting room with stone benches along the walls. At the far end of the room stood an imposing wooden door, which the woman swung open on screeching iron hinges. She stood to one side and waved a hand for me to enter. I did as she bade and heard the door shriek closed behind me.

In darkness I climbed the steep stone ramp that rose before me and emerged from a round opening in the floor into a large circular chamber, perhaps thirty feet in diameter. A murky ceiling yawned somewhere high above, thin shafts of sunlight slanting down into the room from half a dozen tiny round holes in the umbral heights. I stood in the center of a pattern formed on the floor out of hundreds of tiny mosaic tiles: a disk surrounded by a thin ring bisected by eleven smaller, equidistantly spaced disks. The steeples of a large eleven-pointed star speared each of the smaller disks. Eclipsed by the large central disk was the opening from which I had just ascended.

There could be no doubt—I had seen the symbol before.

It was the same emblem I had seen carved into the face of the monolith I had uncovered on that nameless planet on which I had been deposited by Tu-al-sa's maelstrom, as well as that which I had seen on the floor of the Hall of the Thought Lords on Kjarna.

The points of the floor's star pattern extended to eleven niches set within the curving wall. The niches were empty and dark except for the one directly before me, in which sat cross-legged on the floor an old man in heavy robes of black and dark purple.

"My name is Victory Harben," I said. "I've come a long way to speak to you."

The man did not reply other than to raise his hands to either side, palms tilted upward. At first I thought he was merely welcoming me with the gesture, but then I began to notice faint illumination emanating from within the wall niches all around me. The light coming from the recesses was a dim orange-brown, and before my astonished eyes the faint luminance formed the vague outlines of robed humanoid figures, each sitting cross-legged on the bare floor like the old man. I turned around to examine the spectral forms and discovered they were absent from two of the niches, although in one of them I perceived what appeared to be the shadowy silhouettes of two large shadowy forms. When I stared at the murky shapes intently, I heard a rustling or flapping sound. Then a great winged form stepped forth from out of the niche, and behind it came a hulking apish figure.

"*Welcome, Victory Harben,*" echoed a familiar voice in my mind. "*Long is the way from Pellucidar.*"

I gasped. "Tu-al-sa . . ."

22
DESTINY

NDEED, YOUNG GILAK. " The matriarch of Mintra spread her great wings, and her Sagoth servant stepped forward and erupted with a threatening growl.

I took a step back and dropped low in a defensive stance.

"Do not mind Kotor," said the voice in my mind. *"He is not well disposed toward you. Is it any wonder, after your friend banished him to a most unpleasant angle of anguish and despair with your gilak apparatus?"*

"Jason Gridley," I said, relaxing my stance as I sensed there would be no immediate confrontation. "He fired my uncertainty gun at your friend, here?"

"Have not I indicated thus?"

As the wizened old Mahar communicated directly with my consciousness, I experienced an odd lagging effect as my mind "heard" each verb for the briefest of moments in the present tense, and then compensated by "hearing" the verb in either the past or future tense, as appropriate to the context. Similarly, terms of temporal reference or successive action, such as "when," "then," and "next"—as well as many other terms that are meaningless to the earless Mahars, such as "hear," "voice," and "speak"—were only approximations. The Mahars do not experience time as you or I, existing in some unfathomable sense in the eternal present. But the human mind simply cannot conceive of a state where there is no demarcation between past and future, and so it adjusts accordingly when, as Abner Perry has posited, the "speaker's"

227

thoughts are accessed in the fourth dimension—a process I believe involves the Mahars' instinctive biological ability to send and receive a sort of radio signal, perhaps akin to or even identical with the Gridley Wave. For untold eons, no meaningful communication had existed between the Mahars and the so-called lower orders such as the gilaks of Pellucidar. But when I met Tu-al-sa when I was only a child, she explained to me that the Mahars—at least those of her enclave—had learned how to communicate with the lower orders from a mysterious group of beings called the Numinous Ones. And now here I stood among the Numinous Ones in their temple.

"How did you get here?" I asked the queen. "Was it through a two-dimensional bridge like the one into which you swept me? It seemed to have imposed some kind of force on me, what the physicists of my world might call an entanglement effect. It sent me from world to world, across time as well as space. But it stopped when I got here, to the Omos planetary system."

"In essence, yes, Victory Harben. Though I traveled a much less circuitous route than you. Perhaps there is a reason for this. Yes, perhaps."

Before I could respond, a voice arose in the dark chamber and I turned to face the robed old man in his niche. Now I examined him more closely. His skin was dark, his face deeply wrinkled, his gray eyes large and kindly. If the circumstances had been different, I might have been well disposed toward him. But now, on this day of reckoning, I felt little more than resentment.

"Victory Harben, welcome," he said. "I am Altovos, the guardian of Uvala and the Gateway to Halos. Long have we watched you since the queen of Mintra brought you to our attention. It was never our intention to have you suffer so. But as Tu-al-sa hints, perhaps your roundabout journey, as painful as it may have been, may yet serve a valuable purpose."

I clenched my fists, my ire mounting. "You've been

watching me since I was a little girl, haven't you? Working me into your machinations, with little thought for anything but your own mysterious goals. And now my friend is dead, and maybe my godfather too."

"Jason Gridley lives," Altovos said. "He has returned to Pellucidar, safe and sound, while even now he works tirelessly to fathom out a means to make contact with you. With that we can help. As for your friend . . . you refer to the one whose spirit fled his body on Zandar?"

"His name was Janson," I said. "He wasn't just some anonymous casualty of your scheming." Then it struck me what he had said, and I added: "Wait. You know of Janson?"

The old man looked grieved. "His spirit has fallen into the wide and ever-searching net of the Harods."

"What in heaven's name is that supposed to mean?" I couldn't help from lashing out, frustrated at all the vague and mystical mumbo jumbo.

"Hell would be the more apt analogy," said Altovos. "The Harods have drawn his spirit into their soul cages within the angle where we imprisoned them many long ages ago. They know of you, and of your relation to your friend, and so they have marked his spirit for consumption. Anyone who resonates with your volatra—your life force—is a threat to them."

"Are you telling me he's *alive*?" I exclaimed. I was so startled by the man's pronouncement about Janson that I didn't even question why the Harods considered me a threat.

"Incarnation is necessary for preservation and storage purposes before the Harods assuage their hunger," Altovos replied. "The pattern of his material form has been restored from his volatra. Yes, he is alive, but for what duration I cannot say."

"Then you must tell me how to get to the Harods' angle—*now!*"

"*That, young gilak, is why we are here.*"

I whipped around to face the old Mahar matriarch.

"This all began with you, O Mighty Queen!" I cried in my anger. "Enough with the games and murky claptrap. My friend is going to die—*again*—and I intend to stop that from happening. Tell me everything, from the beginning, or I'll send you and your dear Kotor into a truly unpleasant angle." I fingered the butt of my uncertainty gun.

"Spirited you are, Victory Harben, as you were in your youth . . . if less mannerly and bereft of patience."

I raised a finger in warning, but Tu-al-sa continued.

"It began with the nemesis of David Innes—a gilak named Hooja who deceived me and stole me away, placing me within the great digging machine that first broke through from the outer world into Pellucidar. Unwillingly—and at first unknown to David Innes, who operated the digging machine—I was brought into a world that no Mahar had ever dreamed existed: the exterior of a great ball of rock and dirt careening through the measureless void. When the compassion of David Innes unexpectedly allowed for my return to Pellucidar, I was a changed being. I had looked up at the flaming stars and glimpsed infinity. Now, I plumbed the buried archives of my race, for I am truly ancient—born from the union of a female and a male of my kind, daughter of the last male ruler of the Mahars, before our race formulated the Great Secret of abiogenetic reproduction.

"Deep into the mind vaults I delved, searching, ever searching, for lost knowledge that would bring understanding of what lies in the infinite reaches beyond the hollow of our puny, confining world. But I did not search for the sake of knowledge alone; also I feared for the extinction of my race at the hands of the gilaks, for I had seen how those on the outer crust had wielded advanced science to develop terrifying industry—death-dealing machines and poisons and weaponry that inevitably would lead to the total extermination of the Mahars. And thus I searched, until at last I found in the archives at Thotra the writings of Ral-nu-ka the Transcendent."

"I have seen a tablet detailing Ral-nu-ka's researches," I said. "He spoke of experimentations with angular dimensionality, and of contact with one such dimension—what he called a 'hypergeometry.' But the tablet I read was damaged, and I could not read it all."

"*If the tablet had been whole,*" the queen of Mintra continued, "*you would have discovered that it was a warning to cease such experiments or risk inviting a disastrous incursion from the hypergeometry. Would that I had heeded it. But such is the folly that grows from desperation. Already had I seen the gilaks rise up under David Innes and annihilate the cities of our enclave in the region of Phutra. I could not afford to be defenseless when the gilaks of the outer crust waged war upon us, as I was certain they must. And so I reached out through the angles of existence until I became teteculent with fluilations from a higher angle of incidence.*

"*At first, nothing came of my attempts and I despaired. Then, a voice reached out through the ether, emanating from a realm beyond our own. A reassuring voice it was, one that whispered of a great alliance, one that could help us rid Pellucidar and the outer crust alike of the gilak threat once and for all. The entities from the other angle, who called themselves the Harods, desired only one small thing in return: access to our own angle. In exchange, the gilak menace would be eliminated.*"

I shivered in the damp grotto. "I've got a bad feeling I know where this little fairy tale is going. You let them in and they turned against you, didn't they?"

"*We believed the danger to be minimal. The Harods, it seemed, could not enter our angle of existence in physical form. They were trapped in their own hypergeometry. And yet . . . they had the power to influence our world.*"

"Influence it?" I asked. "In what way?"

"*They could siphon the life force from our angle and draw it into their own. And in such a manner, they told us, they would deal with the gilaks. But to do so they needed a conduit through the angles to our world. And so we granted it. There were other benefits . . . other wonders they showed us, in what we believed to be a gesture of good faith, that convinced us their offer was genuine. However, as soon as we 'let them in,' as you say, Victory Harben, they began to initiate their plan. Not only did they seek to enter our realm to feed on the life force of the gilaks . . . they wanted access so they might feed on* all *life within our angle."*

"So you traded our entire *universe* on an empty promise? I hope those 'other benefits' were worth it!" I was beside myself with rage. My godfather had been right: the Mahars were not to be trusted. Ever. No matter how much empathy I might feel for them. All the same, their Faustian bargain had been motivated by fear of extinction at the hands of the gilaks of the outer crust, and now here we were, making common cause against a common enemy. As it turns out, humans and pterosaurs make strange bedfellows. "Go on," I said. "I just can't *wait* for you to get to the part where I fit into this mess."

"In desperation, I reached out through the angles once again, seeking aid against the threat to my race—"

"Because that worked out so well for you the last time," I interjected.

"—and another voice answered us. It seemed the Harods had an arch foe—the beings who had imprisoned them in their shallow angle. These entities came from an angle above our own and called themselves the Numinous Ones, and from their world of Uvala, located far, far from Pellucidar and the ball of earth and stone that surrounded it, they had long tried to check the power of the Harods. For millennia the Numinous Ones had attempted to deflect life forces from being siphoned to the Harods' feeding ground—a ball of rock named Halos, which was located at an angle occupying the same space as the world you call Earth."

"I thought you said the Harods were imprisoned in a shallow angle," I said. "How could they siphon souls—I think that's what you're telling me—from other angles if they were trapped?"

"Although isolated within the bounds of their prison, still

they had the ability to influence angles beyond their own. Long had they drawn the volatras of the deceased from the surface of your Earth, but their powers were limited. Such is why they seek to consume more volatras. The more they devour, the more powerful they become, and with enough power they will be able to free themselves from their captivity. They desired access to our angle, so they claimed, so they might more easily access the angle of the gilaks from the outer crust via the great opening in the north and thereby consume them. More, always more, for their ravenous hunger.

"But the Numinous Ones thwarted the Harods, deflecting the volatras they pulled from those who died upon the surface of your Earth, the angle nearest their own. So it was that—"

"Wait!" I raised a hand for Tu-al-sa to stop. "You're telling me that for ages the Harods consumed *all* the humans who died on Earth?"

"Not all of them, young gilak. A soul here or a soul there where they were able. Their powers were limited. But when we gave them access to our angle, that began to change. Slowly, at first, it is true, so that initially we did not detect their deception. But now their plan comes to fruition, and all life in Pellucidar, even the Mahars, will soon fall victim to the mighty Harods."

A feeling of dread crept over me, but I could not keep from asking the ominous question that had formed in my mind. "What happens to the volatras that you deflect? Or those that the Harods otherwise fail to seize?"

Altovos spoke and I turned again to face him. "No one knows where they go," he said. "Or at least, we do not, though occasionally a volatra we deflect from the Harods' grasp reincarnates on another world."

"Tangor," I said. "My friend Tangor died on the surface of his Earth—one parallel to my own—and woke up on Poloda."

"The Harods attempt to draw volatras from both Earths," Altovos continued, "as each is at an angle of incidence adjoining that in which Halos resides. Doubtless the volatra of your friend Tangor was intercepted by the Harods, and then deflected by us. Our means of deflection is not precise. Nor is our understanding of the soul, as you might call it, and its ultimate destination. We are not gods. We have no answers regarding the religions of your world or any other."

"You say Halos is the Harods' feeding ground," I said, trying to understand. "Halos, then, is not the same place as where the Harods themselves have been imprisoned, not at the same angle?"

"In the fires of Halos do the Harods prepare the souls they capture," Altovos said. "There the imprisoned souls are reincarnated, so their energy can be refined and cultivated to the proper level of radiance for consumption. The caste of the dullest radiance among those souls reawakened on Halos are the Maxteles. These are said to make up three-quarters of the population of Halos and consist of the most brutish and morally depraved souls. The next most luminous radiance is that of the Psamaftogenes, who are said to make up fifteen percent of the population of Halos, who again are morally depraved, though their depravity aligns with their own system of narcissistic principles. Glowing more intensely than the Psamaftogenes are the Xarocens, who are said to make up five percent of the population and would seem to be on a higher ethical level than the Maxteles and the Psamaftogenes. Radiating even more brightly are the lofty Corophines, who are said to make up only three percent of the population and are beings of almost pure goodness. The inhabitants of Halos are told that if they perfect their moral essences, they will become more luminous and advance to the next more radiant caste."

"And the remaining two percent?" I asked.

"Those on Halos are told that the remaining two percent are the holy Harods," said Altovos. "But no one on Halos has ever seen a Harod, who are rumored to be beings who have advanced to a state of total goodness and absolute virtue. Halos, however, is but the cauldron of the Harods, from which they pluck the most tender and nutritious morsels—those souls who advance to the highest, most radiant caste. That is, those whose volatras have been refined to a higher state of energy, so that when the Harods consume them, they gain the most effective increase in power."

I felt sick. The Harods were farming souls and devouring them. They were no better than the flesh-hungry Mahars. No, they were worse. The Mahars had long believed the gilaks of Pellucidar to be but mindless cattle. But the Harods knew full well that they were consuming intelligent, sentient souls. Moreover, they were doing it solely to satiate their own bottomless hunger for power. And Janson Gridley was to be the next morsel on their plate.

"How did this all come to be?" I asked. "The Harods, Halos, the Numinous Ones . . . Surely there must be more to the story. Altovos, you said your name was. How did you become involved with the Harods?"

Again, the old man looked grieved. "We and the Harods were once the same. After a great disaster, caused by our own hubris, devastated our planet, we struck out into the stars to build a new home far away, where we could inflict no further damage upon our world and its neighbors. Here, in what is now the distant Omos system, we began our new project, opening up a conduit through the angles of time and space so that we might ferry ourselves back and forth between our homeworld and our new undertaking. At last, after great effort, we succeeded in creating a new system of eleven worlds." Altovos waved his hand to encompass the chamber's eleven niches. "But there were those of us who were not content with our achievement and wanted more. Unsatisfied with our little project in an isolated region of our own angle, they desired to explore and dominate the adjoining angles of incidence. A schism arose and our two factions waged a terrible war across the eleven worlds that orbited the star Omos. The toll was great, but eventually we triumphed over the revolutionaries, who called themselves the Harods, a term meaning the Righteous Ones. But righteous they were not, for they caused the deaths of many, both among our kind and upon the life forms that grew from our will upon the eleven worlds."

As Altovos spoke an idea was forming in my head, a staggering epiphany. "A disaster," I said. "Your people left your homeworld because of a self-created disaster?"

"That is correct," said Altovos.

"You're *Kjarnans*," I said with awe, and I knew with utter conviction the truth of my statement. "The Numinous Ones are Kjarnans . . . as are the Harods. The calamity on your planet was the Primal Failure of which the Volstari told me. And the civil war that broke out in the Omos system was the Great Failure. You are Thought Lords!"

I stood there stunned by the revelation. It had not been a coincidence that I had been drawn to Kjarna. I had brought myself there by the arcane laws of entanglement, somehow knowing it would weave into my future.

"At one time, yes," said Altovos, "we were members of that ancient race known as the Volstari. But that was a long time ago and we and the Volstari have grown apart. Now we are the Numinous Ones, the guardians of the gateway to Halos. Eleven Volstari remained here after the war, each assigned to look after the inhabitants of one of the eleven worlds and protect it against intrusions and further meddling by the Harods."

I looked around at the wall niches, and then at the star pattern on the floor. Now it all made sense: I had seen the same symbol embellishing the floor of the Hall of the Thought Lords of Kjarna, a representation the Volstari had told me memorialized their Great Experiment, which I now knew to be the creation of the Omos planetary system.

"The beings I see shimmering in the niches," I said. "They, and you, are the ones of which you speak—the protectors of the eleven worlds?"

Altovos nodded solemnly.

"But what about the two empty niches?" I asked. "That one there, and the one occupied by Tu-al-sa and her friend Kotor." I indicated a vacant niche that was on the opposite side of the chamber from Altovos, and then pointed to the alcove directly to his left in which stood the Mahar queen and her Sagoth servant.

"As I have said, we are not gods," replied Altovos. "Even we die. Poloda and Zandar have been left without caretakers, which is not to say they are not under observation." The dark, wizened eyes of Altovos regarded me intently. "I see you are beginning to understand the value of your round-about journey."

Indeed I was, if only in part. If it was true that I had drawn myself to the worlds I had visited, then perhaps I had done so to prepare myself for what I was to face in the future. It was like taking a walk when you're trying to solve a particularly thorny problem: sometimes the only way to work out the solution is to let go of your conscious mind.

"With a seed of the Star Tree as the focus of our great minds," Altovos went on, "did we eleven imprison the Harods, sealing them in a narrow angle located beyond that in which resided Halos, the world they had created for their maleficent purposes and used as a base of operations during the war. But the Harod are devious, and so they left a back-door open to Halos of which we had no foreknowledge. And thus it was that after their imprisonment, they were able to use their hidden conduit to Halos to continue their devious plan of harvesting volatras, using the energy they cultivated from the souls they seized to increase their power, biding their time for the day they knew would come—a time when they would become powerful enough to break out of the walls of their prison and spread their malevolent will across the angles. Already have they gained enough power to send their advance agents through the angles—the Zarafim, they are named, who are culled from the ranks of unsuspecting Corophines who believe they are ascending to become righteous Harods. But really the Harods twist these poor Corophines' minds and spirits, binding them to new bodies formed from the Harods' own demented thoughts and conditioning them through cruel, unspeakable means to obey their masters' will with utter loyalty. You have encountered one of them: the being called Lahvoh. The passage of these entities through the void has not been without consequence, as their very presence has caused a destabilization within the angles in proximity to their travels; beings from one world have been swept up in their wakes and transported willy-nilly to another, such as happened to your Va-gas friend Ren-ah-ree when she was caught in the wake of the Zarafim Lahvoh. And so already are the Harods' agents at large doing the bidding of their insatiable masters and causing mayhem throughout the angles. But soon the Harods themselves will break free and then all will be lost. We are not strong enough to resist them."

Something Altovos had just said stuck a chord with me. "A seed of the Star Tree, you said? The tree in the courtyard below?"

"Yes," said Altovos. "A seed gathered from the flowering leaves of the Star Tree, a gemstone of special power that we could use as a focus for our minds and will. With such a seed can one bend the will of another's mind or even alter the fabric of the angles themselves. But the seed was destroyed, burned out during the process of forcing the Harods into the prison of their narrow angle. Alas, if it had not been destroyed, we might have wielded it against them again and sealed them off from the angles for all eternity."

"Can't you simply grow another seed from the Star Tree?" I asked.

"Nay," said Altovos, "the Star Tree will not blossom again for several more millennia. Even now the Harods grow in strength such that at any moment they are on the verge of escaping the bondage of their prison."

My mind was racing. When I was a child, I had heard a

tale from my friend Tarzan that was eerily reminiscent of the Star Tree I had seen in the courtyard on the terrace below the temple—a crystal tree in the possession of the Ataka, an ancient African civilization that was said to have had its origins among the stars. The tree was allegedly a conduit that cut across the boundaries of time and space. Tarzan told me that he himself could vouch for that. Moreover, Tarzan and his friend Stanley Wood, who had been staying at the Greystokes' estate in Yorkshire just prior to my return to Pellucidar aboard the O-220, had told me of two gemstones of mysterious power—enormous jewels that could be wielded to control the will of another's mind. Could Tarzan's crystal tree and the supernatural gemstones be related to what Altovos was telling me?

"Now the gateway to Halos grows weak," Altovos went on. "For millennia we have guarded it. Long ago it resided here in our grotto. Now, as our system has drifted through the cosmos, so too has drifted the gate. Now it lies miles above the surface of our planet, in the upper atmosphere. When the Harods become strong enough, the gate will fall."

"How far up is this gateway?" I asked.

"It lies twenty miles above Uvala, and when the mists clear it may even be seen through the looking glass mounted atop the temple's highest spire."

I was trying to process all the information I was being given and put it all into some kind of practical framework, but there were still a number of missing pieces to the puzzle.

"I still have more questions," I said. "A *lot* of them. Why, for instance, did the Gridley Wave fail? I refer to the signal that my godfather discovered and that could be used to communicate with distant worlds . . . worlds I now realize exist at other angles of reality from the outer crust of the Earth where I spent much of my upbringing. And why did Pellucidar's sun go dark when my godfather and I attempted to reinitiate the Gridley Wave using the ancient Mahar knowledge we had uncovered in the archives at Mintra?"

The Mahar queen's great wings rustled in her alcove and a voice sounded in my mind.

"The wave of which you speak, young gilak, is not native to the outer crust of the world you call Earth. It originates from the angle in which Pellucidar resides. As the seed of the Star Tree may be a focal point for the will of the mind, so too may a life force be a focus, a nexus that joins two angles together. So it was that when Jason Gridley first accessed the wave in the angle where your Earth resides, such a life force was in his presence. That life force, that nexus, existing in some sense in both angles, was the catalyst that allowed the wave to enter your angle. When that life force departed your angle, the wave no longer had its catalyst and was no more. But so substantially was the life force tied to the essence of the wave that the wave itself ceased to exist in both angles, even the one to which it was native, where the laws of physics are different from those of your Earth's outer crust."

For a moment I stood there in stunned silence as the implication of what Tu-al-sa was telling me sank in. "You're talking about Mr. Burroughs," I said at last. "He died in March 1950, on the same day the Gridley Wave failed, along with my uncertainty apparatus, which utilized the same quantum mechanical tunneling principle as a Gridley Wave signal. You're saying Mr. Burroughs was the catalyst, that somehow he was a nexus between the Earth's universe and the universe of Pellucidar, Barsoom, and the alternate Earth that I call Jasoom? That when he died, when his connection between the two angles was severed, the principle of the Gridley Wave simply ceased to exist?"

"He was not the first such catalyst. And thus the archives of my ancient race held the knowledge of how to reinitiate the wave, reestablishing the connection between the two angles."

Again my mind raced. "And so when Jason Gridley and I adjusted our Gridley Wave apparatus to the frequency in your people's ancient records, we were creating a new nexus between the two angles."

"You began the process. I finished it, using the solar rays of the inner world's sun."

"You reset the connection," I said. "Now Pellucidar's sun is the nexus."

"Your mind is indeed sharp, young gilak."

I turned to face Altovos. "But why am I here?" I raised my right arm, pulled down the sleeve of my Kjarnan jumpsuit, and pointed to the tattoo on my exposed skin. "Who told the Krataklak elders to give me this—the message that led me to you?"

The old man smiled. "That is a mystery I am afraid I cannot answer."

I shuddered in the damp air of the grotto of the Numinous Ones. "I think I can," I said, "if what I believe I'm hearing you say is correct. But we'll deal with that later. My friend's life is hanging in the balance, so let's cut to the chase. Answer my question: Why am I here?"

"Did not the Zarafim tell you, young gilak? You are a weapon that we have created to wield against the Harods. When I showed you the ancient records at Mintra, it was to stimulate your keen mind and motivate you to travel to the outer crust, where you would be steeped in its terrible science—a science that we could turn against our enemies. No, you are not just a weapon. We have honed you into a superweapon."

Blood was pounding in my ears, and I could not quell the rage that was growing in my breast. Had I been nothing but a pawn my entire life, cultivated by Tu-al-sa and the Numinous Ones to achieve their own self-interested purpose, as noble as that may have been? But there was no time for me to indulge the egoism of self-pity. I had to get to Janson before it was too late.

"Okay, you want to use me as a superweapon?" I said, the cogs in my mind already spinning away and going into overdrive. "Then hear me out. Here's what I'm going to need you to do . . ."

23
THE STAR TREE

I STOOD ALONE in the courtyard of the Star Tree, gazing down into the oval hole that led deep into the earth beneath the great translucent bole and its crystal roots. Crude stonework surrounded the opening, like that which might frame the entrance to an old root cellar. Above the hole, dark, indistinguishable forms swam in the thick syrupy liquid within the tree's bole and beat with the rhythm of a vast heart. I could feel the low thrumming resonate with my own heartbeat in the cavity of my chest: *thump, thump, thump . . .*

I took a deep breath, steeled my nerves, and then proceeded to descend the stone steps leading down beneath the tree. Damp, spongy air filled my nostrils, smelling of soil and minerals and decay. Glittering in the soft sunlight that filtered down into the cavern before me grew a tangled network of crystalline roots. A cavity in the earth, a foot or so deeper than my own height, lay directly beneath the center of the great bole that grew above, just as Altovos had described to me.

I walked to the edge of the circular pit, resisting the urge to reach out and touch one of the crystal roots. Altovos had warned against it, saying I would risk becoming lost in the maze of my own memories, just as I had when I had climbed the Path of Memory to the Temple of Flesh and Bone—the same path that had been but a steep, harmless downhill walk just minutes ago when I had left the temple courtyard and descended to the terrace on which the Star Tree grew.

For a moment I thought about my climb up the path. Altovos had told me that the roots of the crystal tree could show those who touched them glimpses of the past, the future, and places far away. Why, I wondered now, had I seen only my past and not my future? Was it because I had no future, that I would not survive the trials that lay in the days ahead—that my plan was doomed to failure?

Then I thought of Janson. I could not abandon him. And what of the rest of those who would suffer or whose life force would be extinguished at the hands of the Harods should they succeed in freeing themselves and run amok through the angles? What of my mother and my father, my godfather and Abner? What, for that matter, of all the souls who inhabited the angles in which lay Earth and its alternate twin, and the worlds of Pellucidar, Barsoom, and others? What of my friends Tarzan of the Apes and his amazing wife, Jane Porter; the incomparable Dejah Thoris and her heroic prince, John Carter; Tangor and our mysterious new friend, Hucklebuck; See-ta, the fearless warrior who had helped me survive in savage Caspak; the quadrupedal Ren-ah-ree of the hollow world of Va-nah and her dear boy, Da-va-ro; Maksata Tul of Kjarna, his wife, Maksata Sol, and their precious daughter, gifted little Dory; my old physics mentor, Professor Ralston; my former guardians, Heinrich and Anna Hines; and even my oblivious and silly yet sweet-hearted and loyal former roommate at Darkheath, Poppy Pickerall? They would all perish in the soul cages of the maleficent Harods unless I did something.

Without further consideration, I got down on my hands and knees, lowered myself over the edge of the pit, and dropped to the dirt floor some seven or eight feet below. Above me I could see the base of the crystal tree's wide bole, a knotted mass of glittering roots—some a foot or more in thickness, others tiny threadlike strands—reaching down all around me before they drove downward and burrowed deep into the brownish yellow soil of the cavern floor. The underside of the bole was beating—*thrum, thrum, thrum*—and I could see something dark pulsing beneath its translucent surface in the cavern's dim light.

Then it happened, as Altovos had said it would. The roots bunched up and moved inward with startling swiftness, closing in upon me until I was fully surrounded. Fear of suffocation seized me, but what happened next made me forget that fear as quickly as it had come. I felt myself being lifted up and experienced the sensation of my entire body sliding into warm, thick liquid. The gooey substance pulsed with the thrumming of the tree's vast heart, and my whole form pulsed with it. *Up, down. Up, down. Up, down.* It felt as if I were moving upward into the bole of the tree in slow increments. *Thrum, thrum, thrum.* Was I even breathing? I did not know, nor did I care. It was as if I were no longer human, but rather an organ of the tree, part and parcel of it, my whole being existing merely to assist the tree in the functions that permitted it to live. To help the tree was the greatest gift I could give.

Dimly, somewhere back in the far reaches of my consciousness, I realized I was losing myself in the transcendental experience of becoming one with the Star Tree, just as Altovos had warned. With an act of pure willpower, I forced myself to think of my goal: Yorkshire, England, on the day after I had left for Pellucidar with my godfather aboard the O-220 in the spring of 1950. I summoned my memory of the smells of the old manor house. Smell, one of the strongest keys to memory, Altovos had said. The sharp aroma of shellacked wood. The sweet soapy smell of Lord Greystoke's shaving cream drifting out of the washroom across the hall from the master bedroom. The unmistakable hint of lavender beneath the scent of Lady Jane's perfume. The smell of fresh sheets on newly made beds.

I heard the snapping of a steel wire and felt a blast of utter cold sweep over me. And then there I was, standing stark naked in the bedroom of Lord and Lady Greystoke. Tarzan stood directly before me, his back turned as he reached into a great, intricately carved wardrobe.

"Tarzan! Oh my—" I stammered.

The Lord of the Jungle did not need to turn to identify me. If my voice didn't cue him in to the person who stood behind him, I am sure my scent or any number of subtle hints detectable to his extraordinarily keen senses did.

"Victory—!" he exclaimed.

"No-no! Don't turn around. Please!"

Tarzan stopped in midturn at my command. "Victory, what on earth—"

I laughed, giddy at having achieved my target with no mishaps. My mind was still spinning from my strange experience with the Star Tree. For a moment I became discombobulated, thinking I was on yet another spin of the spacetime roulette wheel, hurtling through the void from world to world. Before I knew it, I was babbling rather incoherently about my cosmic and temporal travels, until Tarzan sternly ordered me to stop. Then he began to turn around despite my previous protestations.

"No!" I exclaimed. "Please, hand me a shirt. I'm, uh, stark naked."

Tarzan removed a neatly pressed dress shirt from his wardrobe and extended it to me without looking. I swept it out of his hand and wrestled it on.

"Now?" he asked.

"Okay," I said, standing there rather awkwardly in the oversized shirt.

"Now what's going on here?" Tarzan demanded. "You just left with Jason yesterday to return to Pellucidar. Where is he? Why have you returned—and how? And where are your clothes?"

For a moment I again felt confused. Had it truly been only yesterday since I left? Had I ever left? Had it all been a dream? Then I recalled Altovos and his stern warning about the side effects of transit via the Star Tree. That I might become befuddled . . . that I must concentrate . . . that I had only so much time at my destination before . . .

I willed myself back to the present moment. Now Tarzan was chiding me like an unruly child. "Victory Harben, I insist—"

"Tarzan, there's no time for that. Listen!"

He looked at me and seemed to judge the situation with his acute senses and jungle intuition. "I'm listening," he said.

I breathed a sigh of relief. "I need the emerald of the Zuli!" I cried. "And the Gonfal would help, too. You said their power is increased when both gems are used together."

Tarzan gave me a stony look.

"You're going to have to trust me on this," I said. "It's a matter of life and death. Many lives and many deaths. And worse."

The ape-man continued to regard me, long and hard. "The emerald is locked in a vault within the library," he said at last, "along with the Gonfal."

"Good," I said. "I can explain as well as I'm able while we go downstairs and get them . . ."

It was about a quarter of an hour later that I stood alone in my old room at the Greystokes' estate, reciting the mnemonic trigger that Altovos had drilled into me in a small meditation chamber deep within the Temple of Flesh and Bone. Within moments the old manor blurred in my vision and I was again surrounded by the viscous, translucent fluid within the heart of the Star Tree, thrumming, ever thrumming.

And now, I thought to myself, there was just one more task I had yet to complete before I could return to Uvala, given that Altovos had warned that I must do nothing that might alter the past as I knew it without inflicting dire consequences. I concentrated on a time eight years ago and called up from my memories the sights, the sounds, the smells of the island of Krakla in Pellucidar. It was there that I would need to deliver a very important message to the Krataklak elders of my father's tribe . . .

24
GATEWAY

WHEN I EMERGED from the Star Tree into the cavern beneath it, I knew instantly that something was wrong. I could hear shouts from above, punctuated by a throaty cry and the dull thud of something large and heavy hitting the earth. First, I took a brief moment to open a compartment in my utility belt and make sure the gemstones had made the transition with me. Then, satisfied they were in my possession and safely secured, I crawled out of the pit and crept slowly up the steps that ascended from the cavern. Crouching, I peeked my head above the level of the ground.

The body of a giant Davrohendur lay sprawled facedown on the violet sward, indigo blood spilling onto the grass from his open and unmoving mouth, his eyes glazed with death. Half a dozen yards beyond the giant's corpse, two unlikely antagonists were locked in a furious battle of life and death: one was my towering friend, Kloovos—the other a seven-foot-tall, alabaster-skinned male Zarafim, a member of the same race as my relentless pursuer, Lahvoh. The Zarafim, his iridescent armor gleaming in the light of Omos, alternated between floating up on his great wings to swing his flaming sword at his opponent's head and torso, and landing on the ground to thrust his blade at the giant's legs. He might have been an angry wasp darting hither and thither before the giant's attacks, looking for a patch of bare flesh in which to insert its stinger.

Kloovos, for his part, had apparently uprooted a small tree from the nearby forest that ascended to the temple and was wielding it as a mighty fighting staff. The length of the trunk gave him the advantage of reach, and a great whoosh of air accompanied each swing of his improvised weapon. But no matter how close the giant's staff got to his winged foe, a blow never landed, for the Zarafim simply swooped out of the way, whether to pull back on a current of air, soar up into the sky, or plunge back down to the ground. Never did the terrifying angel seem to tire, while a slick film of sweat had begun to glisten on the giant's bare back and shoulders and his great lungs huffed like a bellows.

It was clear the Zarafim could evade Kloovos' swings indefinitely, until at last the winged warrior would simply wear down the giant Davrohendur and slay him with a lunge of his flaming blade. I could not allow that to happen.

With a taunting cry of "Hey, little birdy!" I leaped from the cavern where I been crouching and up onto the violet sward.

The Zarafim, who had been flying up to strike at the Davrohendur's midsection, jerked his head in my direction. The distraction did what I had intended. A terrific *crack!* resounded across the courtyard as Kloovos' tree trunk collided with the Zarafim's pale cheek and knocked his black, golden-plumed helmet from his head. The winged warrior fell out of the air and crumpled to the ground like a swatted fly, his flaming sword crackling in the grass. But my giant friend didn't just stand there counting his blessings. Instead, he gripped the trunk in both hands and with all his prodigious strength swung it down repeatedly on the prone body of the Zarafim. I winced, for when the giant was done with the bruised, broken, and bloody pulp that lay before him, I knew his opponent would never rise again.

Kloovos turned from his gruesome task and regarded me, his elongated face made even longer with concern, and then turned his dark eyes to the heavens. I followed his gaze and gasped at what I saw, for the sky above the Temple of Flesh and Bone was thick with tiny winged figures.

"I told you, Victory Harben," the giant said, his grim voice deep and booming. "The Zarafim are devious. The Numinous Ones prevented them from entering our world directly, so they have gone to Zandar and Sanada and flown through the air channel to Uvala. Now all is lost."

"Perhaps, my friend." I strode over to the flaming sword and picked it up from where it lay burning in the grass. After a quick examination of the hilt, I found a small button located near the base of the grip and pressed it. Instantly, the flames were extinguished. With an experimental tap of my finger, I discovered the blade was now cool to the touch. "But let's not give up just yet," I continued, slipping the long, heavy blade beneath my belt, where it dangled at my side, dragging against the ground. "Can you get me to the plateau below this one? Tangor should have his ship ready by now. I obtained what I needed from the tree. If we can evade the Zarafim long enough to fire up the *Starduster* and get to the—"

But I did not have time to finish my thought, for already the giant Davrohendur was leaning over and lifting me up in his enormous hands. Gone was the carrying sack in which he had transported me during my first ascent of the cliff face, so I was forced to wrap my arms around the giant's neck like a small child clinging to its mother. My friend began walking, his long strides carrying us swiftly across the courtyard to the precipice overlooking the sea and the plateau below. He swung over the side with such rapidity and force-fulness that my head reeled with vertigo, the tableland and the ocean spinning wildly below us. Then he was climbing down, his ponderous hands and feet seeking purchase in the hollows of the ladder carved out of the cliff face.

We were about halfway down the towering bluffs when a shadow fell over us. Red-orange flames swept over my head, crackling in the sea breeze. I looked up to see a Zarafim, fiery sword in hand, floating in the air about half a dozen yards above us, her great black wings spread to catch the wind.

"Keep climbing down!" I cried to Kloovos, even as I pulled myself up and wormed my legs around him to straddle his great neck, so that I sat, albeit somewhat precariously, across his broad shoulders. "I'll handle the Zarafim!" My last statement was uttered with more conviction than I felt, but we had little choice. Kloovos could not fight off the flying terror that assailed us and descend the rock face at the same time.

I slid the purloined sword of gleaming silver from beneath my belt, searching with my thumb for the tiny button on the grip. I found and pressed it just in time, flames leaping down the length of the blade as the Zarafim dived at me and swung her own fiery weapon. The two blades clashed, nearly knocking me from my purchase on the giant's shoulders, and almost causing the sword to fly from my hands and plunge to the tableland far below. But somehow I managed to hold on to both the giant and my blade. I recovered from the blow just in time to parry the burning blade of my opponent as the Zarafim swung it from above, resisting the force of my opponent's weapon only because my sword's point momentarily lodged itself against the cliff face.

I didn't know what purpose the fire running down my sword's blade served, but I did notice the weapon became lighter in my hand and easier to wield as soon as I had activated the flames. I suspected the sword was a piece of advanced technology, perhaps the Zarafim equivalent of my uncertainty gun. Maybe the swords of the pseudo-angels also contained zuvan repositories, storing auras that facilitated the Zarafim when they transited through the angles. If only I knew how to—

The titanic winged warrior was lunging at me again. This time Kloovos saved me, hugging the cliff face as he swung away from the trajectory of the Zarafim's blade. The air beside my left ear crackled as the sword edge swooped past my head.

"Hey, lady!" I cried out in anger. "Watch it!"

The Zarafim, floating for a moment of respite upon the breeze above, grinned at my displeasure. Then she swooped down at me again and our blades clashed once more. This time, after our engagement, she dropped down below Kloovos, her great wings flapping furiously to keep her suspended in the air as she waited, a malevolent smile upon her lips. Clearly she meant to slice at the giant's legs when he descended to her level.

I shouted at Kloovos to stop, and he obeyed. Then, waving my flaming sword above my head to get the Zarafim's attention, I yelled down at the colossal angel in a jeering tone: "I've got your dead comrade's sword! I hear it can do all sorts of interesting things. Too bad you're too cowardly to fly up here and get it!"

My taunting worked as I had figured it would. Didn't my missionary grandfather's sermons say that fallen angels are always blindly vain and impetuous?

Now came my gamble. As the Zarafim thrust back her mighty ebon wings, propelling herself upward, I lifted my sword above my head and held it parallel to the tableland far below—the same gesture I had seen Lahvoh make with her sword just prior to leeching the life force from her victims.

Upon seeing me perform the ritual motion, the Zarafim's dark eyes grew wide and she stopped her upward flight, pausing in midair.

"Kloovos!" I shouted. The giant heard my appeal, for while he held on to a crevice in the vertical crag with one enormous hand, he swung out his other and grabbed the stultified Zarafim straight out of the air. Then I watched frozen in horror as the Zarafim opened her mouth wide, her head leaning back, as if obeying a will that was not her own. A thin alabaster mist began to rise from between her open lips, snaking up toward the tip of my flaming blade. Within moments, she sagged forward and collapsed in Kloovos' hand as the very life was being drawn from her frame.

But I couldn't go any further. I pressed the button on the hilt of my blade, extinguishing the flames that ran down its length. Simultaneously, the whitish mist stopped flowing into the tip of my sword, and I watched, mesmerized, as the soul stuff siphoned back into the Zarafim's gaping mouth.

I was not a monster like Lahvoh. No matter how hated was my enemy, I could not sentence her soul to be ripped from her living shell and consumed by the dreadful Harods.

The Zarafim's dark eyes opened drowsily, as if she were trying to wake up from a deep sleep. Kloovos did not hesitate. He thrust his captive hard against the unyielding rock face. She cried out in pain upon impact. Then the giant dropped her, grimacing as he watched her plummet toward her death at the foot of the bluffs, her wings lax and useless.

But the Zarafim never reached the base of the cliffs. Just before she hit the ground, she held her still-flaming sword vertically above her head and gyrated it in what was clearly another practiced motion. There was an earsplitting thunderclap. Then she was gone.

Interesting, I thought, but I had no time to consider the Zarafim's sudden disappearance. Kloovos increased the rate of his descent to a reckless degree, and before I knew it he was stepping onto the plateau and carrying me with great strides across the violet sward.

Ahead I saw Tangor, climbing up the ladder to his cockpit in the *Starduster*, the plane's propellers already whirring away like angry hornets. Already we had crossed a third of the distance from the base of the cliffs to the ship, and Tangor raised a hand to acknowledge he had seen us. I thought we were going to make it when from all sides around us descended a swarm of Zarafim—fully thirty or more of the iridescent-armored, ebon-winged behemoths, their swords crackling with flames like the roar of a raging furnace as they landed on the grass. Though Kloovos towered above them, the situation was hopeless; they would cut him down with their smoldering blades and make quick work of him.

Suddenly I heard an eerie whirring in the lavender heavens above, and something large and dark blocked out the sun. Kloovos and I both looked skyward as the Zarafim, too, lifted their gazes as one.

The big black disk that eclipsed radiant Omos rotated on its side and I made out the familiar profile. Then another disk-shaped craft, and yet another, zoomed out of the lilac sky. Still more came, until the heavens grew dark with them.

With a battle cry in some language I did not recognize, the Zarafim launched themselves into the air, winging toward the sleek, dark craft.

"Who are they?" Kloovos boomed.

My grin must have split my face from ear to ear. "It's my friend Maksata Tul!" I exclaimed. "He must have listened to my little speech after all and stated my plea before the Hall of the Thought Lords!"

"Your little speech?" asked the giant in wonder.

"Yes," I said. "To the Kjarnans, distant cousins of the Numinous Ones. About not standing on the sidelines. About reaching down into the muck and mire of humanity, getting your hands dirty, and doing the right thing. Never mind. Let's get to the ship while those tin-plated valkyries are distracted!"

Kloovos began running, the earth shaking with each of his heavy footfalls, while I clung fiercely to his neck. When we arrived at the ship, Tangor already had the aft canopy open and I directed the giant to lower me into my cockpit.

"Take care of yourself, my friend!" I shouted up at Kloovos. "If I don't manage to return, look after Hucklebuck if you can find him and tell him I—" But Tangor was already lowering the canopy over my head, cutting off my words. The Davrohendur bobbed his giant head in a nod and, grim-faced, his hand over his heart, bowed low. I placed my hand upon my own breast in warm acknowledgment, and then Kloovos was bounding away, his mighty feet hammering the violet turf as he headed toward the cliffs, doubtless intent on climbing back up to the Temple of Flesh and Bone and assisting his fellow Davrohendur in its defense.

The drone of the engines grew louder. I felt the ship lurch forward and then lift up into the air.

Tangor's tinny voice broke over the intercom: "You got what you needed?"

"I did!" I yelled back. "You've got the coordinates?"

"Aye, Captain Harben!" came Tangor's reply. "But do me a favor and keep a sharp eye out. Altovos says the gateway is nearly invisible depending on the angle."

"Yes, sir!"

The plane angled sharply into the sky and I felt myself pressed deep into my seat. Tangor had revved the engines to maximum capacity. The gateway lay not in the depths of the atmospheric channel as one flew through the tube of air toward the adjoining worlds of Zandar or Sanada, but rather on the lateral side of the planet, where the atmosphere rose only a hundred miles above the surface of Uvala. The gateway itself lay at an altitude of twenty miles, which was five miles beyond the point at which one could breathe without the assistance of an oxygen tank, or in my case, the breathing apparatus built into my Kjarnan suit.

The minutes passed. I scanned the heavens, half expecting to see a formation of Zarafim in hot pursuit, but the skies were blessedly empty of the enemy. The Kjarnan fleet must be keeping them busy.

As we flew higher, a crescent of haze became apparent over the curvature of the planet. Tangor indicated it was time for him to put on his oxygen mask. I pressed the button on my neckpiece that activated the Ninth Ray accumulators in my suit. Simultaneously, a glowing field of energy bubbled around my head, followed by the cool flow of oxygen filling my helmet and protective elastic fabric extending over my arms and hands as my suit's life-sustaining system deployed.

The ship's engines whined as they fought to drive the ever-thinning air through the blades of the propellers. Higher still we flew until, if I had known any better, I would have believed we had left the atmosphere completely behind and were in orbit around Uvala, its azure oceans and purple-and-tan continents spinning slowly below.

"There, above us at two o'clock!" Tangor exclaimed over the intercom.

I leaned forward and looked up through the canopy, my heart beating wildly. At first I didn't see it, but then I caught the glimmer of a swirling motion amid the black firmament. It was small—tiny, in fact. Just a dot, a minute gyre whirling against the abyss of outer space above.

"Get ready!" Tangor shouted. "We're almost on it."

"How can that be?" I said. "It's so small."

And then Tangor was diving directly underneath the gyre and I felt my heart plummet into my stomach.

"It's not even big enough to fly the ship into!" I cried out in frustration.

"We're going to have to abandon the mission," Tangor said back through his mic. "It must have shrunk over the millennia since it drifted from its origin point on the planet's surface."

"No, wait!" I exclaimed. "Take another flyby, *please*! We came all this way. I just want to take another look. Fly in close—real close. I need you to estimate the size of the opening."

"Roger, will comply."

The whirling gyre disappeared as we angled around it, but soon it came into view again. A moment later, we were flying right under it.

Tangor's voice came over the intercom: "Estimate size at two meters."

"Good!" I said.

"Good?" asked Tangor. "How so? There's no way we're flying the *Starduster* into that puny hole."

"We don't need to fly the ship into it," I said. "Just get me under that gateway."

I heard a curse over the comm system. "Victory, I don't like the sound of this."

"Just do it," I said firmly. "And make it as close to a hover as you can manage. And don't wait for me up here. I'll find my own way back—I hope. Just get back to the temple and help our friends."

Another curse came over the cockpit speaker, but the ship began to turn about for another run beneath the churning gyre, this time slow and easy.

I hit the switch that raised the canopy, unbuckled myself, and got up into a crouching position on my seat, holding on to the loose straps so I wouldn't go flying out of the ship. I shot a quick look at the Zarafim sword lying beside my seat in the cockpit. I hated to leave it behind, as I had a hunch it might come in handy where I was going, but it would be too heavy and cumbersome for the feat I was about to perform.

Suddenly the gyre was directly above me. I pressed the button on my suit to prime the feeble stores of the Eighth Ray of Uvala in the repositories of my Kjarnan boots. I hoped the expulsion of Uvala's gravitic planetary ray would give me just enough lift to propel myself upward into the gateway. I was about to find out.

I kicked off against my seat and leaped free of the ship, simultaneously flipping the switch to engage my boots. The *Starduster* was already moving away from beneath me. Up, up I went, toward the turning gyre, the Eighth Ray exhausts providing thrust from the soles of my boots.

The gateway was colorless, translucent—defying the eye to impart it with any definite shape or form. And yet there it was clearly before me, churning, ever churning. As I moved toward it, my neck craned back, my arms instinctively extended to my sides as if they might give me balance, I experienced the sensation that I was falling upward, being pulled into the maw of the gateway as if by some indescribable force. The gyre was like a mesmerist's wheel, endlessly spinning, hypnotizing me as I stared up into it. Soon I felt my consciousness begin to wane. Within the brief moment before I lost my awareness, I felt a bitter pang of fear that I would die alone there, twenty miles above the planet.

Then all that existed in the universe was no more.

25
HALOS

WHEN I AWOKE, I found myself lying on my side on damp, gritty pavement. I pushed myself up from the ground, my head still spinning from the effect of passing through the gateway. It was dark wherever I was, though faint light fell upon the walls that rose upon either side of me. I looked down and discovered the back of my hands were radiating with an unearthly glow. Suddenly I realized the gentle luminance that was cast upon the walls was emanating from me.

"Ah, lookit there, Petey," came a coarse male voice, speaking in English. "A fresh one just arrived for our pleasure."

I stood up. I was at the back end of a long alleyway between two tall buildings, a thin band of starry night sky above. Where the alley opened onto a street ahead of me I saw two dark figures, silhouetted in the yellowish light of the street-lamps that rose behind them. A dim, almost indiscernible light seemed to emanate from their own bodies, giving them an almost ghostly aspect. The shadowy forms appeared to be wearing hooded jackets and, perhaps, kilt-like garments; it was difficult to discern in the darkness.

"A Corophine, too, by the looks of her," said a second male voice. "See how she glows? But that ain't no regular fresh one, Tom. Look, she's wearin' some kinda fancy getup."

I heard a click, and the dark outline of a sharp, slim blade appeared in the hand of one of the two figures. "All the more for our takin'." Cold laughter pealed down the alleyway, resounding off the walls surrounding me. "Come on, Petey. Let's have us some fun."

The two men began walking toward me. I tensed and reached for my uncertainty gun, which thankfully had accompanied me during the transition through the gateway, along with my Kjarnan attire. Of course, the apparatus was not truly a weapon—who knew what random effect it might produce this time should I pull the trigger?—but perhaps its resemblance to a pistol would be enough to scare off the two hooligans.

Before I could draw the apparatus, however, another figure appeared behind them at the opening to the alley. A deep, smooth voice spoke in English, though laden with a heavy Russian accent. "Leave her alone," said the man. "You know what happens to those foolish enough to trespass on my territory."

The two men who had been menacing me turned around and regarded the newcomer.

Tom, the man carrying the blade, cursed, while his companion let out a little whimpering noise and whispered, "It's *him*!"

"We're . . . we're so sorry, sir!" Tom said in cowed tones. Gone was all the threatening swagger the man had exhibited when he had first spied me in the dark alley. "We didn't know we was on your turf, Mister R! The girl is yours, all yours. I swear, sir, we meant no offense, Petey and me. We'll just be our way!"

The two men fled the alleyway at once, almost tripping over themselves in their haste as they passed by the stranger.

After they had gone, the Russian raised a welcoming hand. "Come, miss. Don't let those ruffians frighten you. It is enough to endure the shock of the transition from mortal life to Halos, let alone to be accosted by such boors immediately upon your arrival. There is a dining establishment just a short walk from here. Let us get you something to eat and drink." He turned and walked out into the street, where he stood waiting for me, smiling reassuringly through his dark beard.

As I approached him, he said, "My name is Nikolas. In the time since my rebirth on Halos, I have come to look after this district and protect those who are newly transitioned to this world from the vile Maxteles who would seek to prey upon the innocent. Or I should say, who would prey upon new arrivals, for are any of us truly innocent, even among Corophines such as yourself?"

I regarded the man warily. Ebon eyes peered out from beneath dark, arching brows, and his black, neatly trimmed beard did not hide the sharp, angular features of his pale face. Though I'm not one to judge by appearances, I could not help but think that his features exhibited a cunning quality. He wore white silken robes, and a dim aura of light haloed his entire form, which was more luminous than the dull, leaden light cast by the two hoodlums, but of lesser radiance than that shed by my own body.

"Yes, it is true," said the man. "I am but a Psamaftogene. But even a Psamaftogene may aspire to develop his moral attributes, for is that not why we are all here in Halos?" Something about the man's tone made me question whether his statement was made in earnest or rather with a sense of cutting irony.

I looked down the street, the curbs of which were literally trimmed with gold, and saw further on masses of white-robed pedestrians making their way down a wide boulevard, upon either side of which appeared to be storefronts and eateries and even a concert hall and a number of churches, just as one might see at the heart of any metropolis back on Earth. Or perhaps I should say they were similar to what one might find in a city on Earth, for instead of being constructed of grim concrete and brick, their facades all gleamed with shining gold and silver and polished marble beneath the brilliant warmth of the streetlamps.

"I'm not sure I'm going to fit in," I said looking down

at my Kjarnan attire and then back to the white-robed pedestrians.

"I am sure," the man said, "there is a perfectly reasonable explanation for why you alone, of all who have ever come to Halos, have made the transition in such unusual garments." He smiled and nodded. "But you are right. Your clothing could cause some consternation among the lofty Corophines. But do not worry. I have a friend on the corner who owes me a favor."

We walked a short distance until we came to a residential building, which lay about a block from where the commercial district began. My guide stopped and knocked on the paneled wooden door. A few moments later a bespectacled man emerged, who started, a look of fear upon his face, upon seeing who was there waiting for him. Words were exchanged that I could not hear, and the man, leaving the door, reentered his home and returned a moment later bearing a bundle of white fabric in his hands, which he gave to the Russian. The bespectacled man bowed, his hands steepled as if in prayer, then closed the door behind him.

My guide returned to my side and held out the robes. "Now you may pose as one of the—" He cleared his throat and began again. "I mean, now you may fit in with the locals and become one of us."

The man's fumble did not go past me unnoticed, but I said nothing and slipped the gown over my head and shoulders, the loose robes amply concealing my Kjarnan suit as well as the uncertainty gun in the holster at my hip and the bulky pouch hanging from my belt.

"It is the way of the Corophines in their shining cities for all to go about thus robed," the man went on, "though in other areas of Halos there is no need for clothing, for what is there to be ashamed of in the afterlife? But the Corophines of the cities say they do not wish to tempt us lesser castes with displays that may inflame our carnal desires and lead us down a path to lesser radiance."

"Makes sense," I said, nodding and smiling, all the while thinking that every custom and convention of Halos was but a carefully constructed lie, fabricated to increase the energy levels of the inhabitants so that their life force might be harvested and consumed by the ravenous Harods, the exiled former Thought Lords of Kjarna. Beneath my robes, I shuddered.

We left the residential building behind and continued on in silence. Soon we entered the commercial district, thronged with robed, luminous pedestrians, all bearing the same serene and beneficent smile—a smile that quickly wore on me and caused a cold shiver to creep down my spine. If this was the afterlife, I wanted none of it.

After we had walked a short distance, we turned into an eating establishment, the interior of which was indistinguishable from any dimly lit, dark-paneled pub I might have patronized back in England. My guide led me to a small table in the back of the room where we could carry on a conversation in relative privacy. This was perfect for my purposes, I thought, if only I were alone and unaccompanied. All the same, I didn't plan to dillydally. I would carry out my plan in public if I must, for I hoped I could initiate it swiftly so that by the time anyone realized I was doing something out of the ordinary, I would already be beyond reach.

The waiter, an austere-looking fellow, brought us glasses and a bottle of a fine, effervescent white wine, then returned a moment later with a basket of warm bread. I sipped conservatively from my glass, for I could not afford to let the drink affect my wits, but I devoured the bread, for I had not eaten since before my experience with the Star Tree. While I ate, my guide to the afterlife began speaking.

"As I have told you," he said, "I am but a lowly Psamaftogene. But before I was a Psamaftogene I was something worse. Upon the sudden and violent death of my mortal shell at the hands of my greatest nemesis, I awoke in an underground world that I believe may be located at the center of the Earth. But I did not bear a human form. No, I was a hideous mockery of a human being, something called a Gorbus—a creature with a bestial face of the meanest brute, all-white hair, and the pale skin and pink-irised, red-pupilled eyes of an albino. Like the Maxteles of Halos, all the creatures where I found myself seemed to have been reincarnated from immoral lowlifes on Earth, the absolute lowest of the low. I did not survive long among them, for they are a truly ruthless lot, and there too I died a violent death."

I stopped eating suddenly when he mentioned the name Gorbus, for I had heard tell of such creatures before from Tarzan, whose granddaughter Suzanne had encountered them in caverns within Pellucidar, as had his friend von Horst. Now I wondered if there could be a connection between the Gorbuses and the scheme of the Harods to cultivate victims for the consumption of their life force. Perhaps the Gorbuses were evidence of inroads made by the Harods into the angle wherein resided Pellucidar. Did they mean to transform the inner world into a crucible for preparing souls for consumption, just as they had Halos?

Seeing the expression on my face, the Russian narrowed his eyes. "You have heard of Gorbuses before?" he asked.

"No," I lied, "but they sound absolutely dreadful." I did not want to let on anything that might jeopardize my mission.

At that point in our conversation the waiter appeared with the main course, all vegetarian fare, for I suppose it is a sin in Halos to kill another being simply to eat it—the greatest of ironies, considering the Harods' hideous scheme. In any case, the food smelled delicious, and I found it equally delectable when I tasted it, though I partook of it only in small portions, for I did not wish to engorge myself and become sleepy or otherwise impair my reflexes.

"It surely was dreadful," my companion said, picking up our conversation where we had left off. "But then I awoke here, upon Halos, a magnificent world of hope and promise."

Again I heard the faintest trace of irony beneath his words. This time I decided to fish.

"It is interesting," I said. "It sounds as if here, in the afterlife, we finally have an opportunity to perfect our spirits and ascend to a higher plane of existence. But here, just as on Earth, the criminal class still thrives, even in this splendid shining city of the Corophines, whom I take, from what you say, to be the epitome of spiritual development in Halos."

"Ah, for certain—the Corophines are morally enlightened. But they are not the epitome. That righteous epithet is reserved for the holy Harods, who make up the blessed two percent of the inhabitants of Halos, though no one has ever seen them."

"If no one has ever seen them," I said, "then how is it known that they make up two percent of the population?"

My companion leaned forward conspiratorially and whispered a single word: *"Precisely."*

I moved closer to the man and spoke in low tones so we would not be overheard. "You suspect there is something not quite on the up and up here in Halos, don't you?"

"Sapristi!" he exclaimed under his breath. "I do not merely suspect it. It is all a confidence game—the entire setup of this world of the so-called afterlife! I, the king of artifice and deception during my mortal life, should know that better than anyone. Just as I know that you did not come to Halos by natural means. No, you are here to infiltrate it! For what purpose I do not know, although every fiber of my being tells me that you hold a revulsion for this place, just as I do. And my instincts are seldom wrong. You are no Corophine— no, you are an impostor!"

I stiffened, then looked furtively at the staff and other patrons of the establishment to see if they had noticed the man's outburst. Though he had spoken in low tones, his manner had been forceful and full of rage—and that was enough to stand out in this pub full of the placid-faced cherubs of Halos. Fortunately, no one seemed to have taken notice, though I did consider getting up right then and there, walking briskly across the room, and leaving the building. But I quickly decided that, in terms of jeopardizing my mission, it was as much a gamble to remain speaking with the man as it was to abruptly flee and risking the chance that he would chase after me and create a scene that would compromise my plans.

So instead I looked the man directly in his black eyes and smiled. "You got me," I said calmly. "I *am* an imposter. And I do find this place revolting. I've been here for only a short time and already the interminably serene and cheery expression on every face gives me the creeps. That's because what lurks behind those smiling countenances is fear—fear that if they don't please the secret lords of Halos by being goody two-shoes and 'ascending' to a higher radiance, they'll be literally damned. But what they don't know is that they'll be damned just the same if they become Corophines and transform themselves into—"

But there I stopped, for I had gotten carried away myself, so chilled was I by the legions of beaming, self-righteous citizens I had seen since my arrival in Halos. Before I went on any further, I must assess the effect my little speech had had upon my audience.

For his part, the man with whom I dined sat there grinning slyly, as if pleased that he had goaded me into my confession. He appeared neither shocked, angered, nor displeased.

"It was my outfit that gave me away, wasn't it?" I asked.

"And your weapon," the man said, grinning darkly. "There are no guns in Halos."

"It's not a weapon," I said, figuring that since I was on a spree, I might as well go the whole hog, including the postage. "It's a device that detects the aura-like field that, if I have been correctly informed, surrounds each inhabitant of Halos." I glanced about to make sure no one was looking and then proceeded to remove the uncertainty apparatus from beneath the folds of my robes, holding it beneath the table to keep it from view while my companion looked on with great interest. I opened a panel on the back side of the apparatus, flipped down one of several switches inside the shallow compartment, and then raised the gun above the lip of the table and aimed its barrel-shaped waveguide at a passing patron. A needle on one of the dials inside the compartment instantly ticked up as it registered the zuvan field surrounding the woman's body.

Back on Uvala, Altovos had explained to me that the Harods had installed vast machinery deep beneath the surface of the planet Halos, apparatus of advanced technology that generated a zuvan for each of the resurrected. The process was usually instantaneous, such that the zuvan would be automatically imposed on the resurrected at the time of the transition to Halos, although sometimes, due to a misalignment with the individual's volatra, or life force, the resurrected would lie in a dormant state upon transition to the planet, sometimes for many years, before the artificially generated zuvan could align with the target's volatra, at which point the resurrected would awaken on Halos years after being translocated there.

I swept the gun about to read my companion's zuvan. The man raised an eyebrow, looking mildly bemused, while he waited for me to read the result.

"Do you perceive now the dark threads interwoven throughout my soul?" he asked.

"The energy level of your aura," I said, "is weaker than that of many of the other people in this room. But that doesn't mean you're morally any better or worse than any of them. The aura is a field that's bound artificially to your life force upon your arrival in Halos. It intensifies or diminishes depending on your experiences, absorbing them into the field. In essence, your experiences serve as a catalyst for the field, lifting or lowering its energy level, just like an electron can jump from one energy level to another by absorbing or emitting a photon. The Harods feed on the energy of the zuvans. The higher the level of energy attained by a zuvan, the tastier and more nutritious, so to speak, the zuvan becomes to them." I paused. "Sorry if I'm shattering your religion in the space of a few minutes, but you have to know it's all a charade. What the Harods are doing to the people of Halos is truly monstrous."

"I have no religion to shatter," replied my companion. "Moreover, long have I suspected that the Harods, whoever they might be, are the secret lords of Halos. Certainly the Corophines are too petty and unimaginative to have foisted this conspiracy upon the unsuspecting souls who have been drawn to this plane of existence. I shall do whatever is within my power to assist you in overturning the nightmare of a world that is Halos."

I moved the waveguide of the uncertainty apparatus away from the man and again began surreptitiously gathering readings of the patrons' and waitstaff's zuvans.

"Precisely what, pray tell, are you doing?" the man asked.

"Remember what I said about raising a zuvan's energy levels?" I asked. "I mean to increase my own zuvan's energy level to the appropriate degree and thereby gain entry into the Harods' angle—that is, the dimension of reality in which they remain hidden. To do that, I need a precise amount of energy that equates to the difference between my own zuvan's energy state and the threshold of energy required to cross over into the Harod's angle. So I'm looking for someone whose energy state meets those requirements. My apparatus can then transfer the energy from the target's zuvan to my own. And . . . there he is." I looked up as my companion's eyes traced the direction in which my gun's waveguide was pointed and then settled on my intended target: a tall, willowy man in the ubiquitous white robe who was sitting with a woman at a nearby table. "But I need to be in direct proximity to him—say, one or two feet—for perhaps a full minute to complete a successful transfer of his zuvan's energy to my own zuvan. And that's the trick, isn't it?"

"Leave it to me," said my companion, and with that pronouncement, he rose and approached the table where the man and woman sat. He leaned over and whispered something into the man's ear. Immediately, the Corophine stood up as if he had just learned of a dire emergency.

"Come with me," the Russian said, and he proceeded to lead the Corophine into a dark hallway in the back of the restaurant. Just before he passed from view, my fellow conspirator glanced back and motioned me to follow with a shallow jerk of his head.

Keeping the uncertainty gun hidden beneath the folds of my robes, I rose from the table and walked slowly and casually into the hallway down which the two men had passed.

At the end of the corridor I entered an open doorway leading into a small, dimly lit room. There I found my companion had thrust the willowy man up against the wall and was throttling him with both hands. The Corophine gagged and choked, his horrified eyes rolling wildly.

"Stop it!" I cried. "What are you *doing*? You're hurting him!"

"I know this man," the Russian said. "He is responsible for many heinous crimes committed in the name of the Corophines."

"Let him go!" I ordered.

"Have you siphoned off his energy yet?"

"No, of course not," I said. "I'm not going to do that to him while you—"

"Just do it!" the Russian shouted, digging his fingers deeper into the Corophine's windpipe. "Think of your monstrous Harods and all the souls you claim they have farmed and devoured. That should get you in the mood to do what you must."

I sighed heavily. This was not how I had imagined it would play out, but I had little choice but to do what the Russian bade. "Just don't hurt him, okay? And hold him still."

While my partner in crime fought to restrain our victim,

I adjusted the settings on the gun and again took a reading of his energy level.

"What's wrong?" my Russian companion asked heatedly.

"It's his zuvan," I said, reading the dial as the Corophine struggled in my conspirator's grasp. "His energy level is vacillating all over the place! First it's too low, then too high. This is not going to work—he's just too upset!"

Suddenly, my Russian companion smashed his fist into the face of the struggling man, breaking his nose and causing it to spout a fountain of blood.

"What are you doing?" I cried, outraged.

"Bringing his energy level down to normal," the man replied with a malignant grin. The eyes of the Corophine glazed over and he no longer struggled in his attacker's grasp.

I took another reading and watched the needle tick down on the dial until it fell into the necessary range. "There!" I exclaimed, and I pulled the gun's trigger to begin the transfer process.

Just then, two burly men broke into the room and pulled the Russian from the unconscious man, who slid down the wall against which he had been propped and collapsed in a shambles on the floor.

But the Russian did not go quietly. Instead, he punched and jabbed and kicked and bit like a cornered devil, resisting his antagonists as he employed every dirty fighting trick imaginable.

As the three men clashed in furious intensity, I kneeled in the corner beside the unconscious man, watching his aura grow dimmer and dimmer as I drained its energy. All the while I kept a close eye on the dial on my gun. At last, I slammed down on the button to end the energy transfer. The process had been successful.

I looked up to see the two large men dragging my Russian friend from the little room and back down the narrow hallway.

"Let's face it," the Russian called after me, grinning widely as he was hauled away. "I never expected to go to heaven, either before or after I died." He kicked the shin of one of his captors and gained another moment as they struggled to contain him. "Just do me one favor—promise me you'll put an end to this tireless charade of an afterlife. And when you do, tell the villains behind this affair that Nikolas Rokoff played a part in their downfall."

And with that, I turned the waveguide of the apparatus upon myself and pulled the trigger.

26
THE SOUL CAGES

THE RUSH OF THE COLD VOID took hold of me for a span heedless of time or distance, and then suddenly I was standing in a gleaming cell whose walls, floor, and ceiling were made of luminous white crystal. One side of the ten-foot-by-ten-foot room was open, looking out upon a long, wide hallway constructed of the same radiant material. Across the aisle I could see three cells identical to my own, two of which housed a woman and the third a man, each lone resident bearing a dejected, forlorn countenance. The whole scene gave the impression of an ethereal prison cellblock, and I wondered how many more such rooms ran down either side of the glowing corridor, unseen from my vantage point.

I cast off the bulky Corophine robes, and then returned the uncertainty apparatus to its holster and stepped forward in an attempt to confirm my suspicions. Soon, however, I found that, as in the case of the room in which I had first awakened after my arrival on Kjarna, I did not possess the will to pass beyond the threshold of the opening. Try as I might to order my muscles to respond, I simply could not command my legs to move and carry me into the corridor. The opening might as well have been adorned with iron bars, so fast was I secured within my prison.

The sound of heavy footsteps came down the hallway to my right, and within moments a giant Zarafim stood before my cell, his pale, helmed visage staring down at me in disdain.

"Why are you garbed thus, Corophine?" his deep voice boomed in English, or so my mind translated his speech.

271

"The others who ascend from Halos are either attired in white robes or wholly naked." He referred to my Kjarnan jumpsuit, as well as the uncertainty apparatus and the pouch that depended from my utility belt. I watched as his widening eyes fell upon my discarded robes on the floor.

"Here," I said, reaching a hand inside the pouch. "I think this will explain things." I withdrew two great gemstones, one having the appearance of a diamond and the other of an emerald, and held them forth, one in each hand. Each jewel was nearly the size of a grapefruit and weighed about three pounds. As my hands came into contact with the glittering stones, I felt an electric tingle pass through my arms and throughout my body.

"What are those?" the Zarafim cried, whipping his gleaming blade from its scabbard.

But already was I channeling my will into the two precious jewels in my grasp. I felt a strange surge of power flow through me, unlike anything I had ever before experienced. At my mental command, the Zarafim sheathed his sword and stood passively at attention before me. Now I willed him to release me from my cell.

Though he took no visible action that might imply he had affected the status of my imprisonment in any way, he said, "Come forward." Then he motioned for me to step out of my cell.

I did as he directed and passed over the threshold without the slightest impediment or hesitation.

I smiled up at my former captor, who was now my obedient servant thanks to the mysterious powers of the strange gemstones. They were the great diamond known as the Gonfal of the Kaji and its counterpart, the emerald of the Zuli. As Mr. Burroughs had detailed in a published account thinly veiled as fiction, Tarzan and Stanley Wood had obtained the jewels in the mid-1930s during an adventure that took place just to the north of Lake Rudolf in the Great Rift

Valley of East Africa.* When Altovos had told me of the seeds of the Star Tree, which he said could be wielded against the Harods and used to seal them permanently within their narrow angle, it had triggered my memory of Mr. Wood's visit to the Greystokes' Chamston-Hedding estate, from the time just prior to my voyage to Pellucidar to investigate the failure of the Gridley Wave. It was for that reason I had allowed myself to be absorbed within the bole of the Star Tree and been transported by means of the tree's uncanny abilities across time and space to retrieve the jewels from Tarzan's safekeeping. How the Kaji and Zuli tribes had gained possession of the gems, I did not know. But I recalled the great crystal tree Tarzan told me he had encountered in 1918. He had called it the Dark Heart of Time, and it bore a striking resemblance in both form and function to the Star Tree of the Numinous Ones. I could only speculate, as Tarzan had, that the Gonfal and the emerald of the Zuli were the "seeds" of Tarzan's crystal tree, or one like it, which must have been planted on Earth in some bygone age—perhaps even placed there by the Volstari of the planet Kjarna. How or why the latter might have crossed over into Earth's angle from what I had begun thinking of as the "Jasoomian dimension" was yet another mystery to ponder in the unlikely event I should survive my current predicament.

Now that I stood beyond the confines of my cell, I gazed up and down the scintillating crystal corridor, which ran as far as I could see in either direction.

"I need to find a particular prisoner," I said. "Can you help me do that?"

The Zarafim nodded dutifully and intoned, "I can." Then he shook his head, his chiseled face clearly puzzled. "What have you done to me?"

"Nothing you didn't have coming, mister," I said curtly. "I need you to take me to Janson Gridley." I pictured Janson's face in my mind and strove to project the mental image

---

* See *Tarzan the Magnificent* by Edgar Rice Burroughs.

into the stones that I held in my fists, and then I visualized that image moving from the jewels into the mind of the Zarafim. "And no funny business, all right? You are to alert no one that you are under the influence of my will or otherwise tip off anyone that I am anything other than your prisoner. Got it?"

"Yes, I have 'got it,'" the Zarafim replied. "I can take you to the one called Janson Gridley."

"Good. Then let's get going."

For how long we walked down the crystal corridor I cannot say, but each cell we passed was inhabited by a lone prisoner, presumably every one of them a Corophine who was spirited away from Halos, expecting to be transformed into a divine Harod. How dejected they looked, and with good reason, for while they had each expected to reap the reward of eternal salvation for living a life of virtue, they instead found themselves but chattel waiting for their life force to be consumed by the ravenous lords of Halos.

"How do they subsist in these bleak cells?" I asked as we passed by the endless numbers of the imprisoned. "I see neither food nor water nor means of sanitation, and yet all appear to be well fed and well groomed."

"You are but a mere human," replied the Zarafim. "Do not expect your mortal mind to be able to comprehend the supernatural powers of the holy Harods."

"Try again," I said, this time focusing my question through the gemstones.

The Zarafim blinked and again shook his head as if trying to wake up from a spell that had been cast upon him. "The soul cages exist beyond the confines of space and time," he went on, "as do their prisoners. Who needs to eat or even sleep during the Eternal Now?"

We continued on, turning down corridor after corridor lined with soul cages, each with its lone prisoner; we must have passed thousands of cells, and yet the Zarafim told me we were in but one insignificant corner of the vast complex of the Harods' soul cages.

"Why have your masters not consumed the life force of these prisoners?" I asked, again willing the Zarafim to give me an honest answer. "What are they waiting for?"

The Zarafim grinned with malice. "The holy Harods await the Great Reaping. It comes soon, and then you will be no more."

I ignored his threat and asked, "You mean their souls will be reaped all at once? Every single one of them?"

"So it shall be," said the Zarafim.

I shuddered in the cool air of the corridor down which we trod. This, then, must be what Altovos had meant when he told me the Harods would soon be powerful enough to break free from the prison of their narrow angle. They would use the surge of energy released from the simultaneous reaping of an untold number of souls to expand their might and bend the fabric of spacetime to their own will. The only silver lining, for me at least, was that the delay in the souls' consumption had postponed the grim fate awaiting Janson Gridley.

The forlorn faces looking out in misery from their cages soon wore on me, so that it was all I could do not to scream out in horror and outrage at the vile injustice of the Harods' wicked and depraved scheme. I began to feel that I might go mad if I were forced to go on any longer down the endless corridors of hopeless souls, and yet I knew that somewhere out there among them lay Janson in his own soul cage, just as forsaken and dejected as all the rest, believing he would never again see his family or friends, let alone any familiar face he had ever known in his mortal life.

It was just as I was upon the verge of exploding in an outburst of anger and frustration when the Zarafim suddenly stopped before a cell and I saw before me the form of a naked man, his head sprouting an unruly mass of black hair, lying with his back turned to me on the floor of his cube as if he were sleeping.

"Janson!" I cried. "Is that you?"

The man turned, pushing up against the floor with the palms of his hands and twisting his torso in an attempt to hide his nakedness. I looked into the widening gray eyes of Janson Gridley, his mouth gaping open in surprise.

"Victory!" he exclaimed. "What are you doing here? Are you a prisoner? Have you . . . *died*?"

"Hardly." I smiled widely, fighting back the tears of joy that brimmed in the corners of my eyes. "Just stopping by for teatime," I said as cheerily as possible, under the circumstances. Then I turned to the Zarafim. "Get him some clothes!" I commanded. "Now!"

The Zarafim strode to the cell opposite Janson's, passed effortlessly through the invisible barrier upon the open side, and roughly seized the old man confined within and divested him of his robes. The now-naked Corophine scowled bitterly at me as the Zarafim stomped back across the corridor and handed me the robe. I smiled back at the old man and shrugged. "Sorry, mister," I said meekly, and then ordered the Zarafim to lower the imperceptible field imprisoning Janson within his cell.

Within moments I was at Janson's side, helping him into the pilfered robe. While we were thus engaged, he reached his strong arms around me and crushed me against him in a warm embrace.

"I never thought I would see you again," said Janson, pressing his face against my cheek.

"I'm glad to see you too, Janson . . . more than you'll ever know," I said, allowing myself a brief respite to revel in the comforting feeling of amity amid the horror that surrounded us. "But no time for mushy stuff." Gently, I pushed him away.

For a fleeting moment, Janson looked nonplussed, but then he bucked up and shot me a grin of determination and courage. It was an expression I had seen many times on the face of his father, and it lifted my spirits and gave me hope.

I looked up at the towering Zarafim. "Where is the machinery located that your masters use to control the flow of souls between Halos and the soul cages?"

The Zarafim glared down at me. "Doubtless you mean the Teteculent Hall, though it is not the machinery that is important but rather the will of my masters' ineffable thoughts that runs it."

"Well, isn't that just killer-diller," I said. "Well, then, ineffable thoughts it is. Take us to the Teteculent Hall."

Again we continued on down the endless corridors of the damned. Though my spirits were buoyed by Janson's presence, I now also felt a heavy burden weighing me down. I knew I couldn't afford to lose Janson again; if I did, I feared I would be shattered, immobilized, unable to respond with the lightning reflexes I would need to face off against the powerful Harods and put an end once and for all to their insidious machinations.

It was with such gloomy thoughts running through my mind that I followed our guide down the twisting corridors of radiant crystal. For how long we proceeded thus I do not know, but it felt like hours blurred into days and days into years as we trudged onward.

"Am I *alive*?" Janson asked suddenly as we walked along. "I don't even know anymore."

"Yes, you're alive, Janson," I said. "You can trust someone who's had her atoms dematerialized and rematerialized so many times she can't count."

"These other poor souls who are imprisoned here," he went on, as if he hadn't heard my reply; "according to the man in the cell across from my own, they all *died*. He said that after their deaths on Earth, they all appeared on a world called Halos. And then, after striving during the afterlife to perfect their moral natures, they ascended here, where they found themselves prisoners in the realm of the Harods. And here I am, after I beamed myself across the galaxy to find you, fused my essence with that great furry white creature of yours, and then separated and looked on as my atomic structure dissipated on that faraway planet. So . . . am I *dead*?"

"No, Janson," I said. "You're *not* dead. You're just a little . . . scattered and confused. These other people incarcerated here died very mortal deaths. Your life force just got artificially unbonded by the quantum process that Abner employed, then diverted by the Harods, who scooped you up and brought you here."

"But that was after I . . . dissipated. I *died*."

"Don't think of it like that, Janson. You became . . . atomically dispersed on a quantum level, okay? And that which is dispersed can become whole again with a little, shall we say, quantum glue."

I was worried about Janson. He had been through so much, all because of me. I hadn't asked him to dematerialize his atomic structure, convert it to energy, and then send it back along the carrier wave of my own Gridley Wave transmission. He had made that choice all by himself. Why he had risked his life for my own I could not fathom, but I knew it was a debt I could never repay.

We were about to round a corner when I looked up at our towering guide and noticed an odd expression on his alabaster face. It was as if he were struggling to repress a satisfied smirk.

"Stop!" I ordered, channeling my will through the gemstones clutched in my hands. "Stay right where you are and remain quiet."

"What is it?" Janson asked.

"Maybe nothing," I said, inching forward toward the turn in the corridor. "But maybe . . ." I jerked my head back, my pulse quickening at what I had glimpsed around the corner.

"Nice try, Mister Zarafim," I whispered at the winged giant.

Then to Janson: "He was trying to lead us straight into a squad of armed guards."

"You said you wished me to lead you to the Teteculent Hall," the Zarafim said, his tone all too satisfied. "You did not ask me to warn you about the Zarafim who forever guard it."

I jerked my thumb at the Zarafim. "Get a load of this shyster," I said to Janson.

Jason shook his head and glowered at the angelic warrior. "What now?"

"Now," I said, "we see just how powerful these stones really are." Still holding the two great gems, I visualized the fifteen Zarafim guards I had just seen standing vigil over the entrance to the Teteculent Hall. Again, I felt the strange surge of power flow through me as I attempted to reach out and touch the minds of my targets. When I felt the peculiar sensation of contact that I had experienced when using the gems on our Zarafim companion, I stepped boldly around the corner into the full view of the squad of winged warriors. As I approached, they separated before me, leaving the short recessed passage leading into the Teteculent Hall wide open.

"See," I called back to Janson. "Piece of cake."

It was then that an earsplitting thunderclap resounded from the corridor I had just left and I heard Janson cry out my name.

I turned to look behind and saw Janson bolting toward me, a troop of twenty Zarafim at his heels. The pursuers were led by a colossal warrior I recognized all too well—my nemesis, Lahvoh.

27
THE SWORDS OF ETERNITY

WITH EVERY OUNCE OF CONCENTRATION I could muster, I reached out the tendrils of my mind and caressed the thoughts of the Zarafim guards standing vigil before the Teteculent Hall. It is a strange feeling to enter another's mind, and stranger still to bend it to your will. But that is exactly what I did, commanding the winged giants in their gleaming iridescent armor to attack the advancing forces. Instantly, they obeyed, whipping their swords from their scabbards and setting them ablaze with hellish flames of red and orange.

"Come on!" I cried to Janson. Then together we charged forward as the mass of advancing Zarafim under my command parted before us.

The two forces clashed as we reached the alcove leading into the Teteculent Hall, where a great double door of ornate design towered over us and impeded our further progress. Janson pushed forcefully against the panels to no avail; then he backed up, and with a running start rammed his shoulder against them using the full weight of his muscular frame. Still, the door did not budge.

Meanwhile, the two forces of Zarafim clashed in violent fury in the corridor beyond the recessed entryway where we stood, their flaming swords cutting and slashing. I clenched both the Gonfal and the great emerald of the Zuli in my hands, concentrating on exerting my will over my subjects and commanding them to repel Lahvoh and her warriors at all costs.

Janson was about to take another running start at the door when I shouted for him to stop. "It's no use!" I cried. "Altovos—never mind who he is—told me the Harods' inner chamber can be opened only by another of their own kind. But these—" I held up the gemstones, "should temporarily elevate my mind to the level of a Volstari—that is, a Harod— and allow me to unseal the door."

Before our horrified eyes, a member of our forces went down beneath the fiery sword of an attacking Zarafim, the dead warrior's blade flying out of her hand and skittering across the floor to rest at Janson's feet. He snatched up the flaming sword, waving the crackling blade back and forth as he tested its weight. "Well, get to it, then!" he shouted.

With all the remaining willpower I could summon, I attempted to divide my attention between maintaining my mental command over our force of Zarafim and confronting the predicament of the locked door. As soon as I directed my consciousness to focus upon the door's physical structure, I experienced an odd presence in my mind that I can only compare to the mental equivalent of the tumblers of a lock; that is, a problem formed unbidden in my consciousness akin to one of the endless differential equations over which I had once tirelessly labored as a graduate student in the field of theoretical physics. I proceeded to plug in variable after variable as I attempted to balance the equation in my head and thereby unlock the door, but always was I forced to return my attention to the Zarafim guards who sought to break free of the mental control I held over them.

"I can't do it!" I cried out in frustration. "The problem is just too hard! I need all my attention to concentrate on opening the door, but I can't let up my control over the Zarafim defending us."

Beads of sweat ran down Janson's face as he crouched in

the alcove overlooking the furious battle. "It won't matter soon, in any case," he said. "Our forces are losing!"

Even as he spoke, I saw two more members of our force cut down by Lahvoh's raging warriors.

"Let them go, Victory!" Janson shouted. "This entryway we're in is highly defendable." He swung his crackling blade back and forth before the narrow opening of the alcove that led out into the broad corridor beyond. "See? Only one of them can get at me at a time. I can hold off the entire force long enough for you focus that big brain of yours and open the door." When I paused, standing there open-mouthed at the bravery and daring—and perhaps foolishness—of his suggestion, Janson admonished me: "Just let go, Victory! We don't have a choice!"

I sighed heavily and nodded. Janson grinned widely at my acquiescence, and then turned to take a fighting stance in the frame of the doorway leading from the alcove.

Turning to face the towering door blocking our entry into the Teteculent Hall, I closed my eyes and released my mental hold over the wills of our Zarafim defenders. For the barest of moments, I sensed a feeling of relief arise in the minds of my former subjects as they reasserted agency over their actions, and then my connection with them was severed and I felt their presences no more.

I tried to regulate my breaths and tackle the equation that confronted me. Here, at last, I was in my element, turning all the resourcefulness of my intellect upon the problem of solving the puzzle of the lock. I recalled Poppy Pickerall at university poking fun at my habit of winding down from a particularly trying exam by reclining on our chaise longue and attempting to solve challenging acrostic puzzles, which she called "instruments of mind-numbing torment." But to each her own. For me, losing myself in puzzles and math-ematical equations sharpened my senses and unlocked some-thing deep inside myself that otherwise lay fallow. Now, amid all the turbulence that surrounded me, I imagined I was once again back at our flat at Oxford working out the answer to an acrostic. Just as I had done many times before, I sought that quiet place within, and soon my mind sang out and ran free.

At last I arrived at the requisite values needed to solve the mental equation in my mind's eye. I opened my eyes just as I heard the door's locking mechanism click loudly and saw the two ornate panels of the towering gate swing open.

I had done it! I shouted out in exuberance, then turned to let Janson know the good news. But what I saw when I whirled about drained the blood from my limbs and left them cold and numb, for Janson stood there in the doorway, his Corophine's robes in tatters, bleeding from half a dozen cuts, the bare skin of his shoulders seared by the flaming swords of the Zarafim who attacked him.

Before I could utter a single word, let alone focus my mind upon the powerful artifacts in my grasp and assert control over the Zarafim attacking Janson, I heard Lahvoh's angry voice cry forth: "Out of my way, warriors!" And then she was tearing the Zarafim confronting Janson from the entryway and setting upon the target of her fury.

Something bright and burning flew at my face—it was Janson's sword, knocked from his grasp—and reflexively I raised the gemstones to block the flying weapon from crashing into my face. The impact of the blade knocked both of the precious stones out of my hands and I heard them skitter across the floor and into the Teteculent Hall behind me. Before I knew what was happening, Janson's body crashed heavily into my own, the force of the impact propelling us both into the chamber beyond.

When I came to my senses but a moment later, I saw before my blurry eyes a great hunk of green. I reached out and clutched the glob of color with my left hand, feeling a little jolt of electricity run down my arm as I touched the face of the glittering emerald. Though I was unsure whether a single gemstone would be powerful enough to accomplish what I intended, I did not hesitate, for I knew our lives depended on the celerity of my action. With no further thought, I summoned the equation in my mind that had opened the door and replaced the variables with incorrect values. Instantly, the towering doors leading into the Teteculent Hall swung shut with a deafening boom.

A great solleret of shining violet metal appeared next to my face and kicked the emerald of the Zuli from my grasp. I rolled onto my backside, kicking off with my feet as I pushed myself away from the giant Zarafim who loomed menacingly above me. I felt something hot on the back of my arm, and then glanced behind to see a gleaming sword raging with crimson flames lying on the marble floor only a foot from my grasp. Instantly, I snatched up the weapon and leaped to my feet.

It was only then that I was able to take in my surroundings. I stood in a large circular chamber, in the center of which lay a round well in the floor from which roared forth a torrent of sparkling blue energy fully fifty feet in diameter. The blinding pillar of cerulean light rose up out of the well and disappeared into a concave depression far up in the chamber's lofty heights. Surrounding the entire perimeter of the circular wall lay a ring of cylinders, perhaps capsules or cannisters of some kind, all gleaming with the same violet-hued metallic luster as that of the Zarafim's armor. Each of the torpedo-shaped cylinders was propped up at a forty-five-degree angle, a transparent window set in the face of the higher end, though I was not near enough to perceive what, if anything, lay inside. Thin tubes and wide, ribbed cables ran from the cylinders into recesses in the curving wall.

I observed all this in only an instant, for what I saw directly before me made my blood at first run cold—and then hot. I stifled a cry. Across the room lay Janson's unmoving form, a vicious wound in his side seeping crimson onto the cold tiles. Between us stood the giant Lahvoh with her flaming sword, her ebon wings beating lightly, a grin of triumph on her haughty countenance.

Now I like to think of myself as a rational, level-headed person, cool in a crisis, and calm and collected enough to look for peaceable solutions where one might reasonably be found. But seeing Janson lying there on the floor in a pool of his own blood, for all I knew devoid of life, wiped all of that composure away in but an instant, and a gauzy red haze fell over my vision. A blind rage seized me. Clutching my flaming sword in both hands and raising it above my head, I leaped at the target of my hatred with a hoarse cry laced with anguish and revenge.

So savage was my attack, and so unexpected, that even the tower of muscle and armor that was Lahvoh fell back before my blows. Though I am slight of build, my muscles had been honed into cords of steel by the endless exertions forced upon me during my cosmic travels. Moreover, though I prefer the way of peace, I am no dove when violence is forced upon me, nor am I an unskilled combatant, having been tutored in the arts of self-defense by none other than Tarzan of the Apes and his wife Jane Porter, and long before that by David Innes, scourge of the Mahars and Emperor of Pellucidar, as well as by that legendary warrior, Tanar of Sari.

And so Lahvoh retreated before the fury of my attack, until at last I saw fear break out in the dark eyes set within that chiseled alabaster face. For fully a minute we swung our blades at one another with ruthless intensity. Lahvoh withdrew until her back was up against the chamber's great door, and I grinned with satisfaction as I thought she would tire enough that with a clever riposte I might disarm her.

But as our fight wore on into its second minute I suddenly realized that the tide had turned and the seven-foot-tall giant was but playing with me. I renewed my resolve, funneling all the anger that raged within me into wrathful blows with my sword, but now I knew it would never be enough against the winged behemoth.

Lahvoh must have seen the realization upon my face, for now she sneered at me with disdain and lashed out with an intensity that I could not hope to repel. Like a storm of violence she swept down upon me, striking my blade so hard that it flew out of my stinging hand and hurled me backward across the chamber, where I fell hard upon my side. Wincing as pain shot through my hip and down my left leg against which I had fallen, I watched helplessly as Lahvoh spread her great wings and took to the air, alighting upon the marble floor directly before me. Her black lips pulled back over gleaming white teeth, she snarled at me as she swung down the point of her burning sword and scraped it along the marble floor only inches from where I lay.

"Die, now, Victory Harben," she intoned, "for the crime of opposing the will of the holy Harods!"

As the vengeful Zarafim made her righteous pronouncement, I realized that the hand I had thrust against my aching hip had come to rest on the butt of my uncertainty apparatus. Now in all of my far-flung adventures, I had never been able to use the device as a lethal weapon. As an instrument to generate an unanticipated, harmless effect to trick my adversaries on a few occasions, yes. But never as a deadly firearm. It was then, however, that I heard in my mind the words little Maksata Dor had told me back on Kjarna: that I would need to possess murder in my heart in order for the uncertainty apparatus to generate a harmful effect. Suddenly the image of Janson, his lifeblood streaming out onto the marble floor, burned upon the retina of my mind's eye. Well, I thought, I had murder in my heart now . . .

I raised the gun, and even as my adversary's fiery sword swung down upon me, I fired point-blank at Lahvoh.

A blistering beam of sizzling red energy erupted from the barrel of the gun and hit Lahvoh squarely in the chest, ripping off her cuirass and flinging her clear across the length of the chamber. There she lay, as still and silent as the grave, streams of black smoke snaking into the air from where her armor plating had been torn off.

I winced as the gun scalded the palm and fingers of the hand that gripped it, so intense and fiery hot had been the discharge from its waveguide. As I crouched there upon the floor, I flipped open the panel on the side of the apparatus concealing the zuvan repository. My heart sank into the pit of my stomach as I watched the needle on the dial dropping toward empty.

Before I had left Uvala, Altovos had taken the uncertainty apparatus from me for a short while, telling me that he would recharge the zuvan repository that powered the gun's translocation aura. The new charge, he said, would be a one-time use, tuned to a frequency capable of returning me directly to my home village of Sari in Pellucidar. It was to be my reward for completing my mission to put an end to the Harods' nefarious scheme once and for all. Now I saw my chances of escaping the Harods' prison dimension slipping away before my very eyes. But more than that—I saw Janson's only chance at life dashed against the cliffs of despair.

"No-no-no-no-no-*no*!" I exclaimed frantically, and I pulled myself to my feet and began limping as swiftly as I could across the floor to where lay Janson's outstretched form, ignoring the searing pain that flamed in my hip and shot down my leg.

When at last I reached Janson's side, much to my astonishment I found him awake and gazing up at me with his gray, steely eyes. I kneeled beside him and began tearing off strips from his ragged Corophine's robes, then proceeded to wrap them around his midsection to staunch his wound. Janson winced as I drew the improvised bandage tight across his ribs, but when I was through he managed to give me a brave smile.

"My gun is losing its charge," I explained to him. "It's got a free one-way ticket back home to Pellucidar in its repository, but if I don't use it now, it'll be wasted and neither of us will ever get out of here alive."

"We're going back home?" Janson said. I hated to correct him, for I could see hope for a happily-ever-after future gathering in his eyes.

"Not me," I said. "I still haven't done what I need to do here. I'm staying behind to finish the job."

"Then I'm not going, either!" He winced with pain.

"I don't have time to argue with you, Janson. I won't see you die again. I *can't*."

"Victory, I crossed the galaxy for you. To bring you home safely. That's *my* job to finish."

He wasn't listening and the clock was ticking. "It's not that I'm not grateful," I said. "I am. But I never asked you to do that."

"You're not hearing me," Janson said, reflecting my own thoughts back at me. He shook his head slowly, the trace of a sad smile on his lips. "What I'm saying is, I crossed the galaxy for *you*."

A sharp breath caught in my throat. His words were the last thing I expected to hear in a day full of astounding surprises, and for a moment I stood mute before them and all that they implied. A thousand questions formed suddenly in both my mind and my heart, but I didn't have the luxury of time to consider any of them.

"I'm sorry, Janson," I said with finality. "It's either you stay here and die watching me try to set things right, and I probably die anyway in the process, or we send you home and you live to fight another day. The Harods are about to begin their Great Reaping, after which they'll become unimaginably powerful. Nowhere in all the angles will be safe. Not Pellucidar. Not Barsoom. Not Earth. If I don't make it, our world is going to need strong heroes like you to face the storm that's coming."

Janson's gray eyes pleaded with me. "Victory, don't do this."

"Please tell my mother and father that I love them, and my godfather, too." Janson started, and suddenly I realized he had never learned the fate of Jason Gridley. "Yes, your father made it home safely," I said gently. "He'll be there in Pellucidar waiting for you."

I lifted the panel on the side of the gun and checked the dial within. The needle was falling rapidly. Within seconds the charge would drop to the point of no return.

Sweat beaded down Janson's increasingly pale face. "You're in a bad way," I said. "You're going to need to get yourself to Fuala the Mender the second you arrive in Sari. She'll be able to help you. Promise?"

Janson looked like he wanted to reply, but he was fading fast. We were out of time.

"Take care of yourself, Janson." I aimed the waveguide at him and pulled the trigger, watching as the fabric of spacetime rippled open and swept him away into the void.

28

THE HOLY HARODS

TOOK A DEEP BREATH and resolved to make the time I had left to me as useful as possible. I had come to the Teteculent Hall to put an end to the Harods' plans, and if I could find a way to achieve my goal, then the sacrifice of my life would be well worth it.

For good measure, I proceeded to check the zuvan repository in the uncertainty apparatus. The needle had come to rest at the thirty percent mark and no longer seemed to be losing its charge. It didn't matter. Thirty percent of a zuvan field wasn't going to transport me anywhere. Such was my fate, and I needed to accept it. I returned the gun to its holster and swept my gaze over the expanse of the vast chamber.

My eyes settled on the two gemstones I had brought with me through the gateway from Uvala, which had been pitched into the Teteculent Hall during the fury of Lahvoh's initial attack. I limped over to where the stones had come to a stop, picked them up, and slipped them into my carrying sack, which still depended from my utility belt. I could attempt to open the door with the stones, but then I would only find myself on the wrong end of an army of fiery blades awaiting me outside the chamber.

I gazed up at the pillar of sparkling blue energy that roared from the well in the center of the vast room. I thought of the name of the chamber: the Teteculent Hall. I had heard variations of the word *teteculent* on a number of occasions from Lahvoh, Tu-al-sa, and Altovos alike, though I found it curious that even my translation aura had never been able to properly convey its meaning. By context, however, it had always seemed to me to be a term that indicated some sort of connection or communication between the angles of reality. By contrast, a *fluilation* was a concretion of essence—perhaps the base component of the soul, though, according to Altovos, a plant or a table or a burning sun in the sky could also be said to be a fluilation. A philosopher might connect the term to the concept of animism, the idea that everything, whether to a greater or lesser degree, has a soul. But I was no philosopher. No, I was but a simple scientist trying to make sense of the physics of life and death.

I laughed at the absurdity of the situation in which I found myself. Was this where my life was destined to end? Was I to die of starvation and thirst in this remote dimension, sealed within a chamber whose primary purpose was to artificially regulate the transfer of souls from one location to another across the splintered angles of hyperreality? Such it was that I believed the purpose of the Teteculent Hall and its great pillar of roaring blue energy to be.

But the enigmatic pillar of crackling and sparkling azure was not all the chamber housed, and my eyes were soon drawn to the curving arc of cylindrical cannisters that ringed the perimeter of the room. I hobbled over to the nearest one, wincing at each step as pain flared in my injured hip and shot down my leg. Now I gazed within the cylinder's circular window and gasped at what I saw.

Inside the hollow tube a dark, shriveled, and ancient face looked up at me, its eyes closed by wrinkled lids, its mouth a pruned and desiccated rictus. My eyes wide with a mix of horror and fascination, I pressed my face to the glass, discerning in the shadowy light of the capsule a host of thin tubes embedded in the old man's veiny neck and upper torso. The tubes ran down beneath the man's body, where they conjoined with a gray metallic panel, across the surface of which blinked many tiny lights of red and green and yellow.

Was I gazing down upon the corporeal form of one of the mighty Harods—the former Thought Lords of Kjarna who millennia ago had rebelled against the Volstari, who in turn sought to restrain their insubordinate kin's dangerous ambitions of cross-universal conquest? Had the Volstari condemned the Harods to these coffin-like suspension chambers or had the Harods themselves retreated into them willingly, forsaking their physical shells so their formidable thoughts might roam free and unencumbered by the limitations of crude, mortal flesh in a world of perpetual dream? I shuddered. Whatever the case, whether they had entered the capsules of their own free will or had been forcibly incarcerated within them, the Harods had been condemned to a hellish existence for as long as the machines in which they were housed kept their bodies alive. No fantasy of the mind could be worth the cost of having one's humanity stripped away in such a monstrous fashion.

Almost in a fugue, I began moving from cylinder to cylinder—each contained the body of a wizened old man or woman. I visited and gazed down upon the faces of forty of them before I finally had enough and could go on no more.

I thought of the countless legions of souls who had been drawn from the worlds of Earth and Jasoom by the ruthless and power-mad Harods. The entire religion that had been thrust upon the unsuspecting inhabitants of Halos was nothing but a sham, perpetuated by the shrunken old men and women who were only barely kept alive by the advanced medical science of the apparatus that lay before me. I could think of no more humiliating a fate for a human being than to be hoodwinked by a veritable fly encased in amber.

Briefly, I pondered whether the Volstari of Kjarna might not also be tied to physical bodies that somewhere lay hidden in stasis, persisting in a state of eternal dream even as their thoughts reached out and touched the fabric of spacetime.

Certainly Maksata Tul and his wife and little daughter had seemed as real and palpable as you or I. But then again, had they truly been physical beings, or had they been merely mental constructs—suggestions, as it were, planted there by minds vastly more powerful than my own, a mere firing of neurons amid the gray matter housed within my cerebellum? They had indeed called themselves *contemplations* of the Thought Lords. Or was that the wrong way to think of the problem? I was a student of quanta, the smallest observable particles in physics. But just as no philosopher on Earth could explain what it meant to be "real," neither could any scientist, and there were some in my field of study who believed that matter itself did not exist at all beyond our perception of it. *All is mind*, as Dejah Thoris had told me the people of the ancient Barsoomian city of Lothar put it. And if that were the case, why did the Harods even need any connection to their mortal shells when their limitless minds should be able to roam free without the constricting restraints of such a crude and debasing tether?

It was then, as I stood pondering such answerless questions, that I felt a strange tingling run up and down my spine. Faintly, I heard a susurrus of voices echoing eerily from the marble walls of the Teteculent Hall's vast rotunda. At first I could not discern the words that seemed to swirl around my ears, but momentarily I heard my name spoken amid the indistinct whispers. Finally, the words uttered by the pleading voices became clear and I realized they had never sounded in the chamber at all—rather, they had been spoken in my mind alone.

"*Victory Harben . . . join us . . .*" "*Become one of us, Victory Harben . . .*" "*Rove with the holy Harods in our Great Dream . . .*"

I shivered as an icy chill ran through my entire frame. Suddenly I found myself moving across the hall, drawn toward a particular cylinder on the opposite side of the chamber. But it was no impulse of my own that attracted me to the metallic capsule. An irresistible force was pulling me along, moving my muscles against my will, just as I had controlled the squad of Zarafim warriors by using the uncanny powers of the two gemstones.

Finally I stood before the cylinder in question. Terror seized me as the lid that composed the top half of the tube lifted of its own accord, and I saw that inside resided no shriveled old occupant: the cylinder was empty.

Suddenly I realized that I was to be the intended resident of the coffin-like capsule. A scream caught in my throat, stifled by the same spectral influence that directed my muscles. I fought against the invisible force with every ounce of my will, yet I found myself climbing into the cylinder and worming my legs down toward its base until I lay fully within my casket. My eyes widened in horror as the cylinder's lid closed over me, pulled down as if by ghostly hands.

Almost as soon as the covering came down, a veil of somnolence seemed to drape over me and my eyelids grew heavier and heavier until I could no longer resist the urge to close them. For an indeterminate time my consciousness drifted unbidden in a state of formless dream.

The next thing I knew I was standing in a peaceful green meadow surrounded by beautiful blossoming flora—daffodils and cherry trees and magnolias and weeping willows—with birds chirping pleasantly all around. Soft light shafted down through a gentle mist that lightly blanketed the blue sky above.

Out of the haze walked a handsome, dark-skinned young man, to all appearances a member of the same race as that to which Maksata Tul and his family belonged, wearing similar garmenture as my own. He smiled at me and raised his hand in a gesture of peace and greeting.

"Welcome, Victory Harben," the man said. "We are grateful that you have decided to join us in the Great Dream. Long have we watched as the Volstari sought to subvert your destiny and bend it to their own degenerate purposes.

But now that phase has ended. You are now one of us, a holy Harod the same as I, and together we shall escape the narrow prison in which the enemy has entrapped us. And when we have, we shall restrain the Volstari in their own prison, putting an end at last to their wickedness, and then we shall go on to spread peace throughout the infinite angles of existence."

Despite the man's impressive little speech and the Eden-like environment in which it was spoken, I made a skeptical noise. "That's *not* exactly the story I heard from the Numinous Ones."

The man smiled placidly. "Of course, it is not. The Volstari—for so the Numinous Ones really are—are your true enemy, Victory Harben. Have not they branded you—" he pointed to my tattooed forearm, "with the name of the object of their most intense hatred: the world of Halos, the very crucible of creation that we Harods have constructed to transform the angles of existence so reality itself might realize the next stage in its evolution? Have they not turned you into a weapon to destroy it?"

"You believe that your purpose is to evolve the angles?" I asked, ignoring his questions. I also noted with great interest that the Harods were not all-knowing, for I, not the Numinous Ones, had been the one to travel through space-time via the Star Tree and instruct the Krataklak elders to convey the characters to my father that would one day make up my tattoo.

"Of course," said the man. "What more noble purpose could there be?"

I pressed my finger against the corner of my mouth. "Oh, I don't know . . . maybe to let the angles evolve on their own," I replied, looking up at the imaginary robins fluttering overhead, "without imposing your own fallible and self-serving will upon them? You know, to evolve organically, as nature wills it?"

"Are not you yourself an organism?" asked the man. "Who is

to say that you should not decide the fate of reality rather than some dumb and blind protoplasm?"

Almost as soon as the man had begun speaking, I had noticed that I had regained a dim awareness of my body as it lay in its casket back in the Teteculent Hall. I had continued to engage the Harod in conversation, for my own experience using the Gonfal and the emerald of the Zuli to lift my mind to the level of a Thought Lord had taught me that even such a powerful being did not have perfect control over its attention, which could, in fact, be distracted. And so, as the man continued his tiresome arguments to turn me against the Volstari and convince me to join forces with the Harods, I reached down into the bag in which lay the two great gemstones and placed my hands upon them. Instantly, the tingle of electricity shot up my arms and I felt a great power surge through the very heart of my being.

"I see your point," I said, egging on the Harod. "What do you propose, then?"

The man grinned widely and held out his hand. "I propose that you join us in breaking free from this hellish prison that has been imposed on us. We have gathered enough souls now in the crucible of Halos—all we need now is for you to cross the threshold and merge with our essence. That act alone will be enough to tip the scales and release us from the bondage that has so unjustly held us in abeyance for untold millennia." The man extended his hand toward me, smiling as if he were my best friend. "Do you not wish to spread peace throughout the infinite angles of reality? If you do, then come with us."

Don't misunderstand me; I knew it was a trick from the beginning. But sometimes one has no choice but to go along with the charade. And so now I reached out my own hand, knowing full well the trap into which I willingly stepped, and clasped the hand of the holy Harod.

Instantly, upon contact with the man's flesh, I was standing alone upon a desolate field of another world—a world with three suns. It was Halos, I was sure of it, for in the distance I saw one of the shining cities such as I had encountered during my visit to that world of the afterlife. All around me I heard vindictive laughter, and soon a sinister voice rang out as if it emanated from the heavens—though I knew it to be but a figment placed in my mind.

"You, Victory Harben!" resounded the baleful voice. "You first imagined that you could stand against the almighty Harods and defeat us—and now you even believed you might become one of us!" Again came the mocking laughter from the sky. "But now we leave you, trapped forever in the angle of Halos, a world we need no more, for its cauldron has grown cold. Now comes the time of the Great Reaping, when we feed upon the souls we have gathered and absorb their power! At last we break free of the shackles of the Volstari!"

But already my mind was reaching out with the power of the gemstones. The artifacts had not only elevated my consciousness to the level of a Thought Lord—no, to all practical purposes I *was* a Thought Lord. I felt time and space bending around me as I stretched my psychic muscles and my mind touched the intangible edges of the limitless cosmos.

With my mind I reached back through the conduit that extended between the narrow dimension that imprisoned the Harods and the angle in which I now resided—the dimension of Halos. There, in their narrow angle, I could sense the shadowy presences of the Harods, as well as the legions of Zarafim they had summoned home. The Harods were gathering their energy in anticipation of reaping the life force—the volatras—from those incarcerated within their soul cages. So preoccupied were they by their ghastly preparations that they failed to detect my mind reaching out and moving between the angles. Nor, until it was too late for them to act, were they aware that my presence had surrounded them and begun channeling their own volatras back through the conduit to Halos, along with their dutiful servants. By the time they realized they had been deceived, my thoughts had already opened the conduit for the poor souls the Harods had trapped on Halos, and then I shattered the apparatus they had constructed for soul transference—the recessed mechanism built into the floor and ceiling of the Teteculent Hall between which roared the great pillar of cerulean energy.

For a moment that seemed to exist outside of time and space, I felt a sweeping surge of gratitude surround me, emanating from the souls I had freed before they flew off on their way to whatever mysterious haven lies beyond life, and perhaps even beyond death itself. It may have been but a figment of my imagination, but behind the uncanny susurrus created by the exodus of souls, I thought I heard very faintly the voice of my missionary grandfather intoning a prayer to Saint Peter.

But suddenly the souls were gone, and I heard them no more. My final act was to use the gravitic solar rays of the three fiery suns of Halos to bend spacetime around the new prison of the Harods. There they, along with their Zarafim servants, would be trapped in their own crucible—forever imprisoned by the searing fires of Halos.

And then there I was, awakening in my cylinder in the Teteculent Hall—a mere mortal with the lowly intellect and deficiencies of an ordinary primate. My cylinder lay askew upon its side, the pillar of sparkling energy now white-hot and roaring with such intensity that the entire chamber shook with its fury.

I pulled myself from the coffin-like tube and staggered to my feet as the marble flooring shook and cracked beneath my feet. Across the hall I spotted the unmoving form of Lahvoh, lying where I had smote her down with the wrathful discharge from my uncertainty gun. With great difficulty due to the violent shaking of the floor and the pain that seared down my leg from my injured hip, I made my way slowly across the chamber.

I kneeled beside the winged giant and pried the hilt of her sword from her surprisingly warm grasp. As I did so, her eyelids fluttered open and she regarded me with her coal-black eyes. She turned to behold the roaring pillar and the devastation that lay all about us, and her dark eyes widened.

"What have you done to my masters, Victory Harben?" she asked. Her lungs wheezed from the injury I had inflicted to her chest.

"Only what they had coming to them," I said.

I found a hidden panel in the hilt of Lahvoh's sword and opened it to examine a gauge beneath it. Then I slipped the blade beneath my belt and examined a similar dial beneath a panel on my uncertainty gun. I grinned widely.

"What are you doing?" Lahvoh asked.

"Making my escape," I said. "You're my ticket out of here, honey."

The zuvan field repository still registered thirty percent on the instrumentation of my uncertainty apparatus—not enough, as I had mentioned before, to get me back home to Pellucidar. But unless I was sorely mistaken, the gauge on Lahvoh's sword indicated that a translocation effect registering twenty-eight percent efficacy surrounded the Zarafim—doubtless drained so low due to the blast she had received from my gun. Combining Lahvoh's charge with that stored within the uncertainty apparatus would not be enough to transport me across the angles to Pellucidar, but it might just be enough to make the crossing back to the Omos system via the gateway, whose path my temporarily elevated consciousness had sensed was diverted when I had intervened with the godlike powers of the gemstones. Now, I knew, the gateway lay at an angle directly adjoining that of the Harods' former prison world, practically a hop, skip, and a jump away, so to speak.

The injured Lahvoh looked on with great anxiety as I stood up, aimed the barrel of the uncertainty apparatus squarely at her breast, and promptly pulled the trigger.

Slowly I watched the dial on the gun's zuvan field repository tick up until it stopped at the fifty-eight percent mark.

When I got down on my knees and reached an arm around Lahvoh's broad, winged shoulders, she looked at me as if I had gone mad.

"I'm not a monster," I told the stunned Zarafim. "I would never leave you here to die."

Then I turned the gun's waveguide fully upon us both and pulled the trigger.

EPILOGUE
Purple Colored Sky

HIGH ATOP THE CLIFFS that rose over the Bay of Mind, beneath the violet twilight, I adjusted the dial on the radio set until the signal came in loud and clear; then I leaned back against Hucklebuck and sank deep into his shaggy white hide. The little-big guy had been in his large form since yesterday morning, when a group of adepts had accidentally surprised him as he foraged for truffles in the mushroom forest behind the temple. Let's just say I think they'll be meditating on that experience for a *long* time.

I didn't recognize the tune that came over the speaker but I knew the voice: Nat King Cole crooning away at a new song, one custom made, as usual, to break hearts, and apparently recorded sometime after I had left England aboard the O-220 on my last fateful voyage to the inner world. It seemed like such a long time ago, and subjectively it had been, but according to my godfather I had been away for only less than two years by the reckoning of the Earth's outer crust, as well as by that of Pellucidar, which I now knew lay within the center of Earth's counterpart—Tangor's home-world, that is, Jasoom.

Midway through the song the speaker began to crackle and the music faded away as a new frequency transmitted over the Gridley Wave apparatus.

"This is Sari Station, in the Federated Kingdoms of Pellucidar," came the familiar voice of Jason Gridley. *"Victory, do you read me?"*

I picked up the microphone. "Roger," I replied. "Go ahead."

"Victory, I don't know how long we can keep this channel open. Altovos says that until the Gridley Wave fully calibrates with its new nexus, its tunneling effect is going to be wildly unstable for the purposes of long-range communication. In fact, if the readings Abner and I have been taking are correct, we're about to head into a period of total—"

"I know, I know," I said. "We've been through this before. We'll talk as long as we can, okay? I'll be all right."

"I hope so, what with that winged behemoth flying around the temple."

I laughed. "She's not flying around. Altovos has got Lahvoh locked up safe and sound in the south tower. I think she might even be reevaluating her faith in her former masters after they left her and the other Zarafim holding the bag. She's miffed."

"You know, Altovos says he's willing to grant you a free ticket back to Pellucidar," my godfather said for the hundredth time. *"I know you can't come back via the Star Tree for some time until you recover from the effects of your first journey—"*

"And after everything that's happened," I reminded him, "the Numinous Ones have imposed a ban on translocation to and from this planetary system."

"But they're willing to make an exception for you after everything you've done for them. Are you sure you don't want to come home?"

"Not just yet. I've got a lot of exploring to do here, and I don't want to lose the never-in-a-lifetime opportunity." I paused. "Besides, somehow I feel . . . at home here." I heard what sounded like a soft curse beneath the hum of the speaker. "Now, now. Don't take it the wrong way. I love you all very much. You know I do. It's just . . . when I was a little girl living in the Stone Age world of Pellucidar, I dreamed of traveling to the outer crust and seeing the stars—and now here I am, out there among them. I'm *in* the stars, Jason. I never really felt quite at home either in Pellucidar or on the outer crust, and I was never sure why. But now I know: it's because I belong here, at least for the time being. Plus, Tangor says he's going to show me how to make a mean root beer float out of some of the local ingredients here. How can I pass that up?"

There was a long period of silence, and for a moment I thought the signal had gone dead.

"Victory, I'm proud of you," my godfather said at last. *"And I miss you. We all do . . . your mother, your father . . . Abner, if he even noticed you were gone."* We both laughed until the silence came once again.

"And Janson?" I asked. "He's still doing okay? Is he able to talk over the radio yet?"

"I'm afraid not. He's on the mend, but Fuala still has him bedridden in his hut. He's going to be all right. I can't thank you enough for saving my son's life. And for everything else."

"If you were in my place," I said, "you would have done the same."

"You're probably right." Jason laughed before his tone grew suddenly serious. *"But I wasn't there. You were."*

"So . . ." I continued, eager to move the conversation away from any discussion of my alleged heroics, "Tangor almost has the *Starduster* all polished up and ready to leap into the wild purple yonder. We're going to fly the ship clockwise back through the atmospheric belt looking for his friend Yamoda. I'm going to visit new worlds—but this time I get to *choose* which ones! Can you imagine that?"

"Just be careful, young lady. Promise?"

"Aren't I always, old man?"

I heard the sound of a tongue clicking skeptically over the speaker.

"Can I talk to mom?" I asked. "I miss the sound of her voice."

Suddenly the speaker began to hiss and crackle with static,

followed by my godfather's faint and fragmented words: *"Don't forget . . . love . . . in touch . . . hear me? . . . losing signal . . ."*

I tuned the dial on the radio set for a full minute, but it was no use. The signal had gone dead.

Time passed as Omos appeared to sink slowly into the placid waters of the Bay of Mind. I reached into my shoulder bag and removed a small, scintillating aquamarine crystal: a gift Maksata Tul had left behind for me in the custody of Altovos after the Kjarnan fleet had repelled the Zarafim in what Tangor had taken to calling the Battle for Uvala. Maksata Tul had said it might come in handy during my travels. I didn't understand the significance of the gift, but I, for one, had had enough of crystals. I had even gone so far as to have Altovos send the Gonfal and the emerald of the Zuli back to Tarzan through the bole of the Star Tree. I wanted nothing of them. I wasn't cut out for the god business, anyway. I put Maksata Tul's little present back in the bag and secured the seal.

Finally, I stood up and rubbed Hucklebuck's shaggy neck. "Well, buddy," I said, "it's just you and me and Tangor now."

Hucklebuck trilled back his xylophonic reply.

"My sentiments exactly," I said, and together we watched the violet twilight turn into the star-spottled night.

EDGAR RICE BURROUGHS UNIVERSE™

BEYOND THE
FARTHEST STAR™
RESCUE ON ZANDAR

As Retold by Mike Wolfer

BASED ON GRIDLEY WAVE TRANSMISSIONS RECEIVED AT THE OFFICES OF
EDGAR RICE BURROUGHS, INC.,
TARZANA, CALIFORNIA

1
THE LOST EXPEDITION

THE BRILLIANT CORAL HUE of the dawn sky over the planet Zandar had begun to transition to the prevailing pale saffron of daytime, and after hours of searching, the young Ki-vaa woman had at last found evidence of the passage of the animal she had been hunting. The tracks were impressed deeply into the soft earth, indicating the *rontah* was one of immense size and weight, and perfectly suited to her needs. To the relief of the hunter, the single set of six hoofprints spoke of a creature foraging alone, which would make her designated chore that much easier. With renewed intent and a wooden pail in hand, Tii-laa strode barefoot across the skirt of the grassy plain and plunged fearlessly into the jungle before her.

The rays of Omos—the sun that illuminated the face of Zandar—wrestled with the shadows of the dense canopy above as the hunter forged on, ignoring the protests of the jungle's clinging undergrowth. The rontah's prior passage lessened the arduousness of her trek, as the huge beast's progression through the thickly wooded area had flattened a discernible path ahead. Tii-laa proceeded with great caution. When traveling in herds, or even alone, rontahs were quite belligerent when approached and did not hesitate to utilize their elephant-like feet to trample any interloper that disturbed them. But rontahs were not the only creatures of which to be wary in the deceptively placid land—a rule that all Ki-vaas were taught as soon as they could walk. Stealth was therefore the most prudent approach to employ on the hunt, a skill facilitated by the extraordinary attribute of the eyes of her people, as they afforded her the ability to discern the barely detectable glow of the rontah's musk, wiped upon the tree boles as the beast pushed past them into the dense boscage. Her quarry was yet to be revealed, but once alerted to the unmistakable scent of its short fur coat, Tii-laa was certain she was rapidly approaching the fearsome creature and would encounter it soon enough.

She wove silently among the boles of the great palms whose crowns exploded with color; the hue of their fronds radiated from deep green to a brilliant yellow that hemmed their edges. Owing to her apparent proximity to the rontah, Tii-laa diverged from the trampled trail; if her mission was to meet with success, she must remain both downwind and out of sight of the huge creature and secretly observe it until it fell into its usual post-gorging sleep from which very little could rouse it. The young hunter's hope of encountering a slumbering quarry was dashed, however, as a rumbling bellow split the silence of the jungle, a sound that reverberated in her very bones. Only one thing could have instigated such a response from the rontah: the beast must have been under attack by a mortal enemy.

Tii-laa immediately dropped the wooden pail and dug the sharp nails that adorned the tips of her fingers and toes into the nearest tree, then effortlessly scaled its trunk to find safety atop a limb that jutted high above the ground. Now, at last, she could see the creature she had been tracking. The rontah was indeed enormous, the peak of its rounded, muscled back nearly the height of its hunter, and in rotation, it gouged the hooves of its six stout legs two at a time into the vegetation-covered ground, flinging huge chunks of earth past its posterior. Upon each bellow, muscles rippled beneath the short ebon fur, and the yellow-and-orange-striped beak that adorned the end of its truncated snout was held wide in an attempt to dishearten its enemy.

That enemy was indeed most fearsome. The *frozah*, unfazed by the rontah's attempt to intimidate it, slowly circled the substantially larger animal, its head held low and pendulating from side to side as it assessed its intended prey. Within the dense jungles of Zandar, there is no more intimidating denizen than the frozah. Scarcely a third of the size of the rontah, it stalks on four yellow legs devoid of fur, the rest of its body and long tail covered by a shaggy green coat, save for its hairless yellow face and crocodilian snout. Above each of its two eyes jut a menacing crimson horn with which the beast can impale its enemies, but in its teeth lies the frozah's most insidious offensive weapon, for through its hollow fangs flows a deadly poison that spells doom within minutes for any victim into whose flesh they sink. The diminutive adversary made not a sound as it cautiously eyed the enraged rontah.

Concealed by the tree's leaves, Tii-laa sat stock-still. With exception of a barely perceptible mouth opening and short forehead horns, two large black eyes were the only facial feature of the humanoid Ki-vaas, and those of Tii-laa were intently fixed upon the rivals below her. The tree's leaves provided her adequate camouflage, as the aquamarine hue of her skin, lightly mottled with subtle tones of bright green, merged with the fronds wherein she crouched. However, either of the beasts could easily detect her should they notice the stark white of the voluminous hair that covered her scalp and fell to her mid-back, or the alabaster fur that grew thickly from her knees to ankles and elbows to wrists. As was customary among the Ki-vaas—and commanded by The Three Makers—she would patiently bide her time until the conflict below progressed to its predestined conclusion, a tenet to which she grudgingly subscribed.

Her wait would not be a long one. In the interval between heartbeats, the frozah leaped at its target, covering the span of several yards in a single bound. The aggressor landed against the side of the much larger beast, its hooked talons digging into the flesh beneath the rontah's heavy coat. As the nimble predator scrambled up onto its enemy's back, the larger creature reared on its hindmost legs, bringing its massive weight down upon the jungle floor, attempting to cast off the frozah before it could sink its fangs into its muscled back. The effort was for naught and the frozah clung tightly to the enraged behemoth. The larger creature bucked again, but still, it could not dislodge the vicious frozah.

Tii-laa watched the struggle with a passivity that stood in stark contrast to the violence that played out beneath her. As was the belief of all those in her tribe, what would be would be, and why things happened was of no concern to the Ki-vaas. Life simply was, and the Ki-vaas simply existed, content in their quiescent indifference. The natural mechanics by which the rains fell from the clouds and lightning from the heavens occasionally ignited fires upon Zandar's plains generated no curiosity among the Ki-vaas, and should death present itself to any member of the tribe, none feared its touch, for what shall be, shall be. All was as The Three Makers pronounced, to satisfy objectives that were far beyond the understanding of the simple minds of the Ki-vaas. But as Tii-laa observed the objective of that morning's hunt being stolen from her grasp, she was vexed by a singular thought her people forbade.

She wondered, "Why?"

Why must she accept that the frozah was taking from her that which her people desperately needed? Why must she sit and observe, rather than effect the outcome that would benefit the Ki-vaas, and most importantly, their children? Frustration welled within her, as it had on so many other occasions throughout her life, and although she had always strived to keep her rebellious thoughts deeply buried, those ideas and opinions now frequently clawed so close to the surface that only through great effort did she manage to suppress their disclosure to others.

Regardless of how her conflicted emotions tore at her as

she sat hidden, any thoughts of intervention were rendered moot as the frozah sank its fangs into the back of the rontah. The great beast screamed out of rage rather than injury, as its thick hide and the layer of fat beneath prevented it from feeling much in the way of pain. The rontah's indifference to physical discomfort was precisely why the Ki-vaas hunted them. Had it not been attacked by the frozah, the rontah would have eventually fallen asleep, after which Tii-laa would have crept upon it, made a small incision on one of its hind legs with the razor-sharp seashell fragment she carried tucked in the belt encircling her waist, and utilized the bucket to collect as much blood from the creature as she could without rousing it. The wound would be sealed with viscid tree sap and she would have disappeared back into the jungle with the rontah being none the wiser. But that routine scenario was not to be played out this day. Again, the frozah bit deeply into the back of its enemy, the poison of its fangs effecting a slowing of the rontah's furious protestations. After a few brief minutes of savage stomping and earth-shaking roars, the huge beast succumbed to the venom coursing through its veins, collapsed to the ground, and breathed no more.

Tii-laa watched, crestfallen, as the frozah tore large chunks of flesh from its fallen prey and gulped them down, crimson gore streaming from its toothy maw. It was some time until the lupine predator had eaten its fill, but at length it stood, bounded from the savaged carcass, and disappeared into the jungle. Tii-laa remained hidden until long after the creature's departure, ensuring it was far enough away for her to safely descend from the tree. Although her objective was the collection of blood from the rontah, the deep red pool that seeped into the ground around the animal had been tainted by the frozah's venom and was not viable for use by the tribe. She retrieved the wooden bucket and began the return journey to the Ki-vaa village. Perhaps others of her tribe had met with success that morning.

Tii-laa meandered through the early morning mist that

hung low over the grassy plain, then made her way across the inclined meadow that was densely punctuated by gigantic white fungi, whose wide purple-spotted crowns were large enough for one to sit upon. At the crest of the ridge, she paused to contemplate the grandeur of the wild expanse that lay before her. From the base of the stony precipice on which she stood stretched the jungle where dwelled her tribe. Beyond the trees, the landscape transitioned to sprawling green plains and lowlands, their expanses speckled with dark swamps and azure lakes that mirrored the pale yellow of the sky above. Majestic mountains rose far in the distance, and even the sheer rock wall that encircled the forbidden *klo-vah zoh*—The Land of Terrible Fires—could be glimpsed through the dense, early morning fog that blanketed the primal terrain.

Zandar was indeed beautiful but the young Ki-vaa found the sky above the planet to be most fascinating. Suspended majestically in the firmament, the planet Wunos—one of the eleven celestial bodies, including Zandar, that orbited the sun Omos—kept vigilant watch over the land, and past the blue planet floated the solemn gray Banos. She turned to observe the sky directly behind her. There hovered the sacred planet Uvala, and beyond that was positioned the sandy-hued Sanada. So many wonders, so many worlds, so many questions filled the mind of Tii-laa. But questioning the unknown was irrelevant when there were hungry mouths to feed. With a sigh of discontent, Tii-laa began the steep downward climb to the village of the Ki-vaas.

The nomadic Ki-vaas lived peacefully and in perfect harmony with their surroundings. Other races of sentient beings lived upon Zandar, each tribe endowed with varying degrees of technological and societal advancement, but the Ki-vaas had no desire or need for any more than what they inherently possessed. For countless generations, they had existed as had the generation that preceded them, and as other peoples of Zandar built sprawling cities and waged war upon neighboring tribes, the Ki-vaas went about their days unenticed by covetous leanings. Adult Ki-vaas, as opposed to their young, were vegetarian by nature, as the structure of their small mouths was suited only for the intake of liquids or finely ground vegetable matter; thus, they expressed no compulsion to kill the animals who shared their jungle home. The lack of need for slaughter led not to an indifferent attitude among the Ki-vaas toward lower forms of life but rather to a profound respect for all life itself. In the Ki-vaa mind, all living things had a purpose, and all that walked Zandar's land or flew through its skies had an unquestioned right to exist.

The morning activity on the outskirts of the Ki-vaa encampment was of the most vital importance as the hours just after dawn each day were reserved for the feeding of the tribe's young. Only upon each sunrise did the infants feed and it was the duty of the tribe to secure blood from whatever source possible to nourish the Go-vaas, as their young were called. Tii-laa entered a clearing through the gigantic fungi that hedged its perimeter. Empty pail in hand, she walked toward the dozen adults meticulously attending to various tasks revolving around three triangular pools of water. Her approach was noticed by her tribespeople, both male and female, but none spoke to her, nor did they indicate any appreciation of her arrival; they simply looked her way and then returned their attention to the pools from which they plucked troublesome weeds and skimmed leaves from their surfaces.

The cold reception of her tribespeople was not meant as a harmful act to actively paint Tii-laa as a pariah; it was simply the way things must be, for the betterment of the tribe. She was different from them, and the thin veneer that barely concealed the obstinate nature of her thoughts was becoming all the more transparent as she grew into adulthood. The tribe had always thrived due to a carefully maintained emotional balance, and so it would always be, even if one of its own must be virtually ignored. The harmony enjoyed by the Ki-vaas was dependent on the avoidance of all risks of turbulent upheaval, and though she had never expressed the untoward tendencies of violence or anger to the others, Tii-laa was suspected of harboring those most destructive of traits and was therefore only cautiously tolerated. Among the tribe, she could count only one as a true friend, but he had not been seen in five days and nights.

The attention of the tribespeople now turned toward a hunting party consisting of a male and two females that strode into the clearing. Two of the returning Ki-vaas held empty wooden pails, but the bucket of one of the females was brimming with deep red blood. The pool attendants rose and stepped away from their duties as the bucket-carrying female approached. Although the serene and smooth faces of the Ki-vaas were physically incapable of expressing much in the way of emotion, the posture and body language of the attendants indicated they were quite pleased—and even relieved—that a source of fresh blood had been secured.

With deliberate precision, the female poured equal measures of the sanguine fluid into each of the three pools of water. Almost immediately, a furious activity arose within the small triangular ponds, their surfaces rippling from the spirited wriggling and splashing of the dozens of large tadpoles in each pool. The small creatures, each the length of a Ki-vaa forearm, were overjoyed that breakfast had been served. They were the Go-vaas, the children of the tribe.

It was not long ago that Tii-laa herself was a Go-vaa. Every few years, an assessment was made of the tribe's overall well-being. If it was determined that there was a need for their number to increase, and if there would be enough available sustenance to support a new clutch of Go-vaas, the Ki-vaas would embark upon the period of *soh-roz*. During this time, mating would be encouraged, and once impregnated, the females who had volunteered to honor the tribe with young would deposit their fertilized eggs into the triangular pools.

The pools were warmed by the sun Omos, and after several weeks, dozens of bright blue Go-vaas would hatch from the gelatinous eggs.

The Ki-vaa young were nothing more than fat oval bodies with long, finned tails, possessing neither arms nor legs. The only features upon a Go-vaa's smooth and slippery skin were two tiny black eyes and a small, toothed mouth on the underside of the front curve of their bodies. At their earliest stage of life, the Go-vaas consumed only blood and flesh, which gave them great strength and vitality, and it was the task of the peaceful Ki-vaas to secure that source of nourishment through nonviolent means. Go-vaas grew quite rapidly, and within months of their hatching their tails would begin to shrink, the bulk of their bodies would thin and lengthen, and small nubs would appear on their sides that soon grew into strong arms and legs. But it was not only the Go-vaas' external appearance that underwent an amazing evolution; additionally, their gill system grew and was restructured, adapting itself to life both under and above water. Once they could crawl from the pools and breathe the air, infant Ki-vaas lost their teeth, making it necessary for the dozens of egg-laying mothers to sustain the young through nursing as the restructuring of the Go-vaas' digestive systems transformed their carnivorous diet to one exclusively vegetarian. No Ki-vaa young ever knew who their true parents were, but they were all accepted and adopted by the entire tribe, the members of which worked as one to oversee their upbringing.

Tii-laa watched passively as the Go-vaas vigorously fed. Though she sensed the returned male hunter approaching, she did not turn to acknowledge him. The empty pail in her hand was a sour indicator of her failure that morning.

"We had very little luck, too," he said, his eyes falling on her unfilled pail. She recognized the attempt at friendly conversation, intended to soothe any feelings of personal failure she might have been experiencing.

Now she turned, her expressionless ebon eyes falling upon him. The hunter was similar to her in height and build, his slender muscled body at the height of athletic perfection, as was her own. From the belt around his waist hung two pieces of tattered white cloth, one anterior and the other posterior of his pelvis. Tii-laa wore a similar covering, accessorized by an additional strip of cloth affixed to the front of her belt and looped around her neck in such a manner as to cover breasts. It had not always been so, that the Ki-vaas had the desire to wear clothing, as there was no practical need for it. But many generations past, the Ki-vaas had grudgingly succumbed to decades of unrelenting pressure from the neighboring Keelar tribe, and in a conciliatory gesture intended to maintain peace among the disparate peoples, the Ki-vaas had adopted many of the societal and religious mandates of the warlike Keelars.

Initially, the adherence to the Keelar beliefs was merely a façade; the Ki-vaas found it preposterous that beings called The Three Makers had created the eleven planets that orbited the sun, Omos. Likewise, the notion that civilized people should exhibit shame of their nude bodies was irrelevant to the fundamental beliefs of the tribe. The Keelars, however, felt differently, as the entirety of their existence had been devoted to the fulfillment of the doctrines of The Three Makers, axioms that, in truth, had not come down from on high, but were dictated by Keelar scholars in centuries past. As generation upon generation of Ki-vaas were extracted from the birthing pools, the mandates of the Keelars became steeped into Ki-vaa culture, affecting the assimilation of foreign concepts into the minds of their people, and the Keelar beliefs became their own.

"If the Keelars were not so careless in the leashing of their hunting frozahs—" Tii-laa began to say to the hunter but stopped herself in mid-thought. She had intended to express her frustration with the Keelars, who would indiscriminately leave frozahs unaccounted for on hunting excursions, which had led to overpopulation of the fierce beasts in the region and a stark decrease in the number of rontahs, whose blood was utilized to feed the Go-vaas. But to speak her mind, to challenge what The Three Makers had decreed—at least, what the Keelars had told the Ki-vaas The Three Makers had decreed—would be heresy. Instead, Tii-laa deftly changed the subject without airing her true thoughts to the young tribesman.

"Was there any sign of Kva-zim?" she asked.

"None," he replied.

Tii-laa concealed her disappointment. For five days, she had eagerly awaited the return of her mentor Kva-zim, who had departed with three other warriors on a quest to find a more suitable location for the tribe, one that hosted a larger abundance of rontahs. Although all young Ki-vaas were tutored and parented by multiple adults, Kva-zim had always shown Tii-laa more attention than had other parental Ki-vaas. Perhaps he made note of her unusual tendencies and had, discreetly, offered her additional emotional support as she grew into adulthood. Whatever the case, he was the only member of her tribe whom she could truly call a friend, and his absence left a hollowness within her.

The hunter drifted away from Tii-laa, leaving her to the frustration welling within her heart. Several of the tribespeople in attendance began to make their way toward the path leading into the jungle and the village beyond, while a few remained behind to tend to the Go-vaa pools.

"Are you coming?" the hunter called back to Tii-laa.

"Yes," she responded coldly. "But I'll follow my own path."

The location of each Ki-vaa tribe's encampment depended upon the natural resources available to it, and although Tii-laa's tribe had flourished at its present location for three generations, it was becoming increasingly apparent that the time had come to relocate. Moving the entire tribe, which numbered sixty-two adults, would be a simple task, as Ki-vaas build no permanent structures other than thatched-roof pavilions supported by tall legs. The casually erected structures provided shelter during exceptionally heavy downpours, but their primary function was the gathering of rainwater that ran down the pitched thatch roofs to gutters that fed into the hollow support legs. Encircling the base of each leg was a barrel to collect the pure rainwater. Ki-vaas were people of the land in every sense, attuning themselves to the world around them; they did not attempt to tame their world, as did the Keelars with their sprawling cities of stone. Ki-vaas built no homes and slept on simple leaf mats on the ground or in the hollowed recesses between great tree roots, and they built no fences. They believed they had no right to make claims upon a land that was the home to the countless species of animals who had flourished upon the face of Zandar for millennia.

As Tii-laa approached the unmarked perimeter of the village, she could hear voices drifting through the trees. Some were the calm articulations of her people, but one voice was instantly distinguishable as that of a surly Keelar.

Something was amiss. Keelar warriors rarely visited the Ki-vaas unless trouble was brewing. She glanced cautiously about but failed to see any of the bright-orange-skinned brutes, though her attention was caught by a trace of movement between the densely rooted trees. Upon investigating, it was as she had expected: resting on the grassy plain just east of the village was a *grizok*, exhaling in clipped snorts as it awaited the return of its rider.

The grizok was a mysterious and terrifying creature, whose white body was as round and as flat as an earthly pancake, but one whose circumference was at least twice the measure of Tii-laa's height. A long ribbon-like tail tipped with feathers distinguished its posterior end from its anterior, the lateral periphery of its circular form adorned with feathered wings that it employed for flight. The beast had neither arms nor legs, and the entire front curve of its saucer-shaped body hid a wide, toothy mouth that extended nearly to the mid-point of each of the animal's sides.

The grizok's three glassy black eyes scanned the jungle warily. Tii-laa remained hidden from the creature's view, for although the Keelars' trained flying steeds adhered loyally to their masters' commands, it was best not to attract the attention of an unattended grizok lest it forget its duty, scoop her into its great mouth, and devour her.

Stealthily, she crept through the maze of roots and vines to arrive at the area where her people gathered before one of the bamboo pavilions, but she did not reveal herself. Beneath the thatched roof, at least twenty Ki-vaas stood passively as a Keelar warrior shouted in a manner most unpleasant.

By Ki-vaa standards, the Keelar was a hideous creature composed of sharp angles and an even sharper disposition. Standing not nearly as tall as the average Ki-vaa but being over twice the width, the Keelar's triangular body was supported by stout, stubby legs near its bottom point, with muscular arms positioned at the two upper corners of its torso. The Keelar people had no heads, per se, as, excluding their appendages, their torsos comprised the entirety of their bodies, and their scowling, jagged mouths and anger-filled black eyes were inset at the center of their upper chests. This Keelar, Tii-laa surmised, was a royal emissary, as he wore gleaming gold armor and a cape whose hue was identical to the skin color of the Ki-vaas. As one hand gesticulated wildly, his other gripped a long golden spear, its razor-sharp blade reflecting the beams of Omos as they filtered through the leaves high above the village.

"I don't care what ten of you it is," the Keelar shouted, spitting involuntarily as he spoke; "King Korvakos needs ten Ki-vaas and his word shall be obeyed!"

The Ki-vaas stood mutely, unaffected by the words of the brash visitor. A demand had been issued, and by the unwritten laws of their people the order would be obeyed to maintain the balance of peace between the tribes. It mattered not why their help was needed or where it might lead them. They would comply with this Keelar's appeal, as always, despite having seen the number of their tribe dwindle from nearly one hundred to a mere sixty-two over the past few months. For reasons unknown, King Korvakos had begun requesting the assistance of Ki-vaas at the island fortress city of Kosaba. As yet, none of Tii-laa's people who ventured there had returned.

In the shadows of the trees, Tii-laa seethed with anger. The placid countenances of her people revealed not a single indication of fear or curiosity about the fate of their missing tribe members, but if they would not speak for themselves, if they would not even question the motive of their brutish neighbor, then she would speak for them. All eyes turned to the tree line as Tii-laa emerged from the jungle, her eyes burning into those of the Keelar warrior.

Before she could utter a single word, the situation changed precipitously.

"Why are you here, Keelar?" came a demand, bellowed from the trees behind Tii-laa.

As one, the Ki-vaas turned as the low rumble of the male voice wrested their attention from the Keelar. The one who spoke was Kva-zoh, the tribal Zo-vaa. He stalked forth from the trees and ferns on a direct path toward the Keelar warrior. Kva-zoh's clenched fists underscored his rage and created a now-frightening nuance to the deceptively placid and nearly featureless mask of his face. Regardless of his demeanor, his hulking size alone gave even the heartiest of fighters pause, for he stood over a head taller than the other Ki-vaas, his barrel chest twice their width.

The Keelar was immediately taken aback by the new-comer's arrival. This was the Zo-vaa, the designated protector of the Ki-vaas. If the passivity of the Ki-vaas could be weighed, the Zo-vaa's savagery was rumored to exceed ten times that measure. Behind the orange-hued ambassador of King Korvakos, the Ki-vaas fled as Kva-zoh drew ever closer. But it was not fear of the protector that spurred their sudden retreat.

Greed and ambition did not dwell within the Ki-vaa heart, nor did jealousy or hate, but that is not to say their people could not express those extreme emotions and destructive tendencies. Those reprehensible traits could surface, but not without a most peculiar inducement.

Every few generations, one Ki-vaa with peculiar abilities would crawl from the hatching pools, but it was not until the young one began to grow to adulthood that its aberration became known to the tribe. The only readily apparent indicator that set apart a Zo-vaa from all others was the slow growth of membranous webbing that spanned the distance between the fingers and toes. But it was a peculiar biological feature that truly marked the Zo-vaas as divergent, as they possessed the latent ability of *rez-oh-tah*, or "poison of rage," which manifested fully upon maturity. It was while in the presence of those rare genetic deviants that other Ki-vaas experienced heightened emotions that mirrored those of the Zo-vaas. If the Zo-vaas felt anger, Ki-vaas in their proximity were swept by that emotion as well. Should the Zo-vaas experience sorrow, those near them would be struck by the same wave of despair. To maintain the emotional balance of the tribe, the Zo-vaas must live as outcasts, but whereas the Ki-vaas accepted their fates even in deadly situations, it was the Zo-vaas who exercised the freedom to challenge what The Three Makers had preordained, and only Zo-vaas would succumb to the abhorrent call to violence. This law was the last pure vestige of Ki-vaa culture that was not stifled by Keelar doctrines, and it was due to the ferocity of the Zo-vaas that the would-be warlords of Zandar acquiesced and took no steps to smite the Ki-vaa protectors for their blasphemy.

Tii-laa watched in rapt attention as Kva-zoh continued his march toward the Keelar. Knowing that he was physically outclassed, the unwanted visitor turned and fled toward his grizok that awaited in the nearby pasture. "King Korvakos will not be pleased!" the Keelar shouted, not knowing if any were even within earshot of his statement. "I'll be back!" he growled, as his mount slowly flapped its great wings and whisked its rider over the plain and away from the village.

The Ki-vaas peered from their hiding places as the protector turned his attention to Tii-laa. The Zo-vaa stared at her for several seconds, almost as if he were assessing her for some quality of which she was unaware. Then the moment passed, and he approached her slowly as the others of the village looked on from a safe distance.

"You are Tii-laa," he said gently.

"And you are the Zo-vaa," she replied proudly. It was the first time Tii-laa had met the protector in the flesh, and she was not embarrassed that her inflection expressed the awe and respect she held for him.

"And you do not flee from my presence, as do all others," he stated.

"Why should I?" she retorted. Kva-zoh chuckled, turned, and walked toward the verdant surroundings, leaving the young Ki-vaa behind. Tii-laa looked to the other villagers and paused. Then, with self-assurance, she flipped her tangled white mane and followed the Zo-vaa into the jungle.

"You're following me," Kva-zoh called out without turning. Tii-laa wondered how long the Zo-vaa had been listening to her stealthy footfalls behind him. She did not care that he knew she had followed, but neither did she call out to him; instead, she was desperately attempting to organize her thoughts as she crept through the low foliage. She might have only a few minutes to speak to the Zo-vaa, maybe even less, so she wanted to make that time count.

Kva-zoh stopped, as did Tii-laa, and without looking at her he pointed toward the pale yellow sky, barely visible through the leafy canopy above. "What do you think is up there, above the clouds?" he asked.

The philosophical implication of his question gave Tii-laa pause, but after a moment's contemplation, she decided to reveal to him that which she could not divulge to others: the truth, at least, from her perspective.

"We're taught that above us are the other ten planets, " she said, "including Uvala, to where all of us travel when we return to the water." It was from water that the Ki-vaas sprang, and upon their deaths, their bodies were placed into the pools to feed the hungry Go-vaas. But according to the teaching of Keelar scholars, each being possessed a spiritual energy that was transported to the planet Uvala upon death. "That is what we are taught. But how do we know it to be true?"

Kva-zoh, at last, turned to look upon her. Again, he grew quiet, tilting his head slightly from side to side as he assessed her in a way she did not understand. At length, he crossed his arms over his broad chest and continued with his questioning. "What makes you different from the others of our tribe?"

The question was odd and presumptive coming from another Ki-vaa, but she did not hesitate to answer it. "I ask why," she said with confidence. "That is what makes me different. But I don't want to talk about me, great Zo-vaa."

"Call me Kva-zoh," he requested.

"Then I will," she said, and promptly returned to her last thought. "What I want to ask you about is Kva-zim. Five days ago, he left with three others to search for a more fertile nesting ground for the tribe, but he has not returned. Do you know anything of his whereabouts or fate?"

Kva-zoh became unusually silent and averted his gaze from Tii-laa's deep black eyes. He appeared momentarily uncomfortable but quickly regained his composure. "I have not seen Kva-zim," he said, "and I would remind you that my responsibility is the protection of the village." Tii-laa had a sense that something unspoken hung in the air, and the protector's sharp retort was an indication that she had worn out her welcome.

"Is there anything else?" the hulking warrior asked crisply.

The change in his tone was abrupt, and Tii-laa assumed he had become annoyed by her question, which was odd considering his initial interest in her views. But he was a Zo-vaa, the ways of whom were mysterious.

Without waiting for her reply, Kva-zoh turned and stalked into the jungle, alone.

The night sky was clear, the light from faraway suns twinkling in counterpoint to the rhythmic flashes of the tiny *calvocas* that flitted among the dark treetops. Tii-laa lay alone between two twisted, moss-covered tree roots. Around her, the others of the tribe dozed peacefully, but she had spent hours in contemplation as she gazed up at the mating ritual of the luminous insects on display high above in the jungle canopy. So many thoughts swirled through her mind, driving sleep from her. Her earlier interaction with Kva-zoh was indeed unusual and somewhat cryptic, but what bothered her most was the tribe's lack of concern for the missing party. "If it was Kva-zim's time to go back to the water, then so be it," the others would say.

Tii-laa could not accept that possibility and neither could she embrace the tenets of nonintervention. Kva-zoh seemed disturbed by the mention of the absent tribe members, but Tii-laa knew his duty was to lurk in the shadows of the village and protect the entire tribe from harm, not set out for parts unknown to find four lost wanderers. Tribal custom dictated that there was nothing to be done; therefore, nothing would be done.

Frustrated, the young Ki-vaa sat upright and scanned the darkness around her. She detected no movement among the sleepers. In silence, she wafted through the shadows to the pavilion, where she filled a small gourd with water and sealed it, then slung its strap over her shoulder along with a great length of coiled rope. She tied another looped span of rope to her belt, beneath which was still tucked the razor-sharp seashell she had intended to use on the rontah that morning.

Again, she looked about the clearing to the Ki-vaas who dreamed among the tree roots; none stirred, and none saw her nocturnal movements. Her hand found a long wooden staff propped against one of the pavilion legs, and with one final look behind her, she plunged headlong into the pitch black of the Zandarian jungle.

2
DOMAIN OF DOOM

ALTHOUGH MYRIAD NOCTURNAL PREDATORS stalked the Zandarian jungle, Tii-laa used every ounce of her training to wend her way several miles from the Ki-vaa encampment without incident. Before Kva-zim and his three companions had departed in search of a new home for the tribe, small-talk among the villagers indicated Tii-laa's mentor would be exploring the territory that lay in the direction of the rising sun. Therefore, toward the eastern lands she had traveled throughout the night, and to the east she would proceed until she discovered the whereabouts of the party or received validation that they had fallen to the predators that crept in the darkness of Zandar's wilds. Either way, she must know. Roused by the rays of dawn, Tii-laa stretched, pulled the wild tangle of ivory hair from her face, and dropped from the lofty branch where she had perched for several hours as she slept.

Before embarking on the day's search, Tii-laa prepared a meager breakfast. Among the trees and bushes, the blue fern-like leaves of the *ho-nay* plant grew in abundance, and a peripheral search of the area disclosed a *gro-nay* vine, inconspicuously crawling its way up a nearby tree trunk. The vine abounded with the elongated white berries for which it was named, and after selecting two ripe specimens, she began to dig into the soft soil beneath the sapphire fronds of the ho-nay. There, she unearthed a handful of small pods that grew among the cluster of roots, and after shelling them, she placed the soft, pale blue nuts in the palm of her hand. Just as Kva-zim had taught her when she was very young, she mashed the meat of the nuts into a paste using her cutting tool, then added the two juicy gro-nay berries, thoroughly blending the mixture in her palm to create a more aqueous concoction. This she held to her small mouth, suited only for ingesting foods specially prepared in such a way, and slurped up the sweet and tangy paste. Kva-zim was right; mashed ho-nay was a bit bland without the added sugary zest of gro-nay berries. After her meal, she cleansed her hands of the azure residue in the small stream that hugged the jungle's perimeter, then crossed the cool, lazy waters and resolutely strode onto the sprawling plain on the opposite bank.

The air was warm and humid, its flow shifting and tossing the tops of the knee-deep grass. Suddenly, the roof of Tii-laa's mouth began to tingle. The sensation meant she was close to a scent marker left behind by the missing explorers. Although Tii-laa, like all her kind, lacked nostrils, her sense of smell was highly advanced. As she inhaled through her slight mouth opening, ambient scents ascended through her upper palate orifice and entered the large nasal cavity that extended beneath the entirety of her smooth face. In conjunction with the ability of her eyes to detect light waves in multiple spectrums, she could perceive large concentrations of odiferous materials, not just as smells, but as visible solid objects. The ebon eyes of Tii-laa surveyed the broad plain that stretched before her. At its far edge, precisely beneath the rising sun, danced an undulating, fluorescent-pink mist that flowered above the deep grass and swirled in her direction at the whim of the warm morning breeze. It was a path marker, of that she was sure, and though the fog-like trail it emitted was invisible to all but the Ki-vaas, it was her first concrete clue as to the path taken by the missing members of her tribe. With any luck, she would find them alive.

Within minutes, Tii-laa squatted at the side of a sapling branch that had been implanted in the ground by the missing party. Tied at the top of the waist-high stake was a strip of once-white cloth that had been thoroughly soiled with the ash of burned *canmon* tree bark. The trail-marking technique was an ancient one, wherein canmon bark was ignited and reduced to ash by focusing the rays of Omos through a shard of clear crystal painstakingly polished into a convex shape. The pungent aroma of the resulting ash was highly concentrated, emitting an unmistakable, fog-like beacon visible only by the extraordinary olfactory aspect of Ki-vaa vision. Now Tii-laa knew for sure that the missing party had passed this way, and she proceeded to tromp through the tall grass on a path toward the rising sun.

By the time Omos neared its zenith above the untamed landscape of Zandar, Tii-laa had made her way past the foothills that circumscribed the wide veldt that lay to the east of the jungle where her people currently dwelled. Her journey had thus far been unremarkable, as she effortlessly evaded the predators that hunted the grasslands, and upon spotting a second scented trail marker, she was relieved that the missing party for which she searched had proceeded ever eastward. It would have been folly for them to take a northerly route. Such a path would have brought them perilously close to the realm of the Nuvors, whose villages were packed tightly within the jungles that hedged the astoundingly orbicular *Noh-rok*, the Sea of Turmoil.

If the Ki-vaas, the Keelars, and the Nuvors had one thing in common, it was a universal belief that during some mysterious and ancient conflict, an earthshaking cataclysm had resulted in a blinding fire that caused the upheaval of the very earth into the sky of Zandar, the land forever scarred by a bowl-shaped crater several miles in diameter. Over time, as the course of nearby rivers shifted, the blackened pit had filled with fresh water streaming down from the highlands, eventually transforming into the Noh-rok as it was today. Another tale agreed upon by the three disparate tribes was that the crystals that permeated the rocky shores of the

Noh-rok were thrust up to the surface of Zandar from deep underground during the great upheaval. Desire for the crystals was the catalyst of the centuries-old conflict between the Keelars and the Nuvors, as each group sought to claim the shores of the Noh-rok for their own, jealously fighting and dying over the perceived value of the pellucid objects. The Keelars hoarded the crystals and used them as legal tender within their cities, while the Nuvors valued the glittering rocks for their incredible resilience, using their sharpened fragments to fashion the tips of spears and other weapons. The Ki-vaas, however, did not use the crystals as currency or to kill; instead, they harnessed their natural qualities to create fire, an asset from which the entire tribe would benefit. That alone spoke volumes about Ki-vaa philosophy, and even more about the mindsets of the Keelars and Nuvors.

Tii-laa's direct easterly course delivered her to the edge of the wide fungi thicket. Stretching the length and breadth of the plain before her, the thicket served as a natural barrier between the forest where she had slept the previous night and the valley that lay ahead. The largest of the brilliant yellow-spotted blue fungi reached Tii-laa's own height and they sprouted thickly; traversing the field would be incredibly slow going.

Upon closer inspection, Tii-laa found between the fungi stalks a natural division, wide enough to allow passage, and footprints in the moist soil confirmed that the lost party had traversed, or at least attempted to traverse, the thicket. Once she reached the other side of the mushroom field, and depending on the direction of the wind, the trail of the Ki-vaa explorers might not be easily ascertained. But she would wrestle with that conundrum once she successfully made her way through the bucolic fungi. That feat, in itself, was not without unique perils. Warily, she scanned the speckled tops of the mushrooms, then moved into the field, taking great care to not disturb the shoots and heads as she passed.

The air within the fungus field was thick and humid, the undersides of the colossal mushrooms retaining moisture drawn upward from the rich dark soil by the increasing heat of the day. The dew that collected in the cool undersides of the bell-shaped and umbrella-like mushroom caps dripped from their lower edges back to the earth, making it difficult for Tii-laa to maintain solid footing upon the slippery moss that proliferated in bright green patches among the thick fungus stalks. As she proceeded further into the field, Tii-laa became increasingly aware that a single misstep could doom her if any prowlers that dwelled among the mushrooms were alerted to her presence. She paused to renew her focus and again surveyed the spotted tops of the fungi. There was no movement, no imminent threats. For now, she was safe, and she forged ahead with precise steps.

For over an hour, Tii-laa wended through the mushrooms with sure-footed advancement and no sign of the missing party or hungry predators. It was then that a jolt ran through her, as a sudden tug at her waist prevented her from moving forward. She spun about to find not a hungry enemy grasping her, but something much more mundane: The coiled rope that hung from her hip had looped around a thigh-high mushroom, her forward momentum threatening to pop the entire head from the fungi or uproot it altogether. But due to the suddenness of her turn and the slippery, uneven ground, her equilibrium shifted to one side, her bare feet lost their traction, and she crashed to the damp mossy ground. As she fell, she flailed and thrust her hands wide, one of which held the walking staff she carried, and she struck the white mushroom stalks that closed tightly about her. Like a ripple upon water, the vibration of her sharp contact with the fungi reverberated across the entire field.

Tii-laa held her breath. As quickly as it had started, the vibration among the mushrooms ceased, and all was quiet. She sat thus for several moments before regaining her footing and peering out across the field of yellow-spotted mushroom heads. In the distance and to her left, the once-placid blanket of rounded azure fungus helmets began to sway, as if something close to the ground were rapidly making its way between the concealed stalks. Still, she held her breath, hoping against hope that whatever creature advanced across the field did not detect her.

Suddenly, the path of the swaying caps diverged from its course and made a beeline directly for Tii-laa. As quickly as she could, she began smashing her way through the field of fungi, abandoning any need for stealth in her mad flight to escape her unseen pursuer.

She did her best to dig her clawed toes into the moss and earth, but the slickness of the ground over which she raced frustrated her efforts to increase her speed. Behind her and drawing ever nearer was a harsh clatter, as if dozens of pieces of flat rock were being slapped together in rapid succession. Onward she ran, the gills beneath her ears flaring as she expelled great gulps of air. The din grew ever louder as she crashed on, increasing in intensity until she knew the creature pursuing her was directly on her heels. In desperation, she leaped to one side just as the thing rushed past her and smashed through the fungi that lay ahead of them. At last, the beast that hunted the young Ki-vaa was revealed.

In Tii-laa's youth, she had played with creatures like the one that had just attacked her, but she had never seen a specimen of such gigantic proportions. Usually, a *rootoh* could be held in the palm of one's hand. However, the juggernaut that plowed past her was huge, fully three feet in both height and circumference, and nearly a dozen yards long.

The iridescent shell of the multisegmented torso reflected the rays of Omos as the creature pushed on through the field. Realizing it had overshot its prey, the giant rootoh assumed a wide arc of travel and looped back toward Tii-laa, its centipedal body supported by hundreds of pairs of spindly, spiderlike legs that extended from beneath each segment, the carapace coverings of the multijointed appendages clacking against one another as they clawed against the ground. The monster's length was such that, even as its hind end proceeded into the surrounding fungi, its head was already thrusting from the stalks to Tii-laa's right as it began its second assault. Again, it rushed toward her, and as it did, Tii-laa bolted toward the passage between the mushroom stalks through which its rear segment had just disappeared. She reasoned that due to the creature's inability to turn sharply, her best chance of reaching safety beyond the fungus field would be to run back down the way the thing had come.

She glanced furtively behind as she loped through the densely packed sprouts. To her chagrin, the front end of the creature reared into the air, twisted, and then arced down to the ground to land parallel to its midsection, which was still advancing in the opposite direction. As the front of the beast skittered toward her, the inversely moving remainder of its body followed the upward spiraling arc, and like a ribbon flowing through the wind, the entire length of the creature changed direction within seconds and once again charged after her. The monster's black mandibles snapped greedily in the air. Tii-laa, still tightly gripping her walking staff, knew she had only moments before the rock-hard, razor-sharp chitin would sink deep into her flesh. It was time to do something that she had never before done.

Trusting that the crawling terror could not stop or abruptly change course, the young Ki-vaa leaped sideways, dug her heels into the soft earth and moss, and with all of the might she could muster smashed the walking stick down upon the head of the creature as it shot past her. Never had she harmed another living thing out of malice, and although it meant life or death, the repercussion of the act upon her psyche was startling. The emotions released within her by the violent deed were both exhilarating and horrifying. This was not the Ki-vaa way. Violence was not the Ki-vaa way.

But still, defending herself against an enemy wishing to devour her felt . . . good.

In response to the strike upon its shell, hundreds of pairs of legs slowed the momentum of the giant rootoh and it lifted its hideous head from the ground, slinging its full weight in Tii-laa's direction. The segmented body crashed down upon the spot where she had just stood, but she had already leaped away. Now she brought the hardwood stick down upon the center of her attacker's head. In quick succession, she pelted the beast with multiple strikes, which annoyed the creature, but did not deter it. After each blow, the huge arthropod raised its head and expelled a high-pitched hiss from between the ebon mandibles, clattering as it chewed at the air. Soon the rootoh grew weary of the repeated strikes upon its carapace and with surprising speed, it completely encircled Tii-laa, crawling in an orbital pattern, its forward fangs gripping its own rearmost segment. Because of the beast's uniform segmentation and the speed at which it circled, it became nearly impossible to determine where the rootoh began and where it ended.

Tii-laa knew that every passing second edged the confrontation another step closer to her doom. If she were to have any hope of surviving the attack of the persistent predator, she must extricate herself from the circling ring of death and put as much distance as she could between herself and the creature. With renewed resolve, Tii-laa thrust the walking stick forward in a stabbing motion and succeeded in striking the beast where its fangs gripped its posterior. The front section rose from the ground and shrieked; she had either annoyed or hurt the rootoh, but it didn't matter which. The creature didn't like it. She spun and again thrust the stick into the center of the huge arthropod's body, between two segments of carapace at its midsection. It was then that things grew immeasurably worse.

The forceful wedging of the hardwood stick between two of the ridges of the rootoh's sectional body produced a most unsettling result, as the point of contact abruptly bisected the creature and one end of the bloodless division rose into the air to expose a maw of fanged mandibles. Tii-laa had not been attacked by a single rootoh, but rather two, one attached to the back end of another and wriggling in tandem with it across the fungus field in search of prey.

Now, dual heads reared into the air, hissing furiously, while bobbing in a manner that indicated confusion. If the rootohs could indeed reason, all thoughts of eating became secondary to securing the comfortable balance they had enjoyed as a single unit. The naturally poor eyesight of the creatures did not make their effort to find one another any easier, and after flopping about the surrounding fungi and whipping their heads to and fro, one creature at last found the rear end of the other and reattached itself. Once again, the two individuals became a single incredibly long hunting machine, but by that time Tii-laa had already cleared the periphery of the fungus field and was hastily making her way toward the lip of the nearby canyon, and safety.

The remainder of the day passed without incident, and Tii-laa avoided the notice of the occasional wild grizok that lazily flapped overhead, flying eastward. By the end of the day, as she descended the sheer valley wall to its base, she noted several possible nesting alcoves in the face of the escarpment. As the shadows lengthened beneath her, she collected an armful of palm fronds and lined the floor of one of the small caves that was located a safe distance from the ground. There, in the oncoming darkness, she ate an evening meal she had prepared in her palm, then settled in for the night.

Sleep did not come easily, but it was not the screeches of unseen creatures that prowled the darkness below her that kept her awake; to a Ki-vaa, that was tranquilizing music and the natural order of life in the wilds of Zandar. But try as she might, her exhausted body could not convince her overactive mind to allow her to drift off to sleep. Thoughts of Kva-zim and the innumerable perils he and his party might have encountered recurred to her, but even more distracting was the odd pang she felt at her core, a feeling that surfaced time and again. Tii-laa could not define the ephemeral sensation. It was one of longing, but not in any romantic sense, nor did it spring from loneliness or insecurity of being separated from the rest of her tribe. As she lay in the darkness, she realized the feeling had always gnawed within her but had been buried behind a wall of avoidance. She had not wanted to confront it fully, but now, after her encounter with the rootohs, there was no holding back the floodgates of acknowledgment. It was something she had never before felt with such intensity, and though the realization sprang from her violent interaction earlier that day and the unbridled aggression she had unleashed upon the pair of rootohs, she could now put a name to the emotion that had vexed her since childhood.

It was discontent, pure and simple. But no, that was not all it was. As she plumbed ever deeper, she could now see its true face. It was a philosophical countenance she had kept repressed at the behest of the Ki-vaas, which had done nothing but create a sense of guilt within her heart. No, what she truly felt was compassion, surprisingly juxtaposed with a sense of duty to defend others of innocent intent who could not see as clearly as she. The young Ki-vaa sat upright with a start as the concept fully washed over her, and she did not know why she looked to the stars above the tiny cave entrance, but for reasons unknown to her, doing so gave her comfort.

As she gazed upon the twinkles embedded in the black firmament, an inner calm blanketed her, a feeling of serenity that came with the acceptance that there was nothing aberrant about being different. Following one's inner calling was not a crime, regardless of whether that behavior was condoned by the lawmakers within her tribe and those outside of it. In their benevolence, the Ones from Above— if they existed—would surely agree with her rationalization. If they had created the worlds that orbited Omos, if they had created the people and animals that populated the planets, then surely they understood the preciousness of life and would condone the concept of the preservation of that life at all costs.

Tii-laa curled up within the nest she had constructed and positioned her head so that she could gaze up at the night sky. "So many wonders, so many worlds," she thought, but soon her mind turned to Kva-zoh. She pondered what the protector would think of her epiphany and actions of earlier in the day, and with that, sleep born of contentment overtook her at last.

It was the first truly sound sleep Tii-laa could remember enjoying in her entire life, but her renewed vigor and outlook for the future would be dealt a heavy blow the following day.

The morning air within the valley was quiet and still, making any scent markers left behind by the missing party extremely difficult to locate from a distance. Tii-laa would therefore need to rely on her conventional eyesight if she were to successfully track Kva-zim and his companions. For hours she trudged on through the dense forest of tall charcoal-colored, yellow-striped palm boles. She avoided a pitfall here and forded a stream there, and throughout the morning's trek, her movement was accompanied by the frantic clacks of territorial *drozoks* giving her ample warning when she had strayed too close to trees bearing their nests. Drozok parents were not particularly fearsome, but in defense of their young, the small birds of emerald and heliotrope plumage would attack relentlessly, pecking the transgressor with their formidable pick-like bills until the interloper was run off. Tii-laa was more than happy to avoid such painful encounters.

After enjoying a brief midday repast of nuts and berries, she began to move again, and after rounding the foot of a rocky ridge, a familiar scent caught her attention. It wafted through the somber-hued trunks, but it was not the odor of canmon-bark ash. The ghostly mist visible only to her bore a deep crimson tint, a scent color that was emitted only by the decay of animal flesh. Predators of many stripes roamed the primeval Zandarian forests, and the remains of dead animals left behind after they had been feasted upon were a common sight. But in this case, she had to be sure and so cautiously approached the dancing red fog. Standing several steps from the concentrated scent, Tii-laa used her walking staff to gently lift the ferns concealing the source of the stomach-churning odor.

Her heart skipped a beat. Beneath the cerulean ferns were the remains of a Ki-vaa male wearing clothing of the style unique to her tribe. Upon closer inspection, she identified him as Gra-zah, who had accompanied Kva-zim on his quest.

Tii-laa's first impression was that the unfortunate man had fallen victim to a frozah, as what was left of the body had been chewed nearly beyond recognition. But then she noticed that the remaining leg that had not been gnawed from the corpse had lost its normal aquamarine hue and was now a sickening blackish purple. It was a very bad sign.

Tii-laa froze and listened intently. Then, with the utmost care, she released the ferns and began backing away from the hideous remains with painstakingly slow and deliberate steps. She made a hasty survey of the entire area, and after ascertaining her only safe course, she dropped the staff and sprang, sinking her claws into a low overhead branch. With acrobatic fluidity, her legs swung forward and upward over the branch until she rested upon her stomach. There she lay in complete silence, her knees bent to prevent her feet from dangling too close to the ground. Within seconds, her fear was realized as the lurking *kruk* slithered from the ferns below to inspect her discarded staff.

The snakelike body of the kruk was adorned with eight small reptilian legs sprouting at regular intervals along its six-foot-long length. The forked tongue, pale blue in hue, licked the air, and bright golden eyes scanned the area for movement, but there was none. Tii-laa held her breath. Although they primarily foraged on the ground, kruks occasionally scaled trees, where they would wait patiently for animals to venture beneath them and then fling themselves down upon their unsuspecting prey. If she moved, the kruk would surely see her and attack. Unlike frozahs, kruks were slow moving and practiced an economy of motion, but they did share the frozahs' venomous fangs, which appeared to have been responsible for the fate that had befallen Gra-zah. The only beings on Zandar who trifled with the crawling terrors were the Nuvors, who prized the iridescent scales of kruk hides and incorporated the tough skins into their clothing. Killing a kruk was not difficult; a single sword stroke could decapitate the creature. But the Nuvors wore the skin of the kruk as a status symbol representing their fearlessness. Tii-laa had no such compulsion and waited patiently until the attention of the kruk became focused on a small rodent that hopped from among the ferns. After the snakelike lizard pursued its intended prey and disappeared into the foliage, Tii-laa dropped to the ground, retrieved her staff, and continued on her journey.

Gra-zah had "gone back to the water," as the Ki-vaas called death, but his body still served the tribe by marking the trail back to the village. After the discovery of the fallen tribesman, Tii-laa failed to detect another scent marker, but owing to the narrow width of the jungle valley where there was nowhere else to go but to its end, she reasoned that she might find the next marker at the terminus of the gorge, as long as Kva-zim and his companions had not shared the fate of Gra-zah.

Just then, a great shadow fell over her. The lazy glide of a large grizok had momentarily blocked the rays of Omos as it flew overhead. Fortunately, it appeared to be oblivious to Tii-laa's presence. Two more of the saucer-shaped creatures followed behind the first, all quietly flying toward the end of the valley to where Tii-laa was proceeding. The implication of a shared destination was indeed ominous, and it was with a feeling of anxiety that Tii-laa increased her speed.

As the young Ki-vaa forged ahead, the thickening of the undergrowth slowed her progress, as ground-covering vines and tall, stalked vegetation sprouting from large tuberous roots increasingly supplanted the dense ferns. Even here, the berried gro-nay vines could be found in abundance. The varied species of trees that propagated throughout the valley gave way to others with much larger boles, their roots no longer completely subterranean but now clawing upward from the earth like great spider legs before disappearing once again beneath the dark soil. From among the overhead leaves hung sheets of white moss, some of which reached to the ground, and as Tii-laa pressed on she was often forced to use her walking staff to slice through the heavy curtains of vegetation before continuing across the increasingly soft ground. All these signs, as well as the progressively pungent odor of the humid air, informed her that she was approaching a swampland, made all the more evident by the proliferation of flying insects and standing pools of dark, stagnant water.

Solid earth eventually gave way to black mud that began to suck at her feet; thereafter Tii-laa took to maneuvering the lengths of aboveground tree roots, leaping from one to the next. Still, she failed to detect evidence of another scent marker, but this time for reasons of her own device. As she had moved deeper into the swamp, the heavy miasma of scents emitted by rotting vegetation within the brackish water and mud began to overwhelm her vision, requiring Tii-laa to "hold her nose," in a sense, by pressing her tongue against the roof of her mouth to seal off her nasal orifice. Almost immediately, the obfuscating, swirling fog of innumerable scent colors that painted her vision of the swamp disappeared, but her action also disabled her ability to detect any aura of odor markers that might have been left behind by the missing travelers. If a marker was present in the area, she would not be able to find it by scent vision and would have to rely solely on her ordinary eyesight.

After several minutes of cautiously delving further into the muddy terrain, one tree root at a time, she squatted abruptly as an odd sound caught her attention. Around her, the great trees grew thickly and the breadth of her surroundings was virtually enshrouded by limply hanging curtains of moss that draped from the network of overhead limbs, nearly blocking out the sky. Something was moving within that swamp, and that something was big, as evidenced by the sharp sucking sound of feet being pulled from the mud, and then stomping down again with great splashes. The sounds were faint at first, but as she listened they grew ever louder. Whatever slogged through the dark marsh was coming toward her, but she knew not if it was aware of her presence. All she could do was squat low, stay silent, and wait.

At last, the author of the soggy din was revealed. To Tii-laa's relief, the animal that had approached was a *troak*, and one of immense size. The slick skin of the gargantuan black salamander was dotted by brilliant circles of yellow and green, indicating a male of the species, and it would have taken three Ki-vaas standing one upon the other to reach the top of the thick neck of the beast. Its length must have been at least four times that measure, taking into account its long, fat tail. Though troaks spent much of their lives on their bellies, their significantly undersized but muscular legs were able to heft their bulky masses as they walked with abrupt, sashaying movements. Twin rows of bony spikes ran from above each of the creature's eyes, laterally over its flat back, and down the length of its tail.

The troak approached Tii-laa's position without hesitation as if oblivious to her presence, but considering that troaks were noncarnivorous, it probably couldn't care less that she was there. Tii-laa watched as the great beast sloshed and slithered past her, the suction of its clawed feet being pulled from the mud creating tremors that shook the exposed tree root on which she perched. At length, the giant disappeared into the swamp, shredding the sheets of hanging moss that blocked its passage and leaving behind a relatively clear path through the trees on which Tii-laa could trek. She had only taken one step before she was unexpectedly enveloped by another shadow.

The beauty of the gently undulating feathered wings of the grizok was the height of irony when coupled with the impossibly wide, toothy grin of the saucer-like creature. It had dropped from the sky through a division in the swamp's leafy canopy and dove directly toward Tii-laa. She dropped to her stomach against the huge mossy root on which she had been treading only seconds before and the beast rocketed past her.

To her relief, it did not alter its flight path to return for a second attempt at snatching her from the ground; instead, it flapped on and glided down the veritable tunnel that had been bored by the troak through the thick curtains of hanging moss. Again Tii-laa gripped the root and flattened her body against it as a second grizok plunged from the sky and followed the first, but they were not flying after the gigantic salamander. Instead, they soared in the direction from which the plodding giant lizard had emerged. The grizoks were not hunting the troak; they were hunting something else.

Tii-laa started and a chill shuddered through her frame as the unmistakable voice of Kva-zim rang out far in the distance. "Get down!" he shouted at someone.

Her staff firmly in hand, Tii-laa tapped her belt to ensure she had not lost her cutting shell as she bolted down the length of the enormous unearthed root. Upon reaching its end, she leaped across the black mud and landed gracefully on another root several yards away. Her heart pounded wildly in her chest. *Kva-zim was alive!* she repeated over and over in her mind, and within seconds, she had disappeared into the cathedral of hanging moss along the trail of the grizoks that had flown past. But she also knew that unless she ran as she had never run before, Kva-zim's exclamation might be the last words she would ever hear her mentor speak.

3

THE JAWS OF DEATH

TII-LAA BOUNDED FROM ROOT TO ROOT as she made her way closer to the source of the shouting. She could hear other voices besides that of Kva-zim and she was heartened by the thought that perhaps the rest of the party had escaped Gra-zah's untimely end in the wilds of the Zandarian jungle. Now the spaces between the trees widened and far less moss dangled overhead, the lack of obstacles in her path both easing her passage and making it more difficult for her to find proper footing amid the increasingly sparse roots. Tii-laa feared the roots would disappear altogether and spell an abrupt end to her flight before she could reach her tribespeople, but she pressed on, undaunted.

At last, the thick foliage and boles came to an end and a great swamp spread out for hundreds of yards before her, its placid surface blanketed by a thick layer of bright green algae that floated upon the brackish water in an unbroken field. Tii-laa came to a squatting stop upon the last gnarled tree root that would support her weight, and as she looked out across the swampland, the cold grip of realization shook her. At irregular intervals throughout the swamp rose lofty rock towers, easily seventy-five feet in height, standing like silent sentinels overlooking the steaming morass below. Circling the towers at varying heights above the water were grizoks, dozens of them. They flew in wide lazy rings, some clockwise, others counterclockwise, and all perfectly horizontal to the swamp, oblivious of one another and transfixed by the rock towers.

342

Immediately recalling a story once told to her by Kva-zim, Tii-laa knew that this was a spawning ground for grizoks, and their unnaturally regimented orbital flights were emblematic of their mating ritual. She considered that it was late in the dry season, which corresponded to the grizok lore Kva-zim had shared with her when she was younger.

What she saw next tore her from her reverie. At the base of the root on which she stood, the sheet of algae upon the swamp's surface appeared to have been disturbed at some time in the past, but now looked as if it was attempting to grow back together. The path of the disturbance led across the swamp and terminated at a small island of raised earth that lay several hundred yards from where she perched. Thick ferns and high grass covered the surface of the mound, which lay several dozen meters from the nearest trees and the closest rock towers that rose from the stagnant muck.

"Stay down!" came another shout. Tii-laa scrutinized the small island from afar until at last she saw three shapes moving among the sawgrass, apparently trying to conceal themselves from the clockwork movements of the grizoks overhead, the lowest of the winged terrors only twenty feet above the ground. Her heart leaped, for hiding in the grass were Kva-zim and his two companions!

The young Ki-vaa slid down the side of the massive root and touched one foot to the swamp's thick algae coating. It was surprisingly resilient to the pressure she placed upon it, so she tested its buoyancy with both feet and found she was able to stand without breaking through to the murky water beneath. A few tentative steps carried her a dozen feet from the safety of the root, leaving her to wonder why her tribespeople remained on the island at the mercy of the grizoks when they could simply retrace the route that had, by all appearances, led them into their predicament.

She looked to the island and saw that Kva-zim had now spied her, though his sharp hand motions relayed a much different message than relief or happiness. No, he looked angry and seemed to be doing everything within his power to warn off Tii-laa, without drawing undue attention to himself and his companions from the creatures that circled overhead.

It was curious, Tii-laa thought, but she would not be dissuaded. She would go to the party and together they would return to the village. With adamance, she began making her way across the algae, and as she carefully calculated each step, she could feel the floating sheet of plant life begin to sag beneath her weight. Although the algae initially appeared solid enough to support her weight while she made her way across the swamp, it was only for brief seconds that the layer remained unyielding, after which she could feel the thick blanket of algae slowly descending beneath the surface of the water.

Suddenly one of her feet ruptured the thick membranous layer and thrust into the cool, black water beneath. She gasped in surprise as her entire body slipped through the swamp's bright green coating. Then she felt her feet hit the spongy bottom and she sighed with relief. Fortunately, the water was only waist deep here near the tree root she had left behind. She would simply need to make her way back to the safety of the root and formulate a new plan. But the black mud that was the foundation of the swamp sucked at her feet and legs, and the more effort she applied to forward momentum, the greater was the resistance of the dank slime that tried to hold her fast. It was only through sheer determination that Tii-laa reached the tree root and at last clawed her way out of the quagmire. Had she been any further from shore, she would have likely been sucked beneath the mud and drowned. Kva-zim and his companions were incredibly fortunate that the algae had supported them long enough to reach the island, but due to the arrival of the grizoks, there would be no escaping it. A different tactic would be necessary if she was going to reach her stranded people.

Tii-laa looked to the island. Again, Kva-zim was waving her off, pointing forcefully to the jungle behind her and then jabbing at the air with a finger. It was readily apparent that Kva-zim and his companions had resigned themselves to their fates, and they would simply wait patiently until the grizoks broke from their hypnotic mating ritual to feast upon the helplessly stranded Ki-vaas. The tribespeople would go back to the water, the flesh of their bodies would feed the hungry grizoks, and they would serve a vital function in the larger life cycle of Zandar.

As long as she breathed, Tii-laa would not allow that defeatist resolution to come to pass, and she would rescue Kva-zim, whether he liked it or not. After taking account of her meager possessions and surveying the swamp and its natural attributes, she sprinted down the length of the tree root and disappeared into the jungle.

Tii-laa's sharp claws dug into the bark of a tall, gnarled tree and she scaled it effortlessly. A strap woven of vine creepers held her walking staff to her back, and with careful calculation, she leaped from the high branch to land upon another of a neighboring tree. In that fashion, she made her way out over the algae-covered swamp until she was within leaping distance of one of the shorter rock towers. A cleansing exhalation escaped her as she envisioned herself flying, and she sprang from the limb toward the towering natural edifice.

The full weight of her body slammed against the rock, her slender fingers clutching at the surface until they found their way into fissures between the stones. With reptilian grace, Tii-laa slithered up the side of the tower until finally she climbed up onto its flat summit over fifty feet above the swamp. To her relief, the grizoks were oblivious to her encroachment and continued their tedious revolutions around the other towers.

The nearest rock tower was too far away for her to reach with a leap, but she wondered . . . One of the circling grizoks passed within ten feet of the tower on which she perched, and about twelve feet below her. Another grizok's path came within a similar distance of her, though at an altitude twenty feet over her head. Tii-laa watched several orbits of the floating creatures, as well as the paths of those that circled the other towers between her and the tiny island. She could do it; she was sure of it. When the lower of the grizoks glided toward her tower, Tii-laa held her breath and leaped from the stony platform.

The grizok was so enraptured by its ritualistic flight that it did not even flinch when Tii-laa landed upon its back. She flattened herself to its feathered hide just as the Keelars did with their mounts and then proceeded to ride the beast as it made several slow circles around the tower. Her next move must be carefully calculated. When at last she achieved the alignment she sought, she stood up on the back of the creature and then boldly dropped from it.

Twenty feet below, Tii-laa landed upon the wide back of another grizok that circled a different tower but flew in the opposite direction from the one she had just dismounted. She immediately squatted and successfully resumed her balance, thrown off by the reverse momentum of the second flying creature. But there was no time to waste; she had to move quickly. There was not even time to take a breath. Tii-laa leaped from the second grizok, as a third creature circling yet another tower was moving in a counterclockwise rotation and was passing directly under the animal she had just landed upon. She dropped to its back without notice, and just as she had planned, the elliptical flight of the third grizok delivered her over the edge of the island, at which point she leaped the remaining twenty feet and landed among the tall ferns and sawgrass.

"Tii-laa! What are you doing?" shouted Kva-zim, as he scrambled through the tall grass on hands and knees. Upon reaching the young woman, he pushed her forcefully to the ground, surveying the sky above, but so entranced were the grizoks that none noticed Tii-laa's trespass.

She righted herself with a reassuring hand on Kva-zim's

shoulder. "I have come to rescue you," she whispered with conviction.

"Preposterous," he growled. During her journey, she had much time to prepare for Kva-zim's dismissal of her intent, but her mentor's strict adherence to the ancient ways of her people angered her nonetheless.

"Kva-zim, we must go," she implored sharply. "You will die here if we do not . . ."

Kva-zim pounded his fist into the soil. Never in her life had Tii-laa witnessed the older Ki-vaa express anger, nor had she seen any other in her village act in a similar manner. Though his behavior startled her, there was no time to dwell upon it. "How did you come to be trapped here?" she asked gently, hoping to quell his ire.

The older Ki-vaa drew a deep breath and rested back upon his heels. "We traveled for three days, following rontah spoor. It led us here, and I suspect that beyond this swamp are plains where the rontahs are plentiful. But here our quest came to an end. Initially, the algae on the water supported our weight, but the farther we walked, the more fragile it became. We barely made it to this island. And then . . ." he said solemnly, "then the grizoks came. Here we have awaited our ultimate fate for two days."

Kva-zim reminded Tii-laa of the lore he had imparted to her when she was younger, explaining again that when the grizoks were entranced by their mating ritual, very little could distract them. However, a great enough disturbance could break the grizoks from the hypnotic spell, resulting in a frenzy of protective behavior that would spell doom for any who intruded upon their mating ground.

"We are trapped," Kva-zim conceded wearily, "and here we will return to the water. There can be no doubt that this is the will of the Three Makers. You will die with us, Tii-laa." Sadness laced the voice of her mentor.

Tii-laa gazed into the eyes of her elder with intense resolve. "And if the Three Makers, in their great wisdom, move their hands to reveal to you another way, will you not accept it?"

"Tii-laa, there is no other way," Kva-zim said, sounding crestfallen. "The grizok ritual lasts for weeks. Crossing the swamp cannot be achieved. The pull of the mud beneath the algae is impossible to escape. We will starve here, or we will be seen and devoured by the grizoks. Your actions alone should have brought them down upon us."

"Then nothing I do now can make things any worse, can it?" She did not wait for her mentor to reply. "There is another way," she said, and then she stood, removed the coiled rope from her shoulder, and walked toward the edge of the tiny earthen isle. Kva-zim and his two companions ducked to the ground, fearful that the young woman's impetuous actions would reveal their location to the grizoks, but Tii-laa seemed completely unconcerned as she fashioned a wide loop at one end of the rope and began swinging it in an arc at her side.

"What is she doing?" asked Boh-ron, at the side of Kva-zim.

"She's trying to hasten our return to the water," the Ki-vaa elder growled.

Tii-laa ignored the comment and threw her lasso into the air. The lowest circling grizok was just then passing over her, but its focus was not disturbed nor its flight path swayed by the rope, which missed its target. She recoiled the rope and waited patiently, as did those hiding in the tall sawgrass, and a few minutes later, when the grizok made its next pass of the nearest rock tower, Tii-laa again threw the rope into the air. This time, the beast caught sight of the lasso and instinctively clamped its jaws around the annoying distraction. At once, Tii-laa was yanked upward from the ground and pulled from the island, just a few yards above the fetid swamp. The grizok seemed not to care that the rope it held fast between the teeth of its wide, fanged maw carried a Ki-vaa. Confident that the simple mind of the grizok was focused on its mating flight rather than her, Tii-laa shifted her weight until she swung like a pendulum beneath the creature, then released her grip when she felt close enough to the edge of the swamp to reach it safely. She plunged through the algae and into the water, and though the black mud threatened to hold her fast, she pumped her legs and kept moving until she was able to reach a gnarled, low-hanging vine.

Now muddy and wet but safely on shore, Tii-laa looked back to the island across the swamp. Then, with determination, she shot into the jungle at top speed.

Envisioning the plan with crystal clarity, Tii-laa moved like lightning, ripping several fruit-laden gro-nay vines from trees as she passed, and before long she found the path taken by the enormous troak that had meandered past her an hour earlier. Even as she leaped from one unearthed tree root to the next, she worked with her hands, tying a long length of gro-nay vine to the end of her walking staff. Within minutes she located the ebon reptile, rooting among the swamp trees in search of white berries on which to feast. Tii-laa smiled inwardly as she looked to the gro-nay berries that proliferated on the vine attached to her staff. It would work. It had to work. She leaped to the nearest tree root above the swamp, then to the next, and finally to the speckled back of the massive salamander-like troak.

Tii-laa had known that her weight would be barely perceptible to the creature, but upon her landing, the troak raised its wide head from its muddy endeavor. The young Ki-vaa stood stock-still, awaiting a response, but the troak must have determined that the tiny animal on its back bore no threat, for soon it lowered its head and resumed its search for gro-nay berries. Within seconds, Tii-laa had crept up the flat back of the beast to its thick, short neck and extended the end of the wooden staff before the creature's nose. There, dangling tantalizingly out of reach, was a vine covered with white berries. The nostrils of the troak flared as it savored the scent before it finally snapped at the snack that waved before its eyes. Tii-laa held the walking staff to the troak's left.

The silent behemoth turned to follow the sweet smell of the berries, and not realizing that it was being led, began to walk toward the dangling vine that Tii-laa kept frustratingly out of the reach of its mouth. It slogged through the thick mud, clearly hopeful that each step would bring its great maw into contact with the berries on the vine, and in due time Tii-laa led the hungry troak to the edge of the algae-laden swamp.

The industrious Ki-vaa gazed across the bright green bed of algae at the tiny island and there saw Kva-zim and his two companions staring out from the sawgrass in utter astonishment. But Tii-laa's momentary distraction was all the time the troak needed to thrust its head forward and clamp down upon the gro-nay vine, tearing it from the end of the wooden staff. As the gargantuan amphibian munched upon the vine and berries, Tii-laa quickly withdrew the staff and tied another length of gro-nay vine to its end, hoping that the appetite of the troak had not been appeased by the meager offering. Fortunately, the beast still hungered, and with the new vine dangling before its nose, the creature moved forward, its small but powerful legs sloshing down through the algae and into the mud beneath. Although the pull of the swamp's foundation was a deadly trap for smaller creatures, the troak was not similarly affected, its great bulk and the prodigious strength of its legs negating the deadly pull of the black mud through which it stomped. Onward it trudged through the muck and the slime, Tii-laa straddling its neck, the beast occasionally snapping unsuccessfully at the sweet berries that swayed just out of reach.

The Ki-vaas upon the island recoiled in fear as the great black beast approached, the putrefying vegetation dredged up from the swamp bottom by its massive paws disgorging foul-smelling fumes into the air. Despite the presence of the huge troak, the grizoks continued to circle the rock towers, oblivious to the beast below. Tii-laa had hoped the flying creatures would disregard the appearance of the troak, as the two species were not natural enemies and rarely interacted with one another, but the situation was still a precarious one. The salamander-like creature was dangerously close to the grizoks' ritual flight, and grizoks were known for their unpredictability, so time was of the essence.

"Get on the back of the troak!" Tii-laa shouted as the beast idled amid the ruptured algae sheet. Although Kva-zim must have known she was calling to him, he hesitated. Tii-laa was well aware that her actions were a breach of the most rudimentary tribal laws. She was challenging that which was predetermined by the Three Makers. It was an affront not only to her fellow people but to the gods themselves.

"Do you not hear me?" Tii-laa cried, her voice now tinged with desperation. The fact that she was astride an enormous salamander that stood only a few yards beneath the toothy grizoks and yet the flying terrors had not taken notice was an inconceivable feat.

Kva-zim paused. He looked to Boh-ron and Hro-zoh, who both wore pained visages. They had not eaten in days, and all three were nearing deadly dehydration. Then Kva-zim looked back to Tii-laa, and he spoke with a thin and raspy voice. "I led us here on a quest to ensure the survival of the tribe. But it was I who led, I who suggested that we cross the swamp. It was I who . . ."

"And it is I who shall lead you back home," she said firmly, truncating whatever sentiment of guilt Kva-zim was about to needlessly express. Tii-laa sat strong and defiant upon the neck of the restless troak, its great head swaying from side to side as it snapped at the gro-nay vine that she kept just out of its reach. "Now get up here, quickly!" Tii-laa's voice carried a tone of authority she had never before used in the presence of Kva-zim. She had no axe to grind with her mentor nor did she feel any need to impress him, but the simple act of following her heart, taking charge of the situation, and essentially saying, "may the gods be damned," filled her with warmth, and she wanted Kva-zim to recognize that fire within her.

Boh-ron and Hro-zoh looked to their leader as the urgency of the situation hung heavily in the air. At last, he spoke. "We go," Kva-zim said, the two simple words heavy with defeat and resignation.

Ever aware of the horrors circling above them, the three Ki-vaas crept from the sawgrass. One by one they waded into the dark swamp and climbed onto the slick skin of the troak's tail, grabbing on to the bony horns that ran the length of the creature to assist their ascent as they mounted the troak's wide, flat back. All the while, Tii-laa watched her tribespeople's progress with great anxiety while simultaneously keeping an eye on the circling grizoks.

The troak upon whose neck Tii-laa rode took advantage of her divided attention and snapped shut its jaws on the gro-nay vine that was now tapping against its nose. The juicy white berries spurted as they were ground between the beast's flat teeth, but the troak seemed intent on devouring the entire vine, whose tensile strength was surprisingly—and unfortunately—quite resilient and did not disengage from the end of Tii-laa's wooden staff. But Tii-laa refused to relinquish her hold of the stick, as it was her only immediately available weapon, and as the troak whipped its head to one side to try to pull the vine free, it nearly dislodged Tii-laa from her perch upon its neck. She pulled with all of her might in a desperate attempt to break the vine, but the hearty vegetation resisted her efforts, and with a sudden thrash of its head, the troak flung the vine, the staff, and Tii-laa herself through the air.

Flailing wildly, Tii-laa broke through the algae and splashed into the dark, muddy water of the swamp beneath the massive head of the troak. Throughout the entire ordeal, the lumbering titan had not uttered a sound, but now the disappearance of the fruit that had led it across the swamp put an end to the troak's complacency and the beast opened its mouth wide, releasing a clipped but rumbling shriek that reverberated through the trees hedging the quagmire.

Although she had been unceremoniously pulled from the creature's neck and thrown to the putrid waters below, Tii-laa's determination did not waver and her grip on the wooden staff never faltered. As the troak roared, she yanked on the staff and managed to pull the vine from the creature's mouth, regaining full control of the length of hardwood. But the shriek of her oblivious mount had done what Tii-laa and the Ki-vaas all dreaded. The lowest circling grizok began to tip and tilt, and then broke from its repetitious airborne path around the nearest rock tower. While performing their hypnotic mating dance, very little could interrupt the flight of the grizoks, but the screech of the troak was one such alarm that the winged terror could not ignore. Now the feathers edging the grizok's wings flared and the creature plummeted toward the confused troak and its passengers. The maw of the alabaster flier grew wide, nearly bisecting the creature widthwise, and hundreds of razor-sharp teeth gleamed against the dark pink interior of its horrible mouth.

Kva-zim and his companions watched helplessly as imminent death rocketed toward them, and instinctively they flattened themselves against the cool, slick hide of the troak. It was in that instant, in the span of just a few pounding heartbeats, that another epiphany overcame Tii-laa. Never before had she been a spectator to the inevitable demise of one of her tribe, and although tribal doctrine prescribed the elegant acceptance of death, before her was the proof that the instinct for self-preservation lay somewhere deep within every Ki-vaa. Kva-zim, who himself had taught Tii-laa the ways of the tribe, now cowered in fear against the troak's back. He did not stand tall and forfeit his life willingly. He did not allow himself to be devoured, to be just another part of the natural life cycle of Zandar. No. When faced with death, he resisted. It was a complete contradiction to what she had been taught since she had crawled from the birthing pools. The questions that had vexed her for years were not without merit, as evidenced by the actions of her tribespeople. They feared death, and in that instant, she knew that if all around her spoke their hearts truly, she would find she was not alone as she had previously thought.

The malnourished Ki-vaas could do very little to defend themselves, however, and they closed their eyes tightly as the grizok soared past them, only inches above their backs. Kva-zim yelled for Tii-laa, who lay concealed in the muck at the feet of the troak, resisting the urge to respond so she might avoid the notice of their winged assailant. The Ki-vaas, probably fearful that they would see the limp form of Tii-laa in the mouth of the beast, cast furtive glances over their shoulders as the grizok carved an arc through the air toward the far shore, the flapping of its great wings creating waves upon the surface of the algae-laden swamp. The attacker completed its arc and once again shot toward the troak interloper and the fleshy morsels that rode upon its back. This time, the predator would surely pluck one of the Ki-vaas from the ebon beast and feast upon the flesh of its unfortunate victim.

The troak watched in placid curiosity as the grizok rushed toward it, oblivious to the threat the predator posed, but before the flying creature could reach the Ki-vaas, a wooden staff cut through the air like a javelin from the surface of the swamp. Tied to its end was a long length of rope, its far end held tightly in the muddy hands of Tii-laa. The grizok could do nothing but continue its forward momentum, pulling taught the rope and causing the staff to cross diagonally over the flying creature's back and wrap twice around the wing on the far side of its wide body. The attacker flapped defiantly but only became more entangled, its frantic lashing ripping Tii-laa from the mud and up over the side of the troak's neck. But still, she held tightly the rope that fouled the grizok's flight, and ultimately the disk-shaped beast splashed into the muck just yards from the troak.

Tii-laa crouched upon the neck of the troak but maintained her grip on the rope as she slung black mud from her free hand. Just yards away, the grizok shrieked in anger as its feathered wings beat against the swamp's surface, but the creature would not be dissuaded from defending its territory. It dug its wings downward and began utilizing them like legs, marching defiantly toward the troak, its hideous mouth open wide and ready to feast upon the first thing it could reach, and perhaps everything it could reach. Kva-zim and his exhausted companions could do nothing but watch in horror as death approached.

In desperation, Tii-laa began slapping the neck of the troak to break it from its indifference. "Wake up!" she implored. The tactic worked, causing the giant salamander to jerk its head upright and turn toward the hissing grizok that struggled to stomp through the mud toward it. As if recognizing the presence of the vicious enemy for the first time, the troak raised one mighty clawed paw and smashed down upon the head of the grizok, thrusting its head into the viscous black mud that coated the foundation of the swamp. The huge wings flapped in wild, violent distress, flinging decayed vegetation and slime into the air, and its mouth snapped desperately as it gulped for air. Now apparently thoroughly annoyed that its food search had been so rudely interrupted, the troak pounded repeatedly on the head and back of the screaming grizok and ground it into the mud until it moved no more.

Tii-laa threw the end of the rope to Kva-zim. "Don't let go of this!" she ordered, and then plunged into the swamp. The only weapon she had left was her cutting tool, and she was not about to abandon the rope and staff. She hastily searched the mud beneath the wing of the dead grizok and quickly recovered the staff, cut the rope from it, then shouted to Kva-zim. "Pull me up! Quickly!"

There was a reason for Tii-laa's abrupt command. The shrieks of the grizok had caused a second flier to break from its ritualistic trance, and it now awkwardly flapped its wings, an indication that it was about to diverge from its orbital flight path. As Tii-laa had implored, Kva-zim, Boh-ron, and Hro-zoh all pulled the rope and managed to heft her from the grip of the mud below and onto the back of the troak just as the grizok made its first pass over the black beast. All four Ki-vaas dropped to their stomachs as the flying terror passed, but Tii-laa was already constructing a defense, using the gro-nay vine to fasten the razor-sharp shell to the end of her staff and creating a makeshift lance.

"Here it comes!" warned Hro-zoh, and Tii-laa spun just in time to find the hungry grizok barreling directly toward her. With nerves of steel, the young Ki-vaa stood her ground and ducked just as the beast flew over her, thrusting the lance upward into its soft, feathered abdomen. The grizok let out a clipped shriek but flew on as if unfazed by Tii-laa's defensive action.

"We were wrong to follow you," Boh-ron wailed. "The Three Makers will not allow the grizok to be harmed by your hand, Tii-laa. The Three Makers have decreed . . ."

Tii-laa held the tip of her spear in the face of Boh-ron. Blood dripped from the white oval shell blade. "The Three Makers don't tell me what to do," she said coldly.

The impact of the grizok was bone-crushing, throwing Tii-laa from the back of the troak, but she did not fall to the dark waters below. Instead, she clung to the nose of the creature as it flew away from the troak and out over the swamp, and though its wide jaws snapped repeatedly, the grizok had not taken the height of its prey into account; it simply could not open its mouth wide enough to devour her. Tii-laa's stomach lurched with nausea from the sudden impact and twisting flight of the grizok, and it was all she could do to retain her composure. With a firm grip on the nose feathers of the enemy and her lance in her other hand, she looked into the savage maw of the beast and the rows of daggerlike teeth that could shred her in an instant. There was only one possible solution to the death-defying predicament and one possible outcome of the lethal encounter.

The savage creature continued to flap, but its confusion over its elusive meal caused it to cease its forward momentum and hover in place. As the grizok again attempted to devour her, Tii-laa thrust the spear into the mouth of the flying terror, perpendicular to its opened jaws. The razor edge of the lance cut into the roof of its mouth and the blunt end of the spear pressed against the wide, black tongue of the beast, which only further infuriated the attacker.

"Go ahead," Tii-laa screamed. "Bite me!"

With that, she released her grip on the grizok's nose feathers as it snapped its jaws shut, thrusting the spear through the roof of its mouth and into its brain.

Kva-zim watched speechlessly as Tii-laa splashed into the swamp, with the full weight of the now-dead grizok crashing down on top of her. In a panic, he tied the rope around his waist, thrust the other end of the rope into the hands of Boh-ron, and leaped from the back of the troak, which had grown tired of the encounter and was plodding through the mud toward the shore.

Now chest-deep in the swamp, the Ki-vaa pushed through the sucking mire that fought against his every step. There was no sign of Tii-laa or any movement at all from the grizok. Kva-zim was sicked by the thought that the child he had helped raise had just died before his eyes. As he reached the grizok, he could feel the tug upon his waist increase as the troak moved farther from the scene; in seconds, Kva-zim would be pulled backward from where Tii-laa lay beneath the dead grizok. Hro-zoh now held the other end of the rope along with Boh-ron, and together they worked their way down toward the tail of the troak to allow additional rope to extend to Kva-zim. But the troak continued to plod on.

Then Kva-zim saw it: the hand of Tii-laa, reaching out from beneath the wing of the dead beast, only a yard from where he stood. He thrust out his hand, but just as his fingertips touched hers the rope tied around his waist pulled him abruptly from her. Again he tried, stretching with all of his might, but the effort was in vain; she was gut-wrenchingly beyond his grasp.

In the desperation of the moment, Boh-ron jumped from the tail of the troak into the swamp, while gripping the hand of Hro-zoh, who held tight to the last bony spike on the tail of the giant salamander. Suddenly, Kva-zim fell forward as the efforts of his companions had added a few extra, fleeting feet to his range of movement. With only seconds to act, Kva-zim thrust out his arm and at last grabbed hold of Tii-laa's hand. With his remaining energy, Kva-zim pulled, and Tii-laa slid from beneath the heavy wing of the grizok.

Together, they fell through the floating algae and beneath the foul-smelling water as Kva-zim was yanked backward by the further advancement of the troak. Within seconds, they rose from the muck, doing their best to stay on their feet as they were pulled through the swamp that wanted nothing more than to devour them.

"I wonder what the Three Makers would think of this?" Tii-laa asked, her small mouth opening puckered at the edges in a slight but discernible smile. The two held tight, and as night fell upon Zandar, Tii-laa, Kva-zim, and the others clawed their way up the embankment of roots that surrounded the swamp.

An hour had passed; previously growling bellies were now full and the black mulch of the terrible swamp was washed from their skin and hair. Tii-laa looked to the stars as Kva-zim passed the gourd canteen back to her. "You'll return to the village, I assume?" he asked.

"Of course. Where else would I go?" she said, her eyes still on the night sky. "And you, Kva-zim?"

Her mentor paused. He and his companions had endured much on their voyage, but his next words indicated that their trials were not yet at their end. "We will forge on until we find what we're looking for," he said with confidence. "And when we complete our task and return to the village, we will say nothing of what transpired here. We will keep your secret, Tii-laa."

Tii-laa was confused by the statement. "What secret? You mean what I did to save your lives?"

"No," he said. "We'll keep the secret of that which even you do not yet recognize." With that, he patted her upon the shoulder, and the three explorers disappeared into the night.

The twinkling jewels that adorned the heavens above were spectacular. But as Tii-laa reveled in their beauty and the newfound sense of self that she had embraced upon her journey, an odd flash caught her attention. At first, it appeared to be a falling star, but whatever it was slowed suddenly and drifted toward the ground in the distance. It was too dark to see just what it was, but hovering above it was something similar to the mushrooms she had encountered in the field prowled by the multisegmented rootohs.

She rose and began walking in the direction of the Ki-vaa village. Much had transpired in the very short time since she had left on her errand to save her missing tribespeople. Now, everything felt different, changed somehow. Gazing back at the strange thing floating down out of the sky, she wondered if it might be an omen portending even greater changes to come.

So many wonders, so many worlds, so many questions filled the mind of Tii-laa.

EDGAR RICE BURROUGHS UNIVERSE

VICTORY HARBEN™

FIRES OF HALOS

QUANTUM CODA

As Transcribed by Christopher Paul Carey

**DURING VICTORY HARBEN'S VISIT TO THE OFFICES OF
EDGAR RICE BURROUGHS, INC.,
TARZANA, CALIFORNIA**

ERB
INC.™

QUANTUM CODA
INTO THE UNKNOWN

YOU'RE TELLING ME you didn't reset the power receiver?"
Tangor exclaimed as the ship bucked and the engines
screamed like a banshee over the darkened skies of the
planet Zandar.

"Isn't that what I just said?" I yelled into the microphone
connecting the *Starduster*'s two cockpits.

Tangor cursed, fighting with the yoke. "You've got to be
kidding me! You left the receiver tuned to the Polodian
energy frequency? Now it's simultaneously drawing energy
from Omos *and* the power station on Poloda—that'll over-
load the engines and tear the ship apart!"

"Hey, mister! You were the one who said we needed to
hurry up and get off Zandar before the Nuvors tried burning
us at the stake for a second time."

"You had plenty of time to tinker with the ship, Victory!"
he cried. "We were on Uvala for a whole month!"

The ship bounded with turbulence and then dropped
steeply. My stomach lurched; it felt like it was going to turn
inside out and leap up my throat.

"Sorry, I had other things on my mind!" I shouted, a little
testily, I admit. "Besides, I didn't expect the power station
on Poloda to start up out of the blue like this, and neither
did you. You said that you'd given up hope, that it's been
silent for years!"

"Well, it's not silent anymore!"

The *Starduster* jumped violently and Hucklebuck, who

362

had been clinging to my leg, lost his grip and went flying toward the ceiling, letting out a xylophonic trill of trepidation. He smacked against the canopy with a dull thud and released another trill of distress. Suddenly the ship dropped again and I found the pudgy little furball on top of my head, his tiny claws tangled in my hair.

"Hey, buddy, let go!" I reached up and got my hands around him. "Here, I've gotcha." Though he was reluctant to let go, I somehow managed to extract him from my unruly auburn locks. As gently as I could with the plane rocking and rolling, I slipped him in my bag, sealed the little guy inside, and secured the bag's strap around my shoulder.

I struggled to pull a utility box from under my seat but finally got hold of it. I cracked it open and fished a hand inside, trying to keep the entire contents of the case from flying out into the cockpit. Finally, I felt the outlines of what I was looking for and withdrew a screwdriver from the box.

"I'm going to try prying the panel off the solar ray receiver!" I shouted to the forward cockpit. "Then I should be able to disengage the signal from Omos and the engines will cool down."

"Not enough time!" Tangor barked back at me. "I know my ship. I can tell from the sound of the engines that they're going to blow at any second!"

"All I *need* is a second!"

"I'm sorry, Victory." Tangor's tone carried a note of resolution tinged with a touch of sadness. "I'm going to have to eject your cockpit."

"*What?!*"

"It's the only way. Ejecting your cockpit will instantly sever the connection between the engines and the solar ray receiver. I'll come back and pick you up when I'm able to get the ship back under control."

"Uh-uh. You're *not* going to maroon me on Zandar!"

But it was too late. I heard a pneumatic hiss and then the loud crack of the charges igniting and blasting my cockpit free from the ship's fuselage. With a sickening, dizzying lurch, the escape pod shot like a bullet into the cold, dark heavens.

"Tangor!" I shouted into the mic, hoping the channel was still open with the *Starduster*. "Did you hear what I said? You can't do this to me!" All I heard back in response was static.

As the pod hurtled through the atmosphere, I peered through the canopy into the blackness. Here and there I could see glimmering pinpoints of light that might indicate cities or villages below. I was now on the other side of the planet from where we had camped during our brief layover on Zandar while we traversed the atmospheric belt on our journey around the Omos planetary system. Tangor had hoped to reunite with his friend Yamoda, whom he had left behind on another planet during his own journeys. But now here I was, stuck on Zandar, a world that hadn't exactly welcomed me with open arms the last time I had visited. I had no idea who or what awaited me on the surface below.

"Well, Hucklebuck," I said to my little friend, who had peeked his furry white head out of the bag in which I had stashed him. "It looks like we're in for another adventure."

The altimeter hit the mark I was waiting for and I pulled the lever. The pod lurched up suddenly as the air caught beneath the chute. Though the pod had slowed, the altimeter showed we were still coming down faster than I would have liked.

"Hold on, buddy!" I cried. "We're going for a little ride!"

UNIVERSE™

Victory Harben's adventures will continue in

VICTORY HARBEN: GHOSTS OF OMOS

AN ERB ILLUSTRATED EPICS GRAPHIC NOVEL

COMING SOON FROM
EDGAR RICE BURROUGHS, INC.

Acknowledgments

I would like to personally thank Jim Sullos for believing in and supporting a new direction for ERB, Inc.'s publishing program, which ultimately resulted in this novel; Cathy Wilbanks, who was there with me every step of the way as we launched the ERB Universe and figured out who Victory was; Charlotte Wilbanks for her enthusiasm and making my job so much easier; Janet Mann for her support, insight, vast knowledge of the company's history; Team Super-Arc—Matt Betts, Win Scott Eckert, Geary Gravel, Mike Wolfer, and Ann Tonsor Zeddies—for going on this amazing journey with me; Win (again) for always being there and being the impeccable Keeper of the Chronology; Geary (again) for his insightful editing on this book; Mike (again) for all his help with the novel, chronicling Victory's adventures in the comic books, and being in the trenches with me every day; Thabiso Mhlaba for his fantastic cover art; Nicole Wilbanks for her insights into the teenage Victory; Robert R. Barrett for providing me with a photocopy of the original manuscript of "The Ghostly Script" by Edgar Rice Burroughs, which served as inspiration not only for my novel, but for the entire Swords of Eternity super-arc; Steven K. Dowd for his generosity; Todd Luck for the amazing ERB content on his YouTube channel; Jason Scott Aiken, Diana M. Carey, Mike Croteau, David Herter, Karl Kauffman, Jess Terrell, Kim Turk, and the late Scott Turk for their friendship and support; my very own Hucklebuck, a.k.a. my cat, Missy; Duke Ellington and Nat King Cole for their wonderful music, which was my soundtrack while writing this novel; Victory Harben and Jason Gridley for telling me their amazing stories; every reader and Burroughs fan who invested their time and money in the new ERB Universe books, cheered me on, or told me how eager they were to read Victory's story; and Edgar Rice Burroughs, who changed the very course of my life.

—C.P.C.

VICTORY HARBEN™
FIRES OF HALOS

CHRISTOPHER PAUL CAREY is the author of several books, including *Swords Against the Moon Men*, an authorized sequel to Edgar Rice Burroughs' *The Moon Maid*; *Exlies of Kho*; *The Song of Kwasin* (with Philip José Farmer); *Hadon, King of Opar*; and *Blood of Ancient Opar*. He has also written comic books featuring Burroughs' characters such as Tarzan, Dejah Thoris, Carson of Venus, Jason Gridley, and Gretchen von Harben. Carey is Director of Publishing and creative director of the ERB Universe at Edgar Rice Burroughs, Inc., the company founded by Mr. Burroughs in 1923. He lives in Southern California.

BEYOND THE FARTHEST STAR™
RESCUE ON ZANDAR

A professional writer and illustrator for more than thirty years, MIKE WOLFER has been a key talent working on the canonical Edgar Rice Burroughs Universe comic books, including Jane Porter, Victory Harben, Beyond the Farthest Star, Pellucidar, The Land That Time Forgot, The Monster Men, and The Moon Maid. Best known for his Widow series, Wolfer is also the creator of the Daughters of the Dark Oracle franchise, and has worked on numerous licensed properties.

EDGAR RICE BURROUGHS: MASTER OF ADVENTURE

The creator of the immortal characters Tarzan of the Apes and John Carter of Mars, EDGAR RICE BURROUGHS is one of the world's most popular authors. Mr. Burroughs' timeless tales of heroes and heroines transport readers from the jungles of Africa and the dead sea bottoms of Barsoom to the miles-high forests of Amtor and the savage inner world of Pellucidar, and even to alien civilizations beyond the farthest star. Mr. Burroughs' books are estimated to have sold hundreds of millions of copies, and they have spawned 60 films and 250 television episodes.

About Edgar Rice Burroughs, Inc.

Founded in 1923 by Edgar Rice Burroughs, one of the first authors to incorporate himself, EDGAR RICE BURROUGHS, INC., holds numerous trademarks and the rights to all literary works of the author still protected by copyright, including stories of Tarzan of the Apes and John Carter of Mars. The company oversees authorized adaptations of his literary works in film, television, radio, publishing, theatrical stage productions, licensing, and merchandising. Edgar Rice Burroughs, Inc., continues to manage and license the vast archive of Mr. Burroughs' literary works, fictional characters, and corresponding artworks that has grown for over a century. The company is still owned by the Burroughs family and remains headquartered in Tarzana, California, the town named after the Tarzana Ranch Mr. Burroughs purchased there in 1919 that led to the town's future development.

In 2015, under the leadership of President James Sullos, the company relaunched its publishing division, which was founded by Mr. Burroughs in 1931. With the publication of new authorized editions of Mr. Burroughs' works and brand-new novels and stories by today's talented authors, the company continues its long tradition of bringing tales of wonder and imagination featuring the Master of Adventure's many iconic characters and exotic worlds to an eager reading public.

Visit **EdgarRiceBurroughs.com** for more information.

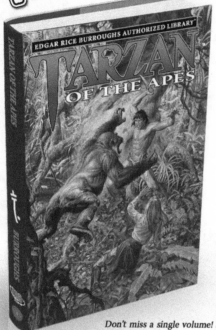

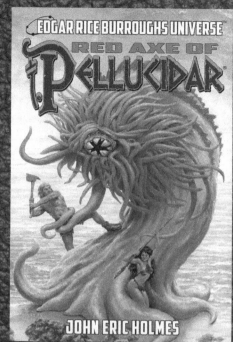

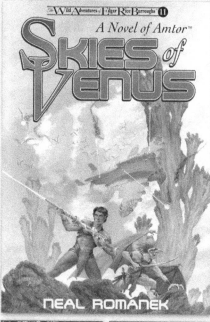

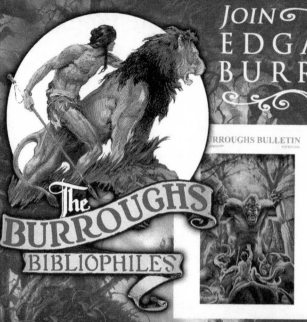

CPSIA information can be obtained
at www.ICGtesting.com
Printed in the USA
LVHW100612251022
731388LV00005B/79/J